Behind the Masks

Sarah drew a sharp breath of air at the sound of his voice and whipped her head around. Keeping his eyes on her, Sebastian ducked his head slightly so that his black felt hat obscured his features more fully.

That small shift in his position threw her masked face into the full light of the lantern that hung from the stern. Behind the glitter of the false gems, her wide eyes sucked the flame reflection into their depths, as dark as the night and as deep as sin.

"It is you," she said, her voice somewhere between an accusation and an epiphany.

"But of course, my dear." Sebastian summoned the appropriate croon easily. Too easily. Even in his own ears it sounded like an exaggerated performance of an uninspired script.

She made a quick, abortive wave—whether angry or dismissive, he could not tell. "What game are you playing at?" Her eyes went as hard as the glass gems, and she swung her legs over the bench so she was facing him squarely.

That question, at least, required no melodramatic declarations in response. "What do you think?"

"I think . . ." She paused, while the sharp-edged look around her eyes softened. "I think that you plan to seduce me."

The Music of the Night

Lydia Joyce

A SIGNET ECLIPSE BOOK

SIGNET ECLIPSE
Published by New American Library, a division of
Penguin Group (USA) Inc., 375 Hudson Street,
New York, New York 10014, USA
Penguin Group (Canada), 90 Eglinton Avenue East, Suite 700, Toronto,
Ontario M4P 2Y3, Canada (a division of Pearson Penguin Canada Inc.)
Penguin Books Ltd., 80 Strand, London WC2R 0RL, England
Penguin Ireland, 25 St. Stephen's Green, Dublin 2,
Ireland (a division of Penguin Books Ltd.)
Penguin Group (Australia), 250 Camberwell Road, Camberwell, Victoria 3124,
Australia (a division of Pearson Australia Group Pty. Ltd.)
Penguin Books India Pvt. Ltd., 11 Community Centre, Panchsheel Park,
New Delhi - 110 017, India
Penguin Group (NZ), cnr Airborne and Rosedale Roads, Albany,
Auckland 1310, New Zealand (a division of Pearson New Zealand Ltd.)
Penguin Books (South Africa) (Pty.) Ltd., 24 Sturdee Avenue,
Rosebank, Johannesburg 2196, South Africa

Penguin Books Ltd., Registered Offices:
80 Strand, London WC2R 0RL, England

First published by Signet Eclipse, an imprint of New American Library,
a division of Penguin Group (USA) Inc.

First Printing, November 2005
10   9   8   7   6   5   4   3   2   1

*In memory of my grandmother Yula,
who was not the least bit shocked.*

ACKNOWLEDGMENTS

Thanks are due to Gabby for watching the Bear when I desperately needed to write and, as always, to my loving husband. I couldn't do it without you!

And I would especially like to thank Giovanna Biscontin for help with all things Venetian. Any remaining errors are my own.

Prologue

He shall not get away with it!

The thought surged through Sebastian Grimsthorpe, Earl of Wortham, as he leapt from the seat of his gig, tossing the traces to the hovering groom the instant his boots crunched down on the cobbles.

"I won't be long." He strode across the fog-stifled street to the discreetly elegant entrance of the Whitsun Club, his steps jerky with scarcely controlled rage.

He flung back the door, ignoring the polite protests of the porter behind his shining mahogany desk, and advanced straight through the vestibule into the dining room. Rich cherry tables dotted the room, modest under the ceiling's embellishments of gilt and crystal that were the remnants of an earlier age. Today, Sebastian had no time to admire the atmosphere of aged dignity and cigar smoke. Today, he had only one thing on his mind.

Bertrand de Lint sat at his usual table just as Sebastian expected, laughing jovially with a friend over port and beefsteak. Sebastian had planned to confront him quietly, hustle him out of the back of the club, and . . . something. He hadn't thought that far ahead.

But coming face-to-face with the criminal for the first time since Adela's attack overwhelmed his discretion. Anger narrowed his vision until everything but de Lint's complacent face was engulfed by darkness, Sebastian's muscles clenching against the furious rush.

"*De Lint, you bastard!*" Sebastian scarcely recognized the roar as his.

Silence fell like an ax. Fifty pairs of eyes looked up from their quiet meals and focused upon Sebastian, but he ignored them all. In the startled hush, the clink of de Lint's silverware against his plate and the muted scrape of his chair across the Aubusson carpet filled the room. The man stood unhurriedly, surveying his accuser with a quiet, sardonic quirk of his brows.

"Really, Wortham," he drawled. "If this is about the prank with that chit of yours again, this is hardly the place—"

"You lying bastard!" Sebastian drowned him out, not wanting to hear what new calumny de Lint had invented to smear his daughter's name. For the first time in the dozen years that he'd known the man, a flicker of uncertainty showed itself in de Lint's amber gaze, and Sebastian took a grim satisfaction in it as he plunged on. "That was a farce of an inquest. How you could have the audacity to come here—"

De Lint's lip curled in contempt. "I said nothing but the truth, which surprised no one, knowing what her mother was. Blood will tell, you know, old boy. You might as well let it go."

"*No!*" Sebastian surged forward, closing the space between them in a heartbeat, his momentum shoving de Lint back until the shorter man crashed against the wall hard enough to shiver the china on the nearby tables. "She is a child, damn you. A child!"

De Lint looked down at his rumpled coat, clenched in Sebastian's fist, then up to his attacker's face. A hard light glinted in his eyes. "She wasn't a child when I had her—"

Sebastian's fist across the man's jaw cut him short. The sudden, violent smack of flesh on flesh unfroze the rest of the room, and the watchers sprang into action. Hands hauled at Sebastian's coat and collar, yanking him away from de

Lint, hustling him across the dining room and toward the door. Sebastian fought on, splitting one man's brow and giving another a sharp elbow in the sternum.

His ears rang with remonstrances against his behavior, all the same old voices saying all the expected things, the things that he might have said himself before the events of the last month: "Quite abominable, old chap." "Not the thing at all, you know." "Really, Wortham, to assault a man in his own club . . ." In their voices, he heard echoes of what his fellows had said ever since he made the accusation on behalf of his illegitimate daughter, and despair welled up black and thick around him.

He stopped struggling.

Sebastian's glare remained fixed upon his adversary as he was jostled through the door. De Lint straightened himself, pulling wrinkles from his clothes and brushing away the signs of their encounter, as if he could clean himself of the smirch of Sebastian's accusations just as easily.

And, deep in his heart, Sebastian knew that as far as society was concerned, he already had. A punch thrown in a venerable and well-respected club—that was a scandal. But a bastard child of a debauched earl and a Spanish whore was nothing to the men of the Whitsun Club or any of their ilk. The rape of such a girl might feed the gossip papers, but she was outside the comfortable world of gentility, and so her fate could have no impact upon it. Not unless Sebastian forced it upon them.

"This isn't over yet." Sebastian didn't raise his voice, but it cut easily through the uproar that came in the wake of the altercation. "Adela will have justice one way or another. I swear it!"

De Lint simply lifted an eyebrow, and that was the last glimpse Sebastian had before he was pushed around the corner back into the vestibule.

"Go away," he growled at the men who crowded around him in the tiny space. His friends, de Lint's friends—he didn't know which, but now they could not be both. The men did not move, and so he turned toward the club's entrance, dislodging the last of the hands that gripped him in the movement. "I am fine. I am leaving. Go."

They fell back as he pushed to the door. He stepped out and let it swing shut behind him as he paused on the stoop, turning his face up to the gray, dirty London drizzle that was just beginning to fall. It suddenly felt cleaner to him than anything he'd experienced in a long time, and that thought stirred a deep disquiet he was loath to examine too closely.

"You'll be banned, you know," a familiar voice said casually at his elbow, and Sebastian gave a sideways glance. Stephen Holland had slipped out after him and was now standing by his side, concern in his eyes despite the way his hands were shoved carelessly into his pockets. A friend still, then.

"I don't care," Sebastian said.

Holland shrugged, in response to the words or to the rain soaking his evening coat, Sebastian couldn't tell. "I really don't see what you intended to accomplish in there."

Sebastian's frustration surged up again. "He's going to get away with it. I cannot permit that."

Holland was silent for a long moment. Then he said lightly, "But therein lies the rub. De Lint may be a scoundrel, but he's never been a liar. And he says there was no assault."

"By God, Holland!" Sebastian spit the words. "If you had been there—seen the blood, the bruises, the tears—you would have known that it could be nothing but a rape, a rape of the foulest sort. She is a child—" He realized he was shouting again, and he bit back the rest of that sentence. "Surely you must believe me."

Holland turned his head slowly and met Sebastian's eyes, his expression troubled. "I've never know you to be a liar, either, Wortham. No more than de Lint. And that is all that I can say about that."

His meaning, the one Sebastian had heard echoed so often for the last month, was devastatingly clear: Sebastian's life had been not one whit more irreproachable than de Lint's. Without the benefit of witnesses beyond one young girl of no breeding and questionable morals and a nurse who hadn't even been there, it became a matter of one man's word against the other's, and the accused should be given the benefit of the doubt.

Sebastian knew then how stupid it had been for him to seek the confrontation, as if he were some sort of knight out of an old romance defending a maiden's honor before the world. As if that could absolve him of his part in her outrage. As he considered it now, the foolishness of it was clear. But when that beggar boy had stopped him outside of his London agent's offices and told him where he might find his enemy, he hadn't stopped to think.

Not trusting himself to utter the nonsensical niceties of leave-taking, Sebastian gave a curt nod, strode down the steps of the stoop, and took the traces of his gig from the waiting groom with the toss of a shilling. He didn't look back as he flicked the reins, sending the horses into first a walk and then a trot. All he wanted to do was go galloping madly away, away from the club and de Lint and his own old life. But he kept the horses to an infuriatingly sedate pace as he wove though the crowded evening streets, leaving the devils that drove him to rage inside his head.

No one but the worst kind of reprobate would host a bacchanal in the house in which he was sheltering an innocent young girl. And no one but Sebastian could so stain a girl by mere blood association that her morals were immediately suspect. It was his fault Adela had suffered from his benign neglect for so long while he'd congratulated himself on his generosity, his fault she was attacked, his fault the attack had not been believed. There was nothing he could do to expiate that guilt, but he could at least bring her attacker to account. He owed her that much.

With the conclusion of those thoughts, he discovered that he had reached the edge of the city, the road opening up near-empty before him. Until that moment, he'd given no consideration to his destination, but now he realized he had unconsciously steered toward Hartwald.

At the thought of that quiet, pristine retreat, his heart warmed, and when he remembered that Daniel was staying there—Daniel, his cousin, the only friend who had shown not the least sign of doubt during the entire ordeal—Sebastian's unconscious decision seemed doubly right. The horses sensed his eagerness through his handling of the traces; they arched their necks, their nostrils flaring, and he gave a flick of the reins that sent them down the road in an eager gallop.

The thoroughfare stretched out in front of him, bare and invitingly uncomplicated. Nothing to do but make his mind equally empty and give himself up to the rattle of the wheels, the drumming of hooves, and the whistle of the wind—

And then the rattle became a crack, and the horses whinnied in panic, and Sebastian was flying through the air. Even then, the peace of the road kept panic at bay, and as he flew toward the hard-packed earth, a corner of his mind thought distantly, *What a stupid way to die.*

And then everything went black.

I stood in Venice, on the Bridge of Sighs;
A palace and a prison on each hand:
I saw from out the wave her structures rise
As from the stroke of the enchanter's wand:
A thousand years their cloudy wings expand
Around me, and a dying Glory smiles
O'er the far times, when many a subject land
Look'd to the winged Lion's marble piles,
Where Venice sate in state, thron'd on her hundred isles! . . .

In Venice Tasso's echoes are no more,
And silent rows the songless gondolier;
Her palaces are crumbling to the shore,
And music meets not always now the ear:
Those days are gone—but Beauty still is here.
States fall, arts fade—but Nature doth not die,
Nor yet forget how Venice once was dear,
The pleasant place of all festivity,
The revel of the earth, the masque of Italy!

—from *Childe Harold's Pilgrimage*
by George Gordon, Lord Byron

Chapter One

It was a perfect day to die.

From Sebastian's bedroom window, the hills of Cornwall undulated in a calico of greens down to the jagged line of the flat, gray sea, visible for the first time in his long and stormy sojourn there. The sky was a fragile china blue, and the light that poured through the thrown-back sash had the sweet, ethereal quality of early spring.

Sebastian viewed it with satisfaction, as if it were some obscure sign that the Fates were smiling upon his unorthodox enterprise. He closed his steamer trunk with a final thud and the certainty that he had folded his shirts wrong. Once it would have irritated him, for he had never packed for himself before. But he was not the man he once was, and dead men did not have valets.

"You're going through with it, then." Daniel's voice came from the doorway, and it was not a question.

Sebastian put a hand on the sun-warmed tin that covered the lid, the tangible evidence of his decision. "Yes," he said without looking up.

The trunk was dark with oxidation and battered from a hundred other trips, more familiar to him than the countless bedrooms he had slept in over the past ten years. His fingers traced the family crest almost of their own volition; it had been a long time since he had paid it much heed. He had, in the various stages of his youth, thought it frightening, hallowed, dashing, or just another signal that he was a bloody important person. But now the swollen, posturing lions seemed a mockery, a twisted joke, and touching them was as automatic and futile as scratching a scarcely healed wound.

"You know how I feel about your scheme," Daniel said.

Sebastian tore his eyes from the trunk and turned around, his sigh strictly mental. The argument was so familiar that he could have recited it almost word for word. Nothing had changed since the last time they had trodden the same tired ground.

Now Whitby stood in the doorway, too. Perhaps Daniel thought he was calling in reinforcements, but Sebastian had never given much credence to the agent's opinions.

"I know you cannot understand, but I must ask you to respect my decision." Sebastian's smile held no humor. "The worst that could happen is that I would die in truth, and then you would find yourself as a permanent earl. I could think of worse fates."

Daniel's expression was an attempt at severity, but he had inherited his father's unfortunate chin, so he managed only to look slightly harried. "I have no wish for your lands or your title. You should know that by now, Grimmy. You've always been a little reckless, perhaps—Uncle was right about that—but who isn't? Still, I've never known you to be foolish. She's a bastard, and you'd risk everything—"

Sebastian's glare, which he had turned on Daniel at the mention of his father, now grew several degrees frostier. "She is my daughter," he said, slowly and precisely.

He looked back at the flaking pictures of the gouty lions, smirking as they reared up on either side of the shield. He wanted to smash them in for all good they and what they stood for had done him. Between Adela and the sabotaged axle that had nearly ended Sebastian's life, de Lint had much to answer for.

"Are my affairs in order?" he demanded of Whitby.

"Yes, your lordship," his thin, balding agent said. He hesitated, his silence laden with unspoken disapproval.

"You wish to make an observation?" Sebastian raised a brow, knowing from experience that he could not avoid the incipient lecture.

Whitby drew himself up. "As the manager of your finances, I feel it incumbent upon my position to express the utmost disapproval of this endeavor. However much you believe in your cousin—and with no disrespect to Mr. Collins—it is most unwise to place all your worldly goods unconditionally in another's hands."

Sebastian snorted. "And don't I already, Mr. Whitby?"

The agent hemmed and hawed for a moment at the pointed question. "It is a matter of trustworthiness, your lordship, and of accountability. I have been your father's agent since my own father died when you were scarcely out of breeches, and our relationship is spelled out in the most precise legal language."

"Whereas Daniel is only my cousin, whom I've known from the cradle," Sebastian finished for him. "I fail to see your point."

"I did not truly believe that you would, your lordship." Whitby sighed. "I have made contacts on your behalf with a very discreet agent in Venice, and I am assured that he will render all assistance that is required."

"Very well," Sebastian said, turning back to survey the flat stretch of gray sea, "then have the carriage brought around, and I'll be off without further delay."

"Do be careful, old chap," Daniel said.

Sebastian smiled tightly, full of the anger that had grown inside him like a cancer for the past three months. His mind went through his meticulous plans, examining them for faults and finding none. Let the world think him dead, and then . . . then he could move without fear of discovery.

"I am not the one who needs to take care."

*   *   *

The ferry dipped and rocked on the choppy waves, its movements more queasily abrupt than the graceful rise and fall of the steamer they had left the day before.

Sarah Connolly stood at the rail between Lady Merrill and Mr. de Lint, straining through the mists for her first glimpse of Venice as the lady's granddaughter chattered with her friends, their backs to the gray view of the Adriatic.

Venice. The name was pregnant with promise. Of Trieste, she carried only an impression of stuccoed houses in failing light as they were driven from the steamer to their accommodations, and their hotel had been disappointingly similar to the one in Southampton. But Venice—surely Venice would not, could not disappoint. Her imagination had feasted on the promise of La Serenissima since her employer first stated her intention of spending spring in that city, and Sarah's quiet, half-desperate gratitude for such an opportunity allowed her to bear the delicate tortures of Mr. de Lint with greater composure than she had thought she possessed.

Sarah stared at the low smear of darker gray that stood as a divider between the undifferentiated expanse of sea, land, and fog. The shoreline looked no different than it had since they left Trieste, still a long, desolate flatland interrupted by the occasional ruin that shot up against the sky for a scant dozen feet before tumbling broken back into the marsh, and she began to wonder if they would ever arrive. Finally, she saw a break in the land ahead, and a few minutes later, the ferry was sliding between the narrow arms of two barrier islands—for she had not been viewing the true shore at all, she realized as she watched the water open out in front of the ferry; at some point, it must have melted into the islets that guarded Venice's lagoon.

Now they were within, and Sarah strained her eyes for the first hint of the glorious city. Hummocks, hillocks, and sea reeds thrust through the silty water everywhere she looked, and between them hundreds of wooden posts were sunk into the lagoon bottom in a baffling pattern. In front of the ferry, sleek black darts pierced the fog, shallow boats sliding among the more wide-flung isles.

For a hundred heartbeats, that was all, until finally a bone-white mass detached itself from the unquiet waters in the mist-shortened distance, resolving as they approached into blocks of towers and colonnades in pale marble and red brick, cut through by avenues of the brackish lagoon.

It was beautiful. It was nothing like she had imagined, but it was beautiful, like some drowned mermaid's city risen from the deep. She let out the breath she hadn't known she'd been holding, and her heart jerked a little inside her chest.

"Isn't it a sight?" Mr. de Lint said with a display of heartiness that Sarah couldn't quite believe was sincere, pulling her out of her reverie.

She did not know whether he was addressing her or his mother; he had used that trick before to embarrass her, so she simply nodded slightly, keeping her eyes fixed ahead.

"I'd wager you never pictured yourself here," he continued in the same too-easy tone.

Sarah looked up sharply to meet his amber gaze. Eyes that color should not be able to look cool, but his did, and they had a glitter that made clear that the reminder of her origins was neither accidental nor careless.

"I am pleased to go where Lady Merrill wishes, sir," she said softly, flushing.

"What virtuous meekness," he murmured, those hard eyes scouring her face, picking out each pockmark that welted her skin with an expression that was almost hungry.

She jerked her head away, the deep brim of her unfashionable bonnet shuttering his view.

"Sarah is quite the perfect companion," Lady Merrill said, oblivious to the tension that thrummed in the air. She patted Sarah's white-knuckled hand on the rail next to hers.

"You are easy to please, your ladyship." Still rattled by Mr. de Lint, Sarah knew her words had a hollow ring. But it was true; Lady Merrill, for all her faults, was a remarkably undemanding mistress. Sarah would be more than happy to spend the rest of her life as a lady's companion if she knew all her future employments would be as pleasant as this one. The lady's flighty granddaughter and her fluttering friends Sarah could bear with equanimity. If only it weren't for the lady's son . . .

"Would you like to see the carnival, madam?" Mr. de Lint asked over Sarah's head, dismissing her as if she had ceased to exist the moment his attention turned elsewhere.

"The carnival?" Lady Merrill asked. "Why, that's three-quarters of a century dead!"

Her son laughed. "Oh, it never truly died, and with Venice's glorious liberation from the greedy Austrian oppressors"—he struck a pose—"certain youthful Venetian elements have decided to revive its more notorious festivities year-round. In private, of course, and with far more taste and discretion than was displayed in times past." From his tone, Sarah could not tell if he thought that was an improvement. "Some are partisans of the new Kingdom of Italy; others wish to relive the days of the Republic. But their reasons hardly matter, for you would make a stunning houri in any of their masques, Mother. If I might be so bold." He adopted a tone of wild flattery.

Lady Merrill laughed girlishly. "Oh, those days of mine are long over. I am done with shocking society! And besides, Sarah might die of humiliation if she were dragged along in the company of a seventy-year-old odalisque, never mind what Anna and her young friends would think."

"What is it, Grandmamma?" Lady Anna asked, turning from her conversation with the Morton sisters at the sound of her name.

Sarah said nothing as Lady Merrill explained, hoping that the girl's interruption would deflect Mr. de Lint's attention. But almost immediately, she felt his eyes light upon her again.

"Our Sarah might just enjoy the opportunity to hide behind a mask and veil," he said, ignoring his half niece. There was no edge in his words, but Sarah could feel their malice biting into her.

I don't care, she told herself. But she did, and he knew it. No matter how many years stood between her and the filthy streets of the rookery, she would always carry the evidence of her origins on her face, bare for everyone to see. Her speech was now flawlessly correct, her education—if not her experience—as good as that of many peeresses, her bearing and etiquette without fault . . . but nothing could erase the smallpox scars that disfigured her cheeks and forehead.

A century ago, those scars would have merely made her plain. But by the time of her birth, all but the poor and a few objectors whose wealth protected them were inoculated, and now that every child in England was required to be vaccinated by law, it marked her as one who had slipped through the cracks—who had a background such that it was possible for her to be invisible, and who had received none of the doctors' various concoctions or treatments for preventing scars when she contracted the disease.

Quite simply, she wore her life story on her face.

And so she would never be more than a lady's companion, and she was remarkably fortunate to have been elevated to that position. It was far more than she had once dreamed of and far more than anyone of her past deserved, and so, she told herself, she would be content.

Resolutely, she shut out Mr. de Lint's continuing acidlaced commentary and turned her eyes to the palazzi that rose from the murky waters like a pale dream.

It was he. There had been no mistake.

A black anger filled Sebastian as he stood in the shadows of the doorway of a draper's shop near the Ponte della Verona, wrapped in an amorphous overcoat and in the swirling fog that now rose from the canals faster than the wind could tatter it. Three crowded gondolas and half a dozen wider batèle buranele rested in the oil-smooth water at the canal door of the palazzo, the wallowing batèle nearly gunwale-deep under the loads of boxes, trunks, and servants.

Through the window of the first gondola's felze canopy, Sebastian could see where de Lint sat with another passenger, his head bare and his chin raised with conceit that radiated across the water. Sebastian watched as the man ducked out of the door and leapt nimbly to the water stairs, much to the irritation of the gondolier, who cursed him roundly in the Venetian dialect as the boat rocked with his jump. His cloaked companion pressed her hands against the sides of the felze and said nothing.

It was obscene that the man could stand there, smiling down like a benevolent deity upon the gondolas that floated at his feet. Even through the distorted lens of Sebastian's implacable anger, de Lint looked every inch the gentleman, from the top of his perfectly smoothed hair to his shining short boots. Nowhere did the filth lying under that veneer betray itself; he was a picture of refinement and moderation, and Sebastian's hands balled into fists at the very sight of him.

Ignoring both his companion and the gondolier, de Lint called up to a servant who had issued a challenge from an upper window of the palazzo. As the great wooden doors were opened in response to his reply, he waved his boat away and ordered the next gondola up, holding out his arms theatrically to a white-haired woman within—Lady Merrill, Sebastian saw when she turned toward him, recognizing her through the twining mist. He allowed himself a surge of dark satisfaction; his sources had proven correct thus far.

The lady flashed her son a dazzling smile and allowed herself to be helped up, laughing as he fussed over her extravagantly. As soon as she was shooed within the palazzo's tall carven doors, he turned back to assist the second passenger. The pretty blonde who emerged was exactly whom Sebastian had expected, a person as essential to his plan as Lady Merrill or even de Lint himself: Lady Anna Dutton, de Lint's half niece.

The girl and the gondola were dismissed, and the final boat slid into place. Two more young girls—Melinda and Euphemia Morton, his sources had told him, friends and distant relatives of the family—were swiftly assisted out, followed by a third woman who had *governess* written in every line of her stout body. That conveyance, too, was rowed away, and Sebastian was about to turn aside when the first one pulled up again and de Lint held out an imperious arm.

It was only then that Sebastian realized that it still carried de Lint's slender, cloaked companion. And no surprise that he had forgotten; as the woman stood, it became apparent she was a creature whose very meekness made her small body seem even smaller. Hunched shoulders, ducked head, all clad in a discreet black linsey-woolsey that completed her air of utter insignificance.

And yet . . . His eyes were caught by the tension that radiated through that frame, more like the string of a bow than a lute, threatening danger rather than breakage. Despite the servility of her posture, there was still something—in her movements? her air?—that spoke of strength and a deep, burning anger that was kept in check only by such elaborate displays of subjection, and Sebastian found himself wondering what would happen when that control finally snapped.

She hesitated, standing in the gondola and radiating uncertainty. The deep poke bonnet that she wore was twenty years out-of-date, and it hid her features as effectively as a wall—

—until she looked up as if seeking an exit from de Lint's too-pressing offer. Then Sebastian had a brief impression of a narrow, pale face before her incredible dark eyes lit upon him, capturing his own gaze with their force and sending a jolt of . . . what? . . . surging through him. It wasn't alarm, exactly, or lust . . . something more like recognition, which was strange because he could not think of a single person who resembled that slender, tenuous girl in even the most remote way.

Sebastian realized that he had been unconsciously leaning out from the doorway in interest; now he jerked back, but it was far too late to hide in anonymous shadows. Those eyes, darker than any shadow, followed him, touching every line and plane of his face that was visible beneath his hood.

For an instant, he felt as if some sort of link were formed between them through that intense scrutiny, boring into him and forging a connection by the sheer force of her gaze. Then she looked away, distracted by something de Lint said, and the illusion snapped. Released from the spell of her eyes, Sebastian saw for the first time the scars that marked her face.

Another shock went through him, this more identifiable—a mix of vindication, fury, incredulity, and an instinctive sympathetic pain. The nurse's wail when he had burst into the nursery echoed in his head: *It was that pock-faced strumpet! She told me I was needed!*

And now here was de Lint with just such a scar-faced woman in tow. The marks were not very deep, nor were they truly disfiguring, but they were clear enough that there was no room for doubt. Sebastian brooded as de Lint picked her up by the waist—to the gondolier's further curses—and swung her around once, acting for an instant as if he were going to tip her into the canal. Her hands tightened so convulsively on the man's arms that Sebastian could see the knuckles standing out from her flesh, but if she uttered a sound, he could not hear it. Finally, de Lint set her down. He was laughing. But when the woman turned back toward the gondola, not a trace of levity showed on her face.

Two scarred women. Chance? Unlikely. Yet there was nothing of a whore in her expression as she looked at de Lint. She only looked frightened, shot through with an abiding anger that was so hopeless that Sebastian felt an instinctive mixture of pity and fascination.

Then her head came up: She was looking for him again. Wishing to avoid that disturbing gaze, he gripped the doorknob behind him and pushed, ducking into the draper's shop behind him.

"Posso esserle d'aiuto, signor?" the wizened shopkeeper asked from behind the counter—in perfect mainland Italian rather than the common Venetian dialect.

"No, no, I am just looking," Sebastian muttered back in

the same language, turning toward a stack of silk bolts and trying to show signs of interest. His head was spinning. He had assumed that the anonymous whore had long escaped his grasp, but here she was, just as the nurse described.

Apparently, she had risen in station over the past six months, for even de Lint would not bring a doxy into his mother's company. Nor would he have brought a momentary diversion all the way to Venice with him. The woman must be his mistress now. Yes, de Lint would have the temerity to dress his mistress up as some sober upper servant and put her among his young relatives. The idea would appeal to his sense of humor.

But what if the woman were revealed as a faithless whore who had not even the decency to be loyal to her master while sharing a roof? What if his mother, the holder of his purse strings, found out exactly what he had brought into her household? Then she would lose everything she had gained in a single stroke—and more, for she would have no friends here in Venice to turn to, no knowledge of the place that might allow her to save herself.

And yet, was she truly the whore at Amberley? In that moment when those deep, dark eyes had met his . . . Sebastian shook off his doubts as superstitious imaginings. For there to be one pockmarked woman with de Lint at Amberley Park and a different one here in Venice—that was pushing credulity to the breaking point, even taking into account de Lint's skewed tastes.

That she was here was felicitous. His scheme was complete without her assistance, but it wasn't her help he wanted. It was vengeance, and that required a new plan. She, almost as much as de Lint, had been responsible for what Adela had suffered.

His eyes slid past the tables of fabric to an assortment of outrageous costumes on the back wall, and an idea flashed into his mind.

"What are those?" he demanded, though he was more than half certain he knew.

"Disguises, signor, for the masquerade parties that are so popular now. My wife makes them," the man replied eagerly. "Would you like to see?"

"Yes," Sebastian said, his eyes narrowing. "Oh, yes."

Sarah jerked away from Mr. de Lint the instant he released her. Automatically, she turned to search for the man who had been watching them. Watching her, for she was certain that his eyes had been fixed on nothing else. But he was gone. Half a dozen Venetians loitered around the bridge, but there was no sign of the tall man with the hooded overcoat and shadowed face.

Lady Anna's incredulous laughter rang out from the interior of the palazzo. "The kitchens are on the ground floor!"

"What, did you expect them to be below the waterline?" came Miss Morton's scathing reply.

"Let's pick out our rooms!" Miss Effie interrupted the incipient squabbling.

Their footsteps echoed fleetingly as they went deeper into the interior, and Lady Merrill's voice rose above them, made incomprehensible by distance and echoes.

"It seems we are alone," Mr. de Lint said slowly as behind him, a dozen servants and oarsmen began to unload the wide, blunt boats that held the luggage. Sarah ignored the patent falsity of that statement just as she tried to ignore the way his eyes were searching her face again. He laughed, and she knew she had failed. Again. "You had better hurry inside or they'll be wondering if you aren't testing your wiles on me, defenseless man that I am."

"You are blocking my path, sir," Sarah pointed out as neutrally as she could manage.

"Am I? I beg your pardon." He moved a scant two inches from the center of the water landing toward the yellow wall of the building, then watched her with frank interest. Sarah swallowed against her sudden queasiness. Always before, she had taken care never to be cornered by Mr. de Lint without his mother's presence. She had forgotten her caution this time, and she would pay for it. Though she knew he had no true interest in her, he was the kind of man who enjoyed tormenting the defenseless, and she was as defenseless as anyone could be.

McGarrity, Lady Merrill's maid, cast Sarah a look of pity behind Mr. de Lint's back as she scuttled into the palazzo with a stack of hatboxes, but Sarah knew better than to expect any help from that quarter. And indeed, the rest of the servants studiously ignored her as they unloaded the boats. If she had been one of them, maybe the butler would have said a word or two in Lady Merrill's ear. But she wasn't one of them—she would never be one of them—because she had come from too low and climbed too high.

The sickening mass in her stomach turned hot and hard so suddenly that for a moment, she could see nothing at all but the black wall of Mr. de Lint's coat front, mocking her with her impotence. Without willing it, she took a jerking step forward and rammed into his chest. He lurched against the wall, wrapping a hand around her waist and pulling her with him so that she was pressed against his body.

Her anger was gone in an instant, replaced by too-familiar fear.

"Why, Sarah." He chuckled, leaning his face down toward hers. He was handsome, very handsome, but her body's small, involuntary reaction to his touch only magnified her disgust.

"Let me go, Mr. de Lint," she said, the words crisp over the tremor that she couldn't quite contain. If she could only fight back, hit and scream and bite. But she was a servant; she could do nothing, or she would lose the only thing she had ever earned.

To her astonishment, he released her—so abruptly that she staggered back and one heel struck the edge of the landing. Catching her balance at the brink, she lurched past him and darted into the cool darkness of the Palazzo Bovolo, trying to bury in her hatred of him the cold, sick certainty that their encounter was not at an end.

Chapter Two

"'I am quite sure that you are right and that Elizabeth will see reason soon,'" Lady Merrill dictated. "'Give all my love to Aunt Gertie.' There. That's the last of them!"

Sarah set down the pen and blotted the final lines of the letter, rubbing her aching hand against her knee under the cover of the desk. Lady Merrill's correspondence, always considerable, had expanded to something vast with the backlog of letters that were waiting for them when they arrived. Nor had they been the first missives Sarah had penned that day, for as soon as her single battered trunk had been taken to her room, Sarah had found her ink and stationery and had quickly dashed off notes to those few people to whom she mattered: the Owen sisters, with a special note for Nan's seven-year-old son; Giles, the terror of Harrow; Frankie, who had no permanent address but who could always be reached with a letter sent to the Crow and Lark; Harry, now a schoolmaster; and finally Maggie, especially Maggie, who had known Sarah longer and better than anyone.

As Sarah set aside the blotting paper, Mr. de Lint stirred from where he stood over Sarah's shoulder, leaning against the deep edge of the window frame. He reached across her, deliberately brushing her cheek with his sleeve as he plucked the finished letter from the desktop. She controlled her urge to flinch, staring at the golden wood.

"You have a nice hand," he said, examining the page with a critical air. "From this, one would think that you could write from childhood."

"I could," Sarah said shortly, her pride getting the better of her for an instant.

"Really?" His tone dripped curiosity, and Sarah regretted her admission immediately as her anger withered away, leaving her once again without support.

She stood, retrieved the page, and slid it into place at the bottom of the pile waiting for Lady Merrill's signature. "Yes."

Sarah handed the stack to Lady Merrill, then crossed to the window farthest from her employer's son. Through the open door, she could hear the girls' voices twittering from some other part of Lady Merrill's second-floor piano nobile apartments, and she tried to fix her mind upon deciphering what they were saying. Anything to distract her from her spiraling apprehension of Mr. de Lint.

"Oh, Bertrand, do quit teasing the poor girl," Lady Merrill said absently as she shuffled through the pages to find the ends of the letters. She had become farsighted with age, but she refused to wear glasses on the principle that it would make her look like even more of an old woman, so Sarah did both her writing and her reading for her.

"Our Sarah doesn't mind, do you, my dear?" Mr. de Lint's response sounded genial, but it rasped a warning across Sarah's eardrums. Her hands tightened on the window frame, but she made no reply, knowing that neither truly expected one.

Sarah was used to Mr. de Lint in only small doses; even on the steamer, he had quickly gravitated toward men of his own tastes, and since Lady Merrill forbade hard liquor, gambling, and risqué stories in her presence (rather hypocritically, Sarah thought, since she engaged in all three with her old friends), he had spent most of his time out of his mother's company.

But since his encounter with Sarah at the water door that morning, he had stayed close to her and his mother, finding sudden amusement in seeing to the unpacking personally, much to the exasperation of his valet, the annoyance of his mother's lady's maid, and Sarah's embarrassed anger as he fingered the plain eyelet of her undergarments before allowing the Italian chambermaid to put them away. Sarah had no energy left to guess when his whimsy might lead him away and only hoped it would be soon.

"It isn't quite what one imagines, is it?"

Sarah jumped; she hadn't heard Mr. de Lint approach.

"No," she said, knowing that he meant the view and, by extension, Venice.

It seemed a safe enough reply. Blue Mediterranean skies and marble palaces shining like mother-of-pearl at the edge of a glittering sea: Such images had entertained her on the long, slow voyage from Southampton.

But the waters of the lagoon were dark with silt and reeked of sewage, pungent even to one who had grown up in the rookery of St. Giles, and the sky was hidden by a damp gray pall that wound through the streets, making the soot-marked marble glow a sickly, cancerous white and the red and gold brick loom suddenly as winds shifted the fog.

And yet her first impression of beauty was not contradicted but complicated, made into something both less ethereal and more eerie. Gazing at the magnificent decadence around her, she found it difficult to mourn her half-formed dreams that were lost.

"With any luck, it will be sunny tomorrow," Mr. de Lint said. "Even Venice has foggy days, but they aren't common except in winter."

"That's nice," Sarah said after his silence had stretched out expectantly for several seconds. She wasn't sure that she meant it. There was something menacing in the fog-wrapped streets and the black water of the canals. But there was also something half-familiar and almost reassuring, as if a piece of London had come with them to remind her that they were not, after all, so very far away. London, which she loved and loathed and already almost missed . . .

But London wasn't here, and it wasn't her home anymore, anyhow, nor would it ever be again. What was here, though, somewhere in the mist, was the man in the shadows, with sharp eyes and a dark hood on a day that had only the slightest nip of chill in the air.

A man who had been watching her, as ridiculous as it sounded. She hadn't been able to make out more than the indistinct shape of his features, but she knew, gut-deep, that they were handsome, that the flash of lining in his overcoat's hood was silk. It had to be an accident—the man had been waiting for something, for someone else, and so he had watched the unloading for a lack of anything more interesting in view. Mr. de Lint would surely laugh for days if he knew she imagined such a man would look at her for any other reason than boredom or malice.

But she didn't think it was an accident. And it troubled her and filled her with a sweet strength all at once.

She turned her back to the window, coming around to face Mr. de Lint. With the image of the man in the shadows fresh in her mind, she could smile blandly at her employer's son despite the studied insult of his gaze.

Mr. de Lint gave her such a perplexed expression as she brushed by that a half-hysterical giggle caught in her throat. She swallowed it and retrieved the signed letters, banishing her fancies and turning to the task of addressing the envelopes.

Sebastian looked up from the ledger in front of him as Gian entered his office at the Palazzo Contarini. The young man had been recommended by Whitby's Venetian contact, and so far, he had proved himself worthy of every confidence. He was exactly what Sebastian had requested: discreet, capable, educated, and very, very handsome. It was a good thing, for Whitby always took a holiday in spring or summer, and before Sebastian had left England, the agent announced that he was arranging this year's to coincide with Sebastian's trip, declaring in his dry way that with his employer officially dead, his services would temporarily be superfluous.

"It is done, sir," Gian said without preamble in his near-flawless English. "With any luck, Bertrand de Lint and his mistress will both be at Bellini's masquerade tonight."

"Separately." It was a half question, half statement.

"But of course."

"Good." Sebastian allowed himself to indulge in a moment of satisfaction. "Tell the girl—what is her name?"

"Domenica."

"Tell Domenica to be ready, just in case. I do not want there to be any mistakes tonight."

"Of course not, sir."

"Thank you."

With a curt bow, Gian left.

It was strange not to be addressed as *my lord* or *your lordship* after twelve years of growing accustomed to it, Sebastian mused, turning his attention back to the stack of financial records that, until now, he had never bothered to review. Sebastian had ordered the books to be gathered before Adela's attack out of the vague realization that perhaps he should take more of an interest in his own properties and investments, but he had never actually opened them before. The irony was not lost upon him; here he was, traveling in the disguise of one Señor Raimundo Guerra of Argentina, and yet he was closer to fulfilling his duties as a peer and landowner than he ever had been before.

The last four months had changed him; there was no denying that. Sebastian rubbed the side of his jaw, clean-shaven for the first time since he left Eton for Cambridge. He was not sure if he liked this new identity, but right now, he didn't care.

Or so he told himself. But when he awoke in the dead, black hours of the night and lay staring at the shape of the moldering canopy above him, he was not so blasé.

Sebastian stood abruptly and circled his desk, bracing a hand on either side of the window behind it. Below him, a handful of Venetians passed back and forth along the raised pavement that bordered the canal as boats slipped like slow sharks down its length. Except for the muted sounds of footsteps, occasional bursts of ironic laughter, and the ever-present strains of distant music, he could hear nothing.

Every time he came to Venice, the silence took him unawares. It was something that he remembered in his mind but that could not be felt in the soul until he had entered the lagoon. The half-empty city was wrapped in dreams of grander days like a smothering shroud, its empty palazzi echoing with the faded memories of old glories. There was no clatter of horse hooves and carriage wheels to break that meditative stillness, to disguise the forlorn and faltering heartbeat of the once-great city in the manufactured bustle of modern life.

And on this trip, without the self-conscious raucousness of deliberate overindulgence, there was nothing to muffle the memories of those other visits in happier times that now seemed like another life. In those halcyon days, he and his mother had stayed in the quiet back canals of Venice and moved among the most dignified circles of the international traveling community. They were pleasant, dreamy memories, to be certain, but the taint of later events always encroached upon that golden time until every sunlit, silent moment seemed like an omen of what was to come.

Venice was the problem, Sebastian decided. Its mournful atmosphere caused his doubts and dark thoughts, made him mistrust himself and wonder if he had ever known who he really was. Was he even capable of reformation, or was he only lying to himself because he could not face the soulless reprobate he must always be?

Soon, he would leave, and when he did, all his newfound doubts would be left behind in this troubling city. But first, he must do what he'd come for. No matter what the cost.

*　　　*　　　*

With quiet relief, Sarah slipped out of Lady Merrill's chambers, closing the door behind her. All the rooms of their floor opened onto what Mr. de Lint called the portego, a long central room that ran the entire width of the palazzo from the canal façade to the garden. It was open to the night air on both ends, an intricate loggia standing in place of wall or windows to form a space that was a kind of balcony and a grand reception room at once.

Now the chill night breeze blew through the stone fret-work of that balcony, bringing with it the fresh, salty tang of the rising tide to wash away the stench of old sewage. Sarah shivered, pulling her wool shawl more tightly around her shoulders, and walked toward the end that faced the canal. The sconces on their floor were all unlit, but gaslight from the first piano nobile blazed from the doorway to the grand staircase, throwing her path into a dancing half illumination of shadows and light. When the palazzo had been a single residence, the stairs had been open to the level below. Now, the new, unadorned plaster walls and unassuming door were a sad juxtaposition to the glorious architecture of the room, an intruding rectangle that interrupted the view from one end to the other. The kitchen and servants' quarters for all the suites were still on the water floor, so the door spent most of the day opening and shutting as maids passed back and forth—or standing wide open to the floor below, as it was now when a servant went on a quick errand.

Lady Anna had discovered—through her usual habit of boldly asking anyone she stumbled across anything that suited her fancy—that the rooms on the first-floor piano no-bile had been divided into separate apartments of two to three rooms each, as had the mezzanine floor below that, and the occupants were in the habit of joining together of an evening in the public space of the portego. Sarah wondered, briefly but intensely, what it would be like if she could bor-row one of Euphemia Morton's frothy gowns and descend the stairs to join the genial crowd below, laughing and talk-ing like one of them, perhaps even taking a turn on the ancient and out-of-tune harpsichord upon which one or another occasionally played a brief riff.

But Sarah dismissed the thought almost as quickly as it formed, shaking her head at herself as she crossed the balcony room. She did not belong with those artistic souls and expatriate Bohemians. She knew it, and they would know it, too, as soon as they laid eyes upon her.

All she truly wanted was her bed, she told herself, turning her gaze away from the hypnotic lights below and fixing it upon the small door that led to her bedchamber. Weariness was making her entertain strange fancies—for she *was* weary, wearier than she ever thought a day of tending to a kindly old lady could possibly make her.

It had not been her employer who had exhausted her but the woman's son and the strange, piercing attention that he paid her. Mr. de Lint had stayed through supper, lingering over a postprandial glass of port until Lady Merrill announced her intention of retiring for the evening. Then, finally, he had stood, swept one of his self-consciously ridiculous bows, and taken himself off. Mr. de Lint's interest was unwelcome to Sarah and stirred a cold disquiet deep in her belly, the glint in his eyes a familiar echo of years she wished only to forget.

Even when Mr. de Lint hadn't been dexterously tormenting her, there was the matter of the man in the shadows to keep her mind tied up in knots. Her emotions vacillated from dark foreboding to secret pleasure to disbelief that the man's awareness of her had meant anything at all. He had seemed so *edged,* the antithesis of a casual observer. And then he had disappeared.

Once, the attention would have driven her to terror, but there was no one left from her past who might take such an interest in her now. But why—why, then?

Sarah shoved away her half-formed speculations as she reached her door and unlocked it, pushing it open to reveal the room within. Her chamber was small but comfortably appointed, the asymmetrical plasterwork of the ceiling, higher than the room was wide, showing that it had been divided from a much more imposing chamber. In addition to her steamer trunk, it boasted a long mirror, a desk that doubled as a nightstand, an ancient wardrobe rather larger than the sum of the clothes she had ever owned, and an iron bedstead. A bedstead, she abruptly realized, on which lay something more than a counterpane, something that glowed and glittered in the light of her candle.

Startled, Sarah left the door open and crept forward, half-afraid that it might be some sort of elaborate prank laid by Mr. de Lint. As she approached with the candle held high, the glow resolved itself into the froth of lace and silk, the glitter into the dazzle of glass and paste jewels.

It was a dress, a dress like she had never seen before, glowing in a tangle of blue, pink, and gold. Shamelessly gaudy, luxuriantly tawdry, it was a wonder and horror all at once. Upon it lay a white demimask, encrusted with more false gems, and a note.

Entranced, Sarah picked up the paper. It was plain white stationery, folded once, utterly nondescript. She opened it.

Palazzo Bellini, Campo Morosini. Tonight.
Compliments.

And that was it. No signature, no hint of its origins.

It still could be some sort of convoluted trickery by Mr. de Lint, but Sarah knew his handwriting, and this was not it. He could have gotten someone else to write the note, of course, and his exaggerated show of attention earlier might have been a preamble to this. But he'd had no opportunity to plan it, and it didn't seem his style; besides, this was the first day that he'd ever paid her so much heed.

She trailed her fingers across the fabric. It must be a costume for one of those carnival parties that Mr. de Lint had kept going on about. Tonight, at the Palazzo Bellini. She wouldn't go, of course. That would be sheer folly. Not only would it be ungrateful to Lady Merrill's generosity to sneak out in the middle of the night like some libidinous scullery maid, but Sarah knew only too well what lurked in city streets after dark, and the invitation itself was steeped in the danger of unanswered questions.

Besides, she would look like a proper doxy, dressed up like a false lady with her disfigured face giving her the lie. She of all people knew what every man thought when he saw a woman like that.

She looked at the mask again and noticed for the first time the veil that was attached to the bottom. Her face . . .

Setting down her candle on the desk, she shut and locked the door before taking up the mask and putting it on in front of the mirror. The hard, smooth papier-mâché hid her upper face, leaving only her eyes to shine through the glittering encrustation of paste and crystal jewels, and below, the gold veil was thick enough to hide all detail while thin enough to hint at the shape of her lips, the line of her jaw. She could even eat and drink in total anonymity, she realized. Looking at her reflection, she could easily imagine that the woman behind the mask was a real lady, lovely, maybe even beautiful.

Breathlessly, Sarah shed her dress—and her crinolette, too, when she saw that underpinnings had been provided. Wide panniers in the style of the pre-Revolution French court replaced her partial hoops, and she pulled the dress on quickly over them.

The bodice gaped along the front fastenings, an inch of her corset cover showing at her waist, so she shrugged out of the sleeves and yanked on her corset laces, cursing under her breath, until she had cinched in her waist another inch. The dress was made for a fashionable waistline, which would be nearly impossible to achieve for an average woman without assistance. Fortunately, Sarah was on the thin side of fashion, so it was manageable alone.

There. The hooks on either side of the stomacher fastened easily now, though the deep neckline threatened to expose her modest underclothing. She stuffed the edge of her chemise into her corset top and wiggled experimentally. It still showed, but only if she moved too much.

She turned toward the mirror and caught her breath.

The dress was magnificent. Pink silk bows, each knot clasped in a glittering brooch, cascaded down the stomacher. The rest of her torso was hugged by a rich brocade of blue and gold, flowing down into a gown that was held up in flounces and ruches over an underskirt of pure gold. Everywhere was more pink ribbon, more rosettes of false jewels.

She felt perfect—and invincible. For a long moment, she just stood there, staring at herself, not daring to believe that it could be her body encased in such elegance, her face behind the mask and veil. She was not blind to the tawdry fabric and cheap construction, but whoever had made it had possessed an eye for beauty, because the effect was gracefully dazzling, and it took almost no imagination to make the costume real. The eyes in the mirror glittered with a shine caused by more than the candlelight.

Blinking away the dampness, Sarah turned back to the bed, where a curled white wig and a pair of golden slippers with pink bows awaited her, sitting atop an enormous black cloak. A feeling of unreality settling over her, she put them on.

When she turned back to the mirror to face the vision there, she knew what her decision had to be.

It took only seconds to wrap herself in the enveloping cloak, blow out the candle, and slip out of her room, locking the door behind her. She slid her room key into her corset and drifted along the portego toward the back stairs, her heart singing a song she hadn't imagined that it knew.

She paused only long enough to duck into a drawing room to purloin a map and an exterior door key. The door onto the garden stairs gave with a slight push, and then she was outside.

Whatever moonlight there might have been was smothered by the lowering clouds and the fog that twined up the sides of the buildings like ivy. She felt her way down the spiral staircase, one hand trailing against the stucco wall as her feet reached out gingerly for each step. When her fingers brushed wood at the level of the mezzanine apartments, the voices of two tenants passed close by the door. She froze, catching her breath, but the voices receded again without incident, and moments later, she stepped out onto the flags of the garden courtyard. Holding up her long skirts, she slipped through the gate and emerged in a narrow lane, amazed at her own daring.

Ahead, streetlamps flickered though the rising mist, beckoning her onward.

The map was almost indecipherable in the half-light of the nearest lamp, but it revealed enough to show her the way, and her memory of other midnight passages down other streets guided her past too-dark courtyards and too-narrow alleys, skirting the hunched figures that hurried through the fog or lurked in the shadows between the guttering islands of light.

The night was full of sounds: the barking of dogs, the patter of cats' paws, voices raised in anger or amusement. But the noises were different from those of London—and unnerving, for without the constant rumble of horses and carriages, each sound stood out alone, distinct and separate, instead of fading into the dull roar that for her had always meant a city. Most foreign of all, though, were the songs. Snatches of tunes or whole melodies echoed faintly through the darkness, sung boldly and with an unselfconsciousness that bewildered her. Three voices, four, ten—she couldn't tell how many there were or where they were coming from, but they were all deep, male, and resonant. Who was singing, she wondered, and why? She shivered and hurried onward.

Sarah stopped as she reached an intersection where several of the angled streets met to form a square that the map called a campo. It was like a dozen others she had already passed through, with one exception: a single palazzo that shone with golden lamplight, laughter and music pouring from it to fill the air and drown out other, more distant songs, a hundred familiar and exotic scents flowing out of it all at once to overlay the raw stench of the canals.

This was it. The moment of choice. She could still slip back through the fog-thick night to the comfort of her bed-chamber. Or she could abandon caution and enter—to face adventure, her mysterious sponsor, and answers to the question that had plagued her since she left Lady Merrill's apartments: *Why?*

She stepped forward.

In the crush of the overheated rooms of Ercole Bellini's palazzo, it was hard to believe that the glories of the Republic were a near-century dead. All that was fantastic and much that was grotesque were represented there, from corpulent, bare-chested satyrs to delicate Borgia maidens, from flamboyant peacocks to tall, pale unicorns with silver horns.

Sebastian lounged in a corner of the water-floor entrance hall in a tiny island of space, the marble of the wall cool against his shoulder blades as he nursed his Vin Santo. He was tall for an Englishman, far taller than the mongrel Venetians who made up most of this motley gathering, and he glowered over their plumaged heads at the street-facing doors as he had since he arrived.

A swirl of horns and feathers, false furs and glittering masks heralded the passage of a clutch of revelers who shoved their way down the staircase and out the wide double doors, laughing and shouting drunkenly on the campo before reeling back inside. Forgotten, the flung-back doors swung gently in the night breeze, but by the time that faint wind passed through the crowded front hall, it was no more than a breath of air, rank with scented lamp oil, toilet water, and the sweat of a hundred bodies.

Surely, if she were coming, she would have arrived by now. But what woman could resist such an invitation as the one he had sent?

Maybe de Lint had other plans for her this evening. Sebastian took a swallow of his drink, as if he could chase away the thought with the action. The idea unsettled him, and he didn't know why, which unsettled him even more. There had been something about the way the woman had held herself, something in her expression when she looked at her employer that made thoughts of de Lint's using her uncomfortable.

Which was ridiculous. She was a whore—no more, no less. She might be a clever one, having charmed her way into becoming de Lint's mistress, but her essential character, or rather lack of it, had not changed. She would come.

Suddenly, he caught sight of a familiar towering wig among the crush of admirers around a singer whose prowess relied more on volume than skill. He frowned in disbelief. Until that moment, he had not taken his eyes off the campo entrance, so unless she had arrived by the water door, there was no possible way that she might have entered without his spying her. He cast a glance around the edge of the stairs to make sure that Gian's harlequin back was still planted at his post by the water door. It was.

He shook his head, dismissing the dilemma. How she arrived didn't matter. She was within his grasp now.

Sebastian pressed through the throng, shouldering aside nymphs and soldiers in the wake of that bobbing headdress of white curls. Yes, now that he was closer, he could see that the gown was certainly the one he had chosen from the draper's shop.

And yet . . . its wearer's back was straight with pride, her movements steeped in poised elegance, and even her slow walk as she moved through the entrance hall was almost hypnotic in its sleek, assured grace. Where was the small, insignificant creature of the ferry, wrapped in dignity like a suit of armor? This one needed no such defense.

She reached the stairway just as Sebastian pressed past the last person separating them and extended a hand. His fingertips had hardly brushed the smooth flesh of her shoulder when she jerked away, spinning to face him.

A shock ran through Sarah's body, a jolt that shot from the fingertips on her shoulder into her core as his eyes met hers. They were green, an enchanting green, too perfect to be real, and she knew it must be *him*.

Under a coiled turban, the man's entire face was covered by a blank white mask, the nose a soft hump in the lacquered papier-mâché, the lips immobile, cold and inhuman. But those eyes were anything but cold, and the instinctive recognition she felt could not be mistaken. It should have been impossible for her to recognize the man from a few seconds' half-obscured glimpse, but she knew it must be him with a certainty that shook her.

She had not thought he would be so big. Even though she stood a step above him, he was still slightly taller than she, and her eyes lowered involuntarily to the quilted coat that pulled taut across his wide shoulders. But more overwhelming than his size was his presence. Nuns and jesters jostled her as they passed up and down the stairs, but when they reached him, they simply made room, giving way like water parting around a rock.

He slid his hand from her shoulder down her arm. She stood stock-still, frozen in the force of his attention, not sure if the gesture was a simple movement or a caress. Her body didn't care. Even through the fabric of her sleeve, she could feel the heat of his palm skating across her flesh, and tension wound through her every nerve, making her heart race and her breath catch as her cheeks flooded with heat.

He caught her hand and brought it to those white, frozen lips. The hard mask brushed coldly against her gloved knuckles, but his eyes, those eyes . . .

"Madame Marie, I presume," he said. His voice, pitched low, had a hint of command in it and an edge of darkness that made her breath catch again.

Her lips began to form the first letter in an unconscious echo: "M." His gaze jerked downward to her mouth, and she stopped. How much could he see through the gauze? In her mind, she reflexively reviewed her careful examination in the mirror. Not much, she reassured herself. No, not much at all. She stood in plain sight yet was as good as invisible; for the first time in her memory, she was truly free.

She laughed aloud at that thought, surprising herself. The sound was rusty, hesitant from disuse, but it felt so wonderful that she threw back her head and laughed again. The man's eyes narrowed, sparking with some sinister emotion, but at that moment, she didn't care.

Marie, he'd said. Like Marie Antoinette. She surveyed his own oriental splendor, from the scarlet turban to the emerald knee-length coat, billowing white trousers half covering golden curly-toed slippers beneath.

"So I am. Monsieur Moor?" She smiled at him through the veil. She had no idea if the tailor had meant the costume to be Moor, Moroccan, Turkish, or Arab, but it was close enough.

"Indeed," he said crisply, the hint of authority sharpening to a whip crack. In one quick maneuver, he tucked her captive hand under his arm so that it came to rest on the quilted silk of his sleeve, turning her so that she again faced up the stairway. He stepped up even with her, and his shoulder rose above her eye level. "There is dancing above. Would you care to join me?" It wasn't a question.

She laughed again, knowing that he was trying to intimidate her. Ugly, scarred, frightened little Sarah would have been trembling in her shoes, furious at her own fear and his presumption both. But she was free of all that now. He could have no idea of what lay behind her mask or he would not have invited her. She was not worth the attention of a man bent upon practical jokes—even Mr. de Lint targeted her only because of her convenience. The Moor must have seen . . . something else, something as beautiful, ephemeral, and as false as the mask she now wore—something he wanted. And that was what she was, at least for this night. She tipped up her chin recklessly, but some little part of her still gave a sad wrench at that thought, another small agony in the slow death of a dream she'd never really believed in.

And in answer, cynicism followed, burning away regret. It didn't matter why he'd sent the dress, why he wanted her company now. It didn't matter if he'd be disgusted by her face or if he was some pervert or sadist who enjoyed disfigurement but was better at hiding his pleasure than most. He wanted her for something, false or not, and she wanted him—for the dream, for the memory, for the beauty.

"Indeed," she returned, a conscious echo of his last response, and he looked down at her quickly, surprise in those emerald eyes behind the perfect mask. That revelation of vulnerability sent a surge of confidence through her even as the keenness of his gaze called up a heat that speared downward, through her center, and rose up again to leave her skin feeling flushed and irritated. She stepped up quickly, half fleeing from that feeling, half rushing toward the dance floor that waited for them above.

They arrived at the ballroom just as a schottische was ending, the orchestra barely audible until they stepped inside the door for the cacophony of songs and conversations that filled the palazzo. Surrounded by a perimeter rectangle of columns, the dance floor teemed with revelers in fanciful costumes, and at least twice as many filled the space along the circumference of the room. But the Moor simply forged ahead, and resistance melted away in front of them until he came to a stop in a small clear space in the middle of the floor.

He turned Sarah to face him just as the five-piece orchestra, squeezed under the colonnade by the press of dancers, began a waltz. The Moor bowed, flaring out his cape, and pulled her into dance position before she could react.

"Shall we, your majesty?"

"Certainly, my Sinbad." She laughed again, because she could.

The pressure of his hand on her waist tightened fractionally, and then they were waltzing.

Until that moment, Sarah's dancing experience had been limited to the weekly hour-long lessons at the Dunnefirth Ladies School, where for lack of partners the girls took turns leading. She had never considered how very different it would be in the arms of a man instead of a giggling school-mate. But there was more to the feeling that swept over her than that alone could account for.

It was like something out of a fairy tale, though no blushing Cinderella would feel so light and heated, so impossibly aware. The Moor was a tall man, but through the heady haze that engulfed her senses, he seemed nearly giant, his hands so large that hers felt lost within his grasp, his chest a wall in front of her face so that she had to crane back her head to meet his eyes. And where he touched her, sensation poured through her, and his gaze quickened parts of her that had never before stirred without a dark edge of humiliation as accompaniment.

The floor was crowded, too crowded, and as they whirled within a hairbreadth of a Greek goddess, her Moor pulled her even closer so that she felt the pressure of his legs against the front of her panniers.

I should not trust his skill, she thought, the memories of a thousand clumsy collisions that had occurred under the dancing master's severe glare sharp in her mind. But the steps of the Moor seemed enchanted, drifting them through the crush of dancers as softly as a breath of air, and Sarah found herself surrendering to the fantasy.

A space opened ahead, and he guided them deftly into a momentary opening. But though there was no longer an excuse for it, he did not loosen his hold, keeping her pressed to him so that she could not take a breath without her breasts moving against his chest.

She should object, some distant ladies-school part of her mind told her. She should pull away, reestablish a proper distance, for such treatment was an insult to a lady.

But Sarah also knew, in the depths of her soul, that she was no lady. Clad in her sober browns and blacks, she now held employment as a decent working woman—before, she had not even been that. Never, never could she be a lady, not even dressed in silks and jewels, not even if they were real. Even the other schoolgirls had eventually realized that.

So she did not protest, and she did not pull away, not even when the Moor bent his head down toward hers so that she might have felt his breath on her cheek if not for their disguises. The bald white mask was perfectly asexual, but those eyes, that body, made it seem profane.

Recklessly, Sarah smiled into that perfect white face and asked, "Why did you invite me here?"

It happened so fast that she could barely encompass it. In an instant, their turning progress across the floor became a whirl of motion that ended when her back fetched up against one of the perimeter columns hard enough to knock the wind out of her.

The Moor's eyes glittered, staring down at her as she gasped, trying to catch her breath. His hands were splayed against the pillar on either side of her head like bars of iron, his weight pinning her against the marble, cool on the damp, prickling skin of the nape of her neck. His arms, his body, and her own towering wig effectively held her immobile.

Over his shoulder, she caught glimpses of other couples, flying past in reckless hedonism. If she cried out, surely one of them would come to her aid. But she didn't want to cry out. Even as her head still spun from the force of the contact, even as her shoulder blades protested being ground against the stone column, the thrill that buzzed up her spine had far more to do with arousal than fear.

Somehow, the demon Moor must have read something of her thoughts in her gaze, because the gleam in his eyes changed to something less cutting if no less brittle, and a low chuckle came from behind the mask, as bald and beautiful as the skull of an angel.

"Does it matter?" He answered her half-forgotten question with one of his own, and his voice sent shivers across her skin.

Before she could reply, he drew back slightly, and by the time she realized what he intended, he was already pulling his mask up so that it rested on his turban like the second face of some two-headed oriental god.

And a god he appeared in truth. No Adonis, certainly, for there was nothing golden about him; he was shadow and moonlight, a Pluto so perfect that Sarah could not help but wonder if Persephone had eaten those seeds on purpose, after all. His forehead was broad and intelligent over the tempestuous black sweep of his brows, his glittering eyes as hard as emeralds on either side of the sharp blade of his aquiline nose. But what caught her attention most of all was his mouth—wide and full and twisted in an ironic half smirk, the mouth of a dissipated prince, epicene in its beauty yet terribly, undeniably male.

Her gaze returned to those cynical green eyes, and reflexive humiliation shot through the heat of her too-intimate admiration; her own meager assets were not worth a glance from such a man as that. She wanted to flee—she would have fled if his body had not blocked her. But the mere thought of touching him again, even to push him aside, caused a shudder of pleasure that rooted her to the spot.

He stood still for a moment, as if acknowledging her gaze as an appreciation that was his due, and his vanity summoned a dark sullenness from within her that did nothing but muddle the emotions that already battered her.

He reached for her veil, but she grabbed the edge and held it down, clinging to the fantasy as long as she could.

"No." Whatever strange fancy had made him pursue her surely would not survive that truth.

"As you will," he murmured. He grasped her chin through the gauze, his grip gentle but imbued with a controlled force that sent waves of prickling sensation across her skin. She could feel the seams of his gloves and the heat of his hand underneath.

An instant before his head began to bend toward hers, she realized what he was about. A deep joy twisted low in her belly, setting every fiber of her being ablaze in an anticipation so sharp that she gasped.

Implacably, his mouth descended, and just as inevitably, her lips parted before he even touched them.

And then she drowned.

Heat. That was the first thing her stunned mind thought. Wonderful, impossible, damp heat from soft-hard lips. At that almost tender touch, something within her broke, sending sweet pain through every nerve. He demanded, but he did not steal, and she gave gladly, gladly. The rough gauze of the veil scraped across her lips, a torture and a titillation.

When the Moor pulled back, a small noise of protest escaped her throat, and she opened her eyes to find him staring at her as she pressed herself into his body.

She pulled back, still breathless.

"No wonder—" He broke off abruptly. Sarah was amazed to find that his infernal perfection had been slightly rumpled, his eyes darkened and two faint blooms of color in his cheeks that made him look boyish, almost innocent. But his low chuckle rippled with iniquity. He shifted his grip on her chin to free his thumb, which he passed across her mouth in a slow caress. Reflexively, she took it between her lips through the thin fabric. He gave a deep breath, and Sarah heard a small shudder in it at the end.

"Tomorrow night," he said, a prediction and a promise. Then he took a step backward, into the crowd, and before Sarah could react, he was gone.

She blinked several times, clearing the fog of whatever spell he had cast over her, as the room burst into applause. For one skewed second, she thought that they were clapping for her, and then she realized that the waltz had just ended and everyone was facing the orchestra.

Sarah stumbled into the portego, searching for a scarlet turban and a white mask. None was to be found. Had he really been there? Or was it some pathetic imagining of a forlorn mind?

The damp veil against her lips was its own answer. She caught her tongue darting out to lick it for a trace of his taste. No, she didn't need that to remember him by. Tomorrow. She would see him again tomorrow.

Chapter Three

Sebastian leaned on the second-floor balustrade as the figure in the towering wig passed below him down the stairs toward the water-floor entrance. His skin felt too tight and hot under the smothering layers of silk, his mind disarrayed. Where had de Lint found such a creature?

The image of her eyes, darker than memory, still shook him. Those eyes had held neither the false coyness nor the veiled calculations of a whore. Instead they had been open, impossibly open, filled with a shifting welter of emotions— joy, a strange impishness, and not least of all, fear. He was honest enough with himself to admit that seeing her afraid excited him, filled him with a heady sense of his own power.

Half a year ago, he would have accepted and exploited such a pleasure without a second thought. Now it was an unwanted complication to his plan, but more troubling, it invited the horrible, inevitable comparison: Was that what de Lint had felt when he looked at Adela?

No. Sebastian turned away as the wig finally disappeared from view. No, de Lint's mistress had wanted that kiss at least as much as he had. Sebastian's body tightened involuntarily at the memory. De Lint's outrage could not even be given the elevated name of seduction.

Gian's face appeared between two medieval doctors, smiling under the checkered greasepaint as he beckoned

Sebastian forward. Sebastian shook off his thoughts and fol-lowed. He could not afford any distractions now, however tempting and however troubling. It was time to meet his ad-versary for the first time since his pretended death in the car-riage accident. Sebastian had anticipated this moment for weeks with a dark joy, and he felt the emotion rise within him again. Was this the reaction of an avenging fury or a self-deluded demon? He shuttled that doubt aside and stored it with all the others as Gian opened the door to a small side parlor, motioning Sebastian inside.

De Lint stood with his back to the door, turning with all evidence of mild, idle curiosity as Sebastian entered.

Sebastian felt a small, sick shock. So much had changed for Sebastian since they had last seen each other that he had subconsciously still been expecting to see the same kind of change written upon de Lint at close range, but the man was identical to the urbane gentleman he had confronted at the Whitsun Club, the same even as the close friend Sebastian had drunk and caroused with a scant half year before. As usual, de Lint wore the impeccable evening suit that was his uniform on almost every nocturnal occasion, a plain black mask his only concession to the nature of the festivities.

De Lint held out his hand for a perfunctory, condescend-ing shake, and suddenly Sebastian's shock turned into a rush of anger. How dared he, the monster that he was, dress him-self like a gentleman? How dared he hold himself with such dignity when he was worthy of nothing but contempt? Se-bastian thought of how easy it would be to end it right there, in that room, with a quick knife in the ribs and a shove through the window.

But no. De Lint might deserve all that and worse, but he would not know why he was being killed; he would not have time to appreciate his sins and his punishment, and to the world, he'd die a respected man, foully murdered in the treacherous political and moral labyrinth that was Venice.

So Sebastian pushed down the red heat of his rage and forced himself to return de Lint's handshake firmly, cordially. Even so, it was all he could do not to crush de Lint's gloved hand and smash in the black mask with his fist.

What is wrong with me? That phrase had of late almost become a mantra. He had thought he was prepared for this encounter, had played it out a thousand times in his imagination, but now that he was faced with it, he could hardly keep control of himself.

"I received your note," de Lint said crisply in his word-perfect but heavily accented Italian. "I already had three other invitations for tonight. From *English* gentlemen."

"And yet you answered mine." Despite the anger that still heated his veins, Sebastian had the presence of mind to put a slight Spanish flavor in the Italian of his response. Between the two unfamiliar languages, he had gambled that de Lint would not be able to recognize a dead man's voice.

De Lint made an impatient noise. "It had better be worth it."

"I have heard from a mutual friend that you are a man of discriminating tastes." Sebastian affected an overly delicate pause. He felt like a clown. Surely de Lint would see through him. . . .

"Perhaps." De Lint's eyes shifted distrustfully behind his mask.

Sebastian was caught. He forced himself to stumble on despite that certainty. "My own taste, like our friend's, is also somewhat unorthodox. A beautiful woman is an incomparable adornment to one's bed—unless, of course, she is followed by an even more beautiful man."

De Lint drew in a sharp breath as he realized what Sebastian was saying, and his eyes narrowed. In England, such open talk could lead to criminal prosecution. But they were very far from England, and as soon as his surprise wore off, a spark of intrigue lit in de Lint's eyes. Sebastian began to believe that his charade might work, after all.

"Oh, yes, Venice is a city of pleasure," Sebastian said, making little attempt to hide his eagerness. "*Every* pleasure. Many gondoliers can be as accommodating as any courtesan—for the right price. If you would like, I could introduce you to a few who are appropriately . . . sympathetic."

De Lint laughed, shaking his head, the first of his defenses coming down. "Old Mansfield misled you, I'm afraid. It was Mansfield, wasn't it?"

Sebastian just shrugged noncommittally.

"At any rate, that is one vice I've found no stomach for." De Lint rocked back on his heels, a smile still in his voice.

"Well, then, perhaps there are others? Mrs. Jeffries does not have a monopoly on houses where the pain of love is perhaps a little more literal than is usually conceived," Sebastian offered.

De Lint shook his head again. "Again, my appetites do not lie in that direction, nor can I think of why you would wish to help me even if they did." The last words seemed innocent enough, but de Lint imbued them with a slight edge, as if he only wanted to be convinced.

Sebastian gave a good imitation of a slightly self-conscious cough. "The truth is that I find myself rather embarrassed for funds at the moment, and as I know certain aspects of the city better than any other expatriate, I make myself available to other visitors, to ease their way in any endeavor. I confess that I am compensated for my recommendations."

De Lint burst out laughing. "You are no more than a pimp!"

Sebastian made his back stiffen in a show of offense while trying to keep the triumph out of his voice. "If you don't care for my services, then there are plenty who do." He turned and made as if to leave.

"Come, now, chap," de Lint said easily. "I was just having a bit of a jape at your expense. I didn't say that I wasn't interested."

Sebastian turned back. Under his mask, his smile took on a feral edge. "I am pleased to hear it, signor. Exactly what piques your interest?"

"My interests are . . . various. I have grown bored with

the fetching little whore of sixteen to forty, and I seek to expand my experiences."

"So what do you prefer? A woman who is not a prostitute? Who is ugly, deformed?"

"That, yes, and more. I collect them, you see. The fat, the rail-thin. The old, the very young . . ." De Lint trailed off. "The very, very young . . ." His eyes glittered hungrily from behind that black mask, the dark mirror of Sebastian's own disguise, a demon to his ghost.

"I believe I might know just the girl for your tastes," he made himself say, forcing himself not to grind out the words. "I can have her meet you tonight—"

"There's no hurry," de Lint said.

"Tomorrow, then."

"Yes. Tomorrow would be good. First, though, I would like to see the face of my . . . partner."

It was Sebastian's turn to laugh. "I prefer the mask. You will receive another letter tomorrow, sent with the same discretion as the first. I must bid you farewell, for I have many more plans for tonight."

Sebastian gave his enemy a perfunctory bow and left, old anger and black glee dogging his steps back down the stairs. Still, he could not help but see in his mind an image of a woman's soulful dark eyes superimposed over the memory of de Lint's smiling face.

The next day dawned as bright as Mr. de Lint had promised, and the rain-scrubbed breeze held only a hint of the stench of the day before. From her bedchamber window, Sarah could see a slice of blue sky above the opposite building, and the sun warmed the red tile roof and yellow brick so she could really believe she was in the Italy of her Baedeker's travel guide that she had studied so diligently during the voyage.

In that clear, brilliant light, it was hard to believe the events of the night before had been anything but a dream. Holding a clean chemise, Sarah paused in her dressing to press her fingers against her lips where the Moor had kissed her. She could almost feel it now, the rasp of the gauze, the sweetness of his mouth. Could it have been real? Almost as important, did she want it to be?

The proof remained: When she opened her wardrobe, the fantastic costume still lay inside. The false jewels were lusterless in the frank light of day, the fine damask revealed as a clever print—but unavoidably, undeniably there.

There were no more answers to the questions that had buzzed through her mind since she'd first spied the stranger than there had been the night before, but Sarah still smiled as she dressed, feeling unaccountably lighthearted. She would see him again soon—so he had promised, and so she believed. There was no rational basis for her faith, and indeed, it was against her nature and experience, but it was no less real for that.

She did not know what he wanted of her, but she didn't care. The memory of the night before sparkled like a diamond in her mind, making her feel reckless—and alive. No one had ever wanted anything from her before, not Sarah, herself, and whatever the reason, she was glad for it.

That feeling lasted until Sarah opened her bedroom door to find a table laid for breakfast on the water balcony of the portego—and Mr. de Lint sitting in one of the two occupied chairs. Bracing against the feeling of sickness in her stomach, she greeted them, Lady Merrill with genuine warmth, Mr. de Lint cautiously, aware of how well he could twist anything she might say, and took her seat across from the lady's son.

She needn't have bothered with her care. Whatever mood had caused Mr. de Lint to torture her the day before had left as inexplicably as it came. Lady Merrill was always slow to wake up, so she sat in silence as Mr. de Lint chattered amiably at both of them about the food, the weather, and the sights of Venice, his sudden friendliness making Sarah feel more hollow and cold than any of his measured insults. She hated him, she hated him down to her bones—and on days like this, when he was warm and amicable, her loathing of him made her feel petty and stupid, made her almost believe that all his small cruelties really were just jokes and she was too twisted and spiteful to take them at face value.

She almost wished that she dared speak and confess her adventure of the night before to him, to flaunt it, to see his face when she described how at least one man wanted to dance with her, to kiss her, even, and not for mockery's sake. It was a foolish wish, and so she held her tongue, but visions of Mr. de Lint's reaction entertained her until she finished her meal.

Finally, Mr. de Lint stood from the table, plucked two roses from the arrangement in its center, and threaded one into his mother's coiffure and the other into Sarah's severe bun before retiring to his room. Lady Merrill was still chuckling when Lady Anna and the Mortons burst out of their chambers and dashed down the portego to the breakfast table, the governess Miss Harker frowning as she followed.

Lady Anna carried an enormous sheaf of lilies before her, and she pushed aside the roses to shove them into the center of the vase. Breathless and beaming, she plopped into the chair across from her grandmother.

"Really, Anna," Lady Merrill said mildly. "I can hardly see you for that forest of flowers."

Miss Effie snatched up the vase, and she and her sister examined it for a moment before she set it on the sideboard. Then, casting accusing glances at their friend, they sat down to eat.

Lady Merrill's eyes glinted with amusement. She must be thinking the same thing Sarah was: that the mysterious flowers were from some admirer and that Lady Anna was teasing her friends by not telling them about their origins.

The idea sent a shiver of disquiet up Sarah's spine. First the carnival costume in her room, and now a huge bouquet of flowers—of lilies, of all things, more suited to mourning than to wooing—for Lady Anna. What was happening? Did she . . . could she really believe it was a coincidence?

But Lady Merrill went back to her unhurried eating

without the least sign of being perturbed, so Sarah held her tongue. Her suspicions, however strong, were nothing more than that, and there was no way to tell Lady Merrill of them without revealing far more than she wished.

Sarah could wait. If there were answers, they would come in time. She looked at the three young girls, engaged in a flutter of pointed giggles and whispers, and wondered what the answers might mean to them—and to her.

It was well after noon by the time the three gondolas finally nudged against the water stairs of the Molo and Lady Merrill's party stepped onto the Piazzetta. The three young ladies had lingered over their breakfast, exchanging whispers and nudges when they thought no one was looking. Miss Harker had browbeaten them into sitting sullenly over their lessons for an hour and a half before their determined dullness gave her a fit of nerves that forced her to retire to her bedchamber. Lady Anna was twice as difficult as the Mortons, her expression studiously dreamy, tempting her friends' questions even as she put them off with vague, unsatisfying replies. Silently witnessing the small drama play out from the other end of the portego, Sarah had taken dictation for Lady Merrill's daily correspondence as she wondered what it all meant.

Ahead of Sarah, Mr. de Lint helped Lady Merrill from their boat, and Miss Effie and Lady Anna scrambled out of theirs. Miss Morton, miffed at not being allowed to crowd in with the other girls, alighted with more dignity, and Sarah followed.

She allowed herself to fall behind almost immediately; Lady Merrill was walking on Mr. de Lint's arm and did not appear to want her presence, and Sarah was more than happy to keep her distance from the man. Instead, she allowed herself the luxury of gazing about as blatantly as the girls were doing, staring at the strangely blocky and flat-roofed building that was the Doge's Palace and at the glorious dome that rose beyond it.

"Isn't it perfectly hideous?" Lady Anna exclaimed as she linked arms with the Mortons, motioning toward that dome.

"It's more like some sort of heathen temple than a proper church," Miss Morton agreed.

The relevant passages of her Baedeker's sprang reflexively to Sarah's mind. "It's Byzantine, modeled in the tradition of the Hagia Sophia," she said before she could catch herself.

All three girls stopped in their tracks and turned around with varying expressions of surprise and derision on their faces. Sarah felt her cheeks flame with anger as much as embarrassment. Why did she always speak when she had learned long ago the value of silence? And why—whenever she did—why must people like *them* look at her as if she were a talking pig? It had been six years since she'd left the disgrace of the rookery—four since she'd even allowed herself to think in the slang-ridden and discordant patois of the streets. And yet it was not enough. Nothing would ever be enough.

After a moment's wordless staring, the girls turned away again, relinking their arms and continuing their easy stroll as if nothing had happened.

"I can't imagine why they built such a thing," Miss Effie said, launching an unfavorable commentary in which they compared the building with every cathedral and parish church that they had ever seen in England or France.

Sarah had seen only a few cathedrals before, and all of those in London. But as they approached and she made out the building more and more fully, she decided that the basilica was compellingly exotic, with its fantastical yet substantial domes and its oriental peaked arches, glittering with golden tiles. It would have looked perfectly at home in a color plate of Morocco or Constantinople. In Italy it should not, but somehow, it did.

She slowed, craning her neck to try to make out the mosaics in the front arches and the details of the four horses that surmounted the front of the roof. When she looked down again, the others were disappearing inside. She hurried after them, ducking between the columns of the arcade before stepping down into the church itself.

Gold. That was her first impression—great arched domes of gold. As her dazzled vision adjusted to the dim yet glowing interior, she realized that the entire ceiling was covered with mosaics, hundreds of stylized figures laid out against a gleaming gilt field.

Ahead of her, Sarah caught the words "St. Paul's" in a disdainful tone. The girls were right; it wasn't like St. Paul's at all. That cathedral was a clash of garish colors, the stained glass at war with the awkward mosaics and modern geometric floor.

But the pure light that streamed through the high windows here did not muddy the colors of the roof. Instead, the domes and arches shone with a delicate luster, the fine lines and formalized postures of the figures picked out precisely against the gold above the undulating floor. This was a place of fantasy, of inhuman beauty that belonged in the world of dreams that she had shared with the masked Moor the night before.

At that thought, a small shiver overtook Sarah, and she looked around suddenly, half certain that her abrupt disquiet had its source in *his* eyes upon her. Other groups of tourists gathered in the vast space, and a few Venetians prayed near the altar, but none could have been her Moor in disguise.

The sensation that he was near, once felt, was impossible to shake, however. Sarah imagined his eyes peering at her from every pillar's shadow; she heard his voice in every echo. Even as her reason dismissed it as foolishness, the power of his presence settled over her like a smothering length of velvet, lush and stifling.

Lady Merrill made a circuit of the church on her son's arm, duly commenting upon the Pala d'Oro, the depiction of the theft of the body of Saint Mark, the tabernacle door behind the high altar. The girls followed, but Sarah stood rooted near the entrance, torn between the desire to hide her face and to charge into every shadowed corner until she found her watcher and drag him out into the light.

Finally, Lady Merrill tired of the church and led the girls out of its wide doors and back onto the Piazza. With a surge of relief, Sarah followed, half stumbling back into the day. The glittering blue sky and the broad expanse of mundane cobblestone should have dispelled any lingering sense of foreboding.

It did not.

While Sarah hovered uneasily at Lady Merrill's elbow, the girls exclaimed over the campanile—the oddity of its red brick in a sea of white, its disproportionate folly, and its awkward placement jutting into the Piazza. Lady Merrill just stood under the edge of the portico, watching them with a comfortably indulgent expression across her face and with no sign of the slightest anxiety.

A balmy breeze blew in from the sea, and Sarah shivered as the hairs rose on her arms. She knew at a level deeper than instinct that *he* was there, close by, watching. The others might be blind and deaf to the sense that was sending alarms through her body, but it was real, nevertheless. Gone was any gladness at the thought of seeing the Moor again. Here, she was revealed for what she was, in her made-over bombazine and with her scarred face bare to the sun. Underlying and more powerful than that purely selfish desire to avoid exposure, though, was a new sense of danger, as disturbing as it was unexpected.

Finishing her crushing critique of the campanile, Lady Anna skipped back to her grandmother's side and declared her intention of climbing it.

"You girls run along," Lady Merrill said, laughing at her exuberance. "I'm too old for that sort of thing, but Bertrand shall stay with me, and Sarah shall take my place as the guardian of your maidenly virtue. It's fortunate that she came. After all, who knows what nefarious personage might be hiding up there?" Her eyes sparkled at her own jest.

"Yes, madam," Sarah murmured, hiding her dismay. She

could not think of a task more inappropriate than serving as a chaperone for three innocents, she who had sneaked out for a tryst only the night before. But there was nothing to be done about it, and so she smoothed over her expression and did as she was told.

The three girls hardly spared her a glance before darting ahead, Lady Anna's and Miss Morton's heads close together as they began an intense, whispered conversation, Miss Effie bobbing along behind and trying to hear. Sarah guessed that Lady Anna was finally divulging whatever great secret had kept them all in a tizzy the whole morning. She did not attempt to overhear; since Lady Merrill seemed to be unconcerned, she did not feel that her duty extended to eavesdropping, and she had an innate aversion to being a spy.

Instead, Sarah kept her distance, glancing covertly at the Venetians and foreigners who strolled through the square or lounged at the caffè tables under the long porticos. Could one of them be the Moor? But none of the figures was tall enough; none had his near-palpable presence.

The girls ducked into the open door of the loggia ahead of her, and after speaking briefly to the caretaker in a kind of pidgin mixture of Italian and English and passing him a handful of coins, they continued through to the tower proper and started scrambling up the ramp that served in place of stairs. More sedately, Sarah followed. The caretaker's room was small and shabby, with laundry strung across one side and a snaggletoothed old woman stirring something on the top of an iron stove for an even more snaggletoothed old man. He waved her through—fortunately, Lady Anna had already paid her way—and she started up the ramp with the decorum of any proper chaperone. The picture of propriety, she thought with some irony, since her mind could not abandon thoughts of the man who had kissed her the night before.

It was a long climb to the belfry. From the sounds above her, the girls had flagged in their precipitate progress at least two full turns before the top. Even at her slower pace, Sarah was slightly winded by the time she emerged into the breeze and sunshine. By then, the girls were leaning against the sill of the marble loggia, laughing breathlessly and exclaiming about the view.

Sarah's rigorous schoolgirl constitutionals had dissolved into near-sedentariness since she had entered Lady Merrill's service, and she paused in the doorway to catch her breath. Once she crossed the threshold into the belfry itself, her range of view broadened, and she discovered that they were not alone. On the far side of the belfry, half hidden by the bells, stood a dark, tall, lean figure, and Sarah could barely stifle a gasp of recognition.

It was the Moor. She knew it, though his back was squarely to her. Jet hair—even when it had been hidden by his turban, she had known that he would have jet hair— waved over the back of his collar, and every line of his powerful frame was strung with a self-aware arrogance that was utterly and completely unmistakable.

He must not see me. That thought was an agonized wail. This close, he could not fail to notice her disfigured face, and she could not, would not let that happen. Without thinking, she spun away and started to flee down the ramp, but she had gone only a few steps when she recalled her duty as chaperone and froze. She stood there, torn by indecision, until the sound of movement behind her made her glance back.

He had turned. Sarah's breath lurched in her chest, her hands flying up automatically to hide her scarred cheeks. But his gaze did not seek her out in the darkness of the stairwell, and she would have sworn that he had not noticed her at all except for an infinitesimal quirk of the lips that, though barely discernible, was somehow suggestive.

Precious Lord, did he realize it was her? Or was she imagining things?

As soon as that thought came, though, his attention clearly fixed upon the three girls who still leaned over the loggia with their backs to the room, and his attitude altered minutely, his shoulders drooping, the patrician pride seeming to flow out of him all at once. Then he stepped forward—toward Lady Anna.

For one mad second, Lady Merrill's cheerful warning against tower-top ravishers echoed in Sarah's mind, and she braced to lunge forward, fighting against the panic that welled in her throat. But then he spoke, and his voice startled her into stillness again.

"My lady." The words did not resonate with the beautiful, cultured Englishman's drawl of the night before but were thick with the guttural accent of the Venetian dialect. It was only then that Sarah realized that he wore another costume, another disguise, this time the rough clothes of a local laborer.

The girls turned at his words, staring at him with the contemptuous astonishment that Sarah was all too familiar with.

Despite their reactions, the man's shoulders did not hunch in humiliation. Why would they? He was no more a laborer than he was a Moor. From her oblique vantage, Sarah could see the side of his smooth brow as his extended his hand. "My master bids me give you this."

Unresistingly, Lady Anna stood with her mouth hanging open and allowed a grubby piece of paper to be pressed into her hand. The man swept a bow, and Sarah had just enough time to hide her face against the wall before she heard him turn. The stairwell darkened briefly as he filled the doorway, and a moment later, his long coat brushed against her skirts and he passed. For an instant, she felt the heat of his gloveless fingers against the back of her bare neck, and then he was gone, leaving behind a chill that crept up her spine.

Sarah trudged up the ramp again and into the belfry, knowing that she should do something, say something to somehow make right what had just occurred. But Lady Anna gave Sarah a hard look, a combination of scorn and defiance in her face as she unfolded the note. Sarah's stomach sank. She should order the girl to hand over the letter, but she knew Lady Anna would simply disobey, and Sarah couldn't face the humiliation of tattling to Lady Merrill—and worse, the questions about her own strange behavior that Lady Anna might ask in return.

Overlaying those fears, though, was the sharp knowledge of how deep such hypocrisy would be when her neck still tingled from the Moor's touch. Who was he, and what had that gesture meant? Was it a caress, a warning? Both? And a warning against what? Impotence mixed with shame and anger into a hard, hot ball of emotion that she had to swallow to keep down.

Deciding that Sarah had been properly cowed, Miss Morton and Miss Effie crowded around Lady Anna as she read the letter, whispering fiercely over its contents with the sheet angled so Sarah could not make out a pen stroke. As soon as they were satisfied, they darted past Sarah to clatter down the stairs as if they feared she would try to confiscate the missive had they stayed.

Attempting to catch them up was useless. Accepting that defeat, Sarah lingered for a moment in the belfry to steal a glimpse of the view that the girls had so volubly enjoyed, walking a slow circuit around the perimeter of the room. Far below, the city spread out in a panorama of red brick, white stone, and acres of tiled hip roofs that reached to the edge of the sea. Except for the distant pearl gray of the lagoon, Sarah could not make out even a telltale glint of the water that ran alongside three-quarters of the buildings, the height transforming the maze of the city's canals and alleys into one aggregate mass of masonry. *Mysterious even from this vantage, when all should be made clear,* she thought, and she felt obscurely pleased.

Reaching the stairs again, she ducked back down them, following her charges and the much more immediate mystery of the Moor's letter.

After a long tea at Caffè Florian on the Piazza—within the gilded rooms rather than under the portico because Lady

Anna declared, to Lady Merrill's patent amusement, that eating outdoors in public was a vulgar foreign habit—the group once again retired to their gondolas. Lady Anna and the Morton sisters stepped out ahead, whispering furiously and linked arm in arm.

When they were still a dozen yards from the Molo, Lady Anna stopped dead with a gasp, staring directly at the boats. The other girls looked up for an instant, then ducked their heads and hauled her forward among smothered gales of laughter.

Lady Merrill paid the girls no more heed than Mr. de Lint did, continuing her tranquil stroll across the Piazzetta. But Sarah followed Lady Anna's fixed gaze to one of the gondoliers waiting for them at the steps of the Molo.

Or . . . *was* he a gondolier?

He was holding an oar, certainly, and he tipped his hat at their approach like the others. But his clothes, though of the appropriate white, were far too fine, his face open and full of a boyish handsomeness Sarah knew many young women found irresistible. Looking back at the girls, Sarah was certain she knew the contents of the Moor's letter as surely as if she'd read it.

Lady Anna and Miss Morton scrambled into the first gondola, holding each other's hands and gazing admiringly back at the handsome youth through the rear window of the felze. Sarah cast a half-desperate look at Lady Merrill just in time to see that woman bestow a tolerant smile upon the two girls. Her heart sank. Whatever game was going on here, Sarah was certain it was not innocent. But she could say nothing when Lady Merrill refused to be disturbed, for she had no proof but a few wild suspicions and a tale that pointed only to her own unreliability.

Her mind hummed with questions she had no answers for. Why had the Moor sent for her the night before? Why had he kissed her? Maybe he had been planning to mine Sarah for information as a part of a scheme to kidnap Lady Anna. Maybe he wanted ransom—or maybe he planned to elope with her in hopes of a generous bribe-cum-marriage settlement when they were caught. Or maybe he really did work for that smooth-cheeked gondolier. . . .

Sarah's mind reeled with a dozen possible schemes, each more impossible than the last. But she stepped silently into the second gondola behind the disgruntled Miss Effie as Mr. de Lint helped his mother into the third. As they were rowed back to the palazzo, the sounds of laughter came frequently from Lady Anna's boat, and though Sarah spent the whole trip tensed for the instant the trap would be sprung, they arrived with no incident more notable than Miss Morton opening the felze door to get a better look at some landmark and then accidentally dropping her handkerchief into a canal.

Chapter Four

Sebastian stared out of the window of the Casinò Giallo, a discreet suite of rooms that had performed the venerable but illicit function of a private trysting place before the fall of the Republic had brought the tradition of the casinò and so many other of the old customs of Venice to an end.

A stroke of luck had caused Lady Anna to climb St. Mark's campanile with no company but her friends and de Lint's mistress, making Sebastian's task of passing the note to her trivial when he had originally intended to use the belfry only to spy upon her and predict a convenient moment to present the message. And he was certainly pleased with the results, both what he had witnessed and what Gian had reported. However, it was not that triumph that his memory kept returning to but the haunting mind's-eye image of a small, drab figure in an unfashionable hat with her face turned toward a redbrick wall.

A knock at the door echoed through the parlor, dispelling Sebastian's thoughts.

Shaking his head, he checked his pocket watch. Nine o'clock, precisely on time. De Lint was many things, but he was never tardy. Sebastian snapped the watchcase closed and slid it back into his fob pocket, checking in the mirror over the mantel that his demimask was affixed correctly and the soft hat covered his hair. De Lint had never seen him with less than a full set of fashionable muttonchops; his clean-shaven chin should now be as effective a disguise as any larger mask.

"Come in," he called in Italian, and the double doors swung open to admit the Spanish butler—*Where had Gian found him?* Sebastian wondered—followed by the handsome, immaculately attired de Lint.

"Señor de Lint," the butler intoned, bowing before closing the door behind the man.

This time, it was easier to come face-to-face with the man who had assaulted Adela and almost murdered him. The blast of rage Sebastian had been braced for did not come. There was still a low boil of old anger deep in his gut, but his fury had finally spent itself. Was it a sign of salvation, or was it yet another weakness, another inconstancy, that he could not hate de Lint in every moment the same?

"Honored signor," Sebastian said in Italian, affecting the accent of his character Señor Guerra. "I am so pleased you could come."

"Wouldn't miss it for the world," de Lint replied easily, sprawling into the chair Sebastian offered. He smiled. His face had a ruddy, healthy glow in the gaslight. Sebastian's gut tightened.

"A drink?" he asked, pouring himself a generous splash of rum. He needed it.

De Lint waved him off, and Sebastian took a quick swallow from the tumbler as he settled into the chair across from de Lint.

"I'm usually not so . . . involved in this sort of thing, signor, but I wanted to make sure that you found the arrangements to your taste," Sebastian said, putting the sound of nervous strain in his voice, hoping it would hide sharper emotions. "I should like one of Mansfield's friends to carry back a good report of me."

De Lint laughed. "Because so many of our companions

are equally debauched? Whatever you wish. As long as the girl's here."

"Oh, she is." Sebastian raised his voice so that it could be heard through the closed door. "Domenica! Domenica!"

Sebastian watched de Lint out of the corner of his eye as the whore hurried in. He had it on good authority that she was twenty years of age—and the mother of two, to boot—but she looked no more than twelve. With huge, soft eyes in a delicately rounded face, she looked beautiful, innocent, and painfully young.

De Lint straightened abruptly when he saw her, his eyes lighting. "Hello, Domenica." His voice was soft, as if she were some small animal he did not wish to frighten.

Domenica played her role well, turning her enormous doe eyes toward Sebastian in pretended uncertainty.

"Go ahead," he urged her, swallowing against the ugly tightness in his stomach. Even knowing the whole thing was a sham, he felt dirty as the woman-child walked tentatively up to de Lint. De Lint pulled her onto his lap, bouncing her in a twisted parody of paternal attention. She giggled.

"Very nice," de Lint said appreciatively.

"Then I shall leave you." Sebastian stood a trifle too abruptly.

"Payment?" De Lint arched an eyebrow.

"Her mother will come after you're finished, though I will be back in the morning if you are still here. Good day, signor." Sebastian turned away and walked jerkily from the room, not stopping until the door was closed behind him. He leaned against it.

What was he doing?

But then he thought of Adela and all she had suffered, and he pushed away from the wall and strode firmly down the corridor. He was doing only what he must, though this pittance of penance and retribution would never balance out against his sins.

And yet, it was not Adela's memory but the image of an insignificant woman in black that troubled his mind as he leapt into his sàndolo and sent it skimming away through the canals. Tonight, he hoped, would be the end to that preoccupation.

The portego was dark and silent when Sarah sought her room, for Mr. de Lint had left after luncheon and had not returned, Miss Harker had herded her charges to bed hours before, and Lady Merrill, who always claimed that old women like her needed very little sleep, had finally retired. That lady had wished for half an hour of poetry read from her favorite book—a posthumous collection of Byron's work— while her lady's maid McGarrity readied her for the night, but eventually she had been tucked securely in bed, the gaslights had been extinguished, and Sarah was released from her duties until the next morning.

And now her senses buzzed with the pent-up anticipation of the day, built upon the Moor's promises and the strange events of that morning, which still made no sense to her. Her hands shook so badly that she had to try twice to unlock the door to her bedchamber.

It was the nervous exhaustion from the day that was making her feel pulled so thin and tight, she told herself firmly. But she knew that was only partially true. She wanted to run away from what had happened that day—the letter she didn't tell Lady Merrill about, the suspicions she couldn't tell her about, and the growing feeling that something terrible was going to happen and that it would be all her fault. The promise the Moor had extended the night before hovered in her mind like a blessed escape, which made no sense at all, since he was the cause of all her fears and confusion.

Finally, the key slid in, and she pushed the door open the moment the bolt snicked back. Her heart in her throat, she crossed to the bed, holding her candle aloft.

The counterpane was bare. No new dress, no new letter, nothing.

Disappointment washing over her, Sarah sat down heavily, sinking into the old down mattress. Whatever the Moor had wanted from her, he'd gotten it, and she didn't matter to him and his plans anymore.

"I am relieved," she said aloud. He was trouble, and nothing good could have come from a second invitation. She should be glad to see the last of him and his disguises.

But even as she repeated a hundred sensible reassurances to herself, the image of her future closed in upon her: a bleak, colorless life as a companion nurse to a succession of elderly ladies until she was too old to work and must return with predestined inevitability to the workhouse where she had been born.

Sarah closed her eyes tightly against those thoughts and blindly set the candle upon the night table with quite a bit more force than was necessary. The edge struck the neat stack of books on the corner, and she had to grab for the candlestick to right it. A French primer, an English grammar, and a geography book from the Dunnefirth Ladies School sat under her newest acquisitions, the used copy of Baedeker's Venice she had hoarded her money to buy and the cast-off ladies' magazines that Lady Anna and the Mortons had brought with them. A pile of dreams and disappointments. After sixteen years in the rookery, years made bearable only by the friendship she had forged with Maggie and the companionship of their strange family, she had expected her escape to come with some sort of enlightenment, some sense of purpose like the rest of her family had gained. Maggie had found hers in her husband and the cultivation of her voice. Nan had found it in caring for her little sister and her young son. Harry was a schoolmaster. And Frankie had never doubted that his place was always in the streets where he had been born.

But what was Sarah? That question had haunted her for years, though she had never acknowledged it in those desperate days when it was enough to have a little food and part of a dry bed. She was no one's sister, no one's mother, no one's wife—nor could she ever see herself in terms that were so simple and conventional. She had thought for the two years after Maggie had married and for the four years when Maggie sponsored her at the ladies school that what she truly wanted was respectability, but after her time there had ended in a debacle, she realized that wasn't true. She craved not to be judged, which was a very different thing. She craved to be listened to, to have a place in the world where she fit even without the usual titles of kinship by which most women were identified. And though Sarah herself would never be lovely, she longed to be a part of something beautiful.

That was why she had shunned everything that reminded her of the ugliness of the streets, of the sense of self-loss she had fought against for so long. That was what had drawn her so to the hope of Venice, and that, as much as anything else, was why she wanted the Moor's promise to be true.

With a sigh of resignation, Sarah reached blindly for one of the magazines, but a soft, whispery sound made her jerk around just as a piece of paper fluttered onto the tabletop like a small ghost.

There it was. A sheet of plain stationery, now spotted with wax droplets. Her hands trembling, she slid it out, and something round and smooth rolled across the tabletop, dislodged by that movement. Reflexively, she caught it before it hit the floor.

It was a pearl. She scraped it against her front teeth automatically, as she had learned to do in the rookery. It was real. It must be another gift, like the dress, but why would the Moor have sent her something so extravagant?

She unfolded the sheet of paper, recognizing the handwriting from the night before.

Campo Manin. As soon as you can.

*   *   *

Sebastian slid the sàndolo up to the water stairs, the gondolier's jacket pulling taut across his shoulders as he stopped the boat with a skillful stroke of the long oar. The boat was his fa-

vorite when he rowed himself, a little shorter than his gondola
and with a single straight, open bench without the black hood
of a felze enclosing the passengers' compartment.

Before him lay a bare gray campo, desolate in the
gaslight and fog of the empty night—empty save for a tenuous, cloaked wraith that stood in the halo of lamp-white
mist, a stray cat twining about its ankles. He had thought
that he had been soundless, but the wraith's head turned toward him, and from the darkness of the cloak's hood, he
caught the glitter of jewels.

It isn't her. That was Sebastian's first thought, and it froze
the breath in his lungs and made his head spin with a
strange, sudden lightness. The gamble of that afternoon had
proven too brave, his gift either too paltry or too alarmingly
generous to tempt her, and the whore had confessed everything to de Lint, who had sent someone in her place to trap
the trickster, the plans of months unraveled at a stroke.

But almost as soon as that idea had taken shape, the figure disengaged itself from the cat and began to approach, instantly dispelling his hasty conclusions. Though he had seen
it only once before, he knew that proud tilt of the head, that
graceful sway of the hips beneath the cloak that clung to her
too narrowly to be supported by a crinolette. She was so un-
like the hunched creature he'd left in the campanile only
hours earlier and somehow far more real. His body knew
her, too—recognized her instinctively and responded, his
groin tightening and a hot buzz of anticipation thrilling
across his skin.

Sebastian was still off-kilter from his body's swift reaction when she reached the water stairs. Without a word or
hesitation, she stepped into the boat as mist swirled in tenta-
cled eddies around her booted feet.

She trusted him. The discovery hit him like a slap, knocking away the heat of sensual expectation. Her confidence
was written in her careless step, in her unrestrained movements, in how she easily turned away from him as she pre-

pared to sit on the bench—and he had to catch himself to keep from recoiling.

It was true that Sebastian had planned to seduce her into a complacent confidence in him. But he had prepared for a fight against a well-armed foe, expecting to trick her through devious battles of wills and wits and bodies. This was a surrender he was not prepared for—a surrender to a boatman hired by a mysterious stranger with dubious intentions, for all she knew. Yet she did not seem weakened by it, and that left him all the more unbalanced and unsettled.

He tried to summon those emotions that should be his as a self-anointed avenger—a righteous satisfaction, a holy wrath. But her sleek grace as she settled onto the cushioned bench in front of him dashed any thoughts of sanctity from his mind.

Clenching his teeth, Sebastian slid the oar into the correct notch of the forcola post. The leverage of the oar shaft against it sent the sàndolo slipping into the center of the canal with one smooth stroke.

"You're to take me to him, I suppose." The woman spoke at last, as if their departure were some sort of signal. He looked down at the top and back of her hood, all that was visible from that angle. Her voice was serene, with no more excitability than if she'd been speaking of the weather, its impeccable tones betraying less-than-irreproachable roots in their very perfection.

Where had de Lint found such a creature? And what, exactly, was she?

"*Si,*" Sebastian muttered in reply.

She drew a sharp breath of air at the sound of his voice and whipped her head around. Keeping his eyes on her, he ducked his head slightly so that his black felt hat obscured his features more fully.

That small shift in his position threw her masked face into the full light of the lantern that hung from the stern. Behind the glitter of the false gems, her wide eyes sucked the flame reflection into their depths, as dark as the night and as deep as sin.

"It is you," she said, her voice somewhere between an accusation and an epiphany.

"But of course, my dear." Sebastian summoned the appropriate croon easily. Too easily. Even in his own ears it sounded like an exaggerated performance of an uninspired script.

She made a quick, abortive wave, whether angry or dismissive, he could not tell. "What game are you playing at?" Her eyes went as hard as the glass gems, and she swung her legs over the bench so she was facing him squarely.

That question, at least, required no melodramatic declarations in response. "What do you think?"

"I think . . ." She paused, while the sharp-edged look around her eyes softened. "I think that you plan to seduce me."

That announcement was followed by a strangled moment in which there was no sound but the splash of his oar as he propelled them mechanically between the looming walls of the buildings that crowded the canal. That confounded veil, that cursed mask . . . He longed to tear them from her face, to hold the boat lantern up and read what was hidden behind them. He was supposed to have the control—he was supposed to play at being the master of disguises, not this woman, his victim.

But he did none of those things. Instead, he finally broke the silence by saying, "If that is what you believe, then why are you here?"

"No one has ever wanted to seduce me before." The words were simple, but under them was a rawness that stung him.

No, a scarred whore wouldn't have much experience with the gentler side of lovemaking. The thought was distant, as if it did not belong to him, for his mind was overwhelmed with her presence and her hurt—and the desire they stirred in him.

Sebastian didn't know whether he wanted to feast on that ache or soothe it, and at that moment, he did not care. He tossed the oar into the bottom of the boat, and she jumped at the clatter, her eyes darting down to it for an instant before snapping back to his face.

The sàndolo rocked as he slowly lowered himself toward her, first crouching, then kneeling on the flat deck so close to her that her knees pressed into his thighs. The woman grasped the gunwales against the boat's sway and stared down at him, uncertainty in her eyes. Her movement parted her black cloak, exposing the bodice of a drab traveling dress that was ridiculous yet somehow poignant beneath the tawdry ostentation of her costume mask.

Sebastian reached up slowly, giving her time to stop him, and pushed her hood back to reveal a loose mass of red-blond curls that gleamed in a golden halo in the lantern's light. She sat frozen except for one small white hand, which lifted to cling to the edge of her veil in a mute prohibition. He did not argue but simply clasped the back of her head and pulled it toward his. She yielded, if stiffly, and she did not turn her face away as he sought her mouth with his own.

He found it. Her lips were hard and a little cold through the veil for the space of a breath. Then she made a small animal sound back in her throat, and all at once she melted. Her lips parted under his, welcoming him through the rasping fabric, and she leaned toward him, sliding her feet backward under the bench until she, too, was kneeling with her torso pressed full-length against his.

The boat rocked with that movement, and her body went still, but her mouth . . . her mouth was so hungry, so rich and wonderful, and it took all his willpower to keep from snatching her veil away so that he could taste it all, flesh on flesh. Her lips were small and soft, her mouth sweet and giving, her teeth slick and hard beneath the harsh cloth.

Beneath her clothing, her corset was stiff against his chest, but her shoulders eased under his hands, her neck tilted back in submission to his touch, and the knowledge of his power inflamed him.

When they separated, she stared breathlessly up at him for one long moment. The shadow of his body fell across her face so that her eyes were inscrutable, and he tried to project an air of mystery and calm, though he was acutely aware of the blood that still thrummed through his veins. She shouldn't affect him so. He'd kissed a thousand women, and her lips could not be terribly different from all the others. Was it his plan, then? Did some sick part of him feed upon the knowledge of future cruelty? He shuddered from the thought.

Finally, the woman broke the silence. "You do want me. But having some idea of who I am, you must know that I have nothing to offer you." It was a flat statement of fact, incongruous compared to the kiss they had just shared and the slight inclination her body still had toward his.

"You are a lovely woman," something made him reply.

She leaned away from him, turning her head aside fast and angrily. "Do not mock me."

"I do not mock." The words came out too fast, a schoolboy's fervent defense.

She did not reply. She just levered herself back up onto the bench behind her, the barrier of her knees coming up between them to break the sense of intimacy they had just shared and bringing him back to an awareness of their surroundings.

They were adrift in a canal so narrow that he could almost touch the buildings on either side with his outstretched hands. There was no pedestrian pavement here, just blank white walls rising from water that flashed quicksilver on jet in the light of the boat lantern that still bobbed with her motion.

Sebastian stood and retrieved his oar, slotting it into place on the forcola and sending them down the canal with slow, efficient strokes. She did not meet his eyes, and the mask blocked his view of whatever expression she might have had.

"If you are certain I know who you are, why do you still wear the mask?" Sebastian asked with some asperity. It was hard to gauge her reaction with her face hidden and averted, but it seemed that she flinched at the question.

"It isn't *who* I am that I do not wish you to know." Her voice was rough from some emotion, but he could not decipher it. The delicate emphasis, though, was another matter entirely—if not *who,* then she must mean *what.* And *what* was a woman with eyes that tugged at his soul and a face checkered with scars.

She must truly not apprehend that he knew what she looked like in any detail, he realized, the discovery amazing him and making him ache for her even though the last thing he wanted to feel for that woman was sympathy.

"You would not take it off to let me touch your cheek, your lips?" he asked. "Not even to let me kiss you?"

Her eyes found his in the darkness. "No," she said softly. "Not even for that."

And then she turned away again, and he did not interrupt the silence until they arrived at their destination, leaving those words to hang in the air and pierce him again and again.

He took her to the Palazzo Contarini because de Lint was still availing himself of Casinò Giallo, which Sebastian had rented for the sole purpose of acting out his revenge. He should feel uneasy about bringing her to his residence; it was a weakness in his strategy, and he knew it. She had not been a part of his original scheme, though, and so his last-minute arrangements had none of the polish of his plans for de Lint.

Still, the feeling that roiled inside him was much more akin to defiance than disquiet. What could she do to him, whore that she was, even if she did find the palazzo again? When he was finished with her, she would be abandoned to the lean streets and canals of Venice.

Sarah watched as the Moor stopped the boat in front of one of the broad façades that crowded the narrow canal, no different from a hundred other deteriorated palazzi that they had passed.

"Are we here, then?"

"Yes, madam," he intoned in a dramatic voice she could not quite believe was genuine. Before she could challenge him on it, though, he leapt lightly to the pavement, leaving her alone in the boat as he secured it to a post set into the walkway.

Sarah tried to ignore the swaying of the boat and the lapping of the water at its sides, focusing instead on the building that rose behind him. As she did so, she realized that the narrow circle of the boat's lantern had tricked her into thinking it much smaller than it was.

The palazzo that Lady Merrill had taken was large enough to make seven apartments in addition to the servants' quarters on the ground floor, but this structure was far grander and far, far more forbidding, the antithesis of the golden, airy rooms she had left behind. White stone walls, mottled with grime and canal slime, seemed to pulse with coldness in the lantern's swaying light, and the black doors before her stood closed, thick and blank like a challenge and an omen. Above them was some sort of carving, dark with speckled mildew, and Sarah abruptly realized that it was the representation of a huge spider, crouched above the lintel on a stone web. *"Will you walk into my parlor," said the spider to the fly.* She recalled the line from the child's poem and shivered.

For the first time since she had pulled the mask over her face that evening, she felt like herself again: small, weak, and insignificant. Her host had some plan greater than her in mind; that much she knew for certain. A girl like her could disappear behind those walls and never be heard from again, and no one would ever know or care.

She started as movement in her peripheral vision impinged upon her fearful imaginings. Turning, she faced the Moor, who had descended the water stairs again to extend an arm to her.

Sarah stood gingerly, aware of the unsteady craft beneath her feet. She reached for his hand, the change of position causing the fabric of her veil to brush against her cheek, and she remembered that tonight, she could be whoever she wanted, mysterious and daring and maybe even beautiful.

She stepped out of the boat.

Chapter Five

Later, Sarah was never exactly sure how she and the Moor found themselves in the room he called the grand salon. He had shoved open the battered doors with a theatrical flourish and golden light flooded out, but the rest of their journey had impressed itself upon her only as a great whirl of motion. Upon crossing the threshold, they were descended upon by at least half a hundred servants, who showed no reaction to her mask or their master's costume but set about their manifold tasks with such an air of frenetic diligence that she was left breathless and dizzy. The Moor strode through them all as if he didn't even see them, leaving her to scamper in his wake, dodging the maids and footmen.

Her cloak, his hat, and his ridiculous gondolier's jacket were each whisked away by a different servant. Dozens more candles were lit until their passage was dazzling in its brightness, bows were made, doors opened, refreshments offered. And still the Moor continued without pause up two flights of stairs and through a series of chambers, oblivious to the uproar he had caused.

He finally stopped in the grandest chamber yet, and in the space of a few breaths, a flurry of servants gusted around them and back out, closing doors behind them. Abruptly, they were alone, wrapped in a sudden, deadening silence.

The room glittered in the light of the candelabra and oil lamps that clustered on every flat surface, revealing with stark clarity the moldering oriental rugs, the moth-eaten draperies and water-stained damask that was visible on the walls between dozens of ancient and inexpert oil paintings. The room looked like Hogarth's etchings of dissolution that Sarah had seen once in the ladies school's library, its worn gilt exposed in the unforgiving glare. Everything looked too real, too ugly for a night of fantasy—everything except the man standing in the center of the room.

He seemed taller than at the whirling masque or even a few moments before in the boat, but he was just as fantastic. His marble-smooth skin pulled taut across an aristocratic nose and high cheekbones under the black shadow of his brows, the austere, piercing stare of his green eyes unexpectedly belied by that too-sensual mouth.

Those features were already known to her from the half a minute he had been unmasked the night before, but now she saw the dark smudges under his perfect eyes, the tiny lines that fanned from their corners. They were not laugh lines, for there were no matching creases at his mouth, but the marks of some other tightness or exhaustion, of dissipation or squinting or anger or something far less gentle. But those minute flaws did not make him seem any less otherworldly, for they merely threw the diabolical perfection of the rest of his lean, saturnine features into focus. And if that was not enough to make her feel the stirrings of doubt, Sarah was still certain he had some plan—for her or Lady Anna or perhaps even Lady Merrill—that was far from honorable.

Still, that gaze sent shivers of heat prickling across her skin, and as he looked her up and down slowly, consideringly, the banked desire she saw in his face twisted her midsection with a tight, sweet pang of awareness.

What must I look like in my made-over black bombazine and a paste-encrusted mask? she wondered, not quite trusting that desire. *Better than if I were barefaced,* she told herself brutally, ignoring the soft, familiar pain that thought caused.

He still had not seen her face clearly, of that she was certain, or else he could not desire her—and whatever else he wanted out of her, he also wanted *her*, at least at that moment, and she would not do anything to spoil it. Deep inside, a very small part of her sneered at the desperation of that thought, but she was realistic, and she knew what her chances were of ever again attracting a man who desired something more than a ten-bob lay from any inoffensive dress lodger.

"I am Sarah," she offered, cutting short that line of thought. The voice did not sound like hers. It was rich and confident, not a subdued near-whisper.

"You may call me . . ." He paused for a moment. "Grim."

She smiled under the cover of the veil against the vague sense of betrayal she felt at such a patent invention. "I should have been more creative in naming myself, then. Sarah cannot compete with Grim."

Her host's eyes narrowed. "It is my name. Or at least a part of it." Scowling, he plucked a strawberry from the plate of fruit the servants had left on a side table and twisted off the stem. He offered it to her with an abrupt thrust of his hand, like some childish faerie-prince seized with a fit of petulance.

She took it wordlessly and ate it under the cover of her veil. "Thank you, Lord Grim."

He flinched at the honorific and gave her a hard look from under his heavy brows. "Why did you come?"

Sarah crossed the room and sat on the ancient horsehair sofa next to the fruit tray, a cloud of dust rising as she settled onto it. She plucked a succulent-looking apricot, maneuvering it behind her veil. "Why did you invite me?" she asked before she bit down.

His eyes lowered to her mouth, and she felt herself flush with the directness of his attention. "You've answered that question yourself. To seduce you."

Perhaps it was the influence of his presence, standing there and looking like a fallen angel, but she had a sudden, impish urge to provoke him, to tempt him, to see how far she could push that tension between them before it broke. "A fine job you've done of it so far."

His expression changed, the hardness cracking, and he seemed to flow forward all at once. She didn't have a chance to even gasp before he was upon her, his weight shoving her down flat against musty sofa cushions. She could feel the heat of his body, the solidity of it, pressing into her, his mouth scant inches from hers and his eyes boring into her soul. Distantly, she heard a soft thump as the apricot fell from her nerveless fingers onto the rug.

"Have I now?" he asked softly, the words barely audible above the rush of blood in her ears. "And did you feel nothing when I took your mouth against the column at Bellini's masquerade?"

Putting an elbow on either side of her head to trap it in place, he traced one long, elegant finger across her lips. Her breath caught. Through the thickness of the veil, she could feel its warmth, the subtle roughness of the pad of flesh at its tip that caught slightly at the fabric and rasped it across her lips.

"Did you feel nothing in the boat?" He lowered his face to hers until the veil moved against her mouth with every breath he took, heating the cloth that was still subtly damp from their kiss, torturing and tickling skin that was already impossibly attuned to his body and winding the sensation of the hot need tighter deep in her midsection.

"If I hadn't, do you think I would be here now?" she whispered hoarsely. Her lips and jaw moved against the breath-heated veil with the words, and she bit back a groan.

For a long moment, he just stared at her, his emerald eyes unblinking. He was going to kiss her again. Her senses sang with it, and her head began to tilt involuntarily toward his lips.

Without warning, he stood in a single swift movement, laughing softly. "Oh, no, sweet Sarah. I know when I have done my job well."

She lay sprawled for an instant, shocked at the sudden lightness and cold of the removal of his body from hers, then pushed herself into a sitting position with an angry retort on her lips.

"Eat your apricot," he said harshly before she could speak, motioning to the forgotten fruit that lay on the rug by her feet. "And do not test me again."

The apricot had landed with the half-eaten side up. Feeling suddenly lost, she retrieved it and brushed the skin against her sleeve. Why had she come here? She should leave now, before it was too late. . . . But instead of getting up to go, she brought the fruit to her lips and took another bite.

As she ate, he paced the room like a caged lion. But no, that was a silly cliché, impossible to reconcile with the man before her. Lions were noble and brave and golden. This man was made of moonlight and shadows, lean, dangerous, and sleek, more like a panther suddenly caught in torchlight and seeking an escape back into the night.

Night. The word came as the answer to a question she had not yet put into words—why, instead of a libidinous and reckless assignation, their encounter was turning into something much too real, much too complicated and uncomfortable. What they intended could not survive in the garish light of a hundred candles. It needed darkness, secrecy, and the illusion of anonymity.

With sudden decision, Sarah stood and set her apricot pit on the side of the tray, then reached over and raised her veil just enough to blow out the tapers in the candelabra that stood above it. The Moor—or Grim, or whatever it was that he wanted to be called—turned abruptly at her sudden movement, but he said nothing until she had blown out two lamps and half a dozen more candles.

"Do you intend to plunge us into utter darkness?"

She couldn't tell what emotion was behind those words, but she answered with unaccustomed self-possession. "If utter darkness is possible." She found a candle snuffer beside the next collection of candlesticks and put each flame out in rapid succession. She felt the Moor's eyes still fixed upon her, and she raised her gaze to meet his as her cheeks heated.

"You asked me to remove the mask," she said softly. "When all the candles and lamps are out, I will do so."

He looked at her, his face as cold as marble, his eyes as hot as coals, and without changing expression, he raised the nearest candlestick and blew out the flame in one quick breath of air.

As they worked, obscuring darkness fell over the rotted glory of the room, hiding age and softening the stains of neglect. Giving the Moor's shadowed face one last look, Sarah extinguished the final candle. Then only the faintest light filtered in from the wide window at one end of the room, where a full moon made the clouds glow faintly with its reflected radiance and the distant glimmers of public gaslights shone on the waters of the canals.

Sarah stood frozen, facing the dark shape that was the Moor. She could not see him as her eyes waited to adjust, but in some strange way, she could feel him, feel her attraction to him pulling her mind taut and making her breath go ragged. She could hear his breathing, and she could almost imagine that she could hear his heartbeat too, racing as heedlessly as hers.

Then he moved, shattering the illusion, and she jerked back as three quick strides closed the space between them. One of his hands caught her neatly by the waist, wrapping around her and pulling her hard against him as the other snatched the mask from her face so suddenly that the ribbon snapped.

"I could have done that at any time, sweet Sarah." The words were harsh, meant to frighten.

"I know," Sarah answered simply.

His body was lean and strong against her, full of coiled energy that made a swift chill rise along her spine even as a rich flush of physical awareness started in her center and spread across her skin.

The mask clattered to the floor, startling her, and his hand came up to cradle her face. It was not a comforting gesture. It was possessive—and self-aware in its possessiveness in a way that was even a little cruel. With his thumb, he stroked her gently—her chin, her lips, her cheek, pressing against her eyelid with a force that was slight but contained enough strength to be a warning. *I can do anything I want with you now.*

She should be frightened, one cool corner of Sarah's mind thought. The memories of other rough touches, other threats, other men's hands on her face and body clattered into her mind. Yet this touch with this hand cut through memories like a cold wind through smoke. It should have been the same, but it could not have been more different.

It wasn't yet too late, she reminded herself. She could still leave without taking this to its conclusion.

"It was a mistake to come here," he told her softly.

"I don't think so." She hoped that she meant it. Though she was not certain he wouldn't hurt her, he did not have the ugly air of a man who took pleasure from a woman's pain.

He laughed, a harsh, breaking sound. "Perhaps I do not do so well in my attempts to seduce you, after all. I should be promising you secrets that you have never beheld, experiences that you have never imagined. Instead, I try to scare you away."

"Don't promise me anything." The words spilled out before she could bite them back.

He brushed the back of his knuckles across her cheek. "Don't you like pretty words?" His voice gentled to a counterfeit croon, but she felt a tightening in his body that belied the falsity and sent an answering tingle through hers.

"I have never had a promise from a man that wasn't rotten in the middle." Her hands balled into fists around his billowing shirt, crushing the fine material as if she could hold on to the night's quickly fleeing fantasy. Why was she saying such things to him? "Anyhow," she added quickly, "I shall certainly never get a promise I can trust from you. Just kiss me again, and don't say anything that you don't mean."

"I am sorry, Sarah," he said, and something in his tone cut into her, and she knew he was sincere.

And then he did as she asked.

The first touch of his lips against her bare skin sent a twisting shock through her that was so strong she gasped against his mouth. His only response was to deepen the kiss and smother the sound, his mouth moving across hers in a rhythm that seized her in its grasp, taking control of her body and stirring hot need deep within her.

She hardly sensed the pressure of his thumb against her chin before she opened automatically to him. The touch of his tongue against hers sent a new riptide of sensation roaring through her. Her entire being was awash with it, her limbs turned to molten weights, her mind flowing with fire and her center heavy with it. He was devouring her, taking everything she gave and asking for more, more, and all she wanted to do was empty herself into him so that he could fill her up.

Slowly, the ferocity of his assault lessened, trailing into a series of briefer kisses. The flood of sensation receded, leaving her breathless, and she flushed, but she discovered she had control of her body once more—of her will once more, and what she wanted was him.

Her questing fingers found the smooth buttons of his shirt. They gave way swiftly under her touch, and she was startled to encounter naked, heated skin beneath, as if he were a common laborer indeed with no use or money for such niceties as proper flannel vests. His arms tightened around her as she freed the last button, splaying her hands against his hot, bare skin, smooth and hard under her fingers. She could feel the texture of it, subtly rougher than her own, searing into her palms with a tiny jolt of pleasured awareness. Involuntarily, she made a small noise of appreciation, and he broke away, cursing.

Before she had a chance to gather her wits about her and ask what was wrong, his strong hands settled on her shoulders and spun her away from him. He unfastened the line of cloth-covered buttons down her back with such bleak efficiency that the fog cleared from Sarah's vision and the furnace of her need died down to low, smoldering coals. She pulled away the instant he finished the last and turned to face him again, trying to read something in the pale oval of his face that she could now make out in the darkness.

"Do you want me?" she asked, not bothering to hide either her confusion or her frustration. "Or is this as much a part of your games as your costumes and your invitations?"

She could feel his eyes on her in the darkness. "I want you. I want you more than is good for me."

She drew upon the hoarse fervency of those words and took a shuddering breath, still not quite believing him but wanting to, wanting to believe him worse than she'd ever wanted anything. "Good. Because I want you, too."

With deliberation, she slid her arms from the sleeves of her dress and pulled it over her head. Her petticoats followed. The Moor made no move to reach for her, merely standing an arm's length away as the rustle of layered fabric betrayed her movements. She wondered how much he could see, and she had a superstitious feeling that his night vision was far better than her own. *But still not good enough to make out any details of my face,* she reassured herself. When she reached behind her back and began to fumble with the laces of her corset, her suspicions were confirmed.

"Allow me," he murmured. There was a touch of self-mockery in his voice as he stepped forward and turned her away from him again, this time with great gentleness, the touch of his oar-roughened palms against her shoulders thrilling softly through her.

Goose bumps rose on her neck and arms as he lifted her hair and set it over her shoulder, his fingers tangling the

strands slightly as he disengaged them. She felt the corset
laces come untied with a single tug, and she had to hold
back a shiver as he began loosening the crossed ribbons
slowly, deliberately, working up her back and then starting
over at the bottom again. With every few tugs, his movement would brush her chemise-clad back through the growing gap, leaving her skin flushed with prickling awareness in
its wake. Sarah felt her corset come loose, but she let the
Moor continue to work for several more seconds, savoring
the sensation before she stepped away from him and un-
hooked the busk. She started to push the garment off but
stopped when she felt his hands on the straps. He took it
from her and slid it from her shoulders.

As she turned, she saw him set it on the shadowy shape
of some piece of furniture, then stop again to look at her,
stirring the heavy heat in her midsection so that it licked
outward in every direction, setting her skin on fire.

"And now what?" Her voice was breathless when she finally broke the silence.

"And now," he said, shrugging out of his open shirt, "I
make good on my promises."

He reached for her shoulder again, then slid down the
length of her arm until he held her elbow. Cradling it, he
guided her to the long, low shape of a sofa and urged her
down. She didn't know whether he meant for her to sit or lie,
so she sat stiffly, her body so impossibly attuned to his that
she swore she could feel his breathing.

He made no protest at her choice. Instead, he dropped to
his knees in front of her, pulling off her cheap, elastic-
sided boots with two quick tugs and following with her
coarse stockings. Was he tender or rough, impatient or
teasing? She couldn't tell through the muffling waves of
sensation that assaulted her brain. All she could feel was
him and a welter of emotions so intense and contradictory
that she didn't know whether she would die if he took her
or would die if he didn't, but she was certain at least one
must be true.

His tug on the eyelet edge of the pantaloons penetrated her awareness, and with that mute request she untied them and rocked her weight onto her lower back so that he could pull them off. It was then, dressed in no more than her chemise, that she knew for certain it was far too late to turn back.

And it was then she knew, in her heart of hearts, that she didn't want to.

Chapter Six

Sebastian took the woman's arm roughly. The skin under his fingers was delicate and soft, but she did not protest as he pushed her peremptorily down onto the sofa.

Frustrated despair boiled up inside him. He didn't want to do this, even knowing what she was, and yet for completely different reasons that he didn't care to examine too closely, he also wanted this more than anything. If he were an uncorrupted instrument of pure retribution, his feelings would have no part in the matter, but as he looked at the pale shape lying so helplessly next to him, he wondered just how much of his revenge was for Adela and how much of it was for himself.

"Why did you come here?" he asked for the second time that night. "Tell me the truth."

She held herself very still, and for a moment he thought she wouldn't answer. "Because you invited me," she finally said, her voice so soft he could scarcely hear it over his own breathing. "Because you, this night, everything—it is a kind of dream of beauty. And there is so little that is beautiful in my life."

The too-poignant words rasped against his senses, and he jerked back involuntarily, at the last moment turning the motion into a rise from the sofa. Quickly, he stripped off the rest of his clothing as a welter of impulses, all at cross-purposes, battered at his composure. He did not want to feel for this woman.

He forced himself to recall the memory of her face, her form, and superimpose it upon the dangerously exquisite creature of pale curves and shadows that lay before him now. *She is not beautiful,* he made himself think. No sane man would believe that. Even without the faint scars that marked her face, she was too pale, too pinched, too small and colorless when tastes demanded flowering bounty.

He told himself those things, but the words battled the reality of his desire. Even in the obscuring darkness, wrapped in the enveloping fabric of her chemise, she inflamed him, and he did not want to give in to the lust that made him forget all too easily the reason he had invited her there.

The woman stirred on the sofa, extending her hand to him in mute question and supplication together, and with that small movement, lust won.

He pulled her up long enough to get her chemise off her, then pushed her down again, kneeling between her knees as he kissed her mouth fully. She was ready for him. He could feel it in the way her body trembled when his forearms brushed against her cheek, in the way her hips arched toward his. His erection ached for her warmth to surround it, and he surrendered to the urge. He shifted between her thighs, met the soft curls of her mound first and slid downward into the wet, clefted folds that guided him into her.

Until that moment, Sebastian hadn't realized how rapidly she had been breathing, almost panting, but suddenly her breath caught and her body went from stiff to rigid stillness, her smooth thighs tight around his flanks, making him groan as he bit back the urge to ram himself hilt-deep within her.

Instead, he let his weight slowly bear down into her. But almost immediately, he met tight resistance. He bit back an oath. She made no movement, no sound under him, and if it weren't for the living tension of her body and the heat and too-tight softness under him, she might have been made of wax. She was as hot as a furnace, slick with desire—so what was wrong? He tried another thrust, and this one penetrated a little deeper before her body shut him out.

She began to breathe again, her hands pulling him toward her even as her body resisted. In small, teeth-clenchingly gentle movements, he pushed deeper until he was half sheathed in her body, biting his lip against the desire to thrust hard against the unyielding flesh and break it to him. Then, finally, the inner muscles that had been tightened in defense against him gave way in a long, hot slide, clasping him instead of barring his way.

He hissed against the sensation that surged through him, then looked down into her face, a smear of white in the darkness with huge, black-shadowed eyes. He felt them sucking at his soul, and his body thrummed with his need but for all the wrong reasons. He had to get this over with now before he forgot why he'd brought her there. . . .

He thrust into her, and heat surged through his body. Again he thrust, and again, his strokes building steadily, not daring to kiss her, not daring to touch her. But then she shifted her grip on him, reaching up and pulling his head down against her neck.

He lost all control. He buried his face against her sweet, salt-tanged skin, kissing it, devouring it as he pushed into her, again and again. She made no sound, and her only response was her fingers tightening in his hair. Her stiff, mute passion should have repelled him, but instead, its raw fragility drove him over the edge. She was trying to build a wall against him, trying to keep him on the outside, but he knew it wasn't working any more than he'd been able to keep himself apart from her. He wanted, he *needed* to break through its flimsy barrier, and as he moved within her heat, hurling unstoppably toward the peak, he intensified his siege of her senses.

He assaulted her mouth, followed the line of her jaw to the sensitive place on her neck. He used his lips, his teeth, his tongue, his hands, everything he knew from a decade and a half of debauchery. Her breath raced and her body grew tight, but still she did not move. Finally, with a growl of frustration, he tightened the fingers that teased her nipple into a pinch, and she gave a sudden, gasping moan.

That small sound shattered her restraint and brought her walls tumbling down. Her hands pulled his head to her mouth; her body rocked with him as she made strangled, inarticulate noises that sounded as much like sorrow or pain as pleasure. Then she arched against him with a sobbing cry, and her inner muscles spasmed around him, and he came without warning or control.

Heat seared through him. It came from her, from inside himself, blinding and deafening him to everything but its roar and the sounds from the woman under him. She clutched him, and he pounded against her, with her as they fell, long and hard, shattering together.

Gradually, sensation receded and sanity returned. Sebastian discovered he was still lying on top of the woman, on top of Sarah, and he pulled back when he realized just how much he wanted to stay there. He shoved up from the sofa, and the cold air hit his remaining erection, quickly cooling the lingering heat of his passion.

Remember what she is, Sebastian told himself. *Remember what she did.*

Sarah just lay there, boneless, as still as a corpse, as pale as a sleeping princess. Her eyes were invisible under the shadow of her brows, but he could feel them following him, as if they owned some part of him, and he turned away from her abruptly, finding the white puddle of his shirt and yanking it on.

"What was wrong?" he demanded, wanting her to deny her enjoyment, to crush the strange fragile sense of connection that seemed to be unspiraling him toward her.

"Nothing," she answered quietly, defeating him.

He clenched his jaw as he buttoned the shirt. What was wrong with him? He wanted her more than ever, for the worst reasons, and he was almost frightened to have her want him in return. "It didn't seem that way to me," he lied.

"Why don't you want to believe me?" she said. The words were quiet, carrying no weight of judgment that he could read, but they silenced him more effectively than any shout. "I know you can't have deceived yourself so fully. Not after that."

"How could you know that?" he retorted, realizing too late that his words were as good as a confession, and a childish one at that.

Sarah watched as the Moor turned his back to her again and jerked on his trousers, a jumble of emotions roiling inside her. It had been different, so different, so wonderfully, terribly different. . . . Her mind sang with it, rejoiced in it, recoiled from it. She didn't know what she felt or why, aside from the wall of relief that hit her with a force that made her want to weep.

She shifted, and sticky wetness chafed her thighs, bringing reality back with a stark suddenness.

"Please. I need to clean myself," she said, the words coming out awkwardly. In the room she had used as a dress lodger, there had always been a basin and a rag for afterward, and the men had never stayed longer than it took to pull up their trousers. She did not know if there was some etiquette for this moment between a man and a woman; what she knew from the rookery amounted to nothing more than a few coins on the dresser, secured in advance, and from the ladies school, nothing more carnal than the importance of a chaperone and the danger in a kiss.

The Moor didn't even turn toward her as he buttoned his waistband. "Use your chemise."

There was anger in his words that startled her, but strangely, it seemed self-directed. A small sympathetic response stirred in her, but she refused to give in. Here, she was no whore, whatever else she might be, and she found some sense of pride that would not let her stoop to that.

When the Moor turned to see that she had not moved, he bent jerkily, and a moment later, a soft wad of fabric came flying through the air and hit her on the chest.

"My drawers," he explained curtly. "They should do well enough."

Sarah used them and dropped them to crumple on the floor. That simple, homely act had imbued her with a queer feeling of calm. Every other encounter she'd ever experienced had left her feeling dazed and used, full of guilt or dread or horror and the feeling that she wasn't even woman enough to be a common whore. Now, though, she felt more self-possessed than she could remember, and she had the realization that it was her host who was ashamed, recognizing in his actions all the emotions she had once felt.

"Why did you decide to seduce me?" she asked.

"Do you regret it?" He answered her question with another, too fast and tense.

"Do I look like I regret it?" She laughed unsteadily as it occurred to her how ludicrous that question was in the darkness. "Do I sound like I regret it?" she amended.

"No."

"Well, then, I have an honest voice. I don't."

He stood silhouetted against the window, his long, lean form towering over her, but she felt strangely powerful, as if she held a piece of him in her hand and he was too afraid to snatch it back for fear she might crush it.

"You are trying to change the subject," she said. "Why me?"

"When I first saw you—"

His words were low and fervent—and false. She knew it, could feel it; the shock of it was like cold water against her face, and all her suspicions rose again to the forefront of her mind. "Don't lie to me," she interrupted. "I know I am no beauty to inspire passion in men. You could not have seen much of what I am or I would not be here now."

"I assure you—"

She cut him off again, closing her ears to the note of pain in his voice. "What is it that you want from me?"

He didn't answer, didn't move, though he suddenly seemed to be looming over her.

She took a deep breath. "If you won't tell me, then I will guess. The most likely possibility is access to Lady Anna's ear. You sent her flowers the night you invited me to the masque and delivered a letter to her the next day. Am I just a ploy to get to obtain her beautiful presence and bountiful dowry?" The words shouldn't sting, but they did. Still, Sarah thought that whatever his motives, his passion for her had been real. At least she would always have that.

"Sarah," the Moor said with sudden firmness, sitting next to her on the sofa, "I promise you, tomorrow night you will find out the whole truth." There—finally, there was the sense of truth that she'd been looking for. Sarah steeled herself against her grateful relief.

"Why tomorrow? What is all this? Why do you even plan to see me again at all? If you truly wanted me . . . why, you've got what you wanted, and there is no reason to see me again. And if you want something else, wouldn't it be wisest to tell me now, when I am most inclined to think kindly of you?"

The Moor pushed off the sofa with a frustrated sound. "If this is kindly, I fear to see your unkindliness."

She sat still, not speaking as he looked down at her. His eyes were invisible, but the force of his gaze was like a weight.

"Why do you even ask me these things? You are the one who wants to hide behind masks and darkness. Why ruin the mystery now?" he asked.

The wistful note in his voice seemed to seize her, and for a moment, she just stared at him. "I don't know," she heard herself say finally. "I try to pretend, but I can't forget that the fantasy isn't real. It's all a terrible jumble. I want tonight to be perfect, but anytime it seems too much like a dream, I want to destroy it."

"Why not just live for the moment?"

"Because the moment is a lie. I cannot believe, I don't want to believe—" She broke off, realizing that her voice was beginning to rise. "I want to steal something sweet just for the memories. But I do not want to fool myself."

"Have you ever been fooled?" His voice sounded less strained, more curious, as they moved away from ground that was dangerous to him.

"In this way?" Sarah asked, her wave encompassing everything that had happened between them tonight. "No, certainly not. There is little in this sort of thing that is beguiling enough to be taken for hope in the normal way of things. But whether it is through the bottom of a gin glass or classes on elocution, dreams are sold to the desperate by the bucketful."

He sat beside her again, not touching her but close enough that she could feel the heat of his body, that she could sense his gaze on her face, softening like a caress. She controlled a shiver.

"Perhaps the desperate sell dreams to themselves," he said, and it seemed to her that he was talking about himself as much as anyone.

She shook her head, uncomprehending. "You need no dreams to fill your belly if you have money that would suit the purpose more nicely."

His rejection was immediate. "There is more to dreams than just food. You can't tell me that you came here because your employer was not feeding you."

That reminder of Lady Merrill sent a jolt of guilt through Sarah, recalling herself to the original thrust of the conversation. "Sir," she forced herself to say, "however happy or unhappy I am, I have a duty to my employer, and if you mean to do Lady Anna harm . . . I should know."

"A duty!" He snorted, and suddenly the sense of closeness, of budding comprehension between them, evaporated. Tense sensuality remained, but it was stripped bare of all softening nuances. "Your employer knows nothing of duty."

Sarah gaped. "How can you—"

"We have a little more time tonight before you must return to your duty," he interrupted coldly. He reached for her, pulling her against him, his mouth seeking hers to silence it.

Sarah's body could not deny him—and she was no

longer afraid. His mouth was angry, demanding, and she met his demands with her own need, which rekindled in her center and surged out until all her limbs tingled with it.

He broke away suddenly. "I can't do this!"

Abruptly, Sarah found herself pushed down again into the sofa, but this time prone, her cheek pressed against the damp mustiness of the cushions as he stood and circled behind her. Her back prickled with awareness. She could get up. There was nothing binding her here, not coins, not words, not even his hands, though she knew they soon would be, that he was giving her a chance and if she did not take it, he would offer her no more.

But she did not want to go.

She shivered against a twisting pleasure as he grasped one of her legs just above the knee. He nudged it aside, and she felt his weight on the sofa, his trouser-clad knees between her own naked ones. It was then that she knew for certain what he was going to do, and her breath caught and her heart began to race as the knowledge was immediately met by her body's eager anticipation.

"Give me your hands," he said. No "sweet Sarah" now, nothing but the complete absence of emotion in his voice to tell her this meant anything at all to him. But in his very appearance of indifference, she sensed much, much more, and that deep, unhappy part of her soul rejoiced.

And her flesh burned.

"Take them," she said, worming her hands from under her body and stretching them above her so that her forearms rested against the arm of the sofa.

The Moor cursed again, longer this time and with an edge that cut her. He grasped her wrists in his hands, leaning over her and pinning them to the sofa with his weight. She gasped as his erection pressed against her buttocks, the damp tip meeting heated flesh exposed by her hiked-up chemise. The familiar hollowness opened within her, the need to be filled, and she tilted her hips, and he slid down, along the sensitive crease until he rested at her entrance.

For one long moment, they both held still, and the only sound was their mingled, ragged breaths, like the rush of a hundred winds in Sarah's ears. Then she said, "You cannot—you cannot hide from this!" She did not know where the words came from, but their truth must have rung in him as they did in her, for with a growl, the Moor surged forward into her.

He thrust again, and then again, slowly and deliberately, and she had to swallow back the sounds that built in her throat. Each movement was wonderful, terrible, its pressure awakening nerves that had not been stirred by their earlier passion and reinflaming those that had become quiescent. She lost track of time, of herself in the building glory of it, but she could not lose track of him. He was everywhere, inside of her, on top of her, around her. She wanted to touch him, she needed to touch him, and she pulled against the hands that bound her. But he would not let her go. His pace quickened, carrying her with him, and her frustration built and mingled with her pleasure until all at once, they both broke. A wash of sensation surged out from where she clasped him within her, spearing deeper into her core and igniting her center with a sudden fire that blazed through her entire body until her bones ached with it and she thought her skin would burst into flame.

"Enough!" she managed to say. "Stop!"

But if he could hear her, he ignored her, driving into her relentlessly and taking her beyond even that impossibility to where there was no sound, no sight, no thought, only the rushing fire that went beyond pain and pleasure into a place where such words meant nothing.

She came to herself slowly as the Moor pulled away. He had released her. Still dazed, she shoved herself into a sitting position. Movement in the darkness told her that he was fastening his trousers again, and her hand encountered the drawers he had given her earlier. As he dressed, she put them to use again, feeling more embarrassed by that act than by everything that had come before. When she finished, she pulled on her chemise against the chill and then looked up to discover that he was standing still, watching her. She didn't need to read his expression to sense the tension in him and know that he was glaring, but she found her voice before he could speak, questions tumbling out of her.

"Why did you ever come to Venice? Where are you from? What's your purpose here?" Her voice sounded broken, husky, and the Moor seemed to relax infinitesimally.

"The first is none of your concern. As for the others, you should be able to guess my nationality easily enough, and as to my purpose, I have already told you that you will soon see." His voice was soft, but the words were firm.

She shut her eyes, not understanding, afraid and yet not afraid in a way that she could not quite encompass. "You mean me ill. I am certain of it. You don't hate me, but you wish you could despise me, and I don't know why. It makes no sense at all."

A sudden stillness seemed to grasp him, and tension radiated from him when he spoke. "You see too much," he said stiffly. And then he went silent, and Sarah held her breath against a feeling of deep significance.

Finally, he exhaled all at once and paced over to the window, stripping off his loose shirt and dropping it as he went. "I don't understand you," he said, and he seemed to be talking more than half to himself. "I can't believe . . . but I must believe . . . I am making a bad job of this. I have lost the taste for recklessness, and I never needed it more than I do now."

"What do you mean?" She asked the question quietly, hardly more than a whisper.

But he did not answer. Sarah sat silent as the minutes ticked away, watching him as he stared out the window. His body was silhouetted faintly, the clean lines of his shoulders narrowing to his small hips, and even abstracted as he was, an unconscious air about him declared he was a man who was accustomed to being obeyed. She should be afraid of him, but she was not.

As he stood, his attitude subtly changed, growing gradually more pensive and more marked with pain. She could not guess how much later it was when he finally turned his back to the view. Ten minutes? An hour? Finally, with a slow step, he returned to the sofa, sitting so that his hip pressed into hers. Dulled awareness rekindled within her, but she was not prepared for the feel of his arms around her, not pulling her toward his mouth but simply gathering her to his chest as if he were comforting her—or himself.

"Where are you from, lost little dove?" His voice was scarcely a breath in her ear, and she shivered. "How did you come to this godforsaken city?"

That was not a question that should be asked—not here, not tonight. Sarah had an urge to pull away, but under his words, she sensed that he needed her there against him, and she had never been needed by anyone before. So she stayed where she was, the smooth skin of his chest warm and roughened with sparse curling hairs as his heart thudded under her ear, the sheer sensuality of his body's perfection winding awareness through her even in complete repose.

"Tonight is about dreams, not nightmares," she heard herself say. "Snatching at the dreams we sell ourselves, remember?"

"Is it, dove? Really?" He seemed to be talking to himself as much as to her. "I lied when I spoke of chasing dreams. Those years of mine are long past."

He lapsed into silence, and Sarah could think of nothing to say, for she had no idea of what demons hounded him, and she knew she could not ask.

Finally, he said, "Tell me, do I seem like a brute to you?"

"No." That much she could answer easily and with honesty.

"But I was. And I must be again. When the time comes for stopping, what will be left of me? What the hell will be left of any of us?"

She didn't know what he meant even though it sent a chill through her, didn't know what to answer, but he didn't seem to expect her to, and so they sat without speaking for a very long time until he took her chin, kissed her, and pushed her with great gentleness onto the sofa again.

"It is time," the Moor said finally, rousing Sarah from her half doze.

Some infinitesimal lightening outside must have alerted him to the approach of dawn. Sarah had not noticed, but when she stirred from her comfortable stupor on the sofa to turn her head to look at him, she realized that the shape of his features was vaguely distinguishable in the darkness.

With a feeling of sleepy unreality making her movements slow and clumsy, she dressed without a word and without a light, knotting the broken ribbon on her mask before she tied it back on.

As she finished, a servant materialized at the doorway. Sarah cast one last look at the Moor. He was standing with his back to her, looking out the window over the canal and silhouetted by the first hints of dawn light.

"Good-bye," she said, her voice hoarse with exhaustion. Exhaustion—nothing more, she told herself.

"Farewell, Sarah." His voice sounded so cold and remote that her heart contracted, and she bowed her head, accepting the finality of it.

She left, and the servant led Sarah through a chain of echoing, deserted rooms, his dim lantern casting leaping shadows upon the walls as her heels clicked unnaturally loudly in the silence.

They reached the huge black doors of the entrance, and the servant swung them wide for Sarah to step outside.

It had grown brighter since she left the Moor's chamber, and the shapes of the roofs across the canal formed a rough silhouette against the deep sky. Silently, Sarah stepped into the boat, and silently, the servant rowed her back toward Lady Merrill's apartments. She watched without seeing as they slid past palazzi and shops, the gaslights strung like pearls along the canals, fading in the cool gray dawn.

It had been a night such as she never could have imagined. Much of it had been wonderful, some almost horrible, and all so confusing that she felt as if her head were stuffed with experiences like heavy clouds, slowing her thoughts and hanging before her vision.

When Sarah stepped onto the Campo Manin and pulled off her mask, the buildings around her were picked out in shades of pewter and alabaster. By the time she arrived at the Palazzo Bovolo, colors had returned to the world in a flood of yellowed pastels. Sarah climbed the exterior staircase, pushed open the third-story door, and locked it behind her. With her head still smothered in exhaustion and experience, she drifted through the silent corridor to her room, where she stripped to her chemise and fell into bed.

In the moments before she fell asleep, she thought again, *What could he still want with me?*

But when sleep came, there were no answers in her dreams.

Chapter Seven

It is impossible.

The words thundered through Sebastian's head in an echoing litany until they lost all meaning. He sprawled naked on the couch, watching the sunrise through the mullioned windows and dangling an empty wineglass in his fingers. What was he trying to do? He wanted justice for Adela; that was an unshakable certainty. But even something that should be so simple, so clean, so right, became perverted in his hands.

He had wanted her. Sarah. He'd known it from the second he'd laid eyes on her, but he had thought—foolishly—that his lust would simply make a necessary task more palatable. Instead, he'd found himself forgetting about Adela completely in the hot darkness of the night, taking joy in the act, finding a glory in having Sarah that seemed a twistedly triumphant declaration of everything that was wrong with him.

"Sir?" The voice behind him was soft but firm. "You will want to bathe before your appointment."

Sebastian stirred. "Thank you, Gian."

The servant helped him into a dressing gown before opening the door to more soft-footed domestics bearing a monstrous copper basin and buckets of hot water. Sebastian washed himself mechanically and allowed himself to be shaved and dressed, pushing all thought, all desire aside until nothing was left but an empty shell.

Good, he thought. *This is how it should be.*

"Mr. de Lint awaits," Gian said softly, holding a golden demimask at arm's length.

Sebastian took the mask and tied it on expertly. "Not for long."

He emerged into a brilliant, cloudless morning, the sky so blue that it looked painted on. Fatigue dragged at his senses, throwing the day into a contrast of painful relief in the sunshine and fuzzing grayness in the shadows. He ducked under the hood of his gondola and allowed Gian to row him to the Casinò Giallo.

One of his own servants greeted him at the door and led him up to the suite where he had left Domenica and de Lint the day before. At the servant's knock, de Lint drawled permission to enter.

"Ah, Señor Guerra!" the man said heartily as Sebastian stepped through the door, raising a tumbler in salute. He was still dressed in the clothes he had worn the day before. They were much disheveled, and the usual perfection of de Lint's hair stood in wild disarray about his head. "So glad that you came to check up on a friend." The Italian was steeped in irony. He fished in his pocket for a moment, then flicked a five-sovereign coin at him.

Sebastian caught it automatically, circling toward the chair opposite him as he tried to control his emotions. The anger had seized him again, the need to hurt that smug man, to make him pay, and Sebastian again wondered how much of his revenge was for Adela and how much for himself.

As he came around the sofa, a figure lying upon it caught his eye. Tumbled black hair, slack limbs, the young, too-young face—for an instant, the sight tangled with a memory of another raven-haired girl, but instead of that limp body he saw tears and blood and heard wails of horror. For one gut-clenching moment, he feared that he had done it again, that he had caused a tragedy, that this time a girl was dead—

Then he saw how her chest rose and fell with her breath and a tiny tendril of hair fluttered in front of her mouth.

Breathing again, Sebastian took the other chair. "Was she to your taste, then, signor?" he made himself ask casually. "It seems you tired the child out."

The man sighed luxuriously. "Oh, yes, she is a tempting slip of a girl, and she tired me out just as thoroughly. Everything you promised—except she was no virgin."

"You did not ask for a virgin, nor did I claim that she was one." Sebastian assumed a tone of offended dignity.

"Yes, but I allowed myself to hope. . . . Nevertheless, she was a fine, tempting bit of flesh, and certainly of much more use to me than an ignorant waif would be after the first night. The things that girl can do . . ." He smiled deliciously. "Have you ever sampled a little of her wares yourself?"

Sebastian looked down at the girl, whose eyes stayed steadfastly closed though there was now a subtle tension in her frame that betrayed that she was awake.

"No," he said firmly. "I prefer my women older."

"A shame." De Lint looked down tenderly at her. "I must get her some little trinket, a poppet or a pair of pretty shoes, perhaps. It is not fair that her mother gets everything."

"Then by all means, do so." Sebastian spoke too abruptly, for de Lint's eyes snapped to his face and a crease appeared between his eyebrows. Sebastian forced himself to moderate his tone. "I am sorry, signor. I am just blaming myself for not understanding what you wanted. Virgins are very, very hard to find, you know, and I do not have one in my pocket at the moment, so to speak. There are a few possibilities that I can follow up, if you wish."

De Lint smiled. "Always," he said. "But there is no hurry. This little girl shall keep me quite occupied for several days, I believe."

"I will see to it, then," Sebastian said, springing to his feet as if he were eager to get started. "You may continue to use this little love nest in the meantime, if you'd like," he added, as if it were an afterthought. "For a small fee."

De Lint's expression was cynical. "So that you can make sure you get your cut, yes?" Sebastian gave a self-deprecating shrug. "Well, I shan't deny that you deserve it in this case. If you bring another surprise this pleasant, it would be worth twice as much." He nodded. "I shall use it."

"Good," Sebastian said. "Mansfield said you were an honorable man."

And with those words, he turned and left.

Sarah arrived late at the breakfast table with gritty eyes and an aching head. Sensations from the night before clung to her like ghost fingers, secret and wonderful. When she sipped her tea, the liquid was an echo of another warmth against her lips; when she grasped her cup tightly, it was the hardness of muscle, not porcelain, that her fingers felt.

She felt strange, disjointed, held captive and helpless in that other world while around her everything went on as usual, Lady Merrill gazing out through the loggia as the girls buzzed with eager, relentless energy.

When breakfast was cleared, Lady Anna rebelled from her lessons and paced the length of the portego as her grandmother dictated that day's correspondence. Sarah could feel her tension echoed in her own body and envied the girl her release even as she stoically recorded the same observations for the fifth time. Lady Anna hovered over her shoulder as Sarah addressed the envelopes, and when the last one was sealed, the girl finally burst.

"Oh, Grandmamma! I simply must return to St. Mark's Square again today. I forgot that we didn't even get to feed the pigeons, and yesterday, Miss Connolly told me that her Baedeker's says that every traveler should eat under the loggia or in the square. I feel quite stupid that we wasted our chance at Florian's and ate inside."

Lady Merrill cast a sideways look at Sarah at the blatant lie about her guidebook, but she said only, "Well, I certainly don't see why not."

Naturally, the Mortons were determined to be included,

and when Miss Harker was given the opportunity to remain behind, she took it. Mr. de Lint still hadn't returned since the night before, so the five of them squeezed into two gondolas for the short ride.

Sarah cast Lady Merrill an uneasy look as she passed through the canals for the second time that morning. She knew she had a duty to assure her employer that her granddaughter was indeed lying, yet the girl's minor transgression so paled against what Sarah had done the night before that she did not speak for several long minutes.

Finally, burning with hypocrisy, she managed to say, "Your ladyship, I didn't tell Lady Anna anything about my Baedeker's."

Lady Merrill just laughed. "I may be old, but I am not a dolt."

"I know, madam. It's just that . . . I just had to tell you myself, is all."

The woman grasped her hand and squeezed it briefly. "You shouldn't allow every triviality to weigh so greatly upon your mind. I know when there is a game of love-play going on under my nose. It is what young people do. I wouldn't want you to lie for the girls, but you needn't spy on them, either. It is not fair to any of you, and besides, a young girl needs to feel like she is getting away with something in a situation like this or it is no fun at all."

"Thank you, madam," Sarah said, genuinely relieved.

Soon, they arrived at the Molo, where they stepped out and crossed the Piazzetta into the Piazza proper.

Lady Anna practically danced with impatience as they placed their orders, staring out from under the loggia in front of Florian's and complaining that the pillars blocked too much of her view. Lady Merrill said nothing, sipping her tea in silence when it arrived, and when her granddaughter drank hers in two gulps and stood, announcing her intention of feeding her scones to the pigeons, she merely told her to take Sarah and the other girls with her—"So she won't do anything exceptionally foolhardy," as the lady whispered to Sarah.

"Are you sure that you wish to be left alone?" Sarah murmured back. She honestly didn't want to leave the old lady without a companion, but in addition to a real concern for her employer's well-being, Sarah felt a selfish wish to not be forced into the company of Lady Anna when the memory of their last time together still stung.

"I will be fine," Lady Merrill said cheerfully, and Sarah's heart sank. Without another word, she obediently followed the girls across the Piazza, keeping one discreet step behind them and hoping that nothing she did would attract their notice.

The Morton sisters scattered bits of their scones into the teeming mass of pigeons that immediately gathered at their feet, but Lady Anna dropped hers directly, leaving the plump birds to squabble over it while she gazed fixedly toward the campanile.

"Did he say he'd be here today?" Miss Effie asked innocently. Her sister gave her a baleful stare and sent Sarah a look that not even a blind man could miss. Feeling her face redden, Sarah kept her gaze from dropping to her feet with difficulty. Lady Anna looked at her with less meaning but just as steadily.

Sarah tried to ignore them, hoping that they would soon forget about her, but it was no use. They kept their silence and their unwavering stares until finally, unable to bear their scrutiny any longer, she spoke. "I will say nothing. It is not my place to report your conversations to Lady Merrill," she said stiffly.

"Thank you!" Lady Anna declared rapturously while Miss Morton gave her an uncertain look. Her sister had no such reservations, for she beamed at Sarah and pressed a piece of scone into her hand for the pigeons. Sarah took it reluctantly, realizing that she was being pulled into a conspiracy when all she had wanted was to establish her neutrality.

"I haven't heard a thing from him since yesterday," Lady Anna answered Miss Effie finally. "I was just hoping . . ." She trailed off and began to walk restlessly along the Piazza, wandering closer to the campanile. "Last night was so wonderful. I can't get it out of my mind."

Sarah's heart contracted, thinking of her own night and fearing the inevitable comparison. But as Lady Anna went on, she was soon relieved. What she described was no more than passionate whisperings, with her hanging half-clad out the window and her paramour in a gondola two stories below. "If only Grandmamma had taken the lower piano nobile." She sighed. "Then I might have leapt into his arms, heedless of my own safety. . . ."

Miss Morton laughed. "From that far up, it truly would have been heedless of your safety—and his! You would have sunk his boat and drowned in the canal."

Lady Anna shot her a look of disgust as Miss Effie tried to smother her giggles. "I can swim," she said haughtily. "And besides, that's why I didn't jump. I do have a head on my shoulders, you know."

"What was it like?" Miss Effie intervened as Lady Anna's glare turned to include her, too. "Wasn't it the most glorious experience of your life?"

"It was indescribable," Lady Anna said firmly, in defiance of the fact that she'd just spent the past several minutes describing it. "And now I feel . . . I feel giddy," she confided. "So wondrously light that I could float away. But every instant he is not here with me, I ache, too, so terribly and so sweetly."

It sounded indeed like love to Sarah, or at least what she'd read of it. How pleasant and harmless it seemed, how charming, and yet as Lady Anna went on, all Sarah could think of was her own more bitter ache and the dizzying welter of emotions that still assaulted her whenever her thoughts returned inevitably to the Moor. Compared to that, Lady Anna's descriptions seemed pale and insipid, like tissue paper next to rich silk. The realization both elated and unsettled Sarah. What she felt was certainly not love, but it was more than she'd ever thought to feel.

Lady Anna paused dramatically when she reached the

end of her narrative, then looked at her companions with an air of superiority. "If you haven't experienced it, there is nothing that it can be compared to."

Miss Morton rolled her eyes. "Really, Anna, you needn't act as if you're the only one in the world to have ever been in love."

Lady Anna looked amazed. "Why, Melinda Morton, you can't have had a sweetheart!"

"And why not?" she bristled.

"You've been out scarcely a year. And besides, you've never breathed a word of it."

"Well, you won't come out until next summer. And I don't tell my secrets so freely as some." She slanted a meaningful look at her sister. "Especially when there are those about who can't keep them."

Miss Effie blushed furiously. "That was an accident! Besides, it was only one time."

Lady Anna was staring at them in fascination, but Miss Morton shook her head primly even as her friend opened her mouth. "Never you mind about me. All I meant was that love is probably the commonest thing there is. Even . . ." Her wandering gaze fell on Sarah. "Even Miss Connolly has probably been in love with someone."

Sarah wanted to hide from Lady Anna's astonished gaze. "Is that true?" the girl demanded.

"I am the exception to your rule of universality, I fear," Sarah said, knowing that her cheeks flamed and hating herself for it. The charming shallowness of the girls suddenly irritated her, their complete lack of knowledge of the world grating against her very core. "I have loved a number of people in my life, but I have never been in love, not as you mean, nor do I have any expectations of it."

"Why not?" Miss Effie blurted.

"Hush," Miss Morton whispered furiously.

Miss Effie recalled herself. "I apologize, Miss Connolly. It is none of my concern." Her mouth made a small pouting expression. "But I still want to know," she muttered.

"It is quite all right, Miss Effie." The words were a lie. It wasn't fine at all, but Sarah had the urge to tell her the whole of it, to give her a glimpse into the lives of the people who made her bed, cooked her food, and dressed her hair every day, the hundreds of ordinary lives that were used up in making her own life so blithe and comfortable. "I have long ago come to terms with my position. It is simply a matter of luck and economics. I have nothing that might attract a man of sufficient means to support me, and the occupations open to married women are only the most menial or, at best, distasteful."

"What do you plan to do, then?" Miss Effie asked in surprise. "Be a companion for the rest of your life?"

Sarah made her voice emotionless. "Until I am too old for such duties, yes." *Which is why I snatched the Moor's offer when it was given to me,* she added silently. "By then, if I am lucky, I shall have a tidy sum built up for me to live on." *And if I am not . . .* She refused to voice those fears.

The girls were silent for a moment, subdued by the idea of a life outside of their own carefree sphere. But then the campanile tolled the hour, and the silence was broken, and the girls returned to their conversation as if it had never been interrupted.

Though the perversity that compelled Sarah to make her confession soon fled, she did not regret it, for she knew it was forgotten in the space of a few breaths. The girls had no attention or memory for a creature like her.

She shredded her scrap of scone in her fingers and let it fall to the pigeons at her feet, watching as they squabbled over the crumbs.

They returned to the Palazzo Bovolo for lunch, where Mr. de Lint met them, freshly shaven and perfectly composed. Lady Merrill announced her intention of visiting the few remaining Venetian nobles who were considered good enough to be embraced by the transient foreign population, but the girls demurred, claiming exhaustion, and Mr. de Lint decided to remain with them. It was left to Sarah alone, then, to accompany her employer to the palazzi.

The conversations were conducted in French, of which Sarah understood one word of ten when spoken at speed, or, at times, in German, of which she understood nothing, so she was left with no occupation but to sit quietly and take in the fashionable and deeply inappropriate youthful dress of their aging hostesses and the strange state of the various rooms in which they were entertained—the smooth tessellated floors radiating coolness, the ancient, uncomfortable gilt chairs, the walls whose faded damask was smothered in the paintings of centuries.

Each room was as smooth and echoing as a mausoleum, and each was far, far too much like the Moor's grand salon for Sarah's liking. She saw him in shadowy corners and in the half-glimpsed faces of their hostesses' menservants; she could almost hear his voice in the rotting depths of the houses or on the pavements below. An unsettled, prickly feeling stirred all her slumbering guilt and far too much of her desire and made her long for the stillness of her bedroom.

On the way back to their palazzo, Sarah was silent as usual, but her private thoughts were interrupted by a quiet, interrogatory sound from Lady Merrill. Sarah recognized her employer's desire for conversation and turned toward her, shaking herself out of her reverie.

The lady was gazing at the palazzi that bordered the Grand Canal with a sad eye. "Harold would have loved it here. For that matter, so would Rupert." She cast Sarah a judging look. "You've never asked me about my husbands, you know."

Sarah returned her look with surprise. "If you wanted me to know, I assumed that you'd tell me, madam. I did not consider it my place to ask."

Lady Merrill smiled, her expression surprisingly impish. "Oh, child, don't you know anything about old ladies yet? We love to talk about ourselves. Besides, you're my companion, not my housemaid. You're entitled to ask questions." She paused meaningfully, and Sarah took the implied invitation.

"So what were your husbands like?"

Lady Merrill nodded with satisfaction. "Well, Rupert was the first, a baron and far too old for me. But I didn't care. I was flattered by his attention and his title—my own family was much less distinguished, you see."

"Didn't you love him?" Sarah blurted, then blushed. "I mean, madam, you always speak so fondly of him that I thought—"

Lady Merrill waved her into silence. "Oh, I loved him, most certainly, but that came much later. In fact, I don't think I loved him until Emilia, our eldest, was born. That's Anna's mother, you know. At first, I was in despair because I thought that at least half the reason he married me was to get an heir. But he was so very glad about Emilia for her own sake, and he said he didn't give a fig for whether I ever bore a son, and I quite believed him. . . ." She sighed. "I was fifteen when we married, and even in 1813, it was quite a scandal. We lived quite happily for nineteen years until he died. I had four more children with him, if you can believe it. Me! The county matron! Two are dead now, and one is unmarried, so it fell to Emilia and John—now Lord Breckenridge—to give me Rupert's grandchildren."

"And your second husband?" Sarah asked shyly, genuinely curious now.

"That would be Geoffrey. He was a widower himself. I had my widow's portion and he had his heir already, so many people could not understand why the match was made at all, much less not two years after Rupert's death. But I am a woman who is happiest with a husband, and as much as I loved Rupert's memory, I loved Geoffrey, too. He was a viscount, you know, and in addition to his son, he had two daughters whom I sponsored when they came out and saw to the altar. I was thirty-five by the time we wed, so we had no hopes for more children, but we were both surprised by little Bertrand. Then we had a strange nursery! The future Lord Aughtley and his sisters, my little Lord Breckenridge and Emilia, and then Bertrand, the baby no one expected. The younger of my stepdaughters, Eliza de Lint, married Sir Gerald Morton within a year of Emilia's own marriage. That's why Melinda and Euphemia were allowed to come with Anna—they're practically cousins and grew up almost as sisters."

"But you married again, didn't you?" Sarah asked tentatively.

She smiled sadly. "Ah, yes, Harold. My last husband. After Geoffrey died only ten years after we married, I'd had enough of older men. I was tired of being left behind. Then Sir Harold Merrill came, like an answer to a dream. He was only forty to my forty-six, and he swept me off my feet. But he, too, deserted me eventually. We had twenty-four years together. Still, it didn't quite seem fair. I was supposed to die first this time."

"I'm sorry," Sarah said.

"You shouldn't be," Lady Merrill said, with her characteristic crushing practicality. "After all, it got you this employment."

"I didn't mean—"

Lady Merrill's expression softened. "I know, dear. I was just pointing out that not everything that came of it was bad. We tend to make tragedies out of the unfortunate things in our lives, but it is rare that something is so very bleak that there is nothing good, however small, that could be said of it."

"Oh," Sarah said, uncertain of how to respond. "Thank you, your ladyship, for telling me. I have wanted to ask but I never felt it was my place."

"You are quite welcome, dear," Lady Merrill said, giving her a shrewd look. "If I do not miss my guess, there is something beyond my granddaughter's conduct that is troubling you. I want you to feel that you can share whatever it is that is burdening you with me."

"Thank you, madam," Sarah managed. Share what with her? The night with the Moor? Impossible. Her fears of the woman's son? Even worse!

Just then, the gondola was brought up to the water stairs, the ripples lapping only one step down from the top at high tide. Sarah was grateful for the excuse to say no more and opened the felze door quickly, standing and stepping nervously over the small gap between the boat and the stairs.

She turned back to assist Lady Merrill from the boat. The old woman linked her arm in Sarah's for support and clasped her companion's hand between both of her own. Sarah could not help but wonder how warm her employer would be if she did confess the whole of what preyed upon her, then shunted away the ugly vision that thought spawned in her mind.

Chapter Eight

Sebastian frowned at the stacked ledgers in front of him, the condensed records of more than a dozen various estates and financial ventures that were considered suitable for a peer to take part in. It had been more than a decade since he'd even glanced at them, and in that time, he'd forgotten why he never bothered to look over the books himself. Accounting was like another language—or rather, it was as completely unlike a language as Sebastian could conceive of. With languages, he had a talent, an ear, a knack for sensing foreign patterns and reproducing them.

But numbers, on the other hand . . . His arithmetic was more than competent, but the scores upon scores of figures, written in their multiple columns, cross-referenced and cross-entered, were enough to give him a headache. He wasn't even sure what, exactly, he should be doing. Each account added up in its orderly way to the numbers that had been all he'd ever bothered to remember before: the amounts in his various accounts that were his capital and the amounts he was free to spend.

He wished he could ask Whitby what a conscientious gentleman should be doing with the pile of documents, but that would only confirm the agent's worst opinion of him—and besides, Sebastian had neglected to ask the man how to reach him while on holiday. He could write Daniel, but he knew his cousin would have even less of an idea of what to do with them than he did. His father would have been proud, he thought sarcastically. It was just another way in which he showed how unsuited he was to the task of being the Earl of Wortham.

A nearby church bell tolled the hour, and Sebastian shoved aside the papers. He had no time for such details now. Another duty called him, a duty that he had turned to the tedious intricacies of his accounts to avoid thinking about.

In a few hours, though, the last part of one of his plans would unfold, and he would never need think of it again.

That evening, Mr. de Lint declared his intention of going out to the municipal casino. To Sarah's pleasure, Lady Merrill decided to accompany him, and so Sarah was given an evening to herself.

In an attempt to be more personable, she took her knitting and joined the girls and their governess on the portego. But Miss Harker buried herself in a book and the three friends whispered furiously with one another, ignoring her, so Sarah soon retired to her own room to work by the light of her lamp.

Automatically, she checked the desk-cum-nightstand as she entered, but only the golden wood of the tabletop shone back at her. She shifted the light to fall upon the bed, and for a moment, she thought that it was equally bare. But there, hidden in the shadow cast by the pillow . . .

She reached down into the crease of the counterpane where the pillow met the mattress, and her hand brushed something soft and smooth. She grasped it and pulled it into the light. It was a flower, a single white lily that glowed like a phantom in the orange flame of the lamp, a pearl nestled at its center, the twin to the first the Moor had given her.

She stared at it for a long moment, remembering the sheaf of identical flowers that had been given to Lady Anna only two days before, though without the accompaniment of the jewel. What could be the purpose in such a repetition?

And why a pearl, the symbol of tears? Was it a reminder, a mockery, a gift, a warning? Or was she reading too much into the action—was the lily simply the Moor's favorite flower and the pearl his favorite gem? Sarah couldn't begin to guess. She set them and her lamp on the desk, and she sat down on the chair in front of them, gazing at the blossom and pearl as she resumed her knitting.

Finally, her back aching and her hands growing weary of the repetitive work, she set aside the half-made stocking. From inside the desk's single drawer, she took out her modest stationery set and began to write. Once a week, she sent letters to each of the heterogeneous collection of people who were the only true family she'd ever had, but to one alone she wrote at least twice as often as that, the woman who was both her benefactress and her best friend.

> *Dear Maggie,*
>
> *Thank you again for arranging for me to buy Mrs. C. Radcliff's mourning garments. I do still greatly regret the death of the dowager, for she was a kind and gentle soul, but the cloth has at least been put to good use. I finished altering the last on the* Serafina *little more than a week past. However unconventional my employer is, I doubt she could have but looked askance at a companion dressed in a schoolgirl's uniform!*

The passage rang of forced gaiety, and Sarah winced at it, but whenever she tried to write her friend, the lessons of the ladies school about what passed for proper correspondence for a young woman always intruded between her feelings and her words until the result hardly sounded like her at all. The awkwardness stemmed from coming so late to letter writing—that, and the secrets she and her best friend now kept from each other.

Frowning, she tried to insert a greater measure of openness into the rest of the letter.

> *Lady Merrill is still all that I had hoped—kindly,*
> *easy, and gracious. It is hard to believe that it has*
> *been four months already. Her son is a trial, though*
> *not as much of one as you had feared. Have you heard*
> *any more on the scandal that implicated him? I know*
> *I shouldn't gossip, but it seems best to be forearmed in*
> *a case such as this.*
>
> *Lady Anna and her friends are still very proud and*
> *very silly, but they wish me no ill. Some part of me*
> *even envies them. Isn't that foolish? How you would*
> *laugh at me!*

There it was again, that piping glee that papered over deeper insecurities. She shunted the girls from her mind, and as her gaze fell on the lily, her thoughts automatically returned to the Moor and the strange and glorious seduction of the night before. If she could tell anyone, it should be Maggie. They'd grown up together in that miserable part of London called the Holy Land, and they'd been family until Maggie's marriage to a baron.

But that was just it. Maggie was a baroness now, and so things weren't the same between them, however much Sarah wished they were. And there was something strange and ethereal about her encounter with the Moor that made her fear that doing anything so concrete as writing about it in a letter would make the whole thing disappear. Sarah stared down at the paper, needing to write something, not able to explain the whole truth.

> *I have met the most extraordinary gentleman who*
> *seems to be taking an undue interest in me. I don't trust*
> *his motives, but something in me wishes that I could.*

That was more than enough. Sarah dashed quick a note recounting the sights of Venice she'd seen so far and signed the letter, sealing it in an envelope and addressing it for the morning's post.

With brisk efficiency, she undressed, washed, and donned the plain linen night rail she had brought with her from the ladies school. Then she crawled into bed, tucked the covers up virtuously to her neck, and extinguished the lamp, composing herself for sleep.

But sleep would not come. Instead, she lay motionless, looking up at the off-center plaster medallion on the ceiling and listening to the sounds of the night that were carried through her open window on the back of the breeze. From the open portego, she could hear the giggles of Lady Anna and the Mortons and the quiet, measured, remonstrating voice of the governess, and laughter and fragments of speech drifted out from a dozen other windows of the other apartments in the palazzo and the nearby buildings.

Each individual voice came to her distinctly, for under it all was a deep and abiding silence, like a slow river that bore dancing, golden leaves upon its surface. There was no clatter of hooves, no rumble of heavy wheels to swallow other, smaller sounds, and the waters of the lagoon were utterly still, the intemperate movements of the Adriatic softened to a hush so profound that the noise of an oar landing clumsily in it rang through the canals like a slap.

Slowly, Sarah realized that there was another sound, the strains of music so muddled by distance that she could not be sure at first if there was just one group of singers or two or three. Gradually, a melody grew louder, separating from the rest of the notes, and Sarah realized that the musicians were drawing closer.

Louder and louder it grew, closer and closer, the smoothness of its approach baffling to Sarah until she realized that the players must be on the water, carried along by boat. She rose just as the sounds seemed to draw even with her window, and simultaneously, shrieks of delight erupted from the girls on the portego's balcony.

Consumed by curiosity, Sarah went to her window and looked out. Directly beneath her, at least ten gondolas sat in the water, stripped of their black felzi and turned at every angle to each other. By the light of their blazing braziers—*Braziers!* Sarah marveled—that hung in the place of the usual stern lanterns, an outrageous collection of musicians dressed in outlandish carnival costumes played and sang and struck dramatic poses. Violinists, flautists, pipers of every kind, drummers, accordion players, guitarists, and more—all were piled in five or more to a boat, so crowded that the girls' cries of delight were frequently punctured by shrieks of warning as one or another of them appeared to be on the verge of toppling over the side.

The gondoliers themselves joined in the music, singing in deep, resonating voices, and across the water Sarah could hear other, more distant Venetians pick up the tune, as if such extravagant serenades were commonplace and open to whomever cared to participate.

People from nearby houses gathered at the windows, all laughing, and a glance to Sarah's left revealed Lady Anna and the Mortons hanging in openmouthed delight over the balcony's latticed rail as the motley collection stared adoringly up at them.

The musicians concluded their current song but paused only long enough to gather the shouts of *"bra'i!"* in the local dialect before they launched into another.

By this time, Sarah herself was almost too mesmerized to see the smaller, lightless craft detach itself from the crowd and pull up under her window. It was only when the long, lithe figure unfolded itself from the seat and began to climb the wall that she realized what was happening. In the darkness, she traced the dim line of the rope that he was grasping and realized abruptly that it was tied to an old iron mount at the bottom of her window, meant for a window box that had long since disappeared.

Any decent woman would scream. That was Sarah's first thought, strangely detached, as if it belonged to someone else. But she had never been a decent woman or even a decent girl, and the conjectures that her racing mind made concerning the identity of the acrobat were far from that of a midnight burglar.

Still, she felt a nervous giddiness that was somewhere between joy and dread, and she retreated to the far corner of her room as the men below sang on, reflexively closing her hand around the candlestick that sat upon the desk behind her.

A face appeared in the window, not the Moor's expected features but a visage as white and blank as the moonlight that shone upon it. Sarah's heart skipped a beat, and she had already drawn in a breath to shout when she realized she was once again confronted with the mask the Moor had worn at the masquerade. Her breath turned into a sigh of relief as he pulled himself up and climbed nimbly through the window, walking to the center of her room and standing there as if he owned it.

"I come here in disguise," he said.

Sarah swallowed a hysterical giggle at the dark melodrama of his words. "My lamp is out," she said, finally releasing her hold on the candlestick. "Neither of us needs a disguise now."

"I could not wait to see you," he intoned as if she had not spoken.

Another delighted squeal erupted from the portego, and Sarah's fragile sense of sanity reasserted itself. What was he doing there? What was he thinking? "Then why not send me another invitation like the first?" she snapped. "This is crazy, dangerous."

He chuckled, his eyes invisible in the shadows of the mask. "More than you could believe."

He was trying to unnerve her, to seduce her into unquestioning acceptance of his insane scheme. Despite the thrill that went through her at the realization that his intentions were still carnal, irritation unfroze her, and she crossed the room to jerk the curtains closed, keeping her face turned away from him until the moonlight was muted by the fabric.

"Why have you come here tonight?" she hissed at him. "What more do you want from me? I'd thought you had your fill last night."

"How could I ever have enough of you?" He grabbed her wrist, pulling her against his chest in the same movement. His body was long and hard, and the memories of the night before tangled with present sensations, making her breath quicken and her heart beat faster.

"You're lying," she heard herself say. "This is ridiculous."

"If only I were."

The words were so soft that Sarah half believed she imagined them. But before she could say anything, his mouth came down and covered hers.

Sweet. She is so sweet. Sebastian pulled her against him so that he could feel every curve through the thin fabric of her nightdress. All her resistance melted as their bodies met, and she leaned into him, trusting his strength, trusting him just as he had planned and as he had half wished that she would not. Speculations about timetables and Gian's skill at convincing de Lint to return home at the most opportune moment whirled in the back of his mind, his obligations and desires pulling at him. He wanted her, wanted her so badly that it almost hurt, and he hated what he must do to her—

He would not think of that. He would think only of this woman and this moment. He would give her a night to remember forever, if only to apologize for what he must do.

No. No apologies. No regrets. Only this moment, now, with her. He could forget everything else and have no fear of losing himself, for soon . . . soon it would all be over.

He pulled off his mask and pushed her toward her bed without preamble, and she allowed herself to be laid across it. Ignoring the intruding comparison of Iphigenia being sacrificed on the beach at Aulis, he tugged on her long, shroud-like nightdress, and she wriggled it off without getting up. Moonlight and firelight filtered through the thin curtains to fall across her, too dim to allow him make out details but enough to illuminate the shape of her pale body.

He had felt that body under him the night before, but now, to see it . . . She lacked the plump abundance that was currently fashionable, but she could not be called thin. Her frame was delicate and so were her curves, not subtle but not overripe, either. The faintly darker shadows of hollows at her collarbones were echoed at her waist and her hip bones, shading the expanse of soft white flesh.

He realized that she was looking at him expectantly. "Delicious," he managed hoarsely, and then he joined her on the bed.

Her lips met his eagerly, with none of the hesitation of the night before. Under his hands, her flesh heated with exquisite warmth, and his mouth traced their path, following her jawline down, along the curve of her neck to her collarbone. He kissed the hollow there that hid so coyly, and she made a little shuddering gasp. Chuckling darkly, he teased at the sensitive place with his lips and teeth and breath as she gasped and wiggled beneath him.

"This is only the beginning," he said, and she made a sound between a whimper and a laugh that went right through him.

He moved his attention to her breasts, tantalizing her until she shifted suddenly and thrust her nipple hard against his mouth. Taking the unsubtle suggestion, he moved his tongue across it slowly, teasing the delicate tip with his teeth before finally giving her what she wanted.

Then he moved down, across her belly. She squirmed, her breath ragged with desire and laughter as his touch simultaneously aroused and tickled, but when he reached the soft nest of curls between her legs, her breath caught.

She made no noise but a groan, but in that sound, he heard her hopeful disbelief, and his body buzzed with anticipation.

"You do not know how much I have wanted to do this," he muttered.

In mute answer, she extricated one leg from under his weight and hooked it over his shoulder. He chose not to react, and soon, the second one followed as she tilted her hips upward, the action opening herself to him.

He took the invitation. Without hesitation, he plunged his tongue between her folds, his swift plundering startling another gasp from her. She tasted hot and musky, and his own body tightened as she arched her back, her hands finding his wrists and gripping hard. He urged her onward with his lips and tongue as she whimpered under him. She was attempting to be quiet, to keep her responses low enough that they could be swallowed by the music that still clashed below. With a dark thrill, he felt her go over the edge. Her legs tightened around his head, and a rippling shiver went through her entire body as she made a frantically muffled moan. Her orgasm seemed to tear through him, too, and while she was still in the first throes of its pleasure, he yanked open his trousers with one hand, pulled his erection free, and entered her, all plans and timetables forgotten.

She welcomed him with her hands and her mouth and her body. He drove into her again and felt her climb even higher, and it was all he could do not to follow her right then.

She collapsed into panting bonelessness just as the song below ended—the last song—but when she started to try to push him off, he found her mouth and kissed it gently. "Not yet, little dove," he said in her ear, the words breathless with lust and exertion. He began moving slowly in her, and she let out a stifled moan.

"Criminy," Sarah muttered. The word was so ridiculous in such a context, so banal that it should have quenched his desire, but instead it inflamed him more, and he kissed her hard and began to drive her toward the edge again.

Sarah's whole body felt both emptied out and wonderfully filled with heavy warmth, but the Moor gave her no time to enjoy the lassitude. He coaxed her with his mouth and hands, pulling her up unwillingly out of that valley until she felt fever-hot again and her vision narrowed to his shadowed features, her hearing blocking every sound but their mingled breaths, her skin burning with his touch and needing more, more, more. . . .

Then—there must have been something, the sound of a

key in the lock, the turning doorknob, something. Sarah didn't see it, couldn't hear it, for the first thing that penetrated her mind was the door flinging open.

Light flooded through, surging in to fill all the corners of the room. For an instant, she was blinded, and as her eyes adjusted slowly to the glare, the whole chamber seemed so bright that the shadows were flattened to nothing. And then the first sensation beyond dumb alarm stabbed through her—a stomach-dropping horror as she realized what a picture she must make, with her naked body entwined around her seducer's and her ravaged face bared to his sight.

"No," she whispered, all her anguish in that one word.

All of that took no more than the space of a breath, and then her mind collapsed into numbness. She hardly felt the Moor jerk away, his white mask flashing down across his face before he dove through the window and into the night. She had barely even the presence of mind to cover herself with the counterpane. She couldn't think anymore; she couldn't feel anymore—all she could do was blink against the lamp glare, which was already fading from an actinic brilliance to the mellower yellow of ordinary lamplight.

Ordinary. Ordinary and sordid and disgusting, now that the fantasy had been stripped away.

Slowly, her eyes adjusted. Lady Merrill stood behind a smug Venetian maid, Mr. de Lint at her side. Lady Merrill's expression was sternly disapproving, but it was the smile on Mr. de Lint's face that made her blood run cold.

Not this, she thought, a few shards of panic stirring deep within her. *Please, not this.*

"Sarah, get dressed," Lady Merrill ordered. "I will be awaiting you in my chambers." She turned her back and led the way out. The maid followed immediately, but Mr. de Lint lingered for a second, staring at Sarah's half-covered body in the retreating light of the lamp before he blew a kiss that seemed bizarrely congratulatory and shut the door behind him.

Chapter Nine

The stern, old-woman voice of de Lint's mother came
muffled through the window as Sebastian dangled at
the end of the rope a few feet above the water. He had slid
down it so fast that his palms stung, fleeing with a speed
born of the sudden discovery that part of him did not want
to leave at all. But it was done, and he should be glad. Now
that Lady Merrill knew exactly what her son had brought
into her household, the whore's stint as de Lint's mistress
was over even if de Lint himself should like to pardon her.
Sebastian ought to be gloating, not feeling torn by a sense
of duty such a woman could never deserve. He forced his
mind away from the yearning to return to play the gallant
defender by forcing himself to focus on his current
predicament.

The boat had drifted on its painter so that he could not
ease into it, and one experimental swing triggered a grating
protest from the iron support anchored in the stone above.
He glanced up at the window—there were not yet signs of
a hunt, but that was no promise that there wouldn't be one
soon.

He let go.

He splashed down in water no more than knee-deep, and
he stumbled in surprise, barely keeping himself from
sprawling face-first—he had forgotten how shallow many

of the side canals were. He began to sink into the muck instantly, for there was not so much an end to the water as there was a beginning of a layer of sludge, which grew thicker as it deepened. He took a step quickly, driving one foot deeper into the mud as he pulled the other out, then another, forcing his way to his sàndolo. Reaching it, he hauled himself over the side, the muck making a sucking sound of protest as he pulled himself free. He untied the painter and pushed away from the palazzo with an unnecessarily forceful stroke of the oar.

Sebastian put his weight into the oar, sending the light, nimble craft skimming across the opaque water. He moved blindly through a maze of canals, heedless of the direction he took.

He should feel triumphant. He had achieved his goal, and he was free from that disturbing woman forever while engineering the disgrace she so clearly deserved. But again and again, the vision of her stricken face rose in his mind's eye, blinding him to the turnings of the canals—its naked, defenseless pallor in the instant of lamplight before he leapt through the window, showing her shock that turned with gut-piercing suddenness into the realization of betrayal.

She knew. She deserved to know, he told himself, for what she had done—what she must have done. But his mind was inventing excuses for her—that she was forced, that she didn't know what she was being used for, that it hadn't been her at all but some other scarred trollop.

What is wrong with me? The words echoed in his mind yet again.

Eventually, Sebastian's wanderings ended as he came around a corner and emerged abruptly upon the Grand Canal. His shoulders were aching, his arms burning with his exertions, and so he allowed himself to slow his pace to the gentle glide of the other traffic upon the canal. Even this late, it all but bustled, and in the distance the Piazzetta burned with light. Without making a conscious decision, he let it draw him onward, and he moored his boat next to the others lined up there. Beside him, yet another crowded gondola joined the row.

As he stepped onto the Molo, the bells in the campanile struck midnight. As usual, though, the two adjoining squares were still thronged, and gas lamps turned the surrounding porticoes into flat, surreal versions of themselves, like scenery in a vast play. Half the caffès were still open, many of their patrons watching the small band that played patriotic songs near Florian's. Sebastian stalked by, passing the mostly foreign occupants of the square, devoid for once of pigeons. Following a sudden urge for solitude, he turned aside to seek the quietness of the lesser streets that radiated from it.

Even in the first dark byway, though, Sebastian discovered that he was not alone. The scuffing echoes of other soft footsteps bounced against the walls, near-silent but loud enough to grate against his hypersensitive nerves. He ducked down another alley, so narrow that his shoulders nearly brushed the sides. After a couple of turns, the noises faded, and Sebastian once more immersed himself in his thoughts.

But then the sound of a boot scraping against the cobbles made him pause, and he ground his teeth in frustration as he cast about for an even more obscure place to take himself. Sebastian was just beginning to turn around when a weight slammed against him, knocking him against the alley wall.

The breath rushed out of his lungs as he hit the rough brick, his head snapping back against it with a force that made lights explode in front of his eyes. He struck out instinctively at his assailant, and pain jolted up his arm as his elbow hit something hard. *A knife blade,* he realized as the edge caught on his coat sleeve. He jerked away and felt the cloth rip, but the force of the contact was not enough to dislodge it from his attacker's hand.

Sebastian did not take the time to think. He just kicked out hard, his knee jarring with the force when he connected with something fleshy. With a grunt, his attacker hurled backward—straight into another man, who went down with a curse.

How many were there? How many more had knives? In the moonlight, Sebastian couldn't tell, and he had no intention of finding out. While the fallen men still blocked the alley, he fled, ducking and weaving through the maze of streets until he was certain that any pursuit was lost.

Finally, he slowed, taking a circuitous route back to the Plaza and his boat, but his mind was troubled by the attack. A man of his size was not a likely target for footpads, however much they outnumbered him. Why had they chosen him, this night above all others? Was it fate, wreaking some sort of unholy vengeance against what he'd done to de Lint's whore? Or was it his own conscience, inviting the attack through his unconscious carelessness?

Whatever the reason, Sebastian could not help but believe, as he stepped into the boat and cast off from the Molo, that he had gotten off far too lightly.

Sarah sat for a long moment, staring at the closed door as her mind slowly began to thaw, assembling the fragmented images of the past minutes into a coherent whole. The Moor's face an instant before it disappeared behind the mask, his expression grimly triumphant. The unsurprised maid with the key clasped in her hand and Lady Merrill and Mr. de Lint in obedient tow. Mr. de Lint's terrible expression . . .

Hell. How could I be such a bloody lust-sotted idiot? A fine mark I made, a blooming sheep ready for the shearing. The old words from her old world jumbled into her head for the first time in years. She'd been so vain, so stupid that she hadn't even seen it coming, when anyone would have known that no sane man would want her for any but the worst reasons.

But why, then? Why? Did he enjoy humiliating poor, homely women so much?

It didn't matter now. Sarah looked around the room in the

moonlight, the chamber that she had enjoyed for only a few short days yet had already begun consider her own. It was probably the last time she could think of it as such.

With shaking fingers, she lit the lamp on the desk and slowly pulled on her discarded clothes. Then she opened her trunk at the foot of the bed and carefully laid the rest of her belongings inside. They barely filled the space halfway, looking lost, common, and ugly, and that seemed suddenly to be the most horrible thing of all.

She tried to fix her mind on nothing, but thoughts lurked under the blankness like grotesque furniture looming under a covering of dust sheets. She fixed her hair in a mercilessly severe bun and scrubbed her face in a vain attempt to restore some semblance of color to its deathly pallor. Then, her back as straight as a rod, she left the room and walked down the echoing portego to Lady Merrill's chambers.

The command to enter came immediately upon her knock. She opened the door to find Lady Merrill in her dressing gown, her lady's maid patiently brushing her long silver hair. "That is enough," Lady Merrill said firmly. McGarrity curtsied quickly and left.

For a full minute, Lady Merrill just sat silently and stared at Sarah, and the familiar, sickening sense of humiliation surged up from her stomach, her face burning with it and her muscles aching against the urge to hunch over like a shamed child. Her vision blurred, and she jerked her gaze down to the ruffles on her employer's dressing gown, unable to meet her eyes.

"Well?" the old woman said eventually. "What do you have to say for yourself?"

"I'm . . . I'm sorry," Sarah whispered. And she was. She was sorry for betraying one of the only people outside her family who had ever been kind to her. She was sorry for forgetting what she had worked for and giving in to those wild, abandoned hours with the Moor. She was sorry for believing that anyone could really want her. "I know I can't stay here. I've packed up my things. If I could just have my back wages so I can rent a room for a few days—"

Lady Merrill sighed, and Sarah's head jerked up at the uncustomary sound. For once, the lady really did look like an old woman. Her lively black eyes dimmed a little with disappointment, her face falling into the creases of age as her shoulders slumped slightly, birdlike in their frailty. "Oh, Sarah. Sarah, Sarah, Sarah . . . Why?"

Sarah blinked hard. "Don't you think that I've been asking myself that question? Now, looking back, nothing sounds like a justification, but I did it because . . . because I thought he wanted me. And because he was beautiful." She tried to laugh, but the sound caught in her throat and came out strangled. "I can't expect someone like you to understand. I don't talk much, but I'm not stupid. I've heard all the hints that your friends have made." Lady Merrill's eyebrows rose, but now that she had started, Sarah couldn't stop. "Men have always wanted you—older, younger, it doesn't matter. You've been married three times, and by your own admission, every one of the men loved you and you loved them, too. You were beautiful—you're still more beautiful than I could ever hope to be. I'd never even met anyone who ever wanted to . . . to kiss me before—not just some girl but me. . . ." The last word was swallowed by a sob, and she turned away as mortification and tears overtook her.

"Oh, my," Lady Merrill whispered. Sarah heard a rustle of ruffled skirts, and a few seconds later, she started when a hand touched her elbow, turning her around, pulling her down into the older woman's soft embrace.

Sarah couldn't bear it. Her strangled sobs erupted into a fit of uncontrolled weeping, and she buried her face against the perfumed frills of the old woman's dressing gown. Lady Merrill made small shushing sounds, rocking back and forth as Sarah cried her heart out.

It was a long time later when Sarah straightened and dried her eyes.

"I don't expect for there to be any more of this," Lady Merrill said sternly but with a soft light in her bright black eyes.

"Y-your ladyship?" Sarah asked dumbly.

"You heard me. No more."

"Then you don't want me to leave?"

"Tch, child, as long as one mistake doesn't become a habit . . ." She shook her head. "Go back to bed. You need your sleep. Tomorrow, I'll be visiting more of my old friends. They're terribly respectable, and I expect you to be in best form."

"Yes, madam. Thank you, madam," Sarah said, still not quite believing it, and she fled the room still hiccoughing before Lady Merrill could change her mind.

Chapter Ten

Sarah woke to her breath misting in the air. She sat up for a second, disoriented as she took in the room—the desk, stripped of her belongings, and the chest lying open at the foot of her bed. At that sight, the night before came back to her in all its horror. She got up, wrapping her blankets around her against the chill that bit into her exposed flesh, and crossed to the window. On the bridge that the Moor had once waited by, wool-wrapped pedestrians walked between the shops under a sky as pale and brittle as glass.

Where was the golden sun of yesterday's Italy or the lusty, warbling boatmen of the Venice of the night before? They were like dreams, and this the washed-out reflection of them. The city muffled Sarah in its silence so that the entire view seemed surreal, as if it were taken from the imaginings of a mad artist and brought soundlessly to life.

She dressed quickly, shivering at the icy bite of the water she splashed onto her face. Then she fixed her hair in the severest, most unflattering bun possible and surveyed her reflection, on guard against a single disreputable stray hair or slatternly wrinkle in her skirt. Finally and with great trepidation, she wrapped her heaviest shawl around her shoulders and went to breakfast.

The balcony was empty when she emerged, a cold wind whistling through the loggia, and she followed the sound of

voices to one of the side parlors. She opened the door and
stepped into a frigid dining room, which, like her own room,
lacked even a hearth upon which to lay a fire.

Lady Merrill gave her a piercing look, but the three
young girls, who were just sitting down, didn't spare her a
second glance. Mr. de Lint was nowhere to be seen.

The girls' lack of reaction told her that Lady Merrill had
stopped the news of what had happened the night before
from spreading, and a quick glance around showed a new
maid waiting upon them instead of the one that had led Lady
Merrill and Mr. de Lint to her room. Sarah spared a twinge
of guilt for the maid's possible fate—even if she had been
in collusion with the Moor, it seemed unfair that she should
be dismissed when the greatest blame clearly lay at Sarah's
own feet.

"Pardon me. I overslept," she muttered as she took her
place and tried to sink invisibly into her chair. It was impossible, though, because the girls had recognized her existence as something other than an enemy or a watchdog,
and this morning they chose not to ignore her but seemed
determined to draw her into their conversation, referencing
her as the expert—"Since you hardly put down your
Baedeker's the entire voyage"—on whatever aspect of the
city they chose to debate. In vain, Sarah would protest that
she didn't remember or that Baedeker's didn't say. Each
time she raised that possibility, it was rejected with scorn.
Obliged to give some answer, Sarah replied faithfully
when she could and inventively when she could not as
Lady Merrill watched them all with an indulgent but
slightly guarded smile.

The day before, Sarah would have enjoyed the game, the
almost-acceptance even with its tinge of condescension, the
teasing and gales of merriment when the girls realized that
they had been deceived by her tale spinning. Everything had
changed in a night, though, and the faint amusement that
Sarah was still capable of feeling seemed to belong to another world.

Finally, breakfast was concluded. The girls retired for their studies in the drawing room, which was the only room in their entire suite that had a stove, and Lady Merrill called McGarrity to wrap her in layers of shawls and cloaks in preparation for going out.

The chill, she said, had got into her bones, but that was no reason for canceling her plans, and so she leaned heavily on Sarah as she descended the stairs. Bundled into the gondola, she and her companion were swiftly rowed to a series of houses where more aging lights of the previous generation lived, native Venetians, Germans, French, and even Americans. A few of the chambers were as cold as the rooms that Lady Merrill had taken, but most were retrofitted with ceramic stoves or boasted of the braziers the locals used. One even had an original fireplace—"the builder's fortunate quirk," as the old Frenchwoman who now owned the palazzo said. Lady Merrill spoke gaily with each of her friends, and Sarah tried to make herself invisible, blanking her mind to everything but the warmth.

But as she stepped out of the door of Lady Merrill's last stop, the soothing, somnolent complacency she had fallen into was stripped away with the first touch of the bitter wind. For the news that they were returning to the Palazzo Bovolo brought back the memory of the look Mr. de Lint had given her the night before and the grim promise it contained.

Indeed, Sarah's fears were justified, for when they arrived, she discovered that Mr. de Lint had returned for luncheon, and his expression upon spying Sarah was filled with such a black pleasure that it made her ill.

Somehow, she made it through the meal, and when Lady Merrill retired to the warmth of her bed, her son excused himself until supper. Sarah was almost giddy with relief as she attended her mistress, her gratefulness so keen that she actually enjoyed the afternoon's stiff-fingered letter-writing session with only the warmth of a candle to keep her fingers from going completely numb. When she was dismissed,

Sarah left the lady's chambers with the intention of hiding in her own room until supper.

But she turned away from the closed door only to discover Mr. de Lint waiting for her, leaning against one of the loggia's columns with his back to the canal. Sarah's heart lurched, and she glanced furtively around, but the entire frigid, open portego was empty. *Of course,* a hard, despairing part of her said. *He would have seen to that.*

"My dearest, dearest Sarah," Mr. de Lint murmured. "I have been waiting for you." His tone was almost ludicrously villainous, and the sickeningly familiar glint in his eye told her that he found amusement in embracing such a role.

"Mr. de Lint," she said in stiff acknowledgment. Her hand was still on the doorknob to Lady Merrill's room. In one twist, she could be back inside. And then what? One hundred stories, one thousand excuses flittered across her mind like dry leaves in a wind, but she did not try to fasten onto their dead, fleeing shapes. She might stay with Lady Merrill another ten minutes, perhaps even another hour. And when she came out again, he would still be there, waiting.

Sarah stared at the smirking, handsome man in front of her, bathed in the glow of the afternoon sun and his own smug self-assurance. She had to swallow hard against the thickening panic in her throat. In his coldly amused eyes, she saw the future, and she was helpless to stop it, a marionette controlled by the strings of her position. She would try to walk past him to her room, he would stop her, and then—

Like before, just like before . . . The images of other rough men flashed through her brain, the ones who had paid her and who had done less wrong in the eyes of the world than she, and the others, even worse, who hadn't. She could feel them all against her, pressing her down, smothering her with their weight and invading her, taking, taking far more than her body but a piece of her soul—

"No," she said aloud. It was hardly more than a whisper,

but Sarah felt the force of every fiber of her being in that word.

"Sarah?" Mr. de Lint asked in a tone of false puzzlement, his smile spreading.

"No," she repeated, louder this time. They were half the length of the portego apart—thirty feet, easily, probably more. The interior staircase stood between them, closer to him than to her, but the exterior garden stairs were behind her. The knowledge of them was like a beacon, beckoning her to freedom and calming the frantic beating of her heart.

She backed up slowly along the portego, away from him. He just stood and watched her as she took the first step, the second, the third, but then comprehension flickered across his face, and he pushed himself away from the column and sauntered after her.

He isn't even hurrying, Sarah realized, her stomach knotting. He was that certain that he'd catch her. Teeth clenched so tightly that her jaw ached, she whirled and started walking toward the garden end of the portego, her steps jerky with adrenaline and fear. She could hardly hear Mr. de Lint's footsteps over the pounding of blood in her ears, but she knew they were faster, louder, nearer.

The door was so close now, only a dozen strides away, but Mr. de Lint was far closer. He couldn't catch her, not when she was so near her goal! Knowing that she couldn't outrace him, Sarah broke into a run anyway, her steps jolting and her breath sobbing in her lungs.

Mr. de Lint's hand closed around her shoulder. Sarah made one last desperate lunge for the door. Her body twisted as she wrenched from his grasp, and her side slammed against the painted wood. The handle, the handle . . . Her hands scrabbled for it, turned it—

Her weight was still against the door, but nothing happened.

It opened inward. That realization struck her at the same instant that Mr. de Lint grabbed her elbow and yanked her hand off the knob.

"Don't," she begged, but he strode back up the portego, jerking her behind him with such force that her head snapped back. Her feet caught her instinctively as he pulled her along, and for a moment, her brain spinning, there was nothing that she could do but follow. In that short span of time, he flung open an interior door and threw her inside, straight into the back of an armchair. The chair flew over, and she slammed into the ground, the chair landing on top of her.

The breath rushed out of her as she hit the cold, hard marble, and pain exploded through her knees and hands, which had tried to catch her fall. She forced air into her stunned body, gasping against the pressure that still seemed to be squeezing her lungs, and shoved herself onto her bruised palms. She kicked the chair off her, her legs tangling in her skirts. Mr. de Lint had shut the door, and he strolled leisurely over to where she still struggled on the floor. He reached down and encircled her upper arm with his hand.

Sarah braced for the yank, but instead he helped her to her feet in a manner that was almost gentle. She pulled away from him the second that she had her feet under her, and he let her go. But instead of stepping away from her, he advanced, closer and closer. She stepped back each time he stepped forward, bumping into furniture and stumbling over rugs, until she felt the pressure of the wall at her back and had nowhere to go. Even then, he did not stop until she was wedged into the corner and his legs were pushing against her skirts, the back of her head aching from the pressure of the plaster walls as she strained away.

"Mr. de Lint, I want to go to my chamber now," Sarah said. She hated the tremor in her voice, the way her gaze dropped from his cold amber eyes to his thin black cravat despite all her determination to face him down. Mr. de Lint merely lowered his head even closer to hers. He was going to kiss her. Sarah jerked her face to the side, and he chuckled, low and deliberate, and pushed his forearm against her neck to hold her to the wall.

"You certainly play the timid little mouseling well." Mr. de Lint's hot breath brushed her ear, and his whiskers tickled her cheek, his mouth a mere inch away. She shuddered, feeling an automatic response in her body that even her worst revulsion couldn't suppress, the thick scent of his cologne making her ill. "I had decided that you weren't worth the bother, you know."

"I assure you, sir, I am worth no one's bother." Sarah closed her eyes against the dampness that pricked them and swallowed hard, the action pushing against the arm that kept her pinned to the wall.

"Oh, Sarah," he said softly. "There's no need to pretend now. Now that I know what you really are." She felt his free hand touch her face, featherlight, and she knew he was tracing the scars. She tried to shake her head to knock his hand away, but he pushed into her throat, and she froze before he crushed her windpipe.

"No more games, Sarah." His voice hardened.

She shouldn't fight; she couldn't fight. He was stronger than she; he was her employer's son—one word from him, and she'd be tossed out on the street. But suddenly, she couldn't stand it any longer.

"Stop saying my name!" she ground out, fighting against the pressure of his forearm against her larynx.

"What?" He sounded genuinely surprised, and for a second, his hold loosened.

"Don't say it!" She lunged against him, but he caught her effortlessly. "It's mine, damn you. Mine!"

Mr. de Lint began to laugh, a chilling sound that broke off abruptly when he backhanded her carelessly across the face. Even as she cried out, she used the force of his blow to throw her weight to the side, jerking free of him for the instant it took to get out of the corner. She sprinted for the door, Mr. de Lint a heartbeat behind her. She couldn't reach it in time, she knew it, but she had to try—

Just then, the door opened from the outside, and one of Lady Merrill's English footmen entered.

Sarah heard Mr. de Lint stop behind her, but she kept going until she reached the doorway. There she froze, her back against the wall, and watched the two men warily.

Mr. de Lint looked collected and distantly amused, as always, only a slight rumpling of his clothes and a hard light in his eye betraying that anything was amiss. The footman was openly gaping and wide-eyed at the tableau before him. If he backed out now and closed the door behind him, Sarah would be lost. She stared at him, begging him with her eyes to save her.

Mr. de Lint cleared his throat, and the young man gulped nervously, his eyes flickering from his face to Sarah's.

"I-I'm sorry, sir," he temporized. "I had no idea you'd be in here."

"Just leave," Mr. de Lint said coldly, his eyes promising hell for the servant if he disobeyed.

"Yessir," the man hastily agreed.

"Please, no." Sarah didn't even realize that she had spoken until the words, barely more than a breath, reached her ears.

The footman's eyes dragged back to Sarah. For a long moment, he said nothing. Then, finally: "Lady Merrill wants to see you." The words were slow and grudging, but Sarah's relief was so intense that she nearly gasped.

Mr. de Lint's face darkened at the obvious lie. "I will send her along when I am finished with her."

The man swayed, looking even more frightened, but his expression grew determined. "Lady Merrill asked me to bring her. Lady Merrill wants her now."

For a second, Sarah was afraid Mr. de Lint would attack the footman, but then he muttered an oath and turned away. "You must have got into his trousers, too, I see," he snapped. "But I'll get my chance. You can't play coy with me forever."

Her face flaming with humiliation, Sarah scuttled out the door, the footman hard on her heels.

"Thank you," she said once they reached the portego. "If I can ever do anything for you—"

"I don't need no favors from you," the young man said, his face set in hard lines as his accent suddenly thickened. "No, thank you, miss. I've kept meself out of trouble for the whole five years I've worked for Lady Merrill, but thanks to you, I'll be lookin' for a new job soon enough. No, I don't need no thanks from you."

He turned his back and walked away. Sarah stared at him for a moment, her mouth agape, then ran for the safety of her bedroom, locking the door behind her.

She leaned against it even as her mind mocked her with the memory of the little brass key the maid had wielded the night before, her arms clasped around her roiling midsection. Her stomach rebelled, and she barely had time to jerk the chamber pot from under the bed before she began to heave.

When she was finished, she shoved it back under the bed and washed her face and rinsed her mouth at the basin. Then she wedged a chair under the doorknob and collapsed upon the bed.

She stared unseeing at the intricate plasterwork above her. It was over. The rest of her employment with Lady Merrill would be a farce. She had lost her one chance at decent independence. The only employment that she had ever had that she could be proud of, and she had destroyed it in less than a year. She was an Irish bastard guttersnipe, born to a class of thieves and whores and worse, without the skill of a pickpocket or the stomach for sterner work. It didn't matter that she had no ability for the one occupation left to her, the oldest one of all. It was her only birthright, reflected in her face and the expressions of everyone who ever met her. Her only value to anyone was in what was between her legs, and even that wasn't much. A warm lump of meat, brainless, spiritless, worthless . . .

She felt the tears starting, and it was a long time before she could banish them again. When she emerged for supper, she felt as fragile as a bruised rose. She was not ready to face Mr. de Lint—she'd never be ready to face him—but she had no choice.

He watched Sarah as they ate and took every opportunity to tease her in his old, hateful manner. Lady Merrill, usually so observant, remained deaf to the ugliness of his words, laughing at his little jokes and smiling at his small cruelties while the girls and their governess ignored them all. Sarah kept her silence when she could and answered as briefly as possible when she could not.

As dessert was being served, Mr. de Lint managed to catch Sarah's eye. Smiling, he motioned at something small beside his plate. Sarah's gaze was dragged to it involuntarily. At first, she could not tell what it was, but then her eyes sorted out the glints and shadows, and she realized that it was an all-too-familiar key.

At that moment, something inside her froze, and she knew she could not spend another instant in those apartments.

She stood from the table, not realizing how abrupt the movement was until six pairs of eyes stared at her.

"Excuse me," she muttered. "I don't feel well." Not waiting for a response, she turned her back to the table and fled the room.

She was at her own door when she realized that she still clutched her dinner knife in her hand. She shoved it into a pocket as she searched for her key, unlocking the door with shaking hands and securing it—fruitlessly, she knew—behind her the second she was through it.

After a second to regain her composure, she flung open her chest, wardrobe, and dresser drawers, spreading out her cloak on her bed and piling her belongings into the center of it. When she was done, there was still enough loose fabric that she could tie it easily. She looked around the room for anything of value to slip in, soothing her guilt with the knowledge that she was owed several days' wages and a trinket could mean the difference between a full belly or an empty one. Even the Moor's gifts would not provide much at a pawnshop. Taking the lamp and the candlestick, she swung the bundle onto her back. It wasn't heavy, though it contained everything that she owned in the world. She had not realized that the material detritus of her life could weigh so little.

She reached the portego, shutting the door behind her. She could still make out de Lint's voice among those coming from the dining room, and she crept down the long room with her heart in her throat to the garden stairs. Once she reached the courtyard, she stashed her bundle behind a statue in the center and entered the palazzo again, making her way boldly to the kitchens. With a combination of pantomime and simple words, she bullied a servant into filling a bag with enough food for five or six careful meals, and then she stepped out into the night.

When she swung her bundle onto her back again, the finality of her severance and the desperation of her position hit her. What did she think that she was going to do, with hardly any money, lost in a city where she could not speak the language? There was only one profession in which speech was no barrier, but her mind shuddered away from that possibility before the thought had fully been formed. Despite the black time in her room just after the attack, she was not willing to consign herself to that fate. Even giving in to the pressures of Mr. de Lint would be better than that; he could contrive to corner her no more than once or twice a day, and without her resistance, his interest would soon stray elsewhere.

Sarah did have one friend with power left, one friend who would do anything to help her: Maggie, who would send money and buy her a ticket to return to England the instant she heard the news—first class, even, if Sarah would let her. But the few shreds of self-respect that remained to Sarah would not allow her to be rescued by her friend. She needed no charity now, with her ladies school education and her wardrobe of decent, sober dresses. But both of those seemed a chilly comfort in the uncertainty of the lifetime that stretched ahead of her.

Biting back a sound of despair, Sarah pushed through the

garden gate and onto the campo. Leaving the gate swinging, she chose one of the branching streets at random, letting her feet choose the path among the serpentine lanes and labyrinthine alleys. She moved at a brisk walk, then at a jog, and then she broke into a run, pouring her fear and determination into her legs as she propelled herself away from Mr. de Lint and everything that he stood for.

In the darkness, all the intersections looked alike, the flickering gaslights like so many reflections, the sudden, bizarre shrines in the street corners and out-of-the-way alcoves indistinguishable variations of the same grotesque theme. Sarah moved fast without pausing to think, her legs pumping against the hard cobbles as a remedy against her thoughts. She let the efforts of her body and the bewildering visions that her eyes presented fill her mind until there was no room for reason. Whenever she came to a dead end at a blank wall or a sudden dark-watered canal, she turned around and continued her careering path at random. She had no plan, no clue as to where she might be going except that she was moving away from the Palazzo Bovolo and the man that lurked within it.

Finally, her leaden legs began to flag, and her gloveless fingers, which had gone numb long before, began to lose their grip on her bundle, and she had to admit that she could not continue to run all night long.

Sarah stumbled to a stop, letting the bundle slide to her feet as she found herself blinking at a shadowy campo. Half a dozen of the omnipresent Venetian cats surveyed her loftily from various vantages, and directly ahead of her stood a derelict-looking church, apparently identical to the others that seemed to inhabit almost every campo, its marble façade stained by years of neglect and salt breeze, its once-proud porphyry saints sad now and forlorn.

She had no idea where she was or where she might go, but Sarah thought of the stories that she had read in her history books about churches in the Middle Ages serving as a refuge for the criminal or the persecuted. Popish though this one must be, she doubted that the tradition continued to the present day, and yet what other chance did she have here?

She ascended the five steps up to the church's doors and paused self-consciously. In front of her, under a layer of black oxidation made motley in the gaslight, towered a pair of great bronze doors, cast in tableaux of biblical scenes. She stared at a panel of Susannah and the Elders for a long time, gathering up the courage to try the handle.

A feathery sensation at her ankles made her start. Looking down, she saw a large gray tabby, having condescended to leave off its aloof surveillance, now twining itself possessively around her ankles. Superstitiously taking it for a sign of approval, she reached up to the doors and pushed. They swung inward without even a creak, and in two steps she was inside, the cat padding at her heels.

Aside from a few small votives in a side chapel, the church was pitch-dark and empty. Sarah could make out the shape of an arch here, the faint lines of a painting there. She was surrounded with a sense of empty space that was saturated with a dampness that seeped up from the stones. Logically, she knew the church must be some neglected parish center that had escaped the suppression under the French that her Baedeker's had so meticulously chronicled. But in the living night, the echoes of her boot heels in the nave seemed portentous, and she felt that the gaze of every Madonna icon and carved saint was fixed upon her. In her imagination, the scrutiny did not seem hostile but wary, as if those eyes had seen much to lead them to distrust.

Sarah's hesitant steps led her out of the open corridor of the nave and into the shelter of an aisle, where she sank down with her back to an exterior buttress. She expected to shiver against the cold of the stone, but the floor and wall were gently warm against her half-frozen flesh. For a long moment, she soaked it in, blanking her mind as she watched the cat cautiously investigating its new territory.

I feel just as out of place, she thought. St. Mark's had been made more for the temporal grandeur of the doges than for worship, but this little church was filled with its sense of purpose, and it unsettled her. As far as she was anything at all, she supposed she was a decent Anglican, and the stories of the decadence and impiety of the papists made her feel guilty to invade a space that she could not hold to be holy. But the exortations of the decent Dunnefirth vicar had so little to do with her own life that she knew she embraced the Church of England more from a desire to acquire all the trappings of a decent young woman than from any stirrings of faith.

Slowly, though, the cat's mundane antics dispelled the sense of invasion, and as she warmed and relaxed, she realized that her stomach was rumbling—that it must have been empty for quite some time. With Mr. de Lint torturing her so, she'd hardly managed to take more than a few bites of her supper, and now she was ravenous. She took out the sack of food and used the knife in her pocket to carefully measure off a piece of bread and cheese. Whiskers pricking, the cat approached, and in the candlelight, she saw how very thin it was. Knowing that she had little enough food for herself, she nevertheless broke off a fragment of cheese and offered it to the animal. It gobbled the food without the least sign of wariness.

Sarah ate and then lay in the darkness, considering her future, her thoughts circling, repeating, doubling back upon themselves, all to no avail. When she had worn out that path, her mind turned to the Moor, and the question that had been haunting her since the night before echoed in her head again and again: *Why?*

At some point, she must have fallen asleep, for she was woken by a voice and a light over her. She looked around in confusion, squinting, then realized that she had curled up on the aisle floor, the cat lying on her skirts. Above a priest's frock, confused but kindly eyes stared down at her, and the man said something in Italian.

"I can't understand," Sarah said, scrambling to her feet and dislodging the cat as she did so. The priest looked down at it and frowned. "I'm sorry," she continued. "I was just resting. I'll go now." She scurried away, the feline pacing after her. As she closed the church doors behind them, she caught one last look of the priest's bewildered face.

Sarah sighed and turned away, continuing her wandering progress though the city, the cat trotting behind her. She felt light-headed from the lack of sleep, and the streets took on an unreal quality as her brain tried to slip into dreams even as she walked. She chose a direction and walked that way until she ran out of pavement, and then she turned and walked some more, the cat staying so close to her that it sometimes tangled in her feet. Finally, she found herself facing the Rialto Bridge over the Grand Canal. She crossed over and followed the canal for a lack of a better destination, taking a wandering path through the backstreets when no pavement followed along its edge.

Slowly, it penetrated her numbed senses that the waters were no longer inky with night but a dull pewter from the coming dawn. Looking across the canal, she saw a flotilla of shapes drifting toward her position. For an instant, she was alarmed, her exhausted mind seizing upon the wild idea of pursuit, but then she realized that it was a fleet of small boats, each packed to the gunwales with fresh produce. The effect was of a huge, silent floating garden—until the boats reached the edge of the canal. Then there was a wash of noise and a flurry of activity as the boatmen shouted to men on shore, who pushed past Sarah to unload the boats and clear them out of the way for the next group to come in. Sarah looked behind her and realized that the narrow pavement had opened into a large campo that was cluttered with dozens of market stalls.

Sarah moved to the edge of the marketplace and scooped up her feline shadow, feeling invisible in the tumult as crates of vegetables and seafood were hauled to the stalls following some system she could not decipher. The movements of the laborers and the calls of the gondoliers were cheerful, even exuberant, and she let herself be carried away by the energy of their exertions. In the pale morning light, the cabbages looked like glass, the shrimp like glimmering gray pearls. Before the last of the boats was even emptied, a few Venetian housewives arrived to pick over the produce, and the stall owners began giving Sarah curious, sideways looks, trying to determine if she, too, was looking for the freshest fish, the best radishes. Sarah slid back into a side street and away with the cat purring comfortably in her arms, resuming her aimless, wandering path through the city.

Perhaps half an hour later, it stole upon her that she recognized her surroundings. She had seen that balcony when she was being rowed back from the Moor's palazzo, and yes, she knew the lion carving over that door, too. She let her memory lead her back along the route, detouring once when the pavement disappeared along a small side canal and picking it up again fifty feet beyond. Finally, she found herself at a doorway of a leprous white mansion with a great marble spider carved upon the lintel.

She stopped.

Now that she was there, what on earth did she think she was going to do? she asked herself. The Moor was the engineer of her humiliation. She had no claims on him, no recourse, legal or moral, to force him to pay an indemnity for the harm he had caused. And nothing, absolutely nothing could restore her to her former respectable position.

So she stood there, staring at the door, too aware of her plain, scarred face, bare to the morning light, and her dusty dress, so eloquent of her undistinguished estate. How could she have thought that a woman like her would be anything more than sport to a man who lived in such a place? Why had she even bothered to come?

The flick of a bushy tail against her skirt roused her from her self-flagellating thoughts. She looked down to see the cat twining faithfully around her ankles. With a humorless bark of laughter, she sat down on the pavement, leaning back against the pale, splotched wall as she petted it. It purred in shameless ecstasy, and she gave in, pulling another small bite of cheese out of her precious horde. The scrawny cat gulped it down, looking at her expectantly for more.

"Oh, puss, I don't even have enough for me," she told it softly, stroking its lean, silky sides. It looked at her with a wise expression, then rolled luxuriantly onto its back. She petted its chest tentatively at first, knowing that many cats hated the touch, but it just purred louder.

Throughout that interminable, horrible night, Sarah hadn't shed so much as a tear. She had left her employment as a disgraced woman and a petty thief, knowing that she had no money beyond what the Moor's gifts would bring and no expectations of any kind. And she had not cried for herself—she could not cry for herself, for fear had choked off that release. But now, faced with the blind animal faith of a scraggly alley cat, she felt her eyes prick with moisture and her throat tighten.

"Poor, stupid thing," she whispered to it. "I have nothing to give you. You picked the wrong champion." She felt its ribs as she stroked its length, felt the strong vibration of the purr through its entire body, and she was overcome by the knowledge that she was powerless even to help a single stray cat.

Biting her lip, she stood and slung her bundle over her shoulder, and she was about to walk away when the black doors opened and a dark-haired man stepped through. With a shock, Sarah recognized the boyishly handsome "gondolier" who had flattered his way into Lady Anna's affections. Now he was dressed in the plain, stiff suit of a secretary or clerk, and he frowned when he saw her, demanding something in Italian.

"I am here to see your master," Sarah heard herself say. She blinked at her own words as they registered, and almost turned and fled right then. Only the purring reassurance of the cat twining around her feet kept her rooted to the spot.

"He does not need more servants," the man replied coldly, his English measured and impeccable.

Steeling herself, Sarah summoned her best imitation of Lady Anna. "I am not a servant." She tried to sound haughty but was afraid that her voice was more anemic than aloof. "I am his lover. I was here two nights ago, and I have come to see him again." The statements were all true, but taken together, they created an impression that was patently false.

The man looked astonished for a moment before taking in her hair and her dress in one sweeping look. His disbelief faded as he nodded curtly. "I remember," he said, his reservations still thick in his voice. "I will talk to him." He turned and passed back into the palazzo.

Sarah knew the man meant for her to wait outside for his return, but she also knew the Moor would dismiss her more easily through a lackey than if he had to face her, so she scooped up the cat and slipped inside behind him.

She stepped silently into the vast entry hall. Lit by prosaic daylight instead of the flickering, golden flames of a hundred candles, it seemed vastly colder and more forbidding. Her shoes scraped on the gritty stone under her feet, stained with dirt and lichen. The painted Chinese wallpaper was a startling, rich red, but it was peeling off the walls in wide strips, splotched and discolored with wide water stains. A series of small, insignificant doorways around the perimeter of the room led into the service areas of the house, making the distant ceiling seem even higher. As she glanced up uneasily, Sarah's gaze was caught by the bizarre and fantastic chandelier whose glass flowers glittered green and blue and red in a single broad shaft of sunlight that slanted through the upper window. Only the sweeping staircase was as she remembered it, its curving marble an invitation to ascend above to where she and the Moor had spent the night only three days before and where he undoubtedly waited now.

Sarah gathered her nerve and climbed, reaching the piano

nobile portego just in time to see the Moor's lackey enter one of the side rooms, leaving the door open behind him. Her heart fluttering with sick nervousness, she crept closer. Inside, the clerklike man was speaking rapidly in Italian, and it was with a jolt that she recognized the Moor's stern baritone snapping out a brusque reply.

She hesitated just out of sight of the open doorway, trying to find the courage to enter when all she wanted to do was run away. But the cat chose that moment to wiggle out of her arms, and it dropped softly to the floor and sauntered into the room before she could stop it.

The Moor's speech broke off, and Sarah knew that within seconds his lackey would be at the door, berating her for her impertinence and telling her to take herself off.

So instead, she took a deep breath, squared her shoulders, and stepped into the room.

Shocked silence met her. The Moor was sitting at a desk, facing the doorway with the servant at his side. His patrician face was still handsome enough to make her heart contract—piercing eyes, angular features, wide brow, sensuous mouth. But those eyes were shuttered when they met hers, his expression so blank that he might have been wearing his mask.

Oblivious to the tension, the cat swaggered to the exact center of the room and began grooming itself. Dragging her eyes from the Moor, Sarah fixed them on the feline with relief, trying to make sense of her jumbled emotions. Anger—that was uppermost, the easiest to identify, its metallic taste bitter in her mouth, its heat making her vision dim. But under it, she felt a roiling mass—shame and despair, self-consciousness and a very unfamiliar feeling that made her lift her chin and glare at her seducer: pride.

Sebastian couldn't believe that she had come, that she'd had enough courage to stand with no mask, no disguise, and confront him. Her clothes were plain and mousy, her red-blond hair coming down in slatternly tangled locks around her face. Her face might have been pretty if it weren't for her pallor, her scars, and the lines of strain that now marked it. Surely there was nothing desirable about her now, but in spite of that intellectual assessment, he wanted her with an ache that took his breath away. Even knowing what she was, what she'd done, he wanted to pull her into his arms and kiss some color back into her cheeks, to forget himself for just a few minutes and bury himself in the wash of mindless sensations they had shared. *Mindless,* he repeated to himself. *They were mindless.* Even in the privacy of his own head, it sounded like he was trying to convince himself.

Then her chin jutted out and tilted up, and he found himself caught in her gaze as he had been when they had first seen each other across the width of the canal. Her eyes were more magnificent than his most passion-hazed recollection of her accounted for, not black as he had assumed but a blue as deep as midnight. And they blazed.

"I hope that you enjoyed your little entertainment last night," she said coldly, so haughtily that he blinked. This was not the insignificant mouse of a girl from the campanile—this was the queen of France. He stiffened under the attack, desire and amazement turning into indignation.

"Entertainment? Is that what you think this is about?" He stood, shamelessly exploiting his size to tower over her.

The woman stiffened, but she did not flinch. "I am neither stupid nor naïve, sir. I knew from the moment you stared at me from that doorway that you could have no honorable intentions. I might have guessed that they were not honest, either, but just because I didn't see it then doesn't mean I am blind now." She flushed as she spoke, and it seemed a mocking parody of his earlier lustful thoughts. "I don't know if mine was the first respectable life you destroyed, but by God, I mean for it to be the last."

"Respectable!" He spit the word. "You call whoring yourself to Bertrand de Lint respectable?"

She gaped at him, clearly taken off guard. "Mr. de Lint?" she blurted. "I—I never. Never, *never* . . ." Her voice rose. "How dare you say such a thing? How dare you assume that

I would ever do that with him?" She caught herself on the edge of hysteria and swallowed hard.

Sebastian felt as if he had just been hit in the stomach. Everything was going incredibly wrong. He sat down heavily. "But you told me about your employer—"

"Lady Merrill. I was her *companion*." She stared at him, her midnight eyes wide, incredulous fury written across her face.

"Not de Lint's mistress." Sebastian felt the walls crashing in around him. It all made an awful sense—why she would travel so openly in Lady Merrill's company, why she would be left alone with the lady's granddaughter and their two friends. A companion. Not de Lint's whore. Not a conspirator in Adela's attack.

"If I had stayed, it wouldn't have been long before I became just that, after what you did to me." Her voice was quiet now, brittle, and it cut him to the quick.

"An innocent," he said. "Another innocent. I didn't even—" He broke off, fighting the urge to bury his face in his hands.

"What was I have supposed to have done to you?" The question had the hard edge of a demand in it.

"I had thought you were a willing participant in an evil crime that your master—that de Lint had concocted," Sebastian ground out. "If you had been, you would have deserved what happened to you and worse. As for de Lint . . . after his crimes, death is too good for him."

"What did he do, then?"

"Pray that you need never know," Sebastian said. He looked at her, standing there bedraggled by what misadventures he dared not speculate and with that preposterous, ragged cat curled at her feet. Stains of color still lurked in her cheeks, her eyes sparked with affront and anger, and her lips, the lips he knew so well, were parted a little in a way that made him ache. He should be apologetic, magnanimous, fatherly. He should give her a thousand pounds and send her on the first ship with first-class apartments back to

England and the bosom of her family, whoever they might be.

And that was what he would have done if he were a gentleman. But he was not. He still wanted her, more than ever now that he knew she was not what he'd thought her to be. And, deeper than mere desire, he wanted to keep the reminder of what he had done to her, of what he was and what he continued to be, close to him. She was both his balm and the embodiment of all the demons that haunted him. And so he would offer her another proposition, one that no decent man would ever make.

"Since I have robbed you of one employment, I find that I must offer you another. I could pretend to give you the position of, say, housekeeper or secretary, but it would be a lie because, sinner that I am, I will take no less from you than what de Lint demanded. So we might as well not be coy about it. Stay here and be my mistress. I will treat you better than I have thus far."

The woman stood silently for a very long moment, the fire gone from her eyes, replaced by an expression of bewilderment. "I am not wearing my mask," she said finally. There was a quiet note of longing in her voice that pierced him, but he forced himself to ignore it.

"Do you think that I didn't know what you looked like all along?" He made his voice as harsh as he could.

"But you wanted me." She sounded even more confused. "I could tell—"

"Yes, even when I thought you were de Lint's whore, I wanted you." He said it aloud for the first time—a crime almost as bad as the others he had committed, that he was planning on committing.

A tightness eased in her face. "I don't see what other option I have, so I agree to your offer upon only one condition."

"And what is that?" he asked, taken aback.

"That you tell me your real name."

He looked at her steadily for a long moment, deciding. "Sebastian. That is enough for now."

"Thank you." She accepted it with a stiff nod.

Sebastian had only enough self-control to return the nod before issuing orders to Gian in rapid Italian. With a curt command of, "Follow me," the man led her out of the room. Scooping up the cat, she followed.

Chapter Eleven

Sarah sank down on the bed numbly, and a cloud of dust rose up. The room was enormous, hung with silk, the hard marble floor decorated with brilliant tessellations, dozens of hideous paintings crowded on the wall in a way she was beginning to recognize as typically Venetian. The ceiling arched high overhead, the broad windows reaching up toward it and framing the sagging bed and ancient, moldering hangings that the cat sniffed with a display of grave suspicion.

Her mind was still reeling at the revelations of her meeting with the Moor. He had not hated her. He was not trying to destroy her but some other woman—a criminal, he'd said. And all because of something Mr. de Lint had done.

Sarah believed him. However foolish it might be, the Moor—Sebastian—had never actually lied to her before, and everything Sarah knew of Mr. de Lint pointed to the likelihood of such an event. Her mind burned with the question: What could Mr. de Lint have done to anger a man of his own class so greatly? She could not guess, and she knew she would never dare ask.

Pushing thoughts of Mr. de Lint from her mind, Sarah surveyed the room again, this time seeing not the disrepair but the potential.

"You have three hundred pounds," Sebastian's lackey

had told her before he left. "Decorate the room how you will. Ring the bell if you need anything, and the servants will obey."

Ring the bell . . . She had never rung a bell on her own behalf. Not when she had acted as Maggie's lady's maid—then, she'd been just a servant herself, and Maggie had done the ringing if someone were needed. Not at the ladies school, where there were no bellpulls and few maids. And certainly not in Lady Merrill's employ, though as one of those members of the household adrift between family and servants, she had supposedly had the right. Then, she had just known, deep inside, that if she ever did pull that cord, no one would come, and there would be nothing she could do about it.

Now, as a disreputable mistress, she had more power than she had ever wielded in her more respectable life.

With budding wonder, she pulled the cord.

"Sir?" Gian spoke delicately from the doorway.

Sebastian sat sprawled in the desk chair, his mind churning with thoughts of the woman who had just left. *Sarah*. He allowed himself to think her name with a wash of relief, realizing that he'd subconsciously kept her as "that woman" in an attempt to prevent her from becoming too real to him.

He had failed. Since he had last left her, his mind had been filled with her memory, preying upon him, eating away at him. To discover that she'd been no guiltier than Lady Merrill's housemaids—he did not know whether he wanted to shout for joy or shoot himself for what he'd done. Whatever he felt about himself, he wanted her still, more than ever, and now that he had her, he was not gentleman enough to let her go.

"My God," he whispered, staring up at the plastered ceiling and thinking of the respectable life he'd just robbed from her, "I corrupt everything I touch." He shook his head, then turned a glare on the servant that was meant for himself. "I had no reason to believe I was wrong. She was with de Lint, after all, and she was certainly no innocent. How was I to know?"

"As you say, sir," the man replied noncommittally.

But Sebastian's mind listed much more damning answers to that question. Gian had subverted one of the maids upon Sebastian's orders. How hard would it have been to get confirmation of his victim's status from her? Or, even more directly, why hadn't Sebastian tried to get the answer out of Sarah himself?

The truth stole upon him, horribly and inexorably. He hadn't wanted to believe that he could be wrong about any detail of this entire endeavor because that opened the whole up to questions, questions about himself and his plans that he would rather not examine too closely.

He shook his head, pushing his doubts away. The rest of his scheme was flawless. The first part had failed only because it had been cobbled together so unexpectedly. In the future, he just had to be certain of every detail, provide for every contingency. And until the last part of the plan was executed, he would have Sarah's presence to remind him of the consequences of failure—and would have some opportunity to make up for what he had done.

He remembered her talk of wanting something beautiful when he had first brought her to the palazzo; he realized how little she had controlled in her life, and a possible solution came swiftly to him. First, though, he would have to face her again. And that would not be easy.

"Have her brought to me at luncheon," he said. "Until then, I have much to prepare."

Sarah followed a servant down from her bedroom to the piano nobile. After assuring herself of the reality of the situation, she had written a series of notes to Maggie and the rest of her friends, telling them with no explanation to send all future letters to her new address—one that she had acquired by ringing the bell for a servant and asking. That act alone reminded her of how isolated she was from everything familiar, for the number the maid dutifully recited had been so bafflingly large that Sarah was convinced there had been a mistake until the girl had explained, in halting English, that addresses in Venice were not given by street or canal but issued sequentially to every house in the entire district.

Sending the letters downstairs to be posted, Sarah had ordered a sponge bath, and with the reasoning that she should by all rights be tired, she donned her nightdress. Dutifully, she lay down in the musty bed, certain she would not be able to sleep. And that had been her last thought before a maid had knocked at her door and entered, telling her that she was to prepare for the midday meal.

Now anxiety chased away sleepiness, and Sarah's limbs were alive with nervous energy as she prepared to come face-to-face with her newly official lover and her first day as a mistress. The servant opened a door, and Sarah stepped through. She had expected to find Sebastian waiting for her, but all the chairs were empty. Silently, a hovering footman pulled one out for her, and she sat, staring nervously at the empty plate in front of her.

Abruptly, the door opened again, and her new master stepped through, his hard green eyes sweeping across her under his too-perfect brow, the corner of his sensuous mouth quirked in some ungentle expression that Sarah could not easily identify. A grimace? A sneer? She could not tell. He seemed to fill the doorway, the room, with his presence, and Sarah stood quickly as he neared the table, sending her chair skittering backward with a scrape of wooden legs across the marble.

"I'm sorry," she managed, blushing furiously and twisting her napkin in her hands.

Ignoring both the noise and the apology, Sebastian surveyed her. Sarah's stomach sank at the frozen indifference of his expression, but he only waved her down and said, "Sit, Sarah. Ladies—even mistresses—do not rise for the entrance of a man."

Blushing harder, Sarah dropped to her seat, berating her

clumsy thoughtlessness and hating herself for caring so much about his reaction. But she had to care now, didn't she? He had stolen her honest job from her, seduced her under false pretenses, used her—and now his pleasure was the only thing keeping her from hopeless ruin. However much she depended upon him, though, and however much he made her flesh burn, she would not, must not forgive him for what he'd done to her.

It was only when Sebastian took the chair opposite her that Sarah noticed his lackey had followed him in. Sebastian ordered the meal to begin as the lackey joined them, and then he turned to his employee and launched into a conversation in Italian that Sarah could not begin to understand.

Feeling more invisible than she had ever been as a lady's companion, Sarah forced herself to eat a few bites of food, washing them down with the wine when they caught in her throat. Had Sebastian changed his mind so soon about wanting her there? Everything in her past told her she should not be surprised, but even so, the thought made her so queasy that she stood hurriedly from the table, muttering an excuse.

Sebastian broke off, his eyes fixed coldly upon her. "Please do not leave. I wish to talk to you in a moment."

Numbly, Sarah sank down again, picking slowly at her food while the men returned to ignoring her. Misery formed a tight ball in her stomach that made it hard to swallow, and her weariness came back all at once, overwhelming her. She tried to shut everything out, to sink into herself completely. But it didn't entirely work—it never had—and she found herself wishing desperately for the meal to end.

Finally, when the men's conversation had concluded, Sebastian turned to her.

"I believe I deceived you a little," he said, his expression intense but far from severe.

"Whatever do you mean?" Sarah tried to make her voice cold and brittle, tried to make it sound as if she cared as little about his actions as he had just shown he cared about her presence. She failed, and she knew it.

"I intend for you to be not only my mistress in the coarsest term but also the mistress of this house for as long as I reside here. Matters are completely out of hand, but my business has kept me from attending to them. I rented this palazzo sight unseen with staff, but it seems to me that every footman and housemaid brought all their cousins to pretend that they've worked here all along, and the place is scarcely habitable, and, in short, there are too many servants and not enough work being done. I expect you to remedy the situation."

Sarah cringed from the thought of the dubious honor of so much authority. "You want me to let them go?"

"Let them go or find them work. I leave it entirely to your discretion." The indifference in his voice told her that he didn't care much one way or the other. "Whatever you decide, I am sure that the palazzo will show a great deal of improvement within the next few days."

"Yes, sir." There didn't seem much else to say.

He cleared his throat stiffly. "You will be amply funded, of course. And I also intend that you buy a wardrobe more suitable to your new position. Again, I rely completely upon your discretion. As long as you do not buy jewels or order five full wardrobes instead of one, my exchequer can handle anything you wish to purchase. Maria will take you out today to be fitted."

"Yes, sir," she repeated.

He nodded, seemingly satisfied. "If you wish to leave now, you may do so, but I expect to see you again at supper."

It was a clear dismissal. "Yes, sir." She stood and inclined her head awkwardly, unsure suddenly if he meant her to be his whore or his housekeeper—and unsure which of the two she preferred.

The dark sweep of his brows drew together. "I hope you are not regretting our arrangement already."

The words were such a close echo of what she had

thought just minutes before that she started, staring at him in disbelief that he could have such a concern about her.

His gaze softened, almost involuntarily, it appeared to her, and he spoke slowly, as if his words were being picked with excruciating care. "It seems to me that you've had little in this world that you've been able to control. Consider this to be your chance. Take a few rooms just for yourself and decorate them how you will, and then refurbish the rest of the palazzo. As long as you are not too extravagant, you may do as you wish. You spoke to me of how much you long for beauty. So make it beautiful, Sarah. I trust in you."

Suddenly, Sarah realized that he had been no more comfortable in her presence than she had been in his, and she recognized that his abruptness was due to a guilty self-consciousness he could not apologize for in words. Instead, he'd taken the only thing he'd known of her dreams and made them real.

She had never been good at keeping grudges, no matter how well earned, and with that realization, the hard knot of her resentment eased. Whatever he'd done to her, she'd been complicit in her own downfall, after all. She'd accepted his invitations and embraces—knowing the risks, doubting his intentions, and welcoming them all the same. She did not know what she felt for the strange, devil-ridden man who had been her Moor for three nights, but she knew she did not hate him.

"Thank you," she said, which meant *I forgive you,* and she left.

Maria turned out to be a sly, pretty little maidservant with red hair and black sloe eyes, a combination of the familiar and exotic that was common among the old families of Venice. She spoke English well enough but with a heavy accent, and she explained their various destinations as they were comfortably ensconced against the black velvet cushions of Sebastian's sleek gondola, watching the activity on the pavements from a knee-high vantage through the felze's windows.

Maria declared that she knew all the best shops, and while she had not an ounce of false modesty, she was completely correct in that instance, at least. She ordered the gondola confidently from one location to the next, never hesitating, never flagging as one hour became two, then three, then four.

Using the letters of credit that Sebastian had given her, Sarah ordered everything she knew a lady needed, half disbelieving that she was finally putting to use those lessons of the ladies school she had always assumed she would never need. She matched the dresses in style and form to her favorites in Lady Anna's discarded fashion magazines, tempering the tendency toward froth and ruffles with her own preference for simpler lines, amazed at how easy it was to re-create all the gowns she had constructed in her daydreams.

In addition to the new clothes, Sarah also had three dresses quickly altered from one dressmaker's stock of ready-made gowns he kept on hand for travelers' emergencies. At Maria's urging, she had one fashionable day dress tacked to her shape on the spot and wore it out, promising to return it that night for more permanent alterations.

Armed with swatches of cloth, Maria guided her to a series of shops for all the necessary accessories. By late afternoon, Sarah had bought a wardrobe that took most debutantes several years to acquire. Maria encouraged every purchase, exclaiming over Sarah's taste and the fine materials as if she were the recipient of their master's largesse, not Sarah.

On the way back to the palazzo, Sarah added up the bills in her head and asked hesitantly, "Do you think that Sebastian will be angry?"

"Who?" The girl's smooth forehead creased in confusion.

"Sebastian. Your master. My—my lover."

"Sebastian's his name, is it?" She smiled smugly. "I told

Lucia that he was no Spaniard, whatever he claimed his name to be. He's as English as any man born, and I suppose 'Sebastian' is English enough to be likely."

Sarah looked down at the letters of credit in her lap. *Señor Raimundo Guerra* was the name written on them. Guerra. Like *guerre,* the French word for war, she recalled. What kind of man went about calling himself Mr. War? she wondered, a small part of her apprehension returning.

As soon as they arrived at the palazzo, Sarah announced her intention of retiring to her room. Maria assented, but as Sarah climbed the stairs to the second floor, she realized the maid was following.

"I don't need an escort," she assured the girl.

Maria laughed, her black eyes sparkling. "But you do need a lady's maid!"

Sarah blinked. "You?"

Maria laughed again. "Lucia was so jealous! She was muttering to the cook all morning that I shall make you look as ugly as a toad. But we'll show them all, yes?" She tossed her head, and her curls bobbed.

"I didn't mean to insult you." Sarah cast her a half-shy, half-pleading glance. "I have never had a lady's maid before."

"Benon," Maria said genially, "I've never been one."

Half an hour later, Sarah could hardly recognize herself. The day dress she had deliberately chosen for its flattering color and simple, graceful lines, and over her new corsetry, the soft blue silk hugged curves Sarah didn't know she had and brought color to her pale complexion.

Those changes she might have predicted, had half seen while still at the dressmakers'. But then Maria attacked her hair. In embarrassed awe, Sarah allowed the maid to pile and curl and tease it into a shape that was both fashionable and flattering.

"False hair," Maria muttered as she worked. "That's what we forgot to buy." But even she seemed satisfied with the emerging changes. Still, Sarah drew the line when the maid wanted to cut the front in a stylish fringe.

"Why not?" Maria demanded, impatiently brandishing the scissors.

Sarah could not explain the thrill and horror she felt as every recognizable aspect of her body disappeared under the modish trappings, so instead she just said, "I don't know if he will like it."

Immediately, Maria's face radiated understanding. "But of course," she murmured, and she set the scissors down.

When Maria was finished, Sarah examined the results in amazement. Her hair, enhanced by a few tiny drops of scented oil, gleamed in rich red-blond curls, completely un-like the dull, frizzing mass that she was used to battling into a bun every morning. The coiffure was fashionable, tasteful, and flattering, and Sarah wondered why she could visualize complicated gowns with ease but could have never foreseen this.

Still, her face spoiled the effect of elegance, checkered as it was with the same ugly pox marks that had marred it since she was a child. When Maria's paint pots came out, Sarah recoiled, remembering the layers of cosmetics that her brothel keeper had piled upon her face to disguise her scars when she worked as a dress lodger.

"I don't want to look like a whore," she said, her face flaming at the knowledge that many would call any woman in her current position just that.

Maria clucked her tongue. "Do you think that I look like one?"

"Why— No. Of course not."

She smiled smugly. "But I am wearing paint."

Sarah looked closely and discovered that the youthful smoothness of the maid's face had artificial assistance, and the pink of her cheeks and her black lashes were slightly more dramatic than nature could account for.

"Go ahead, then," she said, without much hope. The marks on her face could not be hidden by anything so subtle, but there was still the ever-present desperate wish that some miracle would happen to make it all go away.

As she worked, the maid lectured Sarah on face washes—curdled milk in the morning, old wine in the evening, and some sort of concoction twice during the day that was apparently beyond her linguistic skills to describe, for she explained more than half of it in Venetian.

"Finished," Maria finally said with satisfaction.

Sarah looked in the mirror—and gasped.

"My grandmother was a courtesan in the last days of the Serene Republic," Maria explained with satisfaction. "She said there was nothing that couldn't at least be helped with a little paint."

Maria was right. The cosmetics were nearly invisible, but half the marks seemed to evaporate under them, and as for the rest, the thin paste and powder smoothed the way the light reflected off her skin so that the marks were no longer the first thing she saw when she looked in the mirror. Maria had done something to her eyes, too, to make them look huge and smoky, and her mouth and cheeks had a subtle glow that seemed fresh and natural and yet at the same time was not.

Sarah stared into the mirror and realized that she had seen faces like hers in dresses like this one on the street—ladies' faces in ladies' dresses, graceful, elegant, and attractive, even if they fell short of beauty. In fact, she'd seen worse scars from the spots, and women of every walk of life suffered from those.

"Thank you," she whispered, blinking quickly so that her tears did not destroy Maria's artistry. "Thank you so much. It's . . . it's wonderful."

"Most of the scars are so faint that it is a shame that you do not hide them all the time. If you follow my advice, many of them will disappear eventually, but no decent woman would begrudge you a little artificial help."

Sarah gave a watery laugh, knowing that Maria's version of a decent woman was far different from what Mrs. Randall, the headmistress of the ladies school, meant. "Thank you," she said again.

With the new confidence of knowing that she looked the part of the mistress of the house, Sarah ordered Maria to get all of the servants to assemble for an inspection in the entrance hall. She waited five minutes and, steeling herself, descended the grand staircase to the water level. There she found Maria smiling gleefully in front of an uneasily shifting, motley crowd of Venetians.

Sarah took a deep breath—and discovered that she wasn't as terrified as she had expected she'd be. Everyone here knew exactly what she was, or they would know soon enough, and so she had nothing to hide from them—and, as their new mistress, nothing to fear.

"I am Señor Guerra's lady," she said without preamble, "and I am to take over the management of the house." Maria began to translate, and after a pause, Sarah kept going. "And so I expect better of you all, beginning today. What is dirty will be cleaned. What is broken will be fixed. What is beyond repair will be replaced. If we cannot find something with which to occupy your time, you will be let go." That caused a stir among the servants when Maria relayed it, but Sarah overrode them. "I do not think it is a surprise to anyone here that you have been taking advantage of your master's domestic indifference, but he is not ignorant of it, and he has asked me to remedy the situation. Who is the housekeeper?"

After a small flurry of motion, a stocky, middle-aged woman came to the front.

"What is your name?"

"Signora Bertolini," she said.

"And the butler?"

A distinguished man, standing slightly apart from the rest of the servants, bowed. "Señor Garza, at your service."

Sarah remembered how Lady Merrill dealt with the servants on the rare occasions that things did not live up to her expectations, and she assumed an expression that, she hoped, blended compassion and severity in the appropriate amounts. "You both are the foremost servants of this house, and as such, it is your duty to keep order here. I will investigate the particulars of the house this evening and summon you to explain my expectations. I assume that I will not have to take up your duties directly." She deliberately put a high-handed threat into her last statement. "I hope to get to know you all by name in time. For now, you are dismissed."

The servants left, flowing out of the room like water released from a dam. It was only then that she realized what she had done—faced a crowd of strangers, many of whom had origins superior to her own, and taken control of the situation, issuing orders as if she had been doing it all her life. And what was even more amazing was that no one had shouted her down as a fraud—no one had even questioned her.

"Oh, signorina, you were brilliant," Maria exclaimed after the last servant had left.

"I . . . I can't believe that I just did that." Sarah laughed suddenly, the sound raw and jangling.

"I can," came a familiar voice.

Sarah started and jerked around, looking up to find Sebastian standing on the mezzanine landing of the staircase, looking as handsome and tempting as sin.

Chapter Twelve

"You are full of surprises," Sebastian continued, descending with masculine grace to the ground floor. His expression was quizzical as he looked at her, as if he'd never seen her before and wasn't quite sure what to make of her.

Faced with Sebastian's unconscious elegance and dignity, Sarah felt suddenly like a little beggar girl playing dress-up in an opera singer's clothes. "I've never been in charge of a house before," she admitted. The words were thin and uncertain, and Sarah cursed herself the instant they were past her lips. She sounded as if she were making some sort of confession—or worse, fishing for compliments. Her face burned, and she looked away.

To her vast relief, he did not insult her with smooth assurances. Instead, he merely quirked a brow at her before turning to Maria and saying, "Thank you for your assistance."

The dismissal was clear even to Sarah. "Thank you, sir," Maria said with a curtsy, and then she ducked through one of the side doors, closing it behind her and leaving them alone.

Sarah swallowed hard against the dryness in her mouth. There were no masks here, no shadows, and she didn't know exactly who she was supposed to be. With the servants, it was easy enough to step into an empty role, but with

Sebastian—her lover, her keeper, and something else that could not be described by such simple terms—with him, she could not say what she was anymore. Not Sally, the girl fresh from the streets one scant step up from the prostitute she'd once been. Sally she knew how to be all too well, but she despised that life and had forsworn it forever, even if she could turn back time. Not Sarah, the silent, respectable lady's companion. Sarah had never been more than playacting, and somehow she knew this man before her realized it as well as she did. If only she knew what she was now, what he meant her to be.

"I thought a little authority might be good for you," Sebastian said, breaking in on her thoughts.

"I—" She stopped. "I would never have asked for it or wanted it, but now, I am very glad you gave it to me. How did you know?"

Sebastian's lips twisted slightly, his expression turning sardonic. "There are more similarities between a poor girl and a man whose purpose in life is to wait for his father to die than you might think," he said dryly. He surveyed her slowly, openly, and she felt her skin flush and prickle in automatic response. "The change of costume suits you."

"Thank you, sir." Sarah's eyes were drawn to the elegant fit his of clothing over his sleekly muscular frame. "You look perfect, as always."

She hadn't meant for there to be any bitterness in her voice, but it was there nevertheless. Sebastian gave her an uninterpretable look, going very still. "Appearances are often deceiving." He grimaced faintly at some private meaning to his words, but all he said was, "I want to reassure you again that if you had been who I thought you were, my actions would have been more than just."

She stared at him just like she had the first time he had made that declaration, trying to read any sign of deception in his earnest face. And again, there was none.

"I believe you," she said quietly. "I may be a fool, but I believe you."

Tension she had not realized was there flowed suddenly from his frame, but at the same time a pained expression flickered across his face. "Tell me, Sarah, why did you accept my proposal?"

She met his green eyes, clouded with some conflict that she couldn't understand, and she heard herself asking in return, "Tell me, Sebastian, why did you make it?"

One brow lifted, and his gaze raked across her. She stiffened instinctively, but it was neither judging nor dismissive. Instead, it was sensual in the way that a mere leer could never be, meticulous, with every shade of his response written on his face. Abruptly, Sarah realized that he truly found her attractive as she stood there bathed in the early evening light that streamed through the high windows—that he had found her attractive even before her sudden transformation, when he'd offered her the position as his mistress, and before then, too, when he had first begun to seduce her. Even though he had sought revenge against the woman he thought she was, in the heart of the night he had wanted her—and he had already known exactly what she looked like.

The knowledge staggered her and filled her with a dark, luscious heat, making her head light and her midsection heavy with liquid warmth. It was all she could do to keep from bursting into a grin even as he regarded her with tense gravity.

"I don't know why I want you here," he said, closing the distance between them in a single step. She stood her ground, looking steadily up at him, and he locked his hands behind her neck and tilted her head back gently so that his eyes bored directly into hers. "A good man would have taken you in and asked nothing in return. An evil one would have sent you away. So what am I? Some angel still suspended in his fall? A soul caught in purgatory?"

His words were light, but she sensed an agony beneath that sent her whirling into deeper confusion. An answer came to her unbidden, and she spoke quietly. "Perhaps it makes you an ordinary man. Nothing more, nothing less. As I, who accepted the offer, am just an ordinary woman."

He lowered his head toward hers until their foreheads met. "You, ordinary? You have no idea just how wrong you are." And then he kissed her.

He took his time, not engulfing her with uncontrollable passion but exploring her mouth slowly, expertly. Desire spiraled up through her leisurely, making her breath catch against his mouth and filling her with a sweetness that was close to pain. Finally he broke away, and she sighed and opened her eyes. He was looking at her with an unreadable expression on his face.

"A lady's companion," Sebastian said musingly. "Why would one as young as you choose such a life? Isn't that an occupation better suited to dry old maids?"

Frowning, Sarah shook her head, the fire within her effectively quenched with that reminder of how she'd arrived. "I wanted to be more than a third housemaid. I wanted to enjoy an occupation that afforded me some position in life, some stimulation. Some opportunity to experience the loveliness of life firsthand, even if only incidentally. For a woman, such things are hard to come by."

"But why not a governess? That's a role more suited to a young woman."

Sarah pulled away from him, flushing with shame. "Do you mock me?"

Sebastian's brows snapped together. "Of course not."

Sarah gave him a hard look, then grudgingly said, "A woman given over to the shaping of young minds should have an unexceptionable background and unquestionable moral character. I have neither."

"You're quite serious, aren't you? Because you have been . . . indiscreet?" His brows lowered farther.

"Indiscreet?" Her shoulders hunched involuntarily against the memories. "You give me too much credit. Since I am no innocent, you might have wondered why I would give in to you so easily. After all, I should be immune to the first rush of recklessness and lust and knowledgeable of the possible consequences of—of succumbing to your charms." She grasped gratefully at that euphemism, pushing aside the vulgarities that rose in her mind at times like this when the vocabulary of the ladies school proved lacking.

"I assumed— Well, you know quite well what I assumed."

"And now?" Sarah asked.

"And now I find myself puzzled, though I would like to believe my irresistible personal qualities overwhelmed your discretion." The words were light, but his eyes were shadowed.

Sarah smiled sadly. "If I could tell you that in truth, I would. However, in all honesty, I have sufficient experience that a few more encounters cannot noticeably tatter my virtue any further, and, more practically, I am reasonably certain any additional . . . indiscretion, as you call it, cannot result in my—in my becoming with child."

"And so you fear to contaminate innocent children through association with you." It was not a question.

Sarah searched his face but could read no emotion, neither of sympathy nor of censure. "Of course. Firstly, my background makes me unsuited to the job. And secondly, if their mothers ever found out—"

Sebastian interrupted her. "Has it not occurred to you that perhaps their well-bred mammas might possess less than pristine characters themselves—that, in fact, after they dutifully produced the first two sons, the rest of their children might very well each have different fathers? Or that their husbands, the legal fathers of the innocent babes, might entertain themselves at any low brothel as their fancy suits?"

Sarah shook her head stubbornly. "Men may do as they like—that is true anywhere—so it is good that they are not inclined toward the nurturing of their children, because they would surely corrupt them."

Sebastian snorted. "Who told you that?"

"What does it matter?" Sarah asked—even as the disapproving face of Miss Stabler flashed across her memory.

"Sordidness is universal to all walks of life," Sebastian said bluntly. "The lower classes have no monopoly upon it. The vices of the nobility are simply more expensive, and because they often write the rules, they often avoid their sins' consequences."

"I, of all people, know that all too well," Sarah replied, thinking of Mr. de Lint. "But however corrupt a mother was, she would still send me away for having morals no better than hers. And that's the heart of the matter. She would still be a lady by virtue of her birth, while I would be no more than a slut."

Sebastian shook his head, frowning. "Little dove, is that what you believe? That you are never to be a lady because you are not virtuous enough?"

"I don't want to be a lady," Sarah said impatiently. "I just don't want to be despised and dismissed." The events of the last four days overwhelmed her all at once, and she felt her throat tighten as she blinked hard against the tears that pricked her eyes. "I don't care about respectability, but I need it. What is a woman like me without it except someone to be used and discarded? A man can manufacture his own success, can carve a place in the world for someone of intelligence and ambition. But a woman is nothing without relations and a reputation, and I have neither. Respectability is my only defense. I want a place for *me,* Sebastian. I want meaning. Can't you understand that?"

Memories flickered through Sebastian's mind—those long, wasted years when he had neither a title nor an occupation, the even longer years after the title finally became his in which he hid from everything his father had valued and that Sebastian therefore instinctively scorned. He would always be an earl, but what could a girl of no background and no money become even with the finest mind, the best education? Her fate, like his, had been locked at the moment of her birth, though far more dismal than his could ever be.

"Is that the wish of your heart, then? To have meaning?" he asked.

Sarah's chin jerked up fractionally, a blush creeping up her cheeks. "As a woman, I can have no occupation in the commercial sense, but I want to be someone . . . someone whom a person might admire. An accomplished woman, you might call it. Someone of worth, of insight, of talent, who has an illuminating mind and sheds grace wherever she goes. I want to create beauty. Mrs. Randall at the ladies school called that being a lady, though I have a suspicion that you would not."

"Does it mean so much to you?" Sebastian persisted.

Sarah's gaze slid away from his, toward the dingy walls with their painted, peeling paper. "I cannot express how much."

"Then make that your mission in the time that you are here, Sarah, and I will help as I can," Sebastian promised impulsively. "You can start shedding grace in the renovation of the palazzo, of course, but we will find other ways as time progresses."

"Do you mean it?" She shot him a hard glance, as if trying to determine whether he were pulling a jape at her expense.

"Of course," he said, shutting away a swift ache at the kind of life her reflexive doubt revealed.

A wary trust dawned gradually in her eyes. "Thank you, sir," she said, softly, almost tentatively. And then she reached up and gently pulled his head down to her mouth, kissing him with a sincerity that took his breath away.

Deep inside, in a place he had forgotten existed, some small piece of him rejoiced.

Sebastian did not come to supper, Sarah was disappointed to discover. To distract her mind, she oversaw the superficial cleaning of a few key rooms before she retired for the night. But although Maria treated her to another perfumed bath and arranged her hair and the lights of the room most fetchingly, he did not come that night, either. Panicked thoughts raced inside Sarah's head—certainty that he had changed his mind about everything, that he was going to throw her out at dawn if not before, until finally exhaustion got the better of her, and she fell asleep between the fresh, lavender-scented sheets.

In the morning, she awoke to discover piles of books on her dresser—works of literature, philosophy, and poetry. What made her heart leap, though, was a stack of identically bound volumes with *THE STONES OF VENICE* written on the spine. With a cry, she seized one and flipped open the cover.

To my Sarah was all the flyleaf read, but it was then that she truly believed.

Chapter Thirteen

"Ah, the master of the house arrives!" De Lint lifted his glass in toast as Sebastian shut the door of the Casinò Giallo's parlor behind him. Dawn was creeping through the windows, but as Sebastian had expected, de Lint looked as if he hadn't slept a wink. "These apartments are so cozy and quaint. It is a pity that the tradition of the casinò died with the Republic. I think that it rather should have been embraced by all nations. The pretense of sobriety and fidelity is so tiresome!" he continued in Italian.

Sebastian felt hardly a lick of fire from his long-burning anger against the man, but he did have to restrain himself from retorting that he had never known de Lint to be one for pretense. Instead, he replied in the same language, "If every gentleman should keep a suite especially for his assignations and less savory entertainments after the old Venetian fashion, signor, should every lady then adopt a cicisbeo?" He took a seat without waiting for an invitation and regarded the man from behind his demimask.

De Lint guffawed and the wineglass sloshed slightly, betraying the depth of his inebriation. "Capital idea!" he crowed before switching back to Italian. "Then my eldest sister wouldn't have to scour Britain for lovers who look like Lord Dartford for fear her bastards might betray her."

Sebastian had the sudden memory of all other rooms in

all the other houses in half a dozen countries where he and de Lint had sat like this and indulged in similar irreverent, desultory conversations. Then, they had been so alike that Lady Merrill had taken to calling Sebastian "my second Bertrand." So alike except for an underlying cruelty of spirit in de Lint that Sebastian had simply ignored or dismissed as his friend's idiosyncratic sense of humor.

Sebastian slammed the door on those thoughts.

"Domenica's mother said she was home early." Sebastian cut to the chase, knowing that in his present state, de Lint would not notice the sudden change of subject. "When I left you last night, you seemed content enough with her."

De Lint shifted restlessly. "I've found that I bored of her more quickly than I expected. The night before last, I almost had a much rarer sort of encounter, and even the thought of it has spoiled my appetite for your whore." He shook his head, looking up at the ceiling. "If I had known that she had flown the coop, I never would have left little Domenica with such high expectations of another tryst. Do you know what a disappointment like that does to a man?" He glared at Sebastian.

"Of course," Sebastian heard himself say as his mind whirled. He remembered the rejoinder Sarah had made when he had asked if she were de Lint's mistress—*If I had stayed, it wouldn't have been long before I became just that, after what you did to me.*—and he was certain that he knew only too well what the man meant. He closed his eyes briefly against his own self-loathing. He had nearly exacted a "revenge" almost as terrible as the original crime. Was fate doomed to show him that even the small difference he saw between de Lint and himself was false?

De Lint nodded, apparently satisfied. "So instead I spent the night making as big a dent in your cellar as I could. Terrible, terrible stuff"—the wine sloshed over the edge again at a too-enthusiastic wave—"but then again, all the local brew is. The sweet cloying, the sour insuperably bitter."

"What type of entertainment would you prefer tonight,

then, signor?" Sebastian asked, steering the conversation back on course.

"Tonight, I will be nursing a raging headache." De Lint laughed as if it were a great joke. "Tomorrow night, though, I will be in the mood for something new. Something a little less . . . pliable than sweet Domenica, if you understand my meaning."

"I believe that I do." It took all of Sebastian's control to say the words at an even pitch.

"Jolly good, then. If you will allow me the use of your rooms for another twelve hours or so, I will gladly recompense you for any inconvenience. I find that my stomach does not agree with the thought of movement even so gentle as that of my gondola."

"Please, make yourself at home." Sebastian stood.

"Thank you."

"Indeed." His jaw clenching, Sebastian sketched a bow and left before he punched the man.

Sarah dressed quickly and went down to the dining room for breakfast, only to discover that Sebastian had returned late the night before and had left again before dawn. So she ate alone, certain that he would walk through the door at any moment.

But breakfast came and went, and as the hours passed and Sebastian still did not make an appearance, Sarah's worries returned in full force. To keep her mind occupied, she decided to oversee the first steps of the palazzo's refurbishment. She began in the grand salon.

By the light of day, the room just looked sad and old— no faded glories to mourn. Ruthlessly, she ordered the rugs beaten, the floor scrubbed, every inch of molding dusted, the windows and chandeliers cleaned, and the hundred or so paintings that cluttered the walls taken down for examination. As a bevy of servants set to work, she sorted the paintings into three groups—those that were so abominable that they must be gotten rid of, those that were tolerable, and those that she found to be appealing. There were scarcely any of the last, for the canvases appeared to have been chosen more for their ability to fill gaps in the wall than for any other feature. They were not unified in skill, subject matter, color, or age, and Sarah was baffled by the jackdaw mentality that the entire Venetian aristocracy seemed to have embraced.

Sarah had no idea how long Sebastian would be staying in the palazzo, but he had chosen her duties with admirable insight, for even if her efforts were enjoyed only a short time, the work itself was its own reward. As Sarah worked steadily through the stacks of paintings, she tried to reassure herself with the visible reality of the bustle around her—the clear manifestation of her new position of authority in the household. But doubts wriggled into her mind, the same uncertainties that she'd lived with for longer than she could remember, and she recalled again and again all her past shames—whoring herself in Haymarket, the ignominy of leaving the ladies school, her narrow escape from Mr. de Lint. The last, as the most recent, was the most raw, and Sarah found herself wondering if maybe he was within his rights after catching her with Sebastian, if maybe he had treated her as exactly what she was and no worse. . . .

She wanted Sebastian to come back, not just to reassure her that he would return to her but also so that she could question him about Mr. de Lint and hear from a source other than her own half-desperate thoughts that he was, indeed, despicable. Finally, she heard the great black doors open downstairs, and she looked out the window just in time to see Sebastian's gray-hatted head disappear within. With her thoughts still weighing on her mind, she pasted a smile on her face and descended the stairs to meet him.

Sebastian moored the boat at the water stairs of the Palazzo Contarini and ducked inside the entrance hall, his mind unsettled by his conversation at the Casinò Giallo— and what had happened after he left.

He had chosen to row himself alone in his sàndolo, but as soon as he stepped out the door of the building in which the casinò was located, he had the sensation that he was not alone. Dismissing it as paranoia, he rowed out of sight of the casinò's windows and pulled off his mask before slipping into more crowded waterways. But the feeling of being watched did not abate.

After several minutes and many turns, he was certain that he was being followed by a low, brown batèla propelled by two burly oarsmen with their caps pulled low over their eyes. They must have seen him emerge from the casinò and get into the sàndolo alone with clothes that spoke of prosperity and of being a foreigner. Sebastian cursed himself for not taking a gondolier. After the attack two nights before, he should have realized that the thieves were getting braver and more desperate. Instead, he had turned a real attack into a manifestation of his own guilt. When he'd last been to Venice, he'd had his pockets picked twice and had once nearly run into a band of street thugs when he'd been drunk and careless late one night. He could have guessed that as time destroyed whatever reserves of caution the criminals had, some would grow brazen enough to hunt a man in broad daylight.

With another oath, he sent his light craft skimming through the canals, weaving among the larger boats as he chose a labyrinthine path. The bulky, wallowing batèla had been soon left behind, and Sebastian had slowed again and made his way back to the Palazzo Contarini.

Now Sebastian mounted the stairs toward the first-floor piano nobile, turning the events of the morning over in his mind. He'd reached only the mezzanine level when the rapid patter of feet on the stairs made him stop and look up.

"You've come!" Sarah's smile was wide but uncertain, as if she were not sure exactly what was the acceptable greeting of a mistress to her lover.

He marveled again at her transformation. She looked . . . breathtaking. Folds of a claret-colored silk redingote draped elegantly over a smoky rose skirt with cascades of white Brussels lace at her throat and wrists, and her hair was tamed into a sleek twist that flattered her face and made her neck look long and elegant. Despite the slight hesitation in her manner, her cheeks glowed and her dark eyes sparkled, her entire air youthful and fresh and vibrant.

She was not beautiful, but that was something he seemed to forget when he was around her, an unimportant detail that was obscured in the sheer vibrancy of her personality. Now that she was no longer so fiercely self-contained, it radiated from her and colored the air around her with her emotions. She might have passed for a fashionable young woman at any one of the society parties he'd occasionally deigned to attend—or a very expensive courtesan.

Strangely, though, even as he appreciated her metamorphosis, a part of him missed the small, plain, shy woman who had called out to him with her need. A need he'd ignored in his blind certainty, he reminded himself, thinking of his conversation with de Lint. And she had nearly paid the price.

Sebastian didn't want to think of that now. He felt weary with an exhaustion that was as much mental as physical, and he was not prepared to have her further tax him with that intensity that seemed to blast through his long-established defenses. So as she looked down at him expectantly, anxiously, from a higher step, he merely said, "How are you this morning, Sarah?"

"Quite well," she replied instantly. "I want to thank you for the books."

He waved off her gratitude. "It's nothing. Why don't you decide which chamber you wish to take as your sitting room and have Maria visit the shops with you to pick out the furniture and fittings today?"

"That sounds lovely," Sarah said, but her smile froze fractionally.

She knew he was brushing her off, but there was nothing Sebastian could do about it right now, not if he wanted to keep his distance. He forced himself to ignore her response as he brushed past her up the stairs. "Be sure to take Gian with you. The thieves are getting braver, and I've been assured that he is quite capable in matters of defense."

"Of course," she said, so softly that her voice was almost lost to him as he continued upward.

Putting Sarah firmly out of his mind, Sebastian reached the piano nobile and spied Gian coming out of his office. He seized with relief upon the opportunity to talk to the man.

"I need another whore," he said without preamble in Italian.

Gian raised his brows and looked over Sebastian's shoulder. With a glance behind him, Sebastian discovered that Sarah had followed him back up the stairs and was now hovering at the head of the staircase with a troubled expression on her face. He bit off a noise of exasperation and turned his back to her again, hoping, rather vainly, he knew, that she would take the hint and leave.

"Not for me," Sebastian continued in the same language. "For the guest of the Casinò Giallo."

"Ah," the man said. "What do you require, then?"

"A girl who is better at seeming to be less *pliable*." The word twisted on his tongue.

"Ah," Gian repeated. After a moment of appearing to consider the matter, he nodded phlegmatically. "Yes, I can understand the difficulty. Do not worry, for I have just the one for you."

"Good. I need her by tonight."

There was a small sound behind him as one of Sarah's shoes scraped slightly against the marble floor, and bracing himself, he turned to confront her.

"What do you need?" he said, the words coming out harshly before he could check them.

She flinched and some of the color left her cheeks, but she did not drop her gaze. "I apologize. I had not realized that my presence was unwanted."

Why had she found such courage at a moment when her

presence could only be painful to him? He needed time before he was ready for any more weighty discussions. He needed sleep. "Mistresses are not usually included in a man's business discussions," he said as crushingly as possible.

Her eyes sparked, and instead of quickly swallowing her irritation as he had seen her do before, she lifted her small chin in defiance. "Business discussions are not usually conducted in front of them," she said, only the smallest tremor in her voice belying her brave façade.

His incipient guilt reared up at her fearful persistence, and Sebastian gave in. "What so concerns you, then?"

She took a deep breath. "The paintings in the grand salon. I want to get rid of most of them."

"Then by all means, do so," Sebastian said, baffled at her insistence upon discussing the matter right at that moment. "There are probably less than a dozen that are not complete rubbish."

She vacillated. "I thought you might like to look at them first—"

"I have given you license to do what you will. I've rented the place for a generous enough quantity that the owner would not care if I gutted it, but if the idea of discarding so much makes you uncomfortable, put anything you wish to be rid of in the attic instead."

"I really would feel better if you looked them over, sir," she insisted, her face clouded.

Sebastian sighed. "Sarah, you do not need me for these decisions. I trust you."

"I see," Sarah said, but still she did not leave, though her shoulders hunched slightly.

He rubbed his forehead with his hand, realizing that he was not going to escape this without feeling like a beast. "Sarah," he said, forcing his tone to be gentle, "this is not what is on your mind. What do you really wish to talk about?"

She straightened slightly and took a visible deep breath. "Why I'm here."

Sebastian shook his head. "You're here because it pleases me—as long as it pleases me."

"That isn't what I meant. I meant, why did all of this happen? Why do you hate Mr. de Lint so much?" Her gaze was steady, her small mouth set in a determined line.

"It has nothing to do with hate," Sebastian retorted. *Perhaps a little too quickly,* some detached part of his mind observed.

"What, then?" she asked with some asperity.

He frowned. "Justice. And revenge."

"If I have been punished for his whore's sins, don't you think I have a right to know what they are?" Sarah asked obdurately. "I wasn't asking for—for abstractions. You know that."

Sebastian raked his fingers through his hair. He did not want to talk about this. Not now, with the memory of the latest meeting with de Lint still fresh in his mind. Not with Gian standing there, listening with poorly concealed fascination written across his boyish features. And not with Sarah, not ever. She had been involved in this too deeply already when the matter should not have concerned her at all. But he knew she wouldn't be satisfied with that.

"Come inside," he said, gesturing to his office.

Her expression of truculence faded slightly, and she preceded him through the doorway. He shut it behind them, blocking Gian out, and turned back around to find her standing in the center of the room, twisting a handkerchief in her hands.

"Why are you really asking me this now?" he asked, hoping that he sounded reassuring, persuasive.

A dozen emotions flashed across her face, too fast for him to read, before she covered them with a careful blankness. "I think I have a right to know, is all," she finally said.

"Curiosity?" Leaning against the door, he folded his arms across his chest. "Do you truly expect me to believe that you are braving my displeasure to satisfy a little curiosity? It doesn't seem like you, Sarah."

Her face crumpled upon itself, and she crossed to the desk chair and sat upon it heavily, her dark red skirts billowing out in waves of silk. "And to think I had almost fooled myself," she said ruefully. Sarah's gaze strayed to her own hands, folded in her lap around the handkerchief. After a long moment, she spoke. "It seems to me that everyone except me believes that Mr. de Lint is a lighthearted, amusing, and harmless gentleman."

"You know that I know better than that."

"Yes," she repeated. "And I want to know—I need to know what he has done."

"Why is that?" Sebastian asked softly, sensing that he was near the heart of the matter.

Sarah stood abruptly, turning her back to him so quickly that he couldn't tell whether the movement was made in irritation or agitation. Facing the window behind the desk, she said, "Have you ever been afraid that there is something dreadfully wrong with you, Sebastian? Because I am terrified that there is something wrong with me."

"What do you mean?" Sebastian asked, even as her words sent a pang of empathy through him that stirred old parts of his mind he didn't want disturbed.

"I mean that everyone loves Mr. de Lint. His mother dotes on him, laughing at his high spirits and his cleverness, and his mother is a very good and generous woman. His half nieces delight in teasing him and being teased in return. And Lady Merrill's friends, all highly regarded, very distinguished ladies, cannot help but adore him as well. He has a reputation as leading a bit of a profligate existence, but so many other young gentlemen do as well that it's hardly exceptionable."

"But you have no liking for him," Sebastian prompted.

"None," she said flatly. "He is cruel to me. He does not hate me—he does not think me of worthy of enough notice to waste the energy of hatred. But he finds great sport in torturing me." Her head bowed slightly, exposing the nape of her neck above her high collar, pale and vulnerable. "If everyone thinks him such an admirable man, and if he takes pleasure in hurting me, does that mean there is something wrong with him or with me? Lady Merrill would have let me stay. I left because he would have raped me, though I know he would not have called it that. He simply believed that as a slut, I have no right to deny my favors to a man of his status and his position as my employer's son." She turned around, raw pain twisting her face. "Is he right, or am I? I who have the respect and admiration of none—do I dare even ask the question?"

Her words echoed in Sebastian's head, and the somnolent memories that she had stirred woke fully, memories from his youth he had forgotten he'd ever had. Or, rather, that he'd tried to forget. His father's sternness, his unbending displeasure at everything that Sebastian was and did—the situation was so very different from what Sarah had suffered, but his self-doubts had had the same tenor as the ones she now voiced. Still, his father had been merely hard-hearted, not hateful nor deliberately cruel, and his mother's warmth and love had reassured him of his own worth for the first fourteen years of his life. How much more fragile must she be than a pampered earl's son? And how quickly had de Lint realized his power?

He spoke on those thoughts. "Sarah. Dove. Bertrand de Lint has many faces, and he only shows the ugliest to those who have the least ability to face him. Lady Merrill is not the first mother fooled by a son's smile, nor is de Lint the first evil man to charm society into loving him."

Some of the anguish on Sarah's face eased. "You think him . . . evil?"

"Absolutely," Sebastian said, imbuing his voice with every bit of the adamantine conviction that he felt.

"I had hoped to find out, though . . ." She trailed off. "If someone else has been hurt by him, too, someone more important, someone *better* than I, then I can know for certain that I am not the one to blame. That he is a monster and that what I am is not itself a justification for his every action against me." She took a deep breath. "That is why I want to know what he had done to you."

"I would not dare call myself better than you," Sebastian said. "Nor would you if you knew the story of my life. But it was not me whom de Lint hurt. It was someone far more innocent than both of us." He knew she wanted more, but he couldn't bring himself to give it to her. It wasn't a question of trust; he simply did not want her to know all the details of the crime, did not want her to judge him as he judged himself, to ask him questions for which he had no answers. Instead, he merely said, "I will not tell you the specifics, but rest assured that if only he had been less charming or I had been more so, I would not be here now, and he would be in gaol."

Sarah stood very still for a moment, her expression turning inward as she appeared to think about what he'd said. "That isn't all I had hoped for, but it is enough." Her face softened as she smiled, the expression still a trifle uncertain. "Thank you."

"You are always welcome." And he realized that he meant it more than he had intended.

Chapter Fourteen

Sarah's attitude shifted subtly, and she advanced upon Sebastian almost shyly, stopping only a couple of feet away. "You were gone last night. I thought perhaps you had changed your mind about wanting me here."

"I had matters that I had to attend to, and when I returned, you were already in bed. Considering your sleepless night, I thought you should be undisturbed," Sebastian said.

"You left me alone out of consideration . . . for me?" She asked the question as if the possibility amazed her.

"Don't expect to become accustomed to it," he said teasingly. Then he frowned. "If I had known what de Lint had attempted, I would have been even more certain of my choice. Coming to you so soon after he'd done that—" He broke off as a thought occurred to him. "You despised him enough to leave the safety of your employment rather than let him take what he wanted, and yet you accepted my offer. Why?"

She shot him a look of surprise. "You are not Mr. de Lint. And also, just as importantly — you asked."

Her automatic rejection of the comparison between himself and his enemy sent relief through him so intense it was like a jolt. Still, Sebastian wasn't entirely reassured. "He didn't hurt you, did he?"

"Did you speak with him today, then?" Sarah asked tentatively.

Sebastian merely looked at her, and after a moment she nodded in acceptance of his silence and answered his question.

"I have a few bruises. Nothing that won't heal." She raised her hand self-consciously to her eye, and he realized that beneath the powder there was a faint purpling. "He didn't get his cock between my legs or anything of that sort." She blushed as soon as the words came out of her mouth, her expression full of chagrin that bordered on horror. She looked at him as if she were terrified that he might cast her out right then for such a slip, and Sebastian couldn't help but chuckle at her exaggerated reaction. Her eyes widened even more at his response.

"Sometimes," he said, smiling, "indelicacy does have the virtue of directness. What would your ladies academy say to that?"

"I don't want to think about it," she admitted, her face still flaming. "I have managed to replace most of my unwholesome vocabulary with better equivalents, but when there is no polite word that I know, it is hard not to say something vulgar."

Sebastian barely managed to swallow another laugh. "I doubt that there is a word for *cock* that is suitable for polite society, though you might have asked your etiquette teacher."

Sarah made a gasping giggle, involuntarily relaxing at the image that must have conjured. " 'Pardon me, Miss Stabler,' " she said in a diffident, schoolgirl voice, " 'but what is the correct form for referring to a man's cock? And should I address it differently if it is turgid or flaccid?' " A wicked gleam belied the innocence of her expression, arousing in its knowingness as her embarrassment faded.

Chuckling softly, Sebastian pulled her against him. "There is a minx's mind behind that decorum and diffidence."

Her eyes shone merrily as she looked boldly at him. "You have no idea."

"I may have exercised temperance last night, but there is no guarantee that I will have such control now," he warned her. "Especially if you tease me with naughty conversations about cocks. You have no idea what that does to me."

"Oh, I think I might have a very good idea." She cast a coy glance down at where their bodies met—and where his erection now pressed against her corset. "You wouldn't protest if I expressed my—my gratitude for your generosity, would you?" Her eyes were warm and her body inclined toward his, but there was a tightness in her frame that warned him that she was not as carefree as she appeared.

His resolution to keep her at a distance had long shattered, but her tension reawakened his feelings of guilt. He closed his eyes with a groan. "Sarah, why are you doing this?"

The question startled Sarah, and she looked at him, trying to read his face, but his dark expression told her nothing except that he was troubled. "I want to. I am your mistress, after all—"

"Please tell me that you are not doing this just because of your new position," he said, opening his eyes and fixing her with a glare.

"Don't . . . don't you still want me?" she asked quietly, afraid of his answer despite the evidence of his arousal that still pressed against her. Maybe he had changed his mind; after all, maybe in daylight, when he was looking more clearly at her face, mere lust was not enough to make him want her anymore—

"Of course I do, you little fool." He shook his head at her. "Will I be forced to convince you of that every day?"

"It couldn't hurt if you tried." She smiled slightly tremulously. "I'm doing this because I want to. I want you. I'm doing it badly because I've never tried to seduce anyone before."

Sebastian made an inarticulate sound, and she couldn't tell whether it was meant to be a groan or a laugh. "Quite frankly, I think that you are doing rather well."

She felt the heat creep up her face, combined of embarrassment and pleasure both, and her smile grew bolder. "Well, then, sir, unhand me, and I will continue."

"Minx," he said as he complied.

"Bully," she retorted, setting to work on his morning coat. He stood still as she unbuttoned it and his waistcoat, reaching up to push them over his shoulders. She loosened his necktie, too, but as she set to work on his shirt, his eyes roved freely across her, his expression so intense that she found herself flushing under his gaze, her fingers growing slow and clumsy as she became more and more aware of the heated contours of his body under his linen shirt and flannel vest. She kept her head down and her eyes locked on her work, and that helped for a moment—until Sebastian bent over and kissed the exposed nape of her neck.

A delicious heat poured through her even as she made a small sound of protest, and for several long moments, she lost track of everything except the feel of his mouth on her body, gentle and slick.

"I have been wanting to do that for the past ten minutes," he murmured against her skin.

"Oh, bother this!" she snapped in frustration, dropping the fabric of his shirt, which she had unconsciously bunched in her fists. She seized his belt, unbuckling it before he could react. She swiftly unfastened the buttons of his fly, drawn tight across his erection, and reached into his drawers. Her palm met hot, silky-smooth skin, hard and soft at the same time.

She glanced up to find him staring down at her, the clean planes of his face sharpened with tension. She remembered how he had reacted to her playacting before and smiled. That was easy—she had spent so long playacting in one way or another that it was a simple thing to bury her feelings of awkwardness in pretending to be someone else. She knelt down in front of him so that her skirts pooled out behind her, keeping her hand against the smooth length of his erection.

" 'Miss Stabler, I believe this cock is most certainly of the turgid sort,' " she piped, widening her eyes in an exaggerated show of girlish admiration. " 'What do you suppose I should do with it?' " She rubbed her thumb across the head, spreading the bead of moisture that had already blossomed at the tip. He groaned slightly, his hands going to her shoulders, where he gripped her hard. Sarah couldn't hold back a slight giggle.

" 'Oh, look, it's talking to me!' " she managed. " 'I suppose the only decent thing to do would be to greet it properly.' "

She maneuvered his erection through the slit in his drawers. " 'That is quite a proper cock,' " she said, this time attempting to imitate Miss Stabler's voice. Sebastian made a choked, sputtering sound, which abruptly became a hiss as she bent forward, her corset cutting into her stomach, and closed her mouth around him.

She'd done this before, for money. Then, she'd tried to shut her mind away, herself away from what she was doing. She had soon learned how to do it quickly and competently, but she had never thought about it—had never wanted to think about it—beyond that.

But now she found the feeling of control to be intoxicating. She felt attuned to him as she circled the head of his erection with her tongue, feeling his reaction through his entire body. Savoring the sensation of power, she followed the ridge of his erection down to its root, and his powerful frame shuddered delicately. She moved on him slowly at first, gauging his response by the subtle shifts of his body, the catch in his breath, the pressure of his hands on her shoulders. Every response that she drew from him aroused her, the carnal, salty taste of his weeping erection calling an answering heat in her own body.

Then she found a rhythm that made him tighten his grip suddenly. Smothering the urge to chuckle, she fixed upon it, stroking him with her mouth over and over again as his breathing spiraled out of his control. Finally, with a shudder and a groan, he pushed her away and grabbed the edge of his shirt, bunching it over his arousal as he released himself into the fabric.

Sarah rocked back on her heels, looking up to meet his eyes. They were dark with lust, the muscles along his jaw corded.

"Sarah, you are a very dangerous woman," he said hoarsely.

Sarah blinked, then burst into incredulous laughter. "If only I were!"

Ignoring her outburst, he pulled her firmly to her feet, a small smile playing at the corner of his lips. "But I am a dangerous man."

Sarah felt a small thrill—of uncertainty? anticipation?—and said breathlessly, "So what are you going to do now that I have spent you?"

He raised an eyebrow, dark laughter in his eyes. "I believe that you underestimate what exactly it is you are dealing with here." In one swift movement, he gathered up her skirts and shoved them into her arms. Reflexively, she grasped them against her chest, and before she realized what he was doing, she felt the belt of her crinolette slip over her hips, the entire contraption landing with a clatter at her feet.

She opened her mouth to make an exclamation, but at that moment he walked forward, pushing her back so that she had to catch herself from tripping over the half hoops. Still he advanced, an expression of such lascivious intent that Sarah felt her skin begin to heat from her reaction to it.

Suddenly her hips fetched up the desk, and instantly Sebastian's hands were around her waist, simultaneously boosting her up to sit on it and pushing her down against it. Papers, ink, pen stand, nib wipe—they all hit the floor with a resounding crash. Sarah wiggled against his hands at the noise.

"Someone will come!"

"What, because they think you might have assaulted me?" He chuckled. "I think not. Lie down, Sarah."

After a moment's hesitation, she obeyed. Her shoulders

hung off the end of the desk, making blood rush to her head and blocking her view of what Sebastian was doing. But she could feel his hips between her legs, could already sense the weight of his renewed erection pressing against the juncture of her thighs. Her skirts bunched around her in a disarray of rose and red, blocking her view completely—and something hard and small on the desk dug into her back between the bones of the corset.

"Wait," she said, and she rolled slightly to the side so that she could slide a hand between her back and the desk to get to the object. Her fingers closed around the barrel of a pen, and she pulled it out and was about to drop it on the floor when Sebastian suddenly said, "Stop," and took it from her.

"What are you doing?" she asked, craning her neck up to see.

"Lie down, Sarah," he said as he came forward into view. His hands were empty, and he brushed a knuckle softly over her cheek, then followed her jawline down to where the high collar of her dress began. Slowly, he unfastened the top button, leaning across the desk to kiss the first inch of skin as it was exposed before moving to the next button. His mouth followed the path of his hands, excruciatingly slow, deliciously soft and damp and hot.

Under his touch, Sarah's sensual awareness heated quickly to lust, twisting pleasure low in her midsection and sending it racing through every vein down to her fingertips and toes. Her corset felt impossibly tight and restricting, her clothes rasping across her skin, but still his mouth moved over her, licking, nipping, tasting. Just watching the taut, intent lines of his face as he moved lower left her breathless, and what he was doing to her body made her skin itch and burn, sending shivers of heat down to pool in her midsection and below, between her legs.

He pulled down her chemise when he reached it, following the edge of her corset and leaving a line of fire in his wake. Slipping his hands under it to cup her breasts, he kissed her fully on the mouth. The heat of his palms, the subtle coarseness of them against the sensitive flesh of her nipples, sent a new wave of desire through her, and his mouth swallowed her groan. The core of her ached with emptiness, and she tried to arch into his hips, but his weight and the corset held her immobile.

When he broke away, he realized that he had neatly slipped her breasts two-thirds of the way out of the fashionably low corset. He disappeared from view, and she felt him move away from between her legs. She began to sit up—

"Lie still, Sarah," he said.

The roughened edge to his voice made her shiver inside. *I caused that,* she thought with a kind of dazed wonder. She obeyed.

She heard him moving and something being lifted from the floor. Then she felt his body between her knees again, nudging them apart.

"Did you know that both the men and the women of the Polynesian culture tattoo themselves?" he asked, his voice casual—too casual. "It is a mark of primitive belonging. Of tribal ownership, you might say."

"What are you doing?" Sarah demanded, tensing.

He chuckled. "I'm not a sadist, Sarah. I wasn't considering anything so permanent." He bent over her so that she could see his face—and his hand, where he held a pen.

She stared at it, mesmerized, her light-headedness from lying with her head hanging lower than the rest of her body making it hard for her to think. The pen was chased gold with an elegant silver nib, and a black drop of ink glimmered at the very tip.

Sebastian smiled, his eyes glinting with wickedness, his lush mouth promising sin. "You won't regret it," he promised.

He lowered the pen to the skin above her right breast. Sarah jerked a little as the cool metal touched her, her hands automatically flying up.

"If I must tie your hands to the table legs with your stockings, I will," Sebastian said.

Quickly, she put them back at her sides, grabbing handfuls of her skirt to keep them still. Sebastian was studying her face, and she shut her eyes to escape that gaze, knowing it was foolish.

With her eyes closed, she was even more acutely aware of the soft pressure of the pen against her breast. It was cold and alien against her heated skin—and bizarrely arousing. She knew she had no control over its path, over its movement—

The pen began to slide across her skin, the ball of the nib hard under the slick path of ink. Sebastian's pen strokes were firm at first, then abruptly turned teasingly feathery and fast, the sharp edges of the nib just brushing her skin in a way that set every discrete nerve aflame. Then he shifted to just the smooth point again, his movements becoming excruciatingly slow, the changes keeping her off balance, sending her into a state of exquisite sensitivity.

The pen danced wetly across her skin, teasing her breasts, promising a fulfillment that he failed to deliver again and again. It approached a nipple swiftly, and Sarah steeled herself for its touch, anticipating the sharp slickness against flesh now preternaturally sensitive. But it swooped away just before it reached the edge, and she had to bite back a noise of frustration. Then he circled the other, drawing closer and closer until he simply stopped, lifting the pen to dip it in ink again. Every time the nib ran dry, Sarah braced herself, but when the fulfillment came, she wasn't ready.

A single chilled drop of ink fell squarely onto one nipple, surprising a gasp out of her just as another drop hit the other. Before she could react, the tip of the pen pressed down on the first as his thumb and forefinger closed over the second. The smooth pen nib drew tiny circles as his fingers rolled wetly in the ink, the two sensations completely at odds with each other and yet doubly arousing for that. Sensation blossomed between her legs, and she hooked her calves around his lean flanks, pulling him hard against her so that his erection pushed against the center of her need as she rocked against him.

"Not yet," Sebastian muttered, as much to himself as to her, it seemed.

Sarah opened her eyes as he pulled away, and through the haze of her desire, she watched him move out of view. A moment later, she felt a pull against the slit in her pantaloons—and then the pen again, this time against her inner thigh. The touch was exquisitely delicate, delicious and terrible. She clamped her lips tight as he moved through her mound of whispery curls and then lower. . . .

"Oh, God," she said as it hit the sensitive nub there. He moved it—she didn't know how he moved it, but her body responded with a jolt of pleasure so intense that it was almost pain. Again, he urged the sensation from her, and again, until she felt herself at the edge of ecstasy—

Then he stopped suddenly and slid the pen down farther until she could feel the sharpness of the nib's edges against her folds of flesh. She wanted it, she feared it. . . .

"Trust me, Sarah," Sebastian said, as if reading her mind.

And then he pushed, and it slid in, the edges rasping faintly, arousingly against her inner skin. She gasped as it could go no farther. She felt her body clasp it, wanting it to be more than it was, reveling in the promise that it held. He drew it out, slowly, agonizingly, and then pushed it in again. Sarah felt a hollow opening in her, a void caused by her own need. She wanted to be filled—she must be filled.

"Please," she begged. "Please."

The pen was pulled away, and as if he'd been waiting for just that, she felt the pressure of his erection against her opening. But only for an instant. A moment later, he had buried himself in her, stretching her, filling her with such wonderful completeness that her exclamation had the edge of a sob in it.

Swiftly, he drove into her, and Sarah had just enough reach to grab his shirt and pull him on top of her, hauling his mouth down as she craned her head up, urging him onward with her hands and mouth and body. Instinctively, he found the rhythm that took her to the brink and over—and just as she began her fall into ecstasy, one of his thumbs found the sensitive nub between her legs and sent her crashing into a wall of sensation so profound that it darkened her vision and filled her ears with a deafening rush. Every nerve of her body assaulted her mind all at once until she could feel no individual part in the complete and total experience of it. It was beyond pleasure, beyond pain, into a place of pure feeling so intense she thought she might die.

Slowly, slowly Sarah came back to herself. Sebastian was slumped, motionless, on top of her, panting into her shoulder, and her own breath came in ragged gasps. After a moment, he shoved himself upright and offered her an arm. She took it, stumbling to her feet. Blinking around the room, she surveyed the disaster they had made.

The desk was a mess, the floor covered with scattered papers and ink. Sebastian's shirt was covered in ink smudges, and so, Sarah realized as she looked down, was her chemise, and her breasts themselves, swirled with abstract, smeared patterns that would take more than a little lemon juice to remove. She should be blushing, she thought, but after everything that had just happened, she couldn't quite manage it.

"That was wonderful," she said instead.

Sebastian smiled slowly, wearily. "Yes, it was," he agreed. "A true thing of beauty."

Sarah almost choked on her laughter.

Chapter Fifteen

The interlude in the office marked a kind of tacit agreement between Sarah and Sebastian. All things physical they could share. But certain subjects were closed, and Sarah sensed that opening them would only bring strain between them without gaining her any more knowledge. And so she remained silent.

However, Sarah sensed that Sebastian's frequent absences had to do with Mr. de Lint, and it took little power of deduction to realize that Sebastian must have plans of retribution upon him just as he'd had upon her—far more intricate, of course, and probably far more terrible. When she thought of those plans, whatever they might be, a sickening mixture of emotions filled her belly.

First there was fear—fear for Sebastian, about what he was doing, that Lady Anna was somehow being drawn into it in her innocence. Then there was worry about what would happen to Sarah when Sebastian's revenge was complete. After Sebastian had no reason to remain in Venice any longer, where would she go? What would she do? She was under no illusions that their relationship was anything but temporary, but the future beyond him reared up in her mind like a blank wall, and her speculations were tinged with the faintest taste of loss.

Finally, though, there was the thought of Mr. de Lint exposed, ruined, even dead. The bleak satisfaction that Sarah felt at that idea scared her and troubled her more than she wanted to admit.

Sarah's letters from Maggie did not help, either. Maggie was traveling again, this time to Yorkshire to see the Duke and Duchess of Raeburn's newly remodeled estate and their newborn child. Neither of those noble figures followed the events of London with more than a passing interest, so Maggie's vague memory of Mr. de Lint's recent feud with another gentleman was unaided by the people she met there. And Sarah was left to wonder.

Sarah's letters to her friend, for their part, were full of Venice—of the sights and sounds and the omnipresent music. She told her of the cat she'd been allowed to adopt, which she gave the illustrious and rather irreverent name of Victor Emmanuel after the new Italian king. She talked of the weather and her enjoyment of riding along in a gondola despite her fear of the water only the thickness of the boat away. In short, Sarah wrote about everything except the all-critical point that she had left Lady Merrill's service and was now the mistress of a man whose full name she did not even know.

Entire days would pass by without a glimpse of him, and she would grow nervous, wondering if he tired of her, wondering if he'd found a pink-cheeked Venetian girl who filled his bed better than she did, who spoke to him more wittily when he teased her in his elegant, urbane way. For as hard as she tried, she could never master the banter that came to his lips without thought, and she knew from long experience how little her body was worth in bed. She'd sold herself for ten bob a tumble; a man of Sebastian's worth could easily find better.

She could not be beautiful, but she tried to be mysterious. She wasn't very sophisticated, but she tried to be alluring. She knew little about the softer side of lovemaking, but she tried to seem wise in the ways of world. And yet every time Sebastian came into the room, every time he touched her, it was as if she were being taken up and shaken. The wrong words came out, revealing the shame she never wanted to acknowledge to herself, and the graceful movements she had practiced all day, the sensual acts described in the books she had Maria secretly buy, all fell away. When he was with her, she felt rubbed raw and yet sizzling with energy, and every touch, every word stung and soothed her at the same time.

Aside from a constant, unsettled feeling deep in the back of her mind, though, Sarah was happier than she'd ever been in her life. Sebastian accepted her muddled aesthetic desires as they were, treating her enjoyment of a beautiful pattern of damask and her craving for intellectual refinement with the same respect. Sarah was baffled by this unprecedented treatment but reveled in it—and in the gifts he showered upon her.

The Stones of Venice was just the first of many. Others arrived on a daily basis. On the second morning, she woke to find even more books of literature, history, and philosophy, almost all rare editions; on the third there was a selection of expensive perfumes; and on the fourth, a stack of excellent Canalettos to take the place of the dozens of amateurish works she'd ordered Maria to take away. And every day, he not only presented her with some extravagant new gift, but he also discussed it with her in all seriousness, debating the positions of various philosophers, explaining the history of various components of perfume and how they were made, telling her about Canaletto's life and gently encouraging her in her shy observations about the artistic merits of the pieces.

Then, on the fifth day, the piano arrived.

The previous afternoon, she'd asked the manservant Gian if there was perhaps a piano stored away in some back room somewhere, and when she came down for breakfast, it had been sitting in the chamber she'd taken—hesitantly at first—as her private sitting room. It was so glorious, so perfect when she played an experimental scale that she almost began to cry.

The gifts were payment for services rendered. Sarah realized that without Maria's whispered explanations. But Sarah knew what she was worth, and it was far, far less than the profligate amount he was spending upon her; even more than a display of generosity, the gifts were Sebastian's way of expiating his guilt for what he had done to her. Still, the choices were so brilliant, so adept, that they frightened her, none more than the piano.

On a quick trip to a music shop, Sarah found several pieces she'd been working on when she left the ladies school, and she hurried back, filled with repressed excitement. The instrument was so perfect that she more than half expected its honeyed tones to imbue her playing with the grace and power that she'd always longed for.

But after an hour's practice, the song was still as it had been when she last played it—mechanically perfect, yet still essentially mechanical. She bit her lip, glared at the notes in front of her, and played on, over and over again, seeking that expression that somehow always escaped her.

When she finally looked up, she discovered that the light in the room had dimmed with the coming of the night, the music sheets in front of her fading from black-on-white to gray. She realized that she must have missed luncheon, and her belly rumbled at that reminder, so she stood stiffly, deciding to make an undignified raid on the kitchen to see what might be readily had to stave off her hunger until dinnertime.

She stepped onto the portego, and the cool wind blowing through it teased at her hair and the light fabric of her skirts. It was at least six hours until high tide would come and cleanse the canals, so the fresh breeze carried a now-familiar stench on its back.

As she moved toward the staircase, she discovered that the door to Sebastian's bedchamber stood half-open, the lamps within forming a warmer slice of light on the marble floor, cutting through the cool dusk. Though she had been his mistress for nigh on a week now, she had not yet seen his own bedroom, and curiosity led her toward it. As she neared the doorway, she heard voices within and froze. Sebastian was not alone.

"I am tiring of these affairs." That was Sebastian's voice. "Midafternoon gatherings in discreet casinòs may have been popular a century ago, but even with masks and a carefully cultivated outré atmosphere, I cannot see the appeal."

"If all goes well, it will be over soon enough, sir." Gian's response was soothing.

"I hope so. Are you certain no one followed the gondola back from the party?" Sebastian's voice was laced with irritation and a deeper concern.

"Absolutely. I maintained a careful distance. Did you see anyone this time, sir?"

"No," came the brusque reply. "I haven't seen anyone since the thugs in the batèla tried to follow me home."

Gian made a noncommittal noise, and their voices dropped low for a moment before Sarah heard footsteps approaching the door. She panicked, but there was no place to hide, and so she steeled herself as the door swung the rest of the way open and Gian stepped out. He paused for a moment, looking at her with surprise, but said nothing. His reaction, though, was enough to cause Sebastian to step out onto the portego.

Sarah blushed as his glare settled upon her, wishing desperately that she could simply disappear.

"Come inside," he said forbiddingly.

Meekly, she ducked her head and obeyed, burning with mortification.

"I'm so sorry," she said as soon as he shut the door. "I was just walking past, and I saw the light, and the door was open. I-I haven't ever seen your bedchamber before, and so I was curious. . . ." She trailed off, aware of how rude and foolish she sounded.

"How long have you been listening?" he asked, his expression grim.

"You complained about casinòs and then asked if anyone

was following you," Sarah said, feeling like a schoolgirl confessing to some childish infraction.

"That is all?" he demanded.

"That is all."

He looked at her critically for a moment, then nodded, as if deciding to accept her story. "Well, you have at least gotten your wish. What do you think of my room?"

She looked around then, disappointed to discover a cleaner version of the chamber she had been led to when she had first arrived at the palazzo. "I think you need me to refurbish this room at least as badly as any other," she said frankly.

Sebastian smiled slightly. "It serves its purpose." He sat on one of the two chairs that made up a tiny sitting area. "I kept my door open to listen to you play," he admitted.

Biting her lip, Sarah took the other chair. "I am not very good."

"Nonsense," Sebastian said breezily—and unconvincingly. "I enjoyed it." That part, at least, sounded sincere.

"Thank you," Sarah said as she studied her hands where they sat in her lap. "I do love the gift. It's beautiful in every way and far, far too expensive for me."

"Of course it isn't," Sebastian said brusquely, ignoring the question implicit in her statement. Why did he spend so much upon her? He didn't know himself, entirely. "Where did you learn to play?" he asked. She had admitted she was from very low origins, which he'd already guessed. If it hadn't been for her occasional mistake and her odd areas of ignorance, her old defensiveness would have been a clue, not to mention her scars, which were likely the work of smallpox since her skin was otherwise blemish-free. Few women of the middle or upper classes caught smallpox anymore, especially those as young as she was.

"At the ladies school," she said.

The mention of that institution threw his mind back to his own school days, where he'd been dwelling far too often of late, but instead of mentally dismissing the memories as he usually did, he found himself leaning back in his chair and speaking about them. "I must confess that I never liked school very much. My father would have made a very good cavalry officer if he hadn't been the eldest. Or at least one with very well polished boots. He believed in the importance of a public school education for the character of the British upper class, and so he sent me as soon as any of the schools would have me. When I turned seven, I was wrenched from the comforts of the nursery and thrust into the barbarity of a boys school."

Sarah looked up at him quickly. "Seven is rather young, but surely it wasn't that bad."

He smiled dryly at her. "Show me a boy who loved school and I'll show you a bully or a boor. I'll have you know that in the first three months, I tried every trick I could think of in hopes of being sent down. But the headmaster was not so stern as to desire to lose my tuition and the prestige of my presence, so instead, all I gained was a reputation for being clever." He shifted in his chair. "It was a fortunate if entirely unforeseen consequence of my schemes. I was a small, sickly child, and if one was not strong enough to be a bully—or give one a good hiding—then being clever was the next best thing."

"Is that where you met Mr. de Lint?" Sarah asked softly, her dark eyes grave. "Is that why you are thinking about it now?"

He smiled with a touch of bitterness. "My little dove, you are too insightful by half."

She frowned. "What was he, then? Brawny or clever?" She shook her head. "No, I can guess. He's never been one for strength without finesse. I say he was clever—but cruel."

"Indeed, I think you might be able to tell this story better than I," Sebastian said wryly. Sarah immediately flushed, and he hastened to add, "I meant that as a compliment of your insight, not a criticism of your speaking. You are right. He was clever, truly clever, far more so than I. He had a knack for making people like him even then." He shook his head at her expression of distaste. "You may be too percep- tive to be taken in by a man such as him, perhaps, but I was not. I thought him a grand chap and a great friend for many years. With the clarity of distance, I see that he originally at- tached himself to me because of my father's influence. Be- tween that and his charm, he was a veteran of more scrapes and japes than any boy in the history of Eton. He loved it there. He was always at the center of things. But even with him at my side, I never could enjoy it. School was not for me."

Sarah nodded, but her gaze slid away from his, a sure sign that she was about to disagree. "I understand your feel- ings, but I do not think that everyone who has found plea- sure in school deserves the censure you would give them. I greatly enjoyed my time at the ladies school."

"Why?" he asked, honestly mystified.

"The girls—they thought I was someone's poor relation at first, close enough to their social class that I was tolerated, if not liked. They were all from good families, being taught useful things, cultivated things. How to make music and read French and study poetry, arithmetic and geography and elocution. And I was allowed to learn, too, though I hadn't their education, and so it was very hard for me at first. Of course, everyone thought that I was a little stupid in the be- ginning even though the teachers had been instructed not to call me out in class. I was older than most of them, too. I started the school at eighteen when most of the girls began it at twelve to fourteen and left four to six years later, but I was still growing then and no one ever realized that I was older. There were bad things, but I didn't mind so much. I was where I wanted to be, and there are many worse things than that."

"Then there were no bullies?" Sebastian asked in dis- belief.

"Yes. Yes, there were," she replied softly. "They were why I had to leave after four years when I had planned to stay for six. But girls don't fight with fists, and there was always plenty to eat. I cannot say as much for most of my life before that point. And besides, there was so much to learn, so much to know."

It occurred to Sebastian for the first time that much of his hatred of school had its root in the idyllic happiness of his life up until that point. True, his father had always been cold and severe, but his mother's abundant, generous love had easily made up for it during his early youth, which in itself had made those first school years that much harder. But now, reaching past the emotion that colored his recollections of those days, he remembered the good-natured boys who preferred school in all its small inhumanities to the isolation of the nursery room with only a governess and servants for company, and he recalled one first-year student, Albert Lowe, who had sobbed when he discovered that he must go home for the Christmas holiday after all and returned with his back covered in welts.

Sebastian could well imagine the relief and joy of a timid, terrified Sarah upon discovering that the sharpest punishment a female student could suffer would be a sharp rap on her knuckles.

He considered asking her about her life before the ladies school, as he had at least a dozen times a day since she had come to the Palazzo Contarini. But he knew how she'd react, withdrawing into herself instinctively with a haunted look in her eyes. Even now, speaking of the school, she had a slight wariness of her manner, as if waiting for the slightest hint of condemnation or condescension from him. But since she had opened that topic herself, he felt that it was safe enough to pursue it a little further.

"How did you come to the school in the first place?" he asked, as close as he could come to voicing his true question without being certain that she'd shy away.

She treated him to a level look for a long moment, then gave a tiny nod, as if she'd satisfied herself of something Sebastian couldn't fathom. "My best friend from my childhood married a—a very wealthy man. I became her lady's maid and companion for nearly two years after, but I wanted something that I had earned myself, not something that was given out of friendship."

"That's understandable," Sebastian said when she paused, remembering the similar feeling he'd once had about his inheritance, before his fights with his father had embittered him so and set him on the path to becoming a wastrel.

Sarah continued. "The only way I could get employment as something other than a menial was to get an education. I already knew how to read and write from sporadically attending a ragged school near where we lived, and I had taught myself how to speak properly." She smiled slightly. "Like a nob, as some might say. I asked my friend if she would do me the one last favor of sponsoring me at a school, and she agreed. Some of what I was could not be concealed, at least not from the headmistress, and so it took a month to find a place that would take me."

Her voice took on a wistful note. "I was far behind the other students when I began, but I worked hard, and by my third year I was at the top of my class in arithmetic and passable in geography, literature, and dancing, though my penmanship, French, drawing, and piano were still distinctly lacking. By the beginning of my fourth, I was the best in the school in arithmetic, geography, and dancing. That was when the rumors started. I had not realized I would be tolerated only as long as I kept my place, and for someone whose background was so clearly inferior to most of the students, my place was not at the head of the class. A few of the cruelest girls claimed I was a discarded rich man's bastard brought back into the fold, and by the time the students' parents heard the story, it was related as fact. When they complained to the headmistress, she did what she had to—she sent me away." As Sarah told this part of her story, she stared blindly in front of her, her tone emotionless as if her tale were from someone else's life. But she had taken her handkerchief from her pocket and was twisting the fine lace tighter and tighter in her white-knuckled hands.

"I was too humiliated to return to Maggie, so I placed an advert for a lady looking for a young, sturdy companion. By some miracle, Lady Merrill answered it. Only then I did I write a letter to Maggie, telling her that I was lured from the school with the promise of the cultivating influence of travel. I'd sold my books one by one to support myself— my school texts and the gifts that Maggie had given me every year. I had only three left when Lady Merrill's reply came, and they would not have fetched even enough money for me to survive another week." She shook her head as if rousing herself from the thrall of her memories. "You can guess what has happened since then."

"Yes, I can." Sebastian hurt for her, wanting to help soothe away those old wounds but feeling helpless to do so.

Part of him wanted to pull her to his chest and tell her that she could cry all she wanted, but his nature and her personality would not allow them such a simple release. Part of him wanted to make love to her, reassuring her with his body, but he did not want her to feel that he was exploiting the fragility of her emotions or the bargain that they'd made. Part of him wanted to assure her wildly right then that she would not be abandoned again, that he would take her back to England when this was all over, but he realized that she might not want to come after his plan was carried through. Most of all, though, he wanted to give her a piece of himself to reciprocate what she had just done for him, to comfort her with the universality of their pain. But what could he say that didn't sound shallow and silly compared to her own trials?

There was one thing at least that he could give to her— his name.

"I think that it is high time I introduce myself," Sebastian said, speaking on that thought. "Sebastian Grimsthorpe, Earl of Wortham, at your service."

Chapter Sixteen

"What?" Sarah blurted. An earl? And a familiar one at that—even in the backwater of Dunnefirth, she was certain she had heard of him. She had known Sebastian to be a gentleman from the start and recently to be a rich one, but she never would have guessed that he would be so very prominent. That she was here now, with a man like him, seemed almost ludicrous. But . . .

"Grimsthorpe," she said aloud, remembering. "You called yourself 'Grim' the first night that we—I mean, the night you brought me here. You weren't lying, after all." The discovery made her feel strangely reassured.

"Grimsthorpe is my surname as well as the name of the barony that was my courtesy title from birth," he said quietly. "No one but my mother ever called me Sebastian until I was out of school. Until then, I was Grimsthorpe to my father and my instructors and Grim to everyone else."

"But why did you tell me even part of the truth when you thought I was in league of some sort with Mr. de Lint? If I had been who you thought I was, it would have been wiser to lie."

His eyes grew hooded. "Yes. It would have been."

Sarah was silent for a moment, absorbing that, a part of her she did not dare to trust ridiculously glad for it. Eventually she said, tentatively, "Should I—would you like me to

begin calling you 'your lordship'? It would be more proper,
but, considering the circumstances . . ."

Sebastian cut her off with a snort. "In this case, propriety
is my least concern."

"My full name is Sarah Connolly," she confessed,
ashamed of her Irish surname as she'd never been before.

"It is pretty," he said.

Sarah could detect no irony in his voice, but she blushed
anyhow. "It is the only thing I have from my parents."

"Sometimes I think I got far too much from mine," Sebastian said dryly. "Venice is a city of memories for me. My
mother and I used to spend springs here with a cousin of
hers who had taken up historical research."

"But not your father?" Sarah blurted, then immediately
bit her lip at her tactlessness.

"You needn't be afraid of asking me questions, Sarah,"
Sebastian said even as his eyes shadowed over. "Traveling
was too frivolous for a man of my father's position. But my
mother loved traveling, though I think some of her enthusiasm was rooted in her husband's hatred of it." He paused.

Sarah knew he wanted her to ask more. She fought the
urge to shy away from such a personal matter, forcing herself to say, "Did your parents not get along?"

"My father never entirely forgave Mother for bearing
only one child," Sebastian answered readily. "Her duty was
to produce an heir and a spare, and since his multitude of
bastards adequately proved he was not at fault for the lack
of a second, he was . . . unkind to her. After it became apparent that I would have no siblings, she began to use every
excuse to escape his company and take me with her until the
year she died."

"What happened?" Sarah found the courage to ask.

Sebastian's expression turned so bleak that Sarah started
to reach out toward him before she recalled herself and
pulled back. He did not notice. "She took ill when I was
fourteen and died a few months later. The doctors said it was
a tumor of the ovaries."

Sarah could sense a great deal left unspoken behind those words, but she said only, "I see."

"No, you don't," he all but snapped, and for an instant, she saw the hurt and confused boy that he had been. "You can't. You don't know the whole of it."

Biting her lip, Sarah did reach out tentatively then and touched his arm. When he didn't jerk away, she said softly, "I can't know unless you tell me."

He shook his head, answering slowly. "We were in England at the time, with my father, but after the diagnosis he refused to see her. He saw it as one final piece of evidence that proved she had been a bad choice—that she wasn't a true woman because her femininity betrayed her. . . ." He trailed into silence, staring hard past her, his jaw bunching in anger at a man who was dead. "I dedicated the next four years of my life to disappointing him, and when his heart trouble finally killed him, I was angry instead of sad because I felt like I had been robbed of another decade of thwarting his plans for me."

"Sebastian, I know it doesn't help, but I am sorry," Sarah whispered, aching for him.

Instantly, his expression eased, humor glinting over the old pain. "Your own past must be much more difficult than mine, but you still have room in your heart to feel for me. You are one of the most sincerely good people I have ever met."

She pulled away, wedging herself in the corner of her chair. "I am not good. Not even good enough. I never have been."

"You are swifter to judge yourself than others, which is a rare thing in this world." The wings of his brows lowered, making him look fierce. "Most of us protect ourselves by blaming everything and everyone else first. But you assume that others are good even if that means you must be bad, and you trust that others are right even if that means you are wrong."

She shook her head. "That is stupid, not admirable."

"It comes from a good heart, Sarah." He said the words

slowly and distinctly. "It comes from sweet if at times misplaced generosity."

Sarah knew better. She knew what was in her heart—how could she not?—and it was nothing to be proud of. "It comes from not knowing what is right and what is wrong and from a lack of moral certitude." Miss Stabler had said as much a dozen times or more.

Sebastian frowned at her. "On the first night that we spent together, when you sensed that my motives were less than pure, you tried to get me to make an admission as to my motivation, risking my anger and destroying the fantasy of the moment, which was clearly what you had sought when you came to meet me."

"I was frightened at what you might have planned."

"You were concerned for your employer's grandchild, whom I know from your stories that you do not like," Sebastian corrected.

Sarah felt herself flush. "Oh, no, I don't dislike her at all!" she protested automatically.

"But you do not like her, either," he said firmly. Sarah was silent, being unable to refute that statement. He continued, "You risked losing that moment in order to be true to a girl you do not care for. That is good."

"A good woman would like her," Sarah insisted. "I cannot. And I still don't know what you have planned for her, and yet I am here, with you."

"What do you think I am going to do?"

Sarah hesitated, not wanting to put her worst fears into words. "I am afraid that you will get Gian to ruin her or may even trick her into eloping with him. I do not know what it is that Mr. de Lint did to you, but those are the only things that I can imagine that you would want to do with a girl like Lady Anna. Though you have known Mr. de Lint far longer and far better than I, I don't think that hurting his niece will cause him much personal anguish. And she is an innocent party."

"Gian is not going to ruin her," Sebastian said firmly. "She is not my target. She is merely a means to an end."

"I'm glad," Sarah said softly. And she meant it.

"Would you like to go to a masquerade tomorrow?" Sebastian asked, changing the subject abruptly.

Sarah looked at him in mute surprise.

"You know now that I don't spend all the hours I'm away from you just gazing at the sunset from the top of St. Mark's campanile," he said dryly.

"I would enjoy it, but I do not wish to meet my former employer again," she said, choosing her words carefully.

"Understandable," he said. "I will make certain that you won't. Would that please you?"

"Yes, but . . . why do you care?" That question had been troubling her since he had first made the offer to make her his mistress, but she was only now able to put her vague unease into words.

Then he did look at her, the brilliant green of his eyes muted with shadows of concern. "Why shouldn't I? Don't you think I owe you something?"

Sarah's face burned. "I don't want your pity, sir, nor do I want generosity out of guilt or obligation."

The muscles in his jaw tightened. "I have too little conscience or compassion left for such a thing to be my motivation. I want to give you enjoyment, and I know that you would have a difficult time accepting what you do not think you deserve."

"I deserve nothing." The words slipped out, soft as a breath but imbued with a truth she could not deny.

"And there, you don't know how wrong you are." He put a hand on her shoulder and shook her gently. "You are a woman of exquisite sensitivity, which I have known for some time, as well as of great goodness."

And in that fragile instant, Sarah's mind did not rebel from the compliment, and they lapsed into silence that was comfortable, almost companionable, listening to the soft sound of the wind blowing through the portego and the faint melody of someone singing far away.

* * *

Their second masquerade together was a rousing success. Sarah had clearly felt glorious, adoring the costume he'd given her, the dancing, the unfamiliar food. She'd taken his guise of Señor Guerra as a kind of game, though there was a slightly tense undercurrent to her play, and he had penetrated even further into the local international society as she had danced and laughed on his arm, a lovely, mysterious woman to add to his mystique.

They stayed until the wee hours of the morning, and then Sebastian had his gondola brought around. Sarah collapsed into the felze's cushions and promptly fell asleep on his shoulder, but instead of ordering them straight back to the Palazzo Contarini, Sebastian told the gondoliers to row out to the edge of the lagoon.

Now, beyond the felze's wide, beveled windowpanes, the marshy line of lidi stretched out as far as Sebastian could see, slumbering along the boundary of Venice's shallow lagoon. Colorless predawn light whispered across the water, picking out the slender clumps of reeds that rose from the murky bottom and a cluster of painted fishermen's sails far away. Beyond the narrow islands was the expanse of the Adriatic, and beyond that, the dark, wooded shores of Dalmatia, clustered with nascent countries still caught between the vanished world of Byzantium and the waning power of the Turks.

Sarah's head rested against his side, her body leaning on him trustingly in sleep. She'd pulled her mask off, and her face was tilted up toward his. In sleep, without the mesmerizing power of her eyes or the vibrant energy of her personality animating her, Sebastian could look at her dispassionately. Most of her cosmetics had worn off during the night—the rest were smeared across her face, making dark circles around her eyes and a red smudge surrounding her mouth.

Her skin was still scarred, of course, but Sebastian realized with some surprise that he hadn't noticed it since she had confronted him in his office two mornings after her disgrace. Without the concealment of powder, there was a light pattern of marks across her face, shallow enough to be nearly impossible to feel but deep enough that they must seem monstrous to a woman of Sarah's sensitivity. And it was sensitivity, not vanity. She was a woman who felt everything deeply and intensely—neither irrational nor hysterical, merely profound.

Her eyelashes were thick and, even without paint, dark for a woman of her coloring, as were her eyebrows, sweeping and expressive. Her nose was, perhaps, a fraction too long, but it balanced the delicate prominence of her cheekbones and her small, pointed chin that had the tiniest cleft in it.

All things considered, it was certainly an attractive face. But it was not remarkable, not so breathtaking that he could not think of half a hundred other women just as lovely. Still he could not imagine any other woman whom he would have happily sheltered against his body for more than two hours. Nor could he remember a time when he'd ever felt this strange mixture of tenderness and attraction, protectiveness and contentment.

They were fleeting emotions, he knew all too well. Soon, his plan would come to fruition, and he would leave Venice and all of its memories behind. For the first time, he truly considered what Sarah's reaction would be when the whole of it was revealed. He shook his head at the terrible images that sprang into his mind. Speculation was pointless, and it hardly mattered, anyhow.

The sky had lit aflame while he'd been thinking, and now the first pale yellow edge of the sun began to push above the magenta horizon. He bent his head, inhaling the scent of Sarah's hair, and kissed her gently on the brow.

Her eyelids fluttered open. "Are we there?" she asked thickly.

"Look," he said softly. "The dawn."

She shifted slightly in the crook of his arm as she tilted her head for a better view. "How lovely."

As Sebastian had expected, she did not ask why he hadn't taken her straight home. She took it as what he intended it to be—a simple gift, one of time and beauty, one that could never be taken away. He suspected that she knew how fleeting their time together was, how impermanent every material gift would be after he left and she was forced to find her way in the world alone. This, though, was the stuff of memories, and he knew it would never be lost.

The sky danced with color as the sun began its slow rise, red chasing away the purple of night, setting the high, furrowed clouds ablaze, and then fading gently into the blue of day. When the lower edge of sun finally cleared the water, Sarah sighed. "I seem to be saying this with great frequency—but thank you." She shifted back into her previous position and closed her eyes.

He kissed her forehead again, tasting salt. "You are always welcome." He ordered the gondoliers to take them back to the Palazzo Contarini.

As the gondola turned its back to the sun that hung in the sky like a new-minted penny, an old phrase rose in Sebastian's mind and hung there like a harbinger:

Red sky at morning, sailors take warning.

And then, before he could stop himself, he wondered if this was the calm before the storm.

Chapter Seventeen

"What news?" Sebastian asked as Gian entered his office a week later. The man still wore the white uniform of a gondolier, his hair ruffled and his eyes shadowed as if he had not slept since the night before. "Have you found another prostitute to suit de Lint's tastes?"

"Yes," Gian said, but he was frowning. "It is the last one I can promise, though. His desires are very specific, and Venice is no longer the city of ten thousand whores. The profession declined when the visitors did."

Sebastian let out a frustrated breath. "He has been through eight already. I cannot be assured that he won't tire of this one as well after a single night."

Gian shrugged. "There is another way, sir."

"And what would that be?" Sebastian distrusted the man's tone.

"Give him what he really wants. Virgins, unwitting girls sold by their mammas. There are plenty who are poor enough to consider it a good trade."

"Absolutely not," Sebastian said flatly. "We must move up the timetable. We will hold the masquerade here in three days—there's no need to rent another location, since Sarah has made such a change in the palazzo. Señor Guerra has managed to attend every masked gathering in the city since he arrived. Since he has become such a prominent and curious figure, many will be eager to attend his party just to find out more about him. How long will it take before you manage to persuade Lady Anna of your good intentions?"

"The Lady Anna proves to be remarkably energetic, sir," the man said without expression. "I was wooing at her window more than half the night."

"I need progress."

"She enjoys small risks," Gian said cautiously. "I have not yet persuaded her into any true indiscretion. She always adores the flowers, but it took most of last week to persuade her to keep the other little gifts you have begun to include, much less get her into my arms."

Sebastian nodded unwillingly. "You are still making headway, I trust?"

"Slower than I expected, sir, but yes. It has been two and a half weeks since you had me begin this game. Perhaps half a week more, a full week at the outside, and she will be ready."

"You have three days." Three days, and it would all be over. Emotions warred within him at that thought—relief, triumph, and under it all, a deep regret that had Sarah's dark blue eyes. What would happen between them when this plot was over? Would she want to return to England with him? Would he even ask her?

"Yes, sir."

"I want that cologne." Sebastian's frown deepened.

"I know, sir. Nothing has changed."

Sebastian shook his head. "Go on, then. Take this list"— he handed the man a piece of paper—"and write the invitations. Have them posted this evening, and you are free until tonight."

"Thank you, sir." The Italian bowed and left, leaving Sebastian alone with the tangled mess of the ledgers and his thoughts.

Another one. Another! How many childlike whores did de Lint think there were in Venice? The entire plan teetered on the brink of failure. If Gian could not make sufficient progress with Lady Anna before the final masquerade . . .

It wasn't just the complications with de Lint and Lady Anna that were rubbing him so raw. Since the incident when he'd been followed from the Casinò Giallo, he had taken care to bring at least one gondolier with him wherever he went; however confident he was in his own strength, he did not feel the need to court danger. Regardless, the sensation of being watched—and followed—did not decrease. On the contrary, every time he stepped outside of the palazzo, he felt certain there were hidden eyes on him until he reached the shelter of his destination. Maybe he should just give up the whole scheme. It was turning him into a paranoid madman. Only when he was with Sarah did he feel as if he were truly alone.

The thought of Sarah made him crave her company. He had given their time together an end date now. Three days. He knew she would not forgive him for what he was planning to do.

Until that moment came, though, she was his, and with that thought, he rose and opened the door to his office, listening for a moment to the muted sounds of Sarah's energetic renovation to discover where she was working that day. He followed the noise onto the portego and toward the canal.

After her initial hesitation, Sarah had taken him at his word and was refinishing at least one room of the palazzo every day. Even more amazing than that breakneck speed were the exquisite results. He never would have thought she possessed such decision and energy, much less taste—in fact, when he had first set her to the task, he had imagined that she would spend two weeks quietly arranging a single room before moving to the next. Instead, she did most of the work for each room in one brilliant, sweeping burst of energy that lasted only a few hours, and then over the next few days, as she moved on to other rooms, workers would finish the tasks that she had already laid out for them.

Being accustomed to the thousand indecisions of women in his own social circle and not wishing to embarrass Sarah with a question she might misinterpret as criticism, he had asked Maria how her mistress managed to make such incredible progress. The maid had replied with unconcealed awe, explaining that Sarah could take in the entire contents of a shop in one brief visit and later bring any item instantly and infallibly to mind. His exchequer was being much more heavily impacted than he had expected, but he found he could not deny her the joy she was having, and the rooms she left behind were so delightful that he had to admit at least part of his generosity came from his enjoyment of the result.

Sebastian found Sarah in the wreckage of what had been, at breakfast, the dining room. The sun streamed though the curtainless windows, illuminating her in a golden halo of dust in the center of the room as a dozen servants worked around her. Today, she wore her hair arranged high upon the back of her head, and her dress was of a vivid green watered silk. It hugged her waist and breasts, and Sebastian found himself thinking how far his hands spanned that waist when they made love, how her breasts filled his hands and tasted when he kissed them.

Sarah stood so comfortably there, directing the efforts of all the workers in an easy, clear voice, that it was hard to imagine that she had given him such a terrified look when he'd first charged her with the task. As always, she radiated her emotions with her entire body—contentment now, and confidence he never could have thought she'd display. As he watched her, he felt his mind ease. There was something infectious about her happiness, and he shied away from the thought that it would ever end.

Sarah noticed him in the doorway and smiled, her dark eyes lighting and her cheeks pinkening softly. "The walls are actually gilded leather!" she said. "Have you ever heard of such a thing? They seem to be in fine enough shape, though somewhat worn, so I've found two workmen who can repair them."

"What is that?" he asked, motioning to a large shrouded rectangle that leaned against the table.

She gave him a look that was almost shy. "It's a painting I found. There was another estate sale, and most of the work was terrible, as it usually is, but I found this one." She lifted the edge of the sheet carefully. "I thought it was beautiful, and so I bought it even though it's unsigned. It—it reminded me of the Titians in the Correr Museum. I know it isn't one," she said hurriedly, "but I liked the same things about it. The use of color, the luminosity . . ."

Sebastian surveyed the canvas with admiration. A red-headed Esther knelt before Ahasuerus, his hand already extended to raise her up. Sebastian had never been one to study the different components that went into the makings of a masterpiece, but even he felt the energy and beauty of the painting, and as she said, it did have the peculiar luminosity of Titian.

"It very well might be from his studio," he said. "No matter who painted it, though, it must be worth a great deal more than any of the bills you've yet presented me. It is lovely."

Sarah's face lit up with abashed pleasure. "Thank you, sir."

She was everything that was bright and fresh, and suddenly the walls of the old palazzo seemed to close in on him. All he wanted was to escape with her to somewhere he could breathe.

"Put on your paletot," he ordered. "We're going on a trip."

Her smile widened even more. "I am finished here anyhow. It would be a pleasure."

After a short flurry of activity, they stepped outside, where their gondola was already waiting. Sebastian stepped in first and, as usual, Sarah gripped his arm tightly before stepping in herself, releasing it only after she was securely seated on the cushioned bench.

"You seem to enjoy Venice a great deal for a woman who

is terrified of the water," Sebastian observed as he shut the felze door.

"I'm not scared of it unless I am standing over it," she retorted.

"Can't you swim?" he asked curiously.

Her expression was amused. "Where would I have learned? I lived in London as a child, not some charming country village with a gristmill and a canal. No one swims in London except the Thames scavengers."

"There are a few canals you should not fall into, then," Sebastian said. "This one and the Grand Canal, to start. But most are no deeper than your waist, many no deeper than your knees."

Sarah smiled. "I don't intend to fall into them and find out which ones are too deep and which aren't, but it's good to know that not every canal would drown me. Where are we going?"

Sebastian had an insane urge to blurt out, "Milan," but caught himself just in time. What was wrong with him? Yes, he had a mounting dissatisfaction, a restlessness, but all he needed was to leave the claustrophobic maze of canals for an hour or two and he would be fine.

"San Michele," he said instead, choosing one of the two outlying church islands, the only one they had not yet visited.

Ever since their talk in his bedchamber, Sebastian had made a point of taking Sarah to see the sights of the city whenever he could steal a few hours from his books and schemes. He had taken her to squint at the grime-obscured Tintorettos in the Scuola Grande di San Rocco, where she had peered at the canvases as if she were trying to see through fog until she spied the masterpiece of the *Crucifixion* in its pristine glory and stopped with a gasp, her reticule falling to the floor in her surprise. He had taken her to the Ghetto on a Friday afternoon when hundreds of geese were being slaughtered for the Jewish Sabbath and the air was filled with drifting down like warm snow. They had even made the long gondola ride to Murano, where Sarah had gaped in horrified fascination at the intricate and hideous works of glass for which the island was famous.

He had many memories of those places, formed over half a dozen visits over nearly a score of years, but now when he thought of them, it was not the places themselves that came to his mind but Sarah in them, the experience of them reflected in her face with a kind of distilled intensity that he never imagined anyone could feel.

He did not speak again until they reached the island, and Sarah maintained the silence. She seemed, as always, to sense his mood and to adapt herself to it, and while the habit made her company restful, her very pliability also made him ashamed, filling him with the sense that he was using her. She glanced over, catching him gazing at her, and she blushed as a slight sensual awareness of him sparked in her eyes, and his groin tightened instinctively. But neither of them attempted to bridge the short distance between them with their bodies. They had time for now, Sebastian knew, though not much longer.

The last of Sebastian's tension had faded away to his now habitual disquiet by the time the boat reached its dock. A short distance away, a gilded black barge rocked gently in the water, surrounded by smaller gondolas that darted around it like dark dragonflies under increasingly lowering skies. A swarm of Venetians milled around on the shore as even more disembarked, the wind fluttering their sable skirts and veils and tailcoats in a parody of festivity. In front of them rose a tall, encircling wall of red brick that looked queerly washed out against the supersaturated colors of the sky and grass. An entrance arch lay a few yards away, and Sebastian guided Sarah toward it while the Venetians were still gathered on shore.

"It's the municipal cemetery," Sarah said in tones of surprise. "I had forgotten which island it occupied."

Sebastian answered her unspoken question: *Why are we here?* "It is also the only open green space in all Venice aside from the ugly park Napoleon ordered to be made, which is what interests me. And it is the site of a significant and historical church, which is what I am sure shall interest you. Come. Let's walk."

Keeping their distance from the funeral, they passed through the arch, which immediately opened onto a vast sweep of verdant lawn dotted with white markers of the dead that lay across the grass like a thousand spilled teeth. Above those modest stones rose the extravagances of the rich, unequal even in death, their Palladian mausoleums, rococo sculptures, and tall tombs lording over the lesser graves.

"It's very different from an English churchyard," Sarah observed. "It's so . . . lovely. And even cheerful. It seems almost irreverent."

"Look there," he said, nodding at a small mausoleum with a broad porch that shaded a group of pleasant picnickers.

"They're eating?" Sarah asked in tones of stark disbelief.

"It's probably the anniversary of someone's death." He smiled at her incredulous expression. "It's easy to forget how truly different the Latins are from us until you see something like that, isn't it?"

She just shook her head. "Why don't they still bury their dead in the churches? We've seen plenty of tombs there."

"They used to be buried in the campi around the churches, too, and the old bones of insufficiently illustrious citizens were carted off to one of the distant islands whenever room was scarce." He gave her a sideways look of suppressed amusement. "But digging up the campi tended to disrupt traffic, and putting bodies in the churches, however conventional, has significant drawbacks in a city built upon mud. There could be no deep cellar-level crypts, and the bodies under the floors of the churches tended to decay quickly in the muck below, leading to occasional odors that could be so foul at times that they drove out even the priests."

Sarah wrinkled her nose. "Then why did they continue doing it so long?"

Sebastian shrugged. "Tradition? Convention? I don't know. But Napoleon put an end to both practices. He declared that the island of San Michele was the only legal place for the Venetians to bury their dead, and the practicality of the arrangement caused it to survive both the French and the Austrians."

"What did the monks think about that?" Sarah couldn't help but ask. "There is a monastery here, isn't there?"

"There is, but I don't know," Sebastian confessed. "I think that the church might have been suppressed for a while. The monks were certainly not in residence by the time the Austrians took over—they used the dormitory as a political prison when I was a boy. I used to sneak as close to the walls as I could get to see if I could catch a glimpse of a prisoner, though I never did. Now the prisoners have been gone for years, and the monks are back in their cells. But the cemetery remains, and it's become so crowded that there is already talk of resuming the practice of hauling the old bones to mass graves unless the family keeps up payments to retain the plot."

Sarah surveyed the city of obelisks and angels, pavilions and mausoleums, and the thousands of humbler markers that stretched out to the limits of the island. Everything was so precise, so very crisp that it was hard to grasp that something as messy as death could be hidden there. White marble glowed vividly against the backdrop of the green sward, and the darker pillars of cypresses stood out in neat columns against the blue-black clouds that rushed in from the east. "It is both peaceful and unsettling at once," she said.

"I was here once on All Souls' Day. You should see it then. They build a bridge of barges from the main island, and everyone streams across with armfuls of flowers to decorate the graves and baskets of food to eat beside them."

Her smile had a impudent edge as she assumed a tone of prim disapproval. "I wouldn't know, but it sounds terribly pagan to me."

"I'd like you to tell that to her," Sebastian retorted,

nodding at a distant woman who was lighting candles on top of a tomb that looked remarkably like an altar.

"I think not," Sarah said.

He led them to the church itself, a vast building in the same faded red brick and white marble as the island's surrounding wall. They were permitted to tour it under the watchful gaze of a Franciscan monk, and Sarah showed all signs of interest during their slow circuit of the nave, as if she had not seen at least half a dozen similar churches earlier that week. Sebastian, who had visited the church many times before, was thoroughly bored by the entire proceedings, but he enjoyed watching Sarah's enjoyment of it and reading the transparent, shifting expressions on her face as she judged every element of the building.

When Sarah finished touring the church, they left with thanks and a small donation. She made an exclamation as they stepped out of the shelter of the church's porch and a gust of damp wind caught her skirt and sent the crinolette swinging. She glanced at the sky, which was almost black now with boiling clouds.

"Don't you think we should go back?" she asked, her voice heavy with doubt.

"No," Sebastian assured her. "I know the perfect place to wait it out. Storms in the Veneto never last long, and we'll be home by luncheon."

He led the way to the east corner of the island, supporting Sarah against the sudden gusting shoves of the wind as it caught in her skirts. "There it is," he said.

Behind an iron fence, the manicured expanse of well-ordered graves gave way abruptly to a tangle of overgrowth threaded with leafy, half-visible trails. Headstones reared through the unchecked abundance of grass and weeds, covered in moss and tilted at crazy angles from the ground.

"What is this?" Sarah asked as Sebastian escorted her through the creaking gate, glancing back at the immaculate acres they had just left behind.

"Where the Protestants are buried," Sebastian said. There

was a forlornness there in the wild neglect that was lacking in the beautiful rolling lawn of the main cemetery. There, death was sterilized, made manageable and matter-of-fact by the careful regulation of its manifestation. But among the shaggy trees and rampant weeds, with the wind making every leaf and blade of grass toss and shake mournfully against its stem, the knowledge of decay and loss was inescapable. "The Protestants are all foreigners—travelers, dignitaries, and the occasional expatriate," he said.

"And so there's no one here who cares to tend their graves," Sarah concluded. "That seems very sad. But I like it better than the main graveyard. It seems more real." She gave a self-conscious smile. "And much more picturesque."

"Yes," Sebastian said, threading a path through the obscured headstones as the first drops of rain began to fall. Vaguely, his memory led the way—around this tree, by this hedge—and yes, through the tangle of branches rose a lone angel on a pillar, marking the place of a girl who was taken too soon. "This part of the cemetery was always my favorite as a boy. It seemed more honest to me. This is what death is—an ending, a forgetting." He looked over his shoulder as he squeezed between two hedges. "Pretending that it's just a pretty picture in marble only cheats it of meaning."

"When I am gone, I want some marker, even if I'd rather forgo the stiff formality of such a place as the Catholics' plots here. I don't want to be thrown away in a potter's field like I never mattered," Sarah said, her voice quiet but firm.

"I wouldn't want that, either," Sebastian agreed, tightening the grip on her arm as his mind conjured up experiences that would lead her to have such an immediate response.

They pushed by the low-hanging branches of a leaning ash, and he stopped at the edge of a clearing. Trees hedged it in, their shade stifling the undergrowth that was rampant in other parts of the cemetery, surrounding a few graves and a squat mausoleum that sat in the middle of the space like an altar to an ugly god. The wind tangled in the branches of the sheltering trees, stirring them into a constant, whispering rush, but a spattering of rain still reached them through the leafy canopy.

"That looks out of place," Sarah observed, frowning.

"Perfectly hideous," Sebastian agreed heartily. "But come around this way." He circled the stubby structure and, just as he had expected, found that the stone slab meant to seal the end still stood ajar. "Let's go."

Sarah's expression grew wary. "There's nothing—no one in there, is there?"

Sebastian smiled at her response. "Of course not. It's been open and empty since the first time I visited seventeen years ago. Someone must have ordered it and then changed his mind about dying in Venice." The rain increased to a drizzle as he spoke. "Hurry! It's dry." Putting action to his words, he slipped through the crack between the slab and the stone wall—or tried to. He was much larger than he'd been when he last passed through that hole, and what had once been an easy slide now cost him a button on his overcoat and several bruises as he broke free with a grunt.

"Are you all right?" came Sarah's worried voice.

"A bit less skin than I had going in, but other than that, I'm well enough." He turned around to face her. "You next. You'll get soaked."

"Sebastian," she said, doing as good a job of portraying good-natured exasperation as could be expected with a drop of water hanging off her nose. "Look at my skirts. I can't possibly fit though that."

"Can you flatten them?" he suggested.

She shook her head. "They won't flatten enough with me still in them."

"Then I guess the crinolette will just have to come off," he said.

"Here?" she sputtered, but there was more than a little amusement under her exasperation.

"It's too cold to get soaked," he pointed out sensibly. "You'll catch your death. No one's looking, and if I have to come out there again and lose even more skin—"

"Very well, then!" Sarah cast a quick look around and then hiked up her skirts, fumbling with the belt for a moment before it came loose. She wiggled out of it. "Are you satisfied?" she asked, shoving the contraption through the gap before sliding gingerly through herself, holding her now-dragging skirts up carefully off the ground.

"Quite," he said, feeling unaccountably smug.

Carefully styled curls had fallen damply into her face, and she slicked them back, looking at him out of eyes now ringed in smudged cosmetics. "This is a convoluted way to get me out of my clothes," she said, pretending severity.

"Ah, my dear little dove, you make it too easy for me," he retorted automatically. Now that Sarah was inside, he took the opportunity to survey the space. It was still dim and small, with two low biers of stone built into opposite walls, ready to accept the owners' bodies that had never come. Perhaps the composting detritus on the floor was a trifle deeper than it had been, and perhaps the green slick spot in the corner where the roof leaked had spread a little, but beyond such minimal changes, it was exactly as he remembered it.

Sebastian sat on one of the biers as Sarah stripped off her damp paletot and draped it across another, pulling off her gloves and rubbing her hands together briskly.

"I used to lie here as a boy and imagine what it would be like to be dead," he said, unfastening the surviving buttons of his overcoat and shrugging out of it.

Sarah looked at him quickly. "That seems rather morbid."

"Not as much as you would think. On my family's main estate in Wiltshire, visible from practically everywhere, there is an enormous Palladian mausoleum that was built in 1725 when the first Earl of Wortham was created. My illustrious ancestor apparently was of the belief that an earl deserved a better resting place than a mere baron—one that commanded a good view of his property, as well. He even had a few of our mutual ancestors who had not managed to achieve a place of honor within a church dug up and moved.

Every earl since him has been buried there, as well as every unmarried child."

"Why do you dislike it so?" Sarah asked, lines of incomprehension between her brows. "To know that there will always be a place for you, that you won't even have to worry about your grave—surely there is comfort in that."

"It is a constraint to me, not a comfort. So much of the course of my life was set before I was born," he said. The words were bitter, but suddenly he could not hold them back, all of his years of confused and angry feelings against his father resolving themselves into crystal clarity at once. "Who I would be, where I would go to school, what I would become. I was to be the Earl of Wortham, and Wortham is always industrious. Wortham improves his lands. Wortham is a solid Whig. Wortham knows his responsibilities and honors them. My father became my grandfather just as my grandfather became his father before him in a line of dutiful mimicry that goes back as far as the records hold out. I don't like what those men were, and I will not become another one of them. I do not want to be finally brought into my proper place at their sides even in death."

Sebastian stopped abruptly, as surprised by where Sarah's question had led him as she appeared to be. Never in his life had he thought through his muddled emotions; never had he attempted to understand his violent antipathy to so much his father had held dear. It had merely been an unexamined fact of his life that Sebastian hated everything his father was and stood for.

"We are so astoundingly different," Sarah said slowly, her eyes fixed on his face as the wind whipped past the entrance to the mausoleum, teasing escaped strands of her drying hair into a frizzing halo around her head. "And yet at the heart of it, what we want is the same. I want a place for myself in a world that has nothing to offer a woman like me. And you want a place for yourself in a world that has always told you what you must be."

"Yes," Sebastian said, realizing how very right she was.

"I know I should not complain. I have wealth; I have prestige; I have power. I do not want to give them up. I will not. But I want more than that, as selfish and shallow and impractical as I may sound."

"I could have spent the rest of my life as my best friend's houseguest if I had so chosen," she said quietly. "I could have had more comfort and luxury than I had once ever dreamed existed. But I, too, wanted more. If you are shallow and impractical, then so am I."

Sebastian laughed without humor. "You at least had the strength of character to relinquish what your friend had to offer."

"But I was elevated to it, not born to it, and nothing she had was mine to keep." She sat down on the bier facing his, looking at him intently, the dim, sideways light from the gap in the stones illuminating her face and softening it as the rain rushed down. "What you have now is your own. What you do with it is your choice. That is the difference between you and me. You now have the means to make more of a choice than I think you realize, while I have almost none."

Sebastian felt a small chill down the back of his neck, as if the disapproving ghost of his father were standing there, and he realized how much he'd allowed that memory to control his life. He'd been defying the dictates of a dead man for over a decade—not because his desires had led him in that direction but because he had still been rebelling blindly, childishly.

"If you are not happy," Sarah added, as if she read his mind, "perhaps you should simply make different choices. The ones you want to make. Surely honor and industry are not bad things, even if your memory of your father taints your view of them. You can choose the virtues and abandon the rest. You are not betraying yourself by embracing your father's most admirable qualities as long as you do not similarly adopt his vices."

Impulsively, Sebastian reached out to cup Sarah's cheeks in his palms. "You are right," he said. "Thank you." He tried to smooth away smudged cosmetics under her eyes with his thumbs, but he only added a smear of dirt from his gloves to the mix.

Suddenly, it struck him that she looked endearingly ridiculous with such an earnest expression on her mud- and cosmetic-streaked face, her windblown hair frizzing around her head in defiance of all attempts to contain it. This was one of the most significant moments of his life, and he should be appropriately grave and severe, but with the lightening of his burdens came the incredible urge to laugh.

He chuckled despite all his attempts to contain it, and that was like a crack in the dam, for immediately he dissolved into laughter—loud and full, his hearty guffaws drowning out the sound of the wind shaking the trees and the steady rush of rain. Sarah's expression of surprise made her look even more ludicrous, and he burst into fresh peals of merriment.

"What is so funny?" she demanded.

"I-I smeared your face," he managed. He held out the gloves that he had managed to strip off. "Mud," he gasped. "So sorry!"

Realization of what he meant dawned. "You just smeared mud across my face?"

He nodded breathlessly, regaining control with effort. "I apologize. Deeply." He managed to stifle the last chuckles that were still trying to escape. "You were so very grave, and so very right. Your words led me to an epiphany. And then, in one of the most meaningful moments of my generally meaningless life—then I wanted to thank you and I ended up smearing mud across your face instead." He looked at her helplessly. "It was funny."

Half a dozen emotions flickered across her face, but he was not prepared for the fistful of damp leaves that she scooped up and flung at his face, bursting into startlingly girlish giggles.

He launched himself at her as she bent to grab a second handful, and after a few seconds' struggle, hindered by laughter on both sides, he had her neatly pinned under him on one of the biers.

"You, sir, are no gentleman," she accused, smiling up at him. "And you have leaves sticking in your hair."

"You, madam, still have mud on your face, and yet you are the only lady I ever want,"

Under him, Sarah's face froze, and a shock went through Sebastian as the words that had escaped his mouth reached his ears. Had he just said that? Had he just meant it? To his own amazement, he realized that he had.

She collected her wits first. "It's fine," she assured him hastily. "Truly. I know that you don't mean it. What I am trying to say is that, in the heat of the moment—"

"Stop." Sebastian cut her off. She did, biting her lower lip in a way that was pure torture for him. "I have made you no promises," he continued roughly. "I cannot make them, no matter how much I want to. But although my confession may have been unintentional, it was no less real for that."

Amazement dawned in her marvelous, black-smudged eyes. "Th-thank you."

"No," he said with a tinge of irony, "thank *you*."

She wriggled an arm free and used it to pull his mouth down to hers. Her lips were small and soft and eager, opening for him, inviting him in to taste her. His body tightened, buzzing heat spearing down into his groin and spreading through the rest of him. Still kissing her, he slid a hand between them and began to pull up her skirts.

Sarah broke away with a startled noise. "Sebastian, we can't! Not here!"

"Who will see?" he challenged. "Who would come here, in the middle of a storm to the most neglected corner of the entire island?"

She glanced past him out the crack of the opening at the rain-lashed trees and grasses, and her expression went from one of alarm to that of slightly unwilling titillation. "Are you certain we won't be caught?" Her voice was doubtful, but her eyes begged to be convinced.

"Absolutely certain," he assured her.

"You had better not be wrong," she said in a dire tone, but she pulled his head down again and shifted her legs so that his hips were clasped invitingly between her thighs. With a groan, he buried his face against her neck, finding her favorite delicate, sensitive places and teasing them with his mouth until her roving hands went slack and she moved against him in small, delighted wiggles, tilting her hips invitingly against his groin. He kissed her again, full on the lips, and she responded with hot, welcoming desire. Reaching between her legs, he found the slit in her pantaloons and followed the tight, smooth muscle of her thigh to the damp nest of curls above. She shuddered as he pressed a finger into her hot slickness, driving deep as she clasped him. He stopped the movements of his mouth and hand, and she made a sound in her throat that was half laugh, half whimper, a plea and a promise of retribution combined.

He pulled back and looked at her face, dirt-smudged and taut with need, her eyes wide and dark and as inviting as sin. "This is the way I love to see you."

"Seba*stian*," she protested breathlessly, tilting her hips against his hand.

He slipped a second finger inside her, and she sucked in her breath sharply. Then, slowly, he began to move them, not thrusting them within her as he knew she expected but just moving, stroking.

"Oh, my," she said, her brows drawing hard together in a grimace of pleasure. "Oh, my . . ."

With a small chuckle, he put his thumb against the hard nub just above her folds of flesh, pausing just long enough for realization to dawn on her face before beginning to move that, too, circling it to the rhythm of the fingers inside her.

Then she truly did whimper. She lay there, tense, and he altered his rhythm until he found the one that quickened her breathing the most, dragging sounds of pleasure from her.

"Wait," she gasped suddenly. "It's coming too fast—"

And all at once, she screwed her eyes shut and arched back her neck, her hands balling into fists around the fabric of his coat, her lips closed hard against the ragged moans that escaped from her throat. He held her there for five seconds, ten, an eternity, his desire fed by her pleasure, but only when she had begun to relax minutely did he pause long enough to fumble the buttons of his trousers loose and free himself.

She was hot and slick, and he braced himself to thrust home—

—and met a tight resistance. He groaned.

"Slowly," Sarah said hoarsely. But he knew that by now. He put a tight rein on his impatience and pushed gently with each stroke, going deeper, until finally there was an infinitesimal loosening, and the muscles that had tried to keep him out now clasped him with welcoming intimacy.

"Oh, God, Sarah," he muttered. "I can't hold on long." And he drove into her, over and over, until she peaked again and he followed just a few moments later, glorious fire washing over him, pounding through him as he released himself into her rocking body.

And then the heat receded, leaving them both breathless and stunned.

"God, Sarah," Sebastian repeated numbly.

Slowly, he levered himself up, lurching to the other bier and sitting heavily again. Sarah sat up, then made a face and grabbed a corner of her petticoat to use between her legs. Her hair was tousled and matted, her face bright red and smudged even worse than before, but at that moment, Sebastian could not think of a time she had looked more appealing.

"Why does that happen sometimes?" he asked, knowing that he need not be any more specific. "Am I too rough? Too impatient?"

She sighed softly, a rueful expression on her face. "No. I have always been this way. Sometimes it is easy, and sometimes . . . it isn't. It's just the way that I am made, I think."

Her tone had a note of apology in it, and Sebastian

hastened to reassure her. "As long as I am not hurting you, you should not think of it as a bad thing." A small shudder ran through him at the memory of her wonderful tightness. "In fact, it has certain advantages."

"So I have been told." She was silent for a long moment. "I worked as a dress lodger from the time I turned thirteen until I was sixteen."

Sebastian hid his surprise. He had known she'd had a past, perhaps an extensive one, as many women from the lower classes did. But a dress lodger was a professional prostitute, one who rented an expensive dress and a room in a brothel from a madam in return for a portion of her earnings, displaying herself in one of a handful of semirespectable locations around London in order to attract men with middle-class wallets. "Forgive me for being presumptuous, but despite your flattering eagerness where I was concerned, you do not seem to be one who would choose that life."

Sarah's gaze went flat. "To be quite blunt, it was better than the beatings. When I turned twelve, the woman who owned my gang of kids died, and her fancy man set himself up as our new boss.

"Johnny, the fancy man, was a mean one. He had a hand in every racket, but with the kids, the only rule was that we had to bring him a pound a week or he'd beat us and make us sleep in the flooded cellar until we made it up. Most of the kids just stole it, even though it meant taking more risks, and a few of the best could beg it. But I have never been quick with my hands, and I'd been making enough money to satisfy the old woman by taking in piecework. But no one can make a pound a week sewing clothes."

"So you did what you must," Sebastian supplied.

Sarah pressed her lips together, her eyes bleak with old pain. "I did as little as I had to. I hadn't been a virgin since Dirty David who they warned all the kids about had caught me in a back alley the week before the old woman died, so I knew something of what to expect. It was hard to convince one of the madams to take me on since I am not pretty the way most of the dress lodgers are, but I soon got a list of regulars. Some liked me just for being a—a tight tail much of the time, as they called it, and others . . . well, they would pay for several hours and would tell me to pretend that I was fighting them. Those I dreaded the most because sometimes I would forget that I was pretending. . . ."

"You must have hated it," Sebastian said, aching for that haunted look in her eyes. Twelve. Sarah had been the same age as Adela when she was also raped, but there had been no one to exact revenge for the street rat she'd been. No one who even cared. He swallowed against the bile that rose in his throat.

"No," Sarah said. "No, if it had been that simple, I would not have so loathed myself. The moralizers like to believe that all prostitutes, deep down, feel a disgust at what they are doing, but that simply isn't true. There are women who say they're not whores but are forced to sell themselves every so often because honest work simply doesn't pay enough to feed a woman alone, much less a woman and her children. They're usually the cheapest because they cannot face the fact that they are putting a price on their own bodies—them and the women who are just a few drinks from their grave. But to the regulars, the professionals, it's a good living for just a few hours' work every day. Some truly enjoy it, but most simply don't mind or care. They can shut themselves away from what is happening to their bodies. Their bodies can be pleasured or abused, and to them, it's no different from a pleasant walk at a park or tripping down a few steps. It doesn't touch who they are."

Sebastian thought of all the whores he'd met during the misspent years of his life, the ones he hired by the carriageful to liven his parties, the ones who had arrived on the arms of his friends, the ones he himself had chosen. He had never before considered what made them choose their profession beyond the money. The common ones were coarse and often flamboyant, the courtesans and opera singers more

selective, coy, and reserved, but the practical, cynical deper-
sonalization of their bodies had been universal.

Sarah continued, "Whoring pays twice as well—at
least—as being a housekeeper, never mind a housemaid.
Did you know that? If some men are rough or have bad
breath or smell, well, cleaning out chamber pots isn't very
pleasant, either."

"You couldn't view it like that, though," Sebastian said.
Sarah, who felt everything too strongly, would never have
been able to separate herself in such a way.

"No," she agreed quietly. "But even I was far from the re-
formers' image of the fallen woman. Because the first thing
a whore learns is that when a man touches you, no matter
what your mind may be thinking, your body still reacts. It is
a muted reaction when there is no true passion, but when
you don't want to feel anything at all, when you just want it
to be over, that small pleasure is one of the most awful
things in the world. Not only could I not hide away inside of
myself from the unpleasant parts, the painful parts, I could
not keep myself from feeling pleasure. I didn't dread it because I suffered from the pangs of a guilty conscience—
quite the contrary. I dreaded it for the most selfish reasons:
because when I went into that room with a man, I always felt
that he walked out with a piece of myself."

"Why did you come to me, then?" Sebastian asked.

"Don't you understand yet?" She made a little gasping
sound that was something between a laugh and a sob. "You
were not looking for any whore who struck your fancy or
who might play out your private fantasy. For whatever reason, you wanted me."

"I wanted retribution," Sebastian said quietly.

"Intellectually, I am sure that you did," she agreed. "But
when you looked, you lusted, and that night it was for me,
not just any woman who could fulfill a twisted fantasy. No
man had ever done that before, and it was all like a beautiful dream to me." She shook her head, as if dismissing the
last ten minutes of their conversation, and continued on a

more practical note. "What I do not understand is that, thinking I was Mr. de Lint's whore, you did not take precautions against whatever diseases I might have."

Sebastian smiled wryly. "De Lint is many things, and among them, he is superbly fastidious."

"And you still thought I was his when you put your mouth . . . there?" A small flush crept up her cheeks.

"I had reason to know where he'd been for the past few nights," he said. "Also," he added, coming closer to the truth, "the thought of what I was about to do pained me. I wanted to give you something that could not be taken away."

She blinked, then shook her head. "I don't understand you sometimes, Sebastian."

He gave her a sideways smile. "If you always understood me, you would be the only one who did."

Chapter Eighteen

Sebastian and Sarah sat in silence as the minutes slid by in a gusting wash of rain. The world beyond their small, artificial cave was a portrait in gray and brown, all colors muted, softened, and cooled in contrast to the vivid wind-tossed energy of the dancing trees and fluttering grasses. Sebastian pulled Sarah into the crook of his arm, and there she sat, wrapped in his arms and his overcoat. A distant sensual awareness teased at her senses, a knowledge of the pleasantness of his body against hers. She enjoyed it as she enjoyed the rain, asking for no more than the moment. Gradually, the wind lessened, and then the rain slackened to a drizzle.

Sarah's stomach rumbled loudly, bringing her back to the present. "Shall we go?" she asked. She gave Sebastian an embarrassed smile. "This is lovely, but I ate only a couple of rolls for breakfast, and I'm beginning to feel rather peckish."

"Of course," he said immediately.

They both squeezed back through the gap, and Sarah put her crinolette on with much muttering and wriggling. Once her damp and mud-stained skirts were smoothed as best as they could be, they walked with some approximation of decorum down to the dock where they had left the boat several hours before.

The hearse barge and its attendant gondolas had left, and so Sebastian's boat bobbed alone in the murky, wind-chopped waters of the lagoon. Their two white-clad gondoliers lounged beside it, straightening as they approached. Sebastian called something in Italian, and the men replied.

"They waited out the storm inside the gondola," he translated.

"Oh," Sarah said. "I'm glad to know they didn't get wet on our account."

In companionable silence, they climbed back into the gondola, settling damply into the cushions. As they were borne back toward the Grand Canal, Sarah stared sleepily out through the gently fogging windows, letting her mind drift. The broken water lapped in mesmerizing, translucent waves only an arm's reach away, extending to a foreshortened horizon swallowed in the misting clouds. The clean scent of rain mixed with the organic smells of the lagoon, and she breathed in deeply.

She was brought sharply back to the present when Sebastian spoke.

"I intend to hold a masquerade at the Palazzo Contarini in three days."

"What?" Sarah blurted, straightening abruptly and staring at him, both her hunger and her sleepiness utterly forgotten. "You must be jesting!"

Sebastian looked utterly serious, showing no signs of having delivered a grand joke. "I had thought to rent a suite of rooms especially for the occasion, but you have done so magnificently with the renovations that I thought it would be a shame not to use our palazzo. Besides, I don't want to rob you of an opportunity to play the grand hostess for the night."

"There is so much to be done yet," she protested. "The entrance hall hasn't even been touched, and I just started on the dining room today. And that's disregarding all the specific arrangements, especially if you are intending on hosting a party of the magnitude of the one at the Palazzo Bellini."

He smiled at her with what seemed to her to be far too much sanguinity. "I have every confidence in you. You choose the theme and arrange for the decorations. I will handle the food and the entertainment myself, as well as deal with the staff over all the details that concern them and their duties. Hire another hundred workers if you need to—whatever it takes. I know you will acquit yourself admirably."

Sarah shook her head, unconvinced that such a thing was possible in such a short time. Despite her misgivings, she knew better than to argue, and she spent the rest of the trip in silence, her head spinning so with everything she must do that she started when Sebastian reached forward to open the felze door.

She blinked and realized they were at the Palazzo Contarini. She had been so absorbed in her thoughts that the gondoliers had moored their boat to its post and disappeared within the palazzo without her even noticing that they had stopped.

In the warm afternoon light and rain-scrubbed air, the building looked much less menacing than it had the first two times Sarah had seen it, the dirty marble quaint rather than cancerous, the uneven cobbles in front of it cheerful with pedestrians. Sebastian had to wait as a tired-looking nurse-maid with a passel of children walked by before he could step onto the pavement and offer Sarah his arm.

She took it, feeling slightly ridiculous to emerge in her stained and disarrayed clothing. She eyed Sebastian's torn coat, stepping aside to let a thin, stooped man shuffle past. She was certain she looked twice as—

Suddenly, the stooped man straightened and lunged toward Sebastian's back. Instinctively, Sarah jerked away with all her strength, her death grip on his arm hauling Sebastian with her. Only then did she see the dull flash of steel, and she opened her mouth to scream just as the knife struck and Sebastian let out a hoarse shout.

The combined force of their momenta slammed Sarah into the marble wall of the palazzo, Sebastian on top of her. She was still trying to draw breath back into her stunned body when Sebastian pushed off her and turned to face his assailant. The thin man looked at Sebastian for an instant, his eyes clearly measuring his height and the breadth of his shoulders. Then, before Sebastian could take more than a single step forward, the attacker dropped the knife and ran, his feet playing a desperate staccato on the pavement.

"Sebastian!" Sarah grabbed his arm. "Are you hurt?"

He grimaced. "Not badly, thanks to you." He looked around. A dozen people stood rooted on the pavement, staring at them. "Let's get inside."

Her heart still pounding, Sarah pressed her lips together hard and nodded, offering her arm for his support. Ignoring it, Sebastian entered the palazzo without assistance. They were met by a flurry of servants on the other side of the black doors, frightened and babbling.

"Mr. Garza," Sarah called as she spied the tall butler in the crowd. "Have some hot water, rags, and bandages fetched."

"Bring them to my office," Sebastian added.

"Are you certain you can walk that far?" Sarah whispered, keeping the fright out of her voice by sheer will alone.

"Absolutely," he assured her. He looked up sharply, and Sarah followed his gaze to see Gian descending the stairs.

"I was nearly killed just now," Sebastian said brusquely. "I want to know who it was."

Gian's expression didn't change. "Of course." Immediately, he began issuing orders in Italian, and the random milling of the servants became abruptly more ordered as several of the brawny men hurried outside and others set about less identifiable tasks.

Sebastian brushed past him up the stairs, Sarah following in his wake. As soon as he reached his office, he flopped into

his chair, grunted in pain, and then shifted so that his back
was not pressed against the padding.

"Let me look at it," Sarah said. "I've bandaged men up
after knife fights before." That was true enough, but when
she'd patched up Frankie, she'd felt worried and exasper-
ated—nothing like the soul-deep fear she felt now.

For a moment, Sebastian didn't move, staring blankly at
the wall in front of him as if it were the only thing in world,
and so Sarah put as much asperity as she could into her
voice to mask her concern and said, "You won't do anyone
any good if you faint from losing too much blood."

Slowly, he stood, unfastening the remaining buttons of
his overcoat. He stripped gradually, removing his coat,
waistcoat, shirt, and vest and dropping them to the floor.
Sarah winced when she saw the red of the blood against the
white linen of his shirt, but once his torso was bare, the in-
jury itself relieved her fears. It was no more than a thin red
line five inches long, scoring the taut muscles of his back.
Already the bleeding had slowed to an ooze except when his
movements pulled at the skin.

"I am going to need to bandage this," she said when the
water and cloths had been delivered. Sebastian made no response, nor did he react when she wet a rag and began to
bathe his wound, moving gently across the smooth expanse
of his back to cleanse away the sticky blood.

"I was right," Sebastian said finally as she paused to rinse
the cloth, his voice toneless. "I am being followed."

"What?" Sarah asked, pausing in her surprise. "When I
overheard you talking to Gian, I thought you assumed it was
ruffians and the incidents were coincidental."

"I had assumed ruffians or paranoia." His voice dripped
with self-mockery. "Clearly, I was mistaken on both
accounts."

"It can't be Mr. de Lint, can it?" Sarah asked with
trepidation.

"No," Sebastian said. "No, I'm certain he has no idea that
I am here."

"Then who else would follow you and try to have you killed?" Sarah wrung out the rag and set it on the edge of the basin, taking up the long strips of cloth. She stamped down her fear with determination—she would not be a hysterical woman, however much she wanted to. "Do you have so many enemies?"

"Six months ago, I would have said I had none," Sebastian said. He raked his fingers through his hair, wincing as the motion pulled at his cut. "I wanted to spare you the story of how I came to be here, but having just saved my life, if anyone has a right to know it, you do."

"I would like to hear it," Sarah said, keeping her voice neutral and her eyes fixed to the bandages as she wrapped them around his chest.

After a moment, he began, "De Lint was once my good friend, as you know." He laughed, a harsh, barking sound. "In fact, I was so blind then that I would not have thought it an insult for someone to comment that we were remarkably alike. After I came into my inheritance, we lived for a time with several other members of our set in Salamanca, where I had a typically meaningless yet torrid *affaire de coeur* with a courtesan of the town. Some five years later, I received a letter from her telling me that she was dying and that she wished me to care for her daughter Adela, whom she claimed to be mine as well. I sent a man to investigate, and he confirmed the woman was on her deathbed and that she did have a daughter of the right age with black hair and hazel eyes who could very well be mine. And so I promised to take her in, and when the woman died, I did just that."

Sarah continue to bandage his chest as he talked, not meeting his gaze, not daring to interrupt him in case he would not start again. But every word contained answers to the questions she had never even dared completely frame in the privacy of her own mind, and she drank in everything he said.

"I met the child and installed her at Amberley Park, one of my minor country estates. I gave her a governess, a nurse, and a few nursemaids, and I felt very smug at what a good, honorable man I was. I sent her presents every Christmas I remembered and occasionally when I was feeling munificent and something caught my eye. Once a year or so, I would swoop down upon her, shower her with gifts, and leave again. I hadn't visited in two years when I saw her last August. To be honest, I wasn't even going then to see her. I'd only come to Amberley because I needed to review some details of property improvement with my agent—though I took little care about the finer details of my finances, I was intelligent enough to review every major capital investment. I rediscovered Adela and learned that she was a pretty, charming, and intelligent young girl of twelve, and I felt pleased with myself all over again that I had stood by my word and provided so well for her."

The bitterness in his voice made Sarah bite her lip against the reassurances that sprang into her mind. Resolutely keeping her silence, she tied off the end of the bandage. Sebastian didn't seem to notice.

"While I was there, my cousin Daniel Collins and de Lint stopped by with some friends, and I had the idea of hosting a house party," he continued matter-of-factly. "On the first day, while everyone was still relatively sober and more or less decent, I had a lark and invited Adela down over the objections of her nurse to show everyone what a pretty little song she had performed for me on the day I arrived. Naturally, everyone declared themselves charmed and exclaimed over my generosity and good nature for taking her in, and just as naturally, I assumed that everyone forgot about her as quickly as I did when I dismissed her again."

Sarah felt sick, certain now where the story was going, but still she did not interrupt.

"Two nights later, when the party had turned much wilder, I was walking along the corridor to my bedroom when I heard screaming and went to investigate. It was the nurse, wailing and holding Adela, who was covered in blood and in a state of shock. I cannot describe to you what I felt in that moment. Everything that I had been for the last thirteen years and more was suddenly revealed to me in its egocentric horror, for I had brought to harm the only good thing I might have done in my life. The nurse had been lured away by one of the whores of the party who matched the description of a woman de Lint had arrived with—and who had at least a passing resemblence to you, as well, which I why I thought you must be she."

My scars, Sarah thought, feeling sick. He'd seen her scars and had assumed she was the woman the nurse meant.

"After the attentions of the doctor, Adela recovered enough to recount what she could remember in the darkness of the nursery and the confusion of the assault," Sebastian continued. "It was little enough, but her description was clear, and the only man in the household who fit it was de Lint."

It had been ten years now, but suddenly Sarah could taste her own fear again, smell the stench on Dirty David's breath as he hauled her into that alley while everyone on the street looked the other way. The foulest curse she knew flew from her lips.

Sebastian physically started at the sound, focusing on her with an astonished look on his face.

"I know what I would like to do to the man," she spit. "Ten minutes alone with a dull knife . . ."

"I had him arrested instead." Sebastian's scowl went black with remembered rage. "During the inquest, he said she seduced him. The case never even went to trial. It was my negligence that allowed this to happen in the first place, and then . . . then I dragged her name through the mud by publicizing it in the courts, and all for nothing. Afterward, I confronted de Lint at the Whitsun Club, and when I left, I discovered in the most unpleasant way that my gig had been sabotaged. I broke three ribs and very nearly pierced a lung, and I hit my head so hard that the doctor feared that I would never wake up or, if I did, that I would suffer from permanent mental impairment. Thank God, I recovered without incident. But during my convalescence, I realized how I had used Adela, keeping my good treatment of her in the back of my mind as a great redeeming virtue to offset whatever selfish and feckless urges I otherwise wasted my life fulfilling. I had failed her twice, but then I swore that I would avenge her upon de Lint and honor my obligations to her in the process. So I had it announced that I had slipped from a coma into death even as I slipped into another life. And I followed de Lint here."

"What are you going to do to him?" Sarah asked, her head reeling from the confession. "You surely could have killed him a hundred times by now."

"If I killed him, it would be his due for attempting to kill me. But he has indelibly stained the rest of Adela's life, and I want to do no less than that to his."

"So what are you going to do to him?" she repeated.

"That, you don't need to know," Sebastian said flatly. Sarah didn't challenge him. He stretched his back experimentally, sending a ripple across the muscles, his expression flat. "What I am concerned about now is who is trying to kill me. It can't be that de Lint has uncovered who I am. He is not that subtle. But very few people know I am still alive. A few servants and employees—and my cousin Daniel, who is my heir presumptive and has been playing the earl for nearly a month now. And only one of them would benefit if I died in truth."

"Your cousin," Sarah said, aching for the bleakness in his voice.

"Yes. The only man who stood by me without question these past six months and more." Sebastian shook his head slowly. "I don't believe it. I can't believe it. Perhaps it is de Lint, after all. I've misjudged him before. But why would he try something so indirect when directness would easily serve?"

Sarah did not answer, for she had no answer to give. Suddenly, Sebastian snorted, breaking the silence.

"Why must someone be trying to kill Lord Wortham?

Why couldn't someone be trying to kill Señor Guerra instead? That is both the most obvious and the most sensible of all—that it is a Venetian procurer, angry at the sudden competition. If Daniel wanted me dead, he could have done it in England, and no one would have been the wiser," Sebastian said firmly. "All of the men who have tried to attack me thus far have been native, as far as I can tell. If I have unwittingly infringed upon the territory of some powerful local criminal, he would naturally send his own thugs after me."

"What exactly have you been doing?" Sarah asked.

Sebastian gave the question a dismissive shake of the head. "Nothing that I deserve to be murdered over, that's for certain. What's important now is bringing this to a satisfactory conclusion as soon as possible so that Señor Raimundo Guerra can neatly disappear and not be hunted by insane Venetian assassins." He raised an eyebrow. "If we wait too long, one might get lucky. Or buy a revolver."

Sarah shuddered. "When will your plans come to an end?"

"Why, in three days, of course," he said. "At the masquerade."

She felt a lurch in the pit of her stomach. Three days? That soon? And when those had passed—then what? "Is there nothing left to be done except for that?"

"Very little," he said confidently. "There is only one obstacle of any significance at all."

"And what is that?" Sarah pursued, not certain if she wanted to be assured that it was trivial or have reason to hope that it might be a serious impediment.

He regarded her steadily for a long moment before speaking, as if deciding whether he should confide in her at all. "I need a bottle of de Lint's cologne," he finally said.

"His cologne?" Sarah repeated stupidly.

"Yes," Sebastian said. "I have been attempting to get it from someone within his household, which has so far proven impossible."

Suddenly, everything fell into place. In England, Mr. de Lint had escaped prosecution because he was a man with many prominent friends and there had been no completely incontrovertible proof, but in Italy, with a staged "rape" of a willing child-whore and a man who looked enough like de Lint to fool dozens of eyewitnesses, it would be easy enough to secure a conviction. Every detail that could be brought to bear that would make the false Mr. de Lint more like the real one was to be paid the utmost attention, and the cologne would be a master touch.

"Lady Anna," she breathed. "That's what you wanted her for. To get you Mr. de Lint's cologne, his clothing, whatever else you might need. Bribing a servant to bring in flowers and gifts is one thing, but they wouldn't steal for you. Lady Anna, though, wouldn't think of it as stealing. She would see it all as a game."

"Most perceptive," Sebastian murmured, his eyes hooded. "She is not cooperating at this moment, but Gian will talk her around."

"I am sure he will," she assured him, remembering how giddy Lady Anna had been over the Italian. In the light of her realization of Sebastian's full plan, a worried weight lifted from her that she had become so accustomed to that she hardly realized it was there. How could she ever have doubted his intentions toward Lady Merrill and Lady Anna? He was no monster. When he had pursued her, it was only because he'd been certain she was the woman the nurse had described. She put a hand on his shoulder. "It will turn out well in the end, Sebastian. Just wait and see."

His eyes were shadowed and fathomless as he looked down at her. "I haven't your optimism, Sarah, but I do hope that you are right."

Chapter Nineteen

Sebastian stared out his window, his swift, circling thoughts a counterpoint to the stillness of the placid canal below. Sunset gilded the black water in orange and gold, reflecting off the white walls of the surrounding palazzos.

He should be thinking over his plans. He should be checking every detail in his mind, looking for any flaw, making sure that every possible outcome was covered. But in the end, he must rely upon chance, and the time for planning was long past. Thoughts of his revenge, too, stirred the uncomfortable welter of emotions that he had been forced to battle since first deciding on this course—the appropriate grim, disinterested satisfaction, of course, but under it, the rage and the bitterness and the joy at the thought of de Lint's disgrace that Sebastian loathed within himself and yet could not eradicate.

Sebastian knew he should also be considering the attacks on him and what they might mean, but his mind shied away from that train of thought. As he told Sarah, he had settled upon the belief that a leader of one of the local criminal elements wanted to dispose of the competition that "Señor Guerra" represented, and that certainly made the most logical sense, but a part of him still feared something more sinister than that, a closer betrayal, and every time his knife wound twinged, he felt a deeper pain and saw the image of Daniel's earnest, rabbitlike face, exhorting him to give up his plan. How sincere had his cousin been then? Had playing the earl changed him, or had he even then been wondering if he could make it a permanent elevation?

There was an end to it all in sight. Sebastian clung to that thought, a relief and a whip sting at once. Soon, he could surrender this obsession that was becoming more distasteful to him by the minute. He could escape the dangers of smiling assassins and become an earl once again—and he could trade the memory-shadowed canals of Venice for the bright, sweet openness of a quiet English country estate.

And what would become of Sarah then? Would he have to let her go, or would she come to England with him? She thought she knew the whole truth now—could she forgive him when she learned she did not?

He stood as the sun slipped finally out of sight, leaving the view outside his window in shadow. The noises of Sarah issuing orders and the servants scurrying to carry them out had provided a backdrop to his private reflections, but now he realized that silence had once again descended over the palazzo.

Sebastian stepped onto the empty upper portego and crossed to Sarah's bedchamber door. Golden lamplight made a soft glow under it, and so he gave a brief knock before going in.

Sarah sat in the center of her bed with her dark green coverlet pulled up to her waist, balancing a heavy book on her knees as her cat curled in a smug gray ball at her feet. Her hair was pulled back into a severe nighttime braid, her face scrubbed pink and bare of all traces of cosmetics. She looked up at him as he entered, her dark eyes wide in surprise. He realized abruptly that he hadn't seen her like that since she'd arrived at the palazzo. Even at night, she had always been softly perfumed, subtly powdered, the disarray of dishabille artfully enhanced with ribbons and the application of hair tongs.

And he had never even noticed, taking things as she chose to present them. Never wondered how or why. Never, he discovered as he looked deeper, particularly cared.

But now that he saw her there, more naked in her frilled and ruffled nightdress than she had been in his arms at any time over the past fourteen nights, he wanted to throw her paint pots and powder out the window. She looked painfully real sitting there, raw and honest . . . and utterly desirable. It was a strange realization to make since Sebastian could still, if pressed, point out her flaws, list each of the imperfections that made her less than beautiful—her scars, of course, and the nose that was a trifle too long, the chin that was a shade too pointed, and the lips that were fashionably small but a touch too full. He could enumerate each, and yet she was still everything he could want her to be.

"I apologize, sir," Sarah said, setting her book aside hastily. "After what happened this afternoon, I did not think that you would come to me tonight. Let me call Maria and make myself presentable to you."

"No, Sarah," he said flatly, sitting down on the edge of the bed and turning to face her. "You are perfect as you are. And quit calling me 'sir.'" He quirked half a smile. "I am sure that if it were a common enough occurrence to be put in etiquette books, there would be a rule against saying 'sir', to a man whose life you have just saved."

"Oh, I did no such thing," she said automatically, or so it seemed to him, her brow furrowing in rejection of the thought. "I didn't have time to think at all. I am sure you would have—"

"—been neatly skewered," he finished for her. "And I and my nearly whole skin thank you that I was not."

"Well, then," she said, looking as though she was containing herself from further protest only with an extreme effort. "In that case, you are welcome, Sebastian."

Sebastian was silent for a long moment as various desires warred inside him. He was not sure what he wanted to say to her or why he had come. He found himself instinctively tracing the shape that her body made under the blanket with his gaze, remembering how those curves looked naked, how her skin felt against his.

When he met her eyes again, they were bright with awareness, her cheeks flushed faintly. He smiled in recognition of what was between them, but he knew he wanted more out of this night than just another quick tumble, however enjoyable, and so he ignored the simmer within him and forced himself to speak insouciantly.

"How have you progressed in your plans for the masquerade?"

"I have decided on a theme, if it meets your approval," Sarah said, looking slightly shy as she always did at the mention of any of her work. "I wish to do Egypt."

Sebastian raised an eyebrow. "Any reason why?"

"Only that it allows so many different opportunities for people to choose their characters and time periods," Sarah said. She gave him a small smile. "And it seemed exciting and exotic without being either too crass or too obscure. If I had chosen China, I might have confused people, never mind that I myself would have had no clue where to start. If I had chosen Arabia or Turkey, I would have certainly offended someone or . . . misled others as to the type of event you were hosting."

"Fair enough," Sebastian acknowledged, amused at her delicate phraseology. "I will have announcements sent tomorrow to elaborate upon the invitations."

Sarah looked stricken. "I hadn't realized that you would have already sent out the invitations. I can change it—"

"No, Sarah," he said gently. "Your idea is good. There is no inconvenience."

"Are you certain?" she asked doubtfully.

"Absolutely."

"Good," she said, looking disproportionately relieved.

"Sarah, why are you so terrified of doing something wrong?" Sebastian asked with some exasperation. "Surely you know by now that I won't be angry if by some strange chance you actually do make a mistake one day."

Defensiveness flashing across her face, she started to open her mouth, no doubt to issue a quick denial, but then she paused. After a moment, she finally said, "I don't know. I am not afraid of you—or anyone, to be perfectly frank. I just don't like being wrong. I shouldn't be wrong. Mistakes can almost always be avoided with enough care and enough preparation. *Mistakes* are wrong. They are . . . bad." She shook her head. "I do not mean to sound simple, but it is how I have always felt."

"Mistakes are human, Sarah, and so are you," Sebastian said gently.

She looked up at him with her soul in her eyes. "But what if I don't want to be human if that is what it means? How can I be happy with myself when there is still so much wrong with me?"

The words echoed so closely with the feelings that arose whenever Sebastian thought of de Lint's disgrace that he was temporarily at a loss. "I don't know," he admitted. "As well as anyone, I suppose." He shrugged. "You seem to have forgiven me for a mistake that I am certain is worse than anything you have done in your life. Forgiving yourself for any error you might make should be an easy task after that."

Sarah dropped her eyes and bit her lip for a long moment, studying her knees intently. His words reminded her, inevitably, of his entire purpose for being in Venice—a purpose that would be fulfilled in three days. "You will be going back to England when this is over."

"Yes," he said simply.

No *Unless you want me to stay.* No *And I would like you to come with me.* He would be leaving, then—and she would not.

Thoughts from the past two weeks that she had barely allowed herself to entertain coalesced in an instant. Now that she had discovered the joys of commanding her own household and enjoying the pleasures of the world, Sarah could not return to a life in service, homeless and poor; nor could she bear the thought of becoming Maggie's dependent again. "I do not want to return to being a lady's companion," she blurted. "Nor would I want to be a governess, even if such a thing were possible."

Sebastian's elegant face froze. "What do you want, then?" His tone was cool, almost indifferent.

Sarah licked her lips nervously. "First, I must know. Everything you've given me—it is truly mine, yes?"

"Of course," he said, his green eyes dark.

Some of her tension fell away. "Then I will at least have a start at a new life. I said a week ago that what a woman needs is family and reputation. I believe that I now might add money and connections to that list, which together can be used to obtain the first two."

"What are you suggesting?" Still there was no emotion in his tone or expression.

Sarah dropped her eyes again, smoothing the fabric of the counterpane over her knees. "I want to see more of the world. I want to live in lovely places and to own beautiful things. I want to meet dazzling people." She took a deep breath. "In short, I believe that I would like to be a courtesan."

"A whore?" Sebastian straightened abruptly. "After everything you have been through? After what you did to escape?" He sounded incredulous—and angry.

"Not a whore," she countered, her head jerking up defensively. "A professional lover. What I am to you now, though I do not expect such generosity or living arrangements with any future . . . future intimates." He was still glaring at her, and she felt a defensive flush creep up her cheeks. "I know I am no beauty—that even if Maria's rejuvenators work miracles, I will never be a beauty. But I have noticed how men look at me now, and I have realized that while beauty might be an advantage, a lack of it is not as devastating as I had thought." She returned his frown with one of her own. "I had thought the pox marks on my face were as disfiguring as if I had been born without a nose. It is stupid, I know, because now I realize that I have seen worse left from a bad case of the spots, and no one can know for certain where the scars came from unless my behavior betrays me. And even then, who cares where a courtesan came from once she is in your bed? It's not like I am going to be any man's wife."

"No," he agreed, an odd expression crossing his face. "No, no one would expect that."

Sarah forced herself to forge ahead. "You have already given me enough wealth to set out on my own. With that, I can buy myself an appropriate mother or maiden aunt for company and all the respectability that goes with such assumed trappings. What I would ask for in addition are connections. Letters of recommendation to men of the world, preferably scattered about Europe, who are of pleasant demeanor and appropriate tastes. If I meet one and we do not take to each other, then perhaps he might introduce me into the proper segment of society so that I might find someone for whom I am better suited."

Sebastian kept his silence, just watching her, and Sarah gave him a fierce look. "A man of my station might seek a rewarding and remunerative professional career, but I cannot," she said. "I have tried other paths to a satisfying life, and they have all come to nothing. If I am to have independence, I must have either a great deal of money to live the rest of my life upon or a protector of my choosing. Only one of those is possible."

The seconds ticked by, and still Sebastian did not speak, his face drawn into an inscrutable mask, studying her intently. What was he thinking? Was he angry with her for suggesting that he help her more than he had already? Sarah admitted to herself that he would be entirely within his rights if he were, but she stubbornly kept her silence.

Finally—finally—he spoke. "Is that what you want?"

"It is the only thing that I reasonably might have," Sarah

replied, drawing her knees up closer to her body, reflexively warding against the old feelings of helplessness.

"God, Sarah—" He broke off those ragged words and then shook his head. "If that is what you want, I will give it to you. I am not now in a position to offer you more."

A sad relief coursed through her at the words that were both an assertion of their end together and a promise for her future. "Thank you," she said. Impulsively, she reached for his hand to draw him to her. "Thank you."

He took the invitation and kissed her, visibly wincing as the skin pulled taut across the cut on his back. Sarah opened herself to him, pulling him in closer, trying to tell him with her body what she dared not express in words—what he meant to her, what this time meant to her. She only hoped he understood.

A long while later, Sarah lay in the darkness of her bed-chamber, staring at the tall, white ceiling far above her as Victor Emmanuel purred at her feet. Sebastian was stretched out next to her, his breathing slow and regular in sleep. In their weeks together, this was the first time he had ever stayed with her after they made love. She savored the sense of the long warmth of him only a few inches away, familiar and yet foreign, a comfort and a bitter irony, for her future was laid out before her now, and it did not include him.

That future was brighter than she had once dreamed of, and so she should have no regrets. Their paths were simple, clean. After Sebastian's revenge was exacted, they would part ways. He would go to back to England, and she . . . she would begin the new career through which she could make her way in the world.

She tried to imagine what her life would be like, dining on Lake Geneva with one handsome protector and then flitting away whenever she got bored to Nice or Brussels or Spa. She could imagine the houses and flats that she would take, could envision the few carefully selected pieces of furniture that she would order carried with her from one residence to the next. The servants, the dresses, the famous sights, the thrilling adventures—all those were vivid in her mind's eye. But every time she tried to imagine the face on the obligatory man next to her, she saw only Sebastian's.

Sarah pulled her mind from thoughts of distant possibilities and forced it back to the present. After all, nothing was certain. Sebastian's plan for the masquerade might fail. Some detail for de Lint's stand-in might be unconvincing, or de Lint himself might not come, or he might escape Sebastian's distraction and be at the wrong place at the wrong time.

Sarah thought of the cologne, the one thing Sebastian was still missing. If Lady Anna didn't get it, then that would be one more piece of the puzzle that wasn't right. And would that be good or would it be bad? From a purely selfish point of view, Sarah wasn't certain. Perhaps Sebastian would stay and try again, keeping her with him until he succeeded. Or perhaps he would give up and leave her, anyway. Sarah wasn't even sure she wanted Mr. de Lint to be punished by Sebastian. What he had done was heinous, horrible beyond imagining, and yet at the same time, something about Sebastian's exacting such a personal revenge chilled a little piece of her soul. Something felt wrong, something was off in the whole scheme, and although Sarah could not quite place the source of her unease, the unsettled feeling remained.

It was the cologne. That must be it. The uncertainty of not having the cologne was preying on her mind, on her divided desires, wanting to help Sebastian, wanting to hinder him. She recoiled from the second thought. Why would she ever hurt him? Why wouldn't she do anything in her power to help him? After all, after everything that he had done for her, expiation or no, didn't she owe him that?

Suddenly, her mind retrieved the image of Mr. de Lint holding an empty cut-glass scent bottle as he strolled into Lady Merrill's cabin on the *Serafina*. She was certain she'd recognize it if she saw it again. And as for the scent itself—

that was burned as indelibly into her as his expression when he had her cornered in the empty parlor at the Palazzo Bovolo.

Tomorrow, she must shop for supplies for the masquerade, but she was determined that she would also find another bottle of that cologne somewhere in Venice and present it to Sebastian. Whatever misdeed of his had brought her to his palazzo, he had given her far more than she deserved, and she would set aside all of her private doubts and vacillations and give him a demonstration of her faith in him to pay back all the generosity he had shown her.

Having made that determination, Sarah closed her eyes and settled deeper into the pillows, preparing her mind for sleep.

Chapter Twenty

Sebastian had already left when Sarah rose the next morning, and so she ate a hurried breakfast and went on a whirlwind trip through the city, visiting every shop that Maria thought might sell Mr. de Lint's cologne. Even at their frantic pace, it was two hours before Sarah recognized both a bottle and scent, but she felt it was well worth her time as she paid for a vial and slipped it into her handbag.

She spent the rest of the morning ordering everything that was needed for the masquerade in just two nights. Her last stop was the dressmaker's, where her own costume was being created at breathtaking speed for an even more breathtaking price. Arranging for work to begin on her dress had been the only trip she had made the last afternoon after the attack on Sebastian. It was self-indulgent, but she could not regret it.

Sarah stepped lightly from the gondola in front of the elegant shop entrance, and Maria joined her on the pavement, Gian following them like a shadow. Since the attack yesterday, Sebastian had insisted that she take two gondoliers and the manservant with her at all times, with the additional proviso that Gian never let her out of his sight whenever she was outside.

She and Maria entered the shop, Gian standing guard by the door. The proprietor greeted her effusively, and in short order she was whisked to a back room and clad in the half-finished dress as a dozen tailors and seamstresses considered and tweaked and discussed the creation.

Anticipating Sebastian's approval of her plan, Sarah had ordered an extravagant and slightly scandalous sheath. She suspected that most of the guests would choose the pleated and draped styles that people thought of as typically Egyptian or perhaps the Roman fashions of Cleopatra's day or even modern Arabian wear. But she remembered an Egyptian dress from an illustration she'd seen in a book in Lord Edgington's library when she had still been serving as Maggie's lady's maid. It had been a form-fitted tube, constructed of a solid material in brilliant bands of different patterns and colors. She could not remember now what the material had been or even if she could have told from such a small color plate, but she had decided to order an imitation of it encrusted completely in tiny glass beads, which was certainly not authentic but would create a dazzling effect in the candlelight. She had no intentions of copying the dress as it had originally been constructed—as she recalled, the skirt was unseemly narrow, never mind that it left the wearer's breasts completely bare—so she had allowed herself a very liberal interpretation of the design, raising the bodice, adding cap sleeves, widening the skirt slightly, and adding a ruched silk overskirt on top of it. The dressmaker swore he'd had twenty people working night and day on it, and looking at how far it had come since the day before, Sarah believed him.

After the fitting was complete, Sarah got dressed again behind a privacy screen and returned to the front room to discuss the timing of the delivery of the dress with the proprietor.

"Do not worry yourself, signorina," he assured her. "It will be there in time."

Sarah nodded in satisfaction and was about to leave when the shop door opened. She glanced at it automatically, expecting to see Gian come in to attempt to hurry things along as he had been doing all morning. Instead, she locked eyes with Lady Anna.

After a long, shocked moment of silence, Lady Anna squealed, "It *is* you!"

The Miss Mortons, who had been busily bickering as they entered behind her, looked up at her exclamation. Their eyes widened, Miss Effie's mouth actually falling open a fraction of an inch.

"I hardly recognize you," Lady Anna gushed. "You look so pretty!"

"Thank you," Sarah said stiffly, reminding herself that the girl meant no insult.

Lady Anna seemed not to notice her coolness. "Grand-mamma has been so worried. She will be glad to know you're doing so well."

Sarah felt the words like a blow. Lady Merrill was no naïve girl—she would be able to guess quite well what Sarah's new occupation must be. "Please don't tell her." To her amazement, the words were firm, more a command than a plea.

Lady Anna must have sensed the change, too, for she paused and frowned instead of dismissing her concern. "If you absolutely insist," she said in the slightly petulant tone she used with her grandmother when she didn't get her way. "I don't see why not, though."

"Just . . . don't," Sarah said even more firmly.

"Very well, then." The girl's expression cleared, burning with curiosity. "What have you been doing since you left us? Working as a salesgirl?"

"No," Sarah said, allowing a hint of asperity to creep into her voice. "At the moment, I am shopping. A friend was kind enough to take me in."

"A friend? Is that who Antonio was waiting for out there? You?" Her eyes sparked with jealousy and disbelief. "He ducked around the corner when I came because we cannot risk being seen together, you know, but my heart would recognize him anywhere."

She must mean Gian, Sarah thought, discovering that even the brunt of the girl's scorn was not enough to shake her anymore. "No," she said, thinking quickly. "Antonio is a friend of my friend. My friend couldn't come, and so Antonio offered to escort me—with my chaperone, of course." Sarah nodded to Maria. "There has been an alarming increase in thieves and pickpockets recently."

"I know," Lady Anna said enthusiastically, appearing to take Sarah's dramatic elevation in station in stride. "We had to take two gondolas because two big menservants came along to protect us from such ruffians." She gave Sarah a considering look. "So you know Antonio."

"I see him at times," Sarah hedged. Now that she had the cologne, she suspected that "Antonio" would promptly disappear from Lady Anna's bedroom window, and she did not wish to imply that she knew anything more than what Lady Anna had told her about the situation between them. "I did not know that he was your . . . your beau."

"Of course not!" Lady Anna declared. "He is both discreet and noble. Is he truly a count? Does he own a great palace of his own? Oh, you must tell me more about him! I hardly know anything because there are so many matters about which it would be far too rude to ask." Her eyes lit up. "And letters— you must carry letters between us, of course!"

Sarah's stomach sank at that demand. "But you see him every night, don't you?"

"That isn't enough!" the girl insisted. "During the day, when I'm away from him, sometimes I think that I might die." She said the last word in a dire whisper, as if even mentioning it could make it happen.

Sarah smothered a smile at the shallowness of the idea of thinking herself near death due to nothing more than a few hours' absence from anyone. Why, even when Sebastian disappeared mysteriously on one of his inexplicable errands, she missed him reflexively, almost like a piece of herself, but she hardly had any thoughts of prematurely expiring. "No, Lady Anna. I cannot be your confidante in this."

"Oh, but you must!" Lady Anna protested.

"No," she repeated, frowning at the spoiled girl. Another solution occurred to her. "Do you know the statue in Campo Manin?"

"The man with the lion with furry wings? I think so," Lady Anna said doubtfully, a touch of petulence in her voice.

"You can leave a message before noon every day, and I will ask Antonio to check it then and send a reply before nightfall," Sarah said patiently. "Surely you can take a short constitutional twice a day."

"Oh, I knew you would be a good friend from the moment I met you!" Lady Anna exclaimed, aglow at the romance of the suggestion. "What a fantastic idea. Thank you ever so much!"

"You are quite welcome," Sarah said, feeling a touch of pity for the girl. But only a very, very small one.

As Lady Anna turned away from her as if she'd ceased to exist, Sarah realized that she didn't feel much of anything at all for the girl—no guilt, no burdensome sense of duty, no smothered aversion. And that was the best Sarah had felt in her company since she had met her more than a month before.

With an unfamiliar sense of satisfaction, Sarah left the shop and went to find Gian for their return to the Palazzo Contarini.

Sebastian opened the door to Sarah's parlor, expecting to find her inside as he so often did. But the room was empty except for her cat, which had draped itself luxuriantly across its favorite chair. He considered hunting Sarah down, but he knew the urge was both selfish and unfair. Whatever confidence he had in her organizational ability, he knew he had given her a daunting task when he asked her to host the masquerade, and she needed time—time without the distraction of his presence—to make and execute her plans.

It wasn't her fault that what he really wanted was to talk

to her after the disturbing ride back from the Casinò Giallo that morning. He didn't know what he could say to her that would make sense of it. That now he was worried about his own sanity? It wouldn't be so far from the truth, for his paranoia had so affected his mind that he could have sworn he'd seen his cousin Daniel in at least a dozen men's faces for half an instant before he realized that they weren't him, after all. Why, when he passed one side canal, he'd even seen old Whitby's tottering step in the gait of an elderly Venetian man as he disappeared around the corner.

Sebastian sat and played a soft scale upon the piano as he tried to sort through his thoughts. His fears were bad enough, but he knew they weren't the real reason he both desperately wished to see Sarah and yet dreaded every minute with her. The truth was that he was consumed by a sense of time running out—for his plan, for her, for them. And the idea of their relationship now having a definite end disturbed him more than he'd thought possible.

In two nights, she would be done with him. Finished forever. It was sufficiently clear that she'd accepted a future without him, and he had no reason to believe that the events of the masquerade would do anything to convince her to take another path that he couldn't even offer to her until his plans had come to an end. So even as half his mind stewed over all his doubts and fears about his plan and the attacks, the other half dwelt upon every memory of every minute that he could conjure up with her, the significant and inconsequential, the intimate and commonplace, each competing for a sliver of his fragmented attention.

It's not like I am going to be any man's wife, she had said the night before. Those words had sparked an idea in him, an idea so ludicrous and impossible that he could not let himself think about it. She would never forgive him, anyhow, not when she knew the entire truth, when she realized how he had let her deceive herself.

As his mind circled, his hands began to move across the keyboard, following the sheet music and the memory of

Sarah's hours at the piano without a conscious thought, echoing his thoughts and his torn heart.

Sarah stepped into the palazzo with the bottle of cologne in her hands. As she started up the stairs, the sounds of piano music met her ears, and she hastened her steps, following them to her parlor. She opened the door, and the unsullied sound washed over her, stopping her dead.

It was amazing. Vaguely, she recognized the piece that she had been laboring so long over, but now it had become something almost unrecognizable. Every note that had been lifeless under her hands now sang, sparkling one moment, clashing the next, dancing and whirling in joy or agony. Sometimes, there were stumbles—sometimes, there were mistakes—but the sheer energy and vitality and beauty of it took her breath away.

And in the center of it all was Sebastian, his hands moving lightly over the keyboard as he frowned abstractedly at the music in front of him. The painful gloriousness of it washed over her, and with it the realization that she would never be able to coax that kind of music from any instrument in her life, no matter how hard she strove or desired.

Just as that hit her, the last notes died away in a wistful falter, and he looked up and saw her there.

Sarah swallowed. "That . . . that was wonderful," she managed. "I never imagined it could sound like that."

Sebastian smiled slightly and said, "My mother used to complain that if I had half as much dedication as I did soul, I would be the finest pianist in all England." He ran his hands lightly over the ivory keys. "I haven't played in years."

Sarah swallowed against the bile in her throat. "When I played, you must have thought—" She broke off, recalling why she had come, shoving everything else aside. "I have brought you something," she said instead.

She crossed to the piano bench and pressed the vial into his unresisting hand. "I found it today, while I was shopping.

I'd seen Mr. de Lint's bottle before, on the ship, and when he tried to—when he attacked me, I smelled the scent of it. I don't think I could forget it even if I wanted to." She stopped, realizing that she was babbling, trying to drown out the voices that still rang with the echoes of music inside her head.

He stared at the bottle for a moment, his eyebrows drawn together, before his expression cleared. "This is his same cologne?"

"Yes," Sarah said. "Now your plan will be more likely to work because you have everything you need."

His hands closed over it. "Thank you," he said, but to her it sounded like a farewell.

"You're welcome," she replied, and then she fled from the room as tears overwhelmed her.

She dashed across the portego and into her bedchamber, shutting the door behind her as she flung herself on the bed. Why had she ever thought that she could sound like that? How could she have deluded herself that all she needed was a chance? The gulf between her and Sebastian had never been clearer—he came from a world of refinement, generations of gentlemen and ladies behind him.

As for her, it was true what everyone had always said, wasn't it? *Blood will tell.* As hers had with her clumsiness at the piano she'd been so delighted in. She cried harder. What more was she deluding herself with? Was she just as clumsy with all the ideas in the books she struggled to understand? Did Sebastian secretly laugh at her—or, worse, pity her?

She bit her bottom lip as a sob shook her. That was the heart of it. The night before, Sebastian had not asked her to stay, to come with him when he left Venice. Why? What was wrong with her? The question had been lurking unrecognized in the corner of her mind, but the music had served as a trigger, forcing her to confront the truth—that after all of Sebastian's protestations of her worth, even after the tenderness he had expressed on San Michele, she was still not good enough to be more than a temporary mistress.

It was just as well that she was to be a courtesan, she told herself. She should end any delusions about what her life might have for her. She would rise as far as any woman of her background and breeding could ever expect to. And she would be content.

But that thought only made her weep harder, and it was a long, long time before she left her room to face the rest of the day and her future.

Chapter Twenty-one

Dazzling.

Despite the lingering feeling that she was made of spun glass, part of Sarah still marveled at what had somehow come together in the space of three days.

The portego of the first piano nobile glowed. A canvas mural of Egyptian figures covered the walls between bottom-heavy false columns painted in a lotus pattern. Discovering the impossibility of obtaining real lotus blossoms or water lilies to decorate the rooms, Sarah had remembered Sebastian's predilection for true lilies and had ordered them by the sheaf. Now they hung everywhere, their flame-colored blossoms scenting the air. Bouquets were tied to every column and bedecked every door, and red and orange garlands swayed across the ceiling, winding around chandeliers below rich, billowing lengths of midnight-blue silk that streamed along the ceiling and down to the floor along one end of the portego.

That dark wall of silk had been Sebastian's idea, and it cut off a dozen feet of the canal end of the portego from the rest of the room—for the grand entertainment, as he darkly put it. Within the space, a second cascade of draperies concealed the ceiling, the loggia, and the side walls, so that except for a single door that led to a side parlor, it was like being within a huge, lightless tent. Sarah felt a small shiver of unease run up her spine as the fabric belled softly in the faint breeze coming through from the garden side.

Pushing away her trepidation, she continued down the grand staircase to the entrance hall, which was arrayed in equal extravagance, her dancing slippers sliding softly across the cool marble as her heavy beaded skirts dragged behind her. To the elaborate pattern of azure and emerald beads, she had added as adornment only two clusters of orange lilies, one threaded through her intricately braided hair, the other fastened to her right wrist over her short white glove.

At the bottom of the stairs, she stopped and tied her mask on, the plain white papier-mâché marked only by a graceful imitation of black kohl around the eyeholes.

"Sarah." The voice was an admiring breath, and she turned to find Sebastian stepping out of the doorway that led to the kitchens to meet her. He was dressed in his Mohammedan costume again, now a contemporary Egyptian rather than a Moor, his mask dangling from one hand. His eyes burned as he surveyed her, the elegant lines of his face taut with a tangle of emotions she could not begin to unravel. She was struck, as she often was at unguarded moments, at just how beautiful a man he was. His wide brow, the lean, patrician lines of his face, rescued from harshness by the sensual sweep of his lips—they were all intimately familiar to her but no less devastating for that.

Her breath lurched a little, her hand automatically going to her stomach, and she smiled at him from behind the mask, smothering the ache of wanting and incipient loss. Tonight was the last night she could count on. Afterward, who knew what would happen?

"Señor Guerra," she returned, for he had taken up that persona for the night.

"I suppose I should call you something more exotic than Sarah," he said, tying on his mask.

"I only know the names of two Egyptian women," Sarah confessed, "and I could not become used to you calling me either Cleopatra or Nefertiti."

"Let's look to the Arabian harem for a name, then. Leila? Zara?" He extended his arm to her, looking at her steadily from behind his blank white mask.

"I think Zara will do," she said lightly as she took his proffered arm, a tingling awareness running through her at the touch. "It has a familiar ring."

The front doors swung open abruptly, and a waiting footman struck a gong beside it so that its noise shimmered through the room as the butler Garza announced two names.

"I believe that our guests are beginning to arrive," Sebastian said.

"Let us greet them, then." Sarah smiled up at him, feeling a small thrill of delight at the idea of her first real audience.

The guests arrived, first trickling in and then pouring. Men in pharaonic crowns and pleated skirts strolled the rooms with women in cobra-headed tiaras. Sloe-eyed Cleopatras rubbed shoulders with Caesars and Mark Antonys, and Arabian concubines smiled beneath their veils at sheikhs and emirs. Among the sea of white-clad Egyptians, Romans, and Mohammedans, Sarah stood out like a sapphire on a bed of pearls. She felt eyes following her wherever Sebastian led her, and she knew for once that the watchers felt wonder and even admiration for the graceful creature on their host's arm, encased in the glittering dress in every shade of blue and green, the heavy, beaded fabric swishing with every step. Behind her mask, she felt powerful, exquisite, glad to greet every guest with a lovely nod and gentle, murmured word.

As the minutes stretched into an hour, the rooms became full, even crowded. Sarah had had no idea Sebastian—or Señor Guerra—knew so many people in Venice. She heard Italian, French, German, and English, all muddled into an unintelligible babble, tied together with a thread of laughter and a bubbling excitement.

"Where did they all come from?" Sarah whispered after Sebastian had greeted at least the hundredth person.

"You know I haven't spent the last two weeks solely in de Lint's company." He sounded amused. "My forays into local society have been arranged to build up such an air of mystery that every straitlaced tourist and resident who craves a slightly outré experience has been feasting on my hints of such an event from the beginning."

Sarah had noticed an edge, an energy to the celebrations that had not been present in any of the parties Sarah had ever witnessed before, neither as Maggie's lady's maid nor Lady Merrill's companion nor even in Sebastian's company. It was as if the event deliberately skirted the limits of propriety, as if everyone were determined to be consciously risqué and daring but no one was precisely vulgar.

"It is a fine line you tread," Sarah said soberly as they passed a young musician singing an amorous song that had the couples surrounding him giving each other coy glances.

"I know," Sebastian said with satisfaction. "The perfect atmosphere. Now I must wait for the perfect moment." He gave her a look steeped with meaning, then abruptly changed the subject. "Everyone seems content enough here. Let's go above. There is dancing, of course."

Sarah smiled, her heart accelerating slightly at the memory of their first dance together. "I wouldn't miss it for the world."

They made their way swiftly up the crowded staircase and into the chamber that served as the ballroom. Already, more than a dozen couples whirled across the floor, and as he stepped through the doorway, Sebastian turned her into dance position with one dexterous tug and launched into a waltz without pausing.

"My dear Señor Guerra," Sarah said, the familiar sensual prickling stealing over her at their proximity, "you are an excellent dancer."

"It is one of the few benefits of squandering one's life in frivolities," he said with false gravity. But there was a darker undercurrent to the facetious words, as if they reminded him of times he would rather forget, and his eyes when they met

hers were full of pain and the now familiar hunger that it
seemed to always call from within him.

A quick thrill shot through her at that look, and she knew
her own eyes betrayed her body's swift reaction, but she
didn't care. She was no longer a lady's companion, trying to
grasp at freedom with one hand and respectability with the
other. She was a most improper mistress instead, and yet she
was suddenly happier than she could ever remember being
in her life.

Sebastian's hand around her waist held her too close, and
she smiled under her mask, tilting her face up so that their
mouths were only inches apart under the papier-mâché.
Without the cage of her crinolette, his legs pressed against
hers as they danced. She reveled at the feel of his long, hard
body against her, at the impropriety of such contact in such
a public place, and she embraced the sensual awareness that
stole across her body in a slow heat until she could hardly
feel her own movement or the floor under her feet—only
him, pressing into her, with eyes like emerald coals.

When the music ended, he maneuvered her through the
crowd and into a dim side room. Leading her swiftly to a
corner, he stood so that his body blocked her from the rest
of the room.

"You are a minx," he said softly, his voice touched with
humor even as it deepened with desire.

"A sybarite," she corrected, still slightly breathless. "A
bacchante. A voluptuary. A maenad. And you have no one
but yourself to blame."

His eyes raked across her, and he pulled his mask up.
Willingly this time, she lifted her hands to her own, but he
stopped her by taking her wrists in his hands.

"Not yet," he said. And then he kissed the hard lips of her
mask.

Sarah froze for an instant as a shock of pure lust went
through her, astonished at how strange an act could affect
her so much. Through the tiny slit between the lips of the
mask, she could feel his damp breath, the hard, smooth sur-

face of it being pressed against her lips and heated by his mouth. It was a tease and a torture, a promise yet to be filled, and she had to bite back a noise of frustration. Finally, he finished and loosened his hold upon her. She shoved up the mask and glared at him.

"You had better make up for that."

He chuckled, low and soft, but he did not smile. Instead, he lifted her chin and brought his mouth down slowly, deliberately to meet hers.

She melted. Her skin had already been brought to unbearable sensitivity, and the force of the first brush of his lips against hers went through her like liquid fire. She closed her eyes, losing herself in the sensation of his mouth against hers, moving softly, then deeply, sending ripples of desire up from her center and into every limb until she was weak with it. And still his mouth moved, his tongue teased, and a familiar ache of emptiness opened in her midsection—

"Sampling your own wares, I see."

The familiar, mocking voice sliced through the passionate fog that had enveloped her. She opened her eyes as Sebastian jerked back from her, pulling down his mask in the same instant, but she could only stand there, frozen, with her heart beating in terror against her chest.

It was Mr. de Lint, clothed incongruously in an ordinary suit amid a sea of pleated skirts and togas. Only his chin, mouth, and bristling muttonchops were visible beneath his plain black demimask, from which his amber eyes glinted as they surveyed her.

As she stood there, a horrific scenario played in Sarah's head—Mr. de Lint dragging her back to the Palazzo Bovolo, declaring that she was a thief and insisting that he take a turn with the procurer's whore lest he have her arrested. Her mind was so caught up in the nightmare that it took several seconds for her to realize that he had not recognized her at all and had already lost interest in her presence.

"Ah, Signor de Lint," Sebastian said expansively, and he followed the words with a flood of incomprehensible Italian.

Mr. de Lint, his attention now entirely upon Sebastian, answered in the same language. Sarah took the opportunity to pull the mask back down over her face, retreating farther into the corner. The conversation continued, back and forth, without Mr. de Lint even sparing her another glance. Their discussion went on for one minute, two, then five, and gradually, despite herself, Sarah began to relax and even grow bored, and as she did so, she began to take in the rest of the room.

To her shock, she realized that the dimness concealed a number of other couples who had chosen discreet places near the walls and were now locked in various passionate embraces. None had gone beyond kissing and a covert groping through clothes, but the realization was profoundly shocking to Sarah—and, contradictorily, slightly titillating as well. The old sense of self-disgust welled up, but she shut it away, studying the chandelier on the ceiling as the men talked on and on.

Finally, Mr. de Lint switched back to English. "Well, I shall leave you and your, ah, companion to return to your dalliance. Good evening, sir." And then he sketched a slightly mocking bow and left.

"Why did you risk—risk *that*, since you knew he was going to be here?" she asked Sebastian as soon as Mr. de Lint was gone.

"I forgot myself," he replied, raising an eyebrow at her and giving her a look that reawakened her desire. "Trust me, I had no intentions of such an encounter when I suggested that we dance."

"He might have recognized me." She pressed on, some of her original panic returning with the thought. "You must have realized when my mask came off—"

"But he did not." Sebastian dropped his voice. "Sarah, you, too, knew he was going to be here. You, too, forgot."

That silenced her for a moment. "I did not want to think of seeing him again," she eventually admitted.

He chuckled softly, sadly, running a finger along the

point where her mask met her jaw. She shivered. "I cannot blame you. I wish I did not have to think of him, either." He held out his arm to her. "Come with me. Let's dance again, and this time, keep your succubus eyes under control or I will not be responsible for my actions."

They danced two more dances in a row together—as Sebastian put it, this was not a party that stood upon ceremony—and then he led her into the dining room, where a lavish buffet was laid. Sarah did not know much about the conventions of sensuality of the upper classes, but the spread of oysters and chocolate, caviar and grapes, tickled something in the back of her mind that a whore who attended a lord's wild party had once said.

"Are you attempting to start an orgy?" she asked, blushing slightly at her frankness.

Sebastian just laughed. "Of course not. I merely want to give the appearance that there might be one. This entertainment is almost perfectly respectable."

"Almost respectable." Sarah smiled back and was about to deliver a retort when a familiar voice arrested her attention and silenced her.

"Look at this! Isn't it so very *fast?*"

Sarah started and jerked around to look at the doorway. It couldn't be, not here. . . .

But it was. Lady Anna—for it was unmistakably Lady Anna under the liberal interpretation of a Roman costume that somehow still allowed her to fit a crinolette beneath— floated into the room, one of the Mortons on each arm.

Pulling away from Sebastian, Sarah turned and all but fled, pushing through the crowd to duck out another door and onto the portego. She felt rather than heard Sebastian behind her, and she whirled to face him once she was securely out of sight. "You invited Lady Anna?" Sarah asked, keeping her voice lowered to an incredulous hiss so that none of the guests who packed the room would overhear.

"But of course," Sebastian said urbanely. "Why ever not? Lady Merrill must be in attendance to see her son disgraced or she would never believe it, and she enjoys events that are perhaps a trifle more risqué than is now fashionable. It was only natural to include her entire party in the invitation."

Ignoring the press of people jostling around her, Sarah looked hard at him as disquiet teased at her mind. But his eyes were inscrutable behind the blank mask that might as well have been a wall. She wondered, with a faintly despairing edge, how well she had ever really known him.

After a minute of heavy silence as she tried to think of something to say, Gian materialized at their side. Sarah was startled to see that he was dressed in the costume of an ancient pharaoh instead of in the ordinary uniforms of the rest of the servants. He cast her only one sideways look before bowing to Sebastian and whispering something quickly to him in Italian.

As Sarah's heart clenched, Sebastian gave her a short bow. "I see someone I must speak to. If you will excuse me for a few minutes, Sarah."

"Of course," she heard herself murmur.

Without another word, he turned away and was swiftly hidden from her sight by the crowd. *This is it,* she thought to herself. *The final step. The end of his plans.*

And she still did not know if she should hope that they would fail or succeed.

Sebastian stalked through the rooms, trying to keep his mind on the business at hand, but it kept wandering—back to Sarah, to the attempts on his life, to his last memory of Daniel, to Adela's attack—everything jumbled together in his memory so that it made no sense. There was something wrong, very wrong, something that he did not yet understand. . . . For an instant, he even thought he saw his agent's stooped form among the revelers, but he blinked, and the illusion was gone.

"I see that you've rid yourself of that fine piece of skirt. Does that mean everything is ready for me?" De Lint's Italian was congenial and slightly too loud.

Sebastian turned to find him leaning against the wall with a tumbler of amber liquid in his hand. The servants whom Sebastian had encouraged to ply him with stronger spirits appeared to have been successful, and Sebastian smothered a grim smile.

"Yes, indeed, signor," he assured the man. "Step right this way."

He led de Lint into one of the side parlors, and from there through a sufficiently complicated array of rooms that he hoped the man would not realize he was guiding him directly back onto the portego—or, specifically, the canal end of the portego, which was isolated from the rest of the room by nothing more than a layer of silken curtains that were rigged to collapse at the tug of a single cord. The noise of the party was such a steady roar everywhere in the palazzo that Sebastian had no fear that de Lint would suspect their location until it was too late.

Gian guarded the last door, and he gave Sebastian a nod as they approached. Everything was prepared, then.

"She awaits within," Sebastian said. "Remember, signor—complete silence. That is the only rule."

"Yes, yes, of course," the man snapped. De Lint opened the door just wide enough to admit his body and slipped inside, closing it behind him.

Sebastian stood, staring at the door's blank wood for a long moment. His part was done. Now everything must be left to chance.

After several minutes of standing on the crowded portego where Sebastian had left her, her mind and her stomach in turmoil, Sarah peeked around the corner into the dining room to scan the chamber for Lady Anna. She quickly spotted the Morton sisters and started to pull back when the wrongness of it hit her. The Morton sisters, but no Lady Anna.

Where was Lady Anna?

Lady Anna, who had been the focus of too much of

Sebastian's attention. Lady Anna, who had been invited to this very inappropriate masquerade . . .

Inevitably, her eyes dragged across to the curtain of gently billowing silk that blocked the far end of the portego. Surely Sebastian wouldn't have . . . he couldn't have . . .

But Sarah saw the logic in it even as she automatically began to push through the crowd. Despoiling a girl from the lower classes, even a seemingly irreproachable one, would not forever destroy Mr. de Lint's position among his peers. But a lord's daughter, *his own niece*—

Sarah tried to break into a run, but there were too many people, too many bodies between her and the seductively streaming curtain. Even as she struggled against them, her mind unraveled other puzzles, producing new and horrific revelations that made her push harder into the pressing crowd. *The cologne.* She had bought Sebastian the cologne thinking it would be used by an impostor at the party pretending to be Mr. de Lint. But it had really been for Gian to wear when he wooed at Lady Anna's window, coaxing her finally into the closeness of his embrace so that she would know the scent—so that in darkness of Sebastian's tent room, Lady Anna would not later be able to tell the difference between her lover and her own uncle until it was too late. Sarah had possessed every piece of the puzzle, but she had put it together wrong because she had been so blind. And now, if she could not stop him, Sebastian was about to make the biggest mistake of his life.

Her breath sobbing in her lungs, Sarah shoved harder through the crowd. She was caught up short as someone stepped on her trailing skirts, but she threw her body weight against the dress and the glorious cloth ripped, dozens of beads cascading down to roll under her feet. Sarah plunged onward, shoving people aside, heedless of the exclamations and curses that followed her.

Closer, closer . . . Finally, she was there. Her hands met silk. A man's elbow caught her in the face as she knelt to grasp the edge, knocking her mask askew, and she shoved it off impatiently, flinging it aside with one hand and yanking up the rich fabric with the other.

The light from the main portego shone into the tiny enclosed room of cloth for an instant, revealing Lady Anna locked in Mr. de Lint's arms. She looked breathless, angry, and was pushing against his chest as he held her against him, his hand down the front of her bodice roughly groping a breast.

"No!" Sarah shouted.

In that instant, the would-be lovers locked eyes in the candlelight, both their expressions turning to simultaneous horror. Mr. de Lint shoved Lady Anna hard, sending her stumbling back. And just then, the walls fell.

Streams of silk billowed down, encasing Sarah in their smothering lengths. She thrashed and kicked, yanking the satiny fabric down and off her, yard after yard, until finally she emerged, blinking, to discover that the silken wall that had divided the main portego from the tent room was gone.

Behind her was an utter silence so profound it was almost palpable, and she spared a glance back to see every guest crowded into the room, watching the scene before them with wide eyes and open mouths. She saw Lady Merrill near the front, her expression astonished, horrified under her demimask. Their eyes met for an instant, and Sarah read amazed recognition there, quickly turning to betrayal. It was only then that she realized how she must look to everyone, her fantastical dress torn, her elegant coiffure destroyed by the cascades of silk, her scarred face stripped of its beautiful mask. And it was then that she realized how little she cared.

Sarah turned away.

In front of her, Lady Anna crouched at the latticework of the newly revealed loggia, sobbing softly into her hands. Mr. de Lint stood across from her, his face set in a mask of fury—every particle of it focused at the man who had just entered the portego.

But Sebastian had his glittering eyes fixed upon Sarah, where she stood caught between the crowd of guests and the strange tableau Lady Anna and Mr. de Lint made.

"Why?" Sebastian demanded, striding to a point in the middle of the open space like a man taking center stage in an opera. "Why, Sarah?"

His voice trembled with anger and the anguish of her perfidy, and Sarah swayed slightly under its force. It was over. He hated her now—how could he not? He must think that she had worked for Mr. de Lint all along, that she had always been planning to betray him— She cut off that thought with a swallow, forcing herself to focus on the truth. "It was wrong. I couldn't let you do it. She hadn't done anything to you or anyone else—"

"I would not have let him rape her," he hissed, low enough that the words reached no farther than her and Gian, who had followed close behind, shadowing his master.

"She would have been ruined nevertheless," Sarah whispered back, aware of all the eyes fixed upon them—upon her, as she stood there, unmasked, her dress torn, yards of silk still tangled around her feet. "Technicalities of virtue have never concerned society. You know that. In the eyes of the world, you would have destroyed her just as Mr. de Lint destroyed Adela."

Even behind his mask, she could read the emotions that flitted across his face at her words: surprise, self-loathing, and a deep, immeasurable rage—directed at her.

Sarah felt sick, but she forced herself to lift her head. "She is an innocent bystander—just like I was," she said clearly, raising her voice. "I could not let you do it, Sebastian. I could not let you make the same mistake twice."

"Sebastian?" Mr. de Lint roared the name, his face flushing with fury under the demimask.

Sarah jerked back, clapping her hands over her mouth, appalled at what she had just said, but Sebastian did not even spare her a disgusted glance. Instead, he tore off his mask and flung it away so that it clattered like a thunderclap when it hit the floor. "I decided to come back from the untimely grave to which you attempted to send me and exact my revenge," he said. "Adela's revenge."

Mr. de Lint laughed, a scornful sound. "If I had tried to kill you, you would have stayed dead. This time, though, you *go too far!*"

With his last words, he launched himself at Sebastian, who leapt into a dead sprint to meet him. They collided with a smack that rang through the portego, and Mr. de Lint staggered back under Sebastian's weight as the watching crowd gave a collective gasp. They pummeled each other with neither skill nor finesse, pitching strength against brute strength. The blows rained down faster than Sarah could track them, and the sounds of fists meeting flesh seemed to fill the room, her mind, with their terrible violence until there was room for nothing else.

Suddenly, Sebastian's leg lashed out and Mr. de Lint fell, pulling his foe down with him. They hit the marble with a force that seemed to shake Sarah's bones. Sebastian pulled away first, rising up just enough to hammer the man in the face with his fist, his knuckles slamming into Mr. de Lint's flesh over and over again as Sarah stood a dozen feet away.

My God, she thought. *Oh, my God, Sebastian's going to kill him!* Sebastian would kill him, and then he would hang—

Sarah's mind rebelled at that thought. With a cry, she fought out of the silk that tangled around her legs and ran forward, scarcely noticing Gian at her side. She threw herself at the struggling men, pulling at their grappling arms, at their clothes, trying to force them apart.

"Stop!" she screamed. "Stop it! Don't kill him, Sebastian. Please, don't kill him. I love you!"

A thrashing leg caught her in the stomach, knocking the breath out of her and sending her sliding crazily across the floor until she fetched up against the carved stone of the loggia. It took two tries to suck air back into her shaken body, and she hauled herself up weakly, coughing and crying in pain and anger.

"Gian!" she managed to call out. "Stop them! You mustn't let Sebastian kill him!"

Gian looked at her for an instant, humor glinting incongruously in his eyes. He stepped up to the fighting pair, reached into the folds of his pleated robe, and began to withdraw a cold metal object—

Sarah flung herself at him before her conscious mind even recognized the shape of the gun in his hand. She slammed into him, yanking his arm down, and he fired wildly. His fist caught her across her face, knocking her back into the loggia railing. She seized it for support to keep from sliding to the floor. Turning away from the struggling men, Gian raised the revolver, this time pointing at her.

Sara thought, *At this distance, he cannot miss.* And then she tightened her grip on the railing, shoved hard, and went over the balcony with just enough time to gather a breath before she plunged into the canal below.

Chapter Twenty-two

Sebastian jerked his head up at the reverberating *crack*. For a crazy instant, he thought a chandelier had fallen, but then he saw the gun in Gian's hands, pointed at Sarah, who was backed against the loggia. . . .

And then, silently, as his heart stopped, she went over the edge.

A second later, a splash in the canal below punctuated the utter silence of a hundred indrawn breaths. Had she been shot? Sebastian had no idea. In a minute, it wouldn't matter. She could not swim. An instantaneous image of her appeared in his mind—a lone outstretched hand disappearing into black water as her weighty, beaded skirts dragged her ever deeper into the muck—

No!

Gian swung back away from the loggia, holding the gun level in front of him, but Sebastian was already lunging for him, the image of Sarah's falling body burned white-hot into his mind. The impact of his body sent the gun flying, Gian staggering back under Sebastian's weight.

"Get him!" Gian shouted.

Sebastian looked around wildly, but a couple of footmen only shifted uneasily at the edge of the crowd, unwilling to commit themselves. With a snarl, he turned back to his quarry and lifted the smaller man up, throwing him over the edge of the balcony in the same movement.

Gian twisted in the air, reaching desperately for the loggia to save himself from the fall. He missed the railing but caught the base of a baluster below, and his body swung like a pendulum to collide with the exterior wall of the palazzo.

Sebastian ignored him. With a leap onto the railing and a push off it, he was arching over the pavement, over the canal, and then plunging down, down into the cold water that smacked against his body and crashed around his ears as he sliced through it.

After only a handful of his racing heartbeats, his feet met the soft mud of the canal bottom. He pushed hard against it, sending himself rocketing back to the surface. His legs straightened fast, but the muck sucked around his feet, holding him down until the force of his push yanked him free and he surged out of the water.

He emerged into a night that was almost black after the brilliance of the portego. *Sarah—where is Sarah?* The stinking water around him was opaque and broken, tiny waves surging out from his position and bouncing off the side of the canal until the choppy interference made it impossible to tell which ripples were from his movement and which from hers, each individual wave casting back broken reflections of the yellow light that streamed from the palazzo above. He cast a quick look up at the portego to judge where she'd fallen from, then took a deep breath and dove under, swimming against the pull of his boots toward the most likely spot.

Holding his breath, he waved his arms and legs, hoping to come in contact with flesh or fabric, but his limbs met nothing but liquid resistance. He stayed under until his lungs burned and he started to see spots in front of his eyes, and he pushed to the surface again—

Only to see two pale hands reaching up through the light-gilded water, waving faintly only a few feet in front of him. He lunged for them, met flesh, and gripped. With a pull, he shot under as she surged up, her sodden, glass-weighted skirts holding him down. He moved his hands along her arm, following it to her body, finding her waist, boosting her up to the surface. After an instant, her hands found his shoulders and clenched hard. *She is fine. She is going to be just fine.*

Half swimming, half flailing, he shoved them toward the side of the canal as his lungs flamed and the blood pounded in his head until he thought it would burst. He was running out of air, and when the last was gone, he would lose consciousness and she would slide into the water again and to her death. . . . The impulse to breathe in was overwhelming. He fought it, fought the demands of his body and the seduction of the liquid around him, and pushed harder in the direction that he hoped would soon bring them to the canal edge.

Suddenly, his burden lightened, and he found that he was no longer holding Sarah up. He pushed away from her entangling skirts and clawed for the surface, coming up gasping at the edge of the pavement. He looked over and found Sarah three feet from him, clinging weakly to the edge, coughing, her paint and hair streaming down her deathly pale face.

"Are you injured?" Sebastian gasped. "Were you shot?"

Sarah shook her head mutely.

Sebastian sucked two lungfuls of air and then forced his oxygen-deprived limbs to haul him heavily out of the water.

It was then that he saw Gian, sitting with his back to the wall of the Palazzo Contarini, his teeth bared in a grimace of pain and one leg stretched out in front of him. He must have lost his hold on the baluster before he could haul himself up and fallen to the pavement below. From the angle at which the ankle was bent, it was clearly broken, and badly. The Italian was not going anywhere soon. Sebastian allowed himself to turn his back for the time that it took to pull Sarah from the canal, his air-starved muscles protesting every movement.

Her face was ashen as he reached for her. She clung to his arms hard enough to leave bruises as he lifted her clear of the edge, then collapsed onto the pavement as soon as her knees cleared the brink, vomiting canal water and weeping. Sebastian had bent to help her to rise when a cry from above made him look up.

It was de Lint, and in his hand was Gian's gun.

Sebastian's heart stuttered, and automatically he straightened so that he was standing in front of Sarah, facing the man squarely. Dozens of guests now crowded around the loggia, watching the scene before them like some sort of grotesque play, but not one of them tried to relieve de Lint of his weapon. Sebastian had the sudden, bizarre image of being murdered on the pavement to his own guests' applause.

"Don't be an idiot, Wortham," de Lint called down. "If I'd wanted you dead, I wouldn't have bothered to take the gun from this queer little man."

Sebastian's gaze slipped sideways, and he realized that the man beside de Lint was being held there forcibly by the collar. The man's mask was gone, his wig askew, and his features were clearly recognizable.

Whitby.

Sebastian looked from his agent to Gian, the man Sebastian had hired on Whitby's recommendation. Gian, who had just tried to murder Sarah . . .

"You want to kill me?" he called up incredulously. "Why?"

"I could claim innocence, but as I had a loaded gun pointed at your back, I doubt it would be believed, and so I will satisfy your curiosity," Whitby said in his usual fastidious tones. He did not raise his voice, but the words were clearly distinguishable in the unnatural silence of the gathered guests.

"The attempted murderer of a peer will not escape a hanging, and so pretending at innocence would yield nothing. You were simply becoming meddlesome," the wizened man continued, frowning at Sebastian as if he were a recalcitrant child. The very calmness of his demeanor sent a chill up Sebastian's neck. "My family has worked for yours for five generations, and the four before me have died poor and without honor. It was only logical that I utilize my position in order to fulfill the debt your family refused to recognize that it owed mine."

"You were stealing from me?" Sebastian asked incredulously.

"Oh, do not think that you are so special," Whitby retorted, a hint of querulousness entering his voice. "Your father was a cleverer man than you, and it took him years to suspect what I was up to. A little foxglove in his tea, and his faulty heart became abruptly lethal." Whitby's frown became severe. "You should have been grateful for what I had done for you, but instead you rewarded my loyalty by asking for the books, so that you might go over them yourself. Now, I am too clever to be caught out by such simple means, but your interest was disturbing. It marked a change that was highly unwelcome, and so I had to think of something. Foxglove would have hardly have been convincing for a man of your age and health."

Sebastian remembered requesting those records only a few weeks before the attack on Adela, and suddenly, everything fell horribly into place—Whitby's need for his presence at Amberley, the assault, de Lint's claims of innocence, the too-convenient beggar child outside his agent's offices waiting to direct him to the Whitsun Club—even the sabotaged axle that had so nearly ended his life. "Then Adela's rape—"

"Was engineered by me, yes." The old man sighed regretfully. "There was no reason for it to fail. I found an unscrupulous man who looked enough like your friend Mr. Bertrand de Lint to fool the child in the darkness, and then I encouraged your cousin to bring a party of your friends to make an impromptu visit to Amberley while you were there. I convinced Mr. de Lint's own current whore to lure away the nurse, though she never knew until too late what she had participated in. I even arranged for a girl with a more than passing resemblance to your little Adela to seduce Mr. de Lint simultaneously. It was a perfect plan. I was certain that you would kill de Lint or he you, and in either case my way would be clear. But you uncharacteristically insisted upon legal means."

Fury and despair washed over Sebastian. He'd had the man responsible for Adela's atttack within his grasp all along, but he'd allowed himself to be deceived, chasing after a man who, however unprincipled, had once been his friend and was innocent of the crime for which Sebastian had tried to punish him.

"Why did you touch Adela?" Sebastian demanded harshly, his hands balling into fists. "She had done nothing to anyone! She was a *child,* damn you!"

"Exactly," Whitby said dispassionately. "She had done nothing, and you kept her like a little princess, spending far more on her every year than you ever spent on my wages despite my years of service."

"Are you satisfied now?" de Lint shouted down with a mixture of anger and triumph. "I told you I was innocent!"

"Yes," Sebastian ground out, his mind still reeling. "Yes, you did."

"Now," Whitby continued, his voice rising slightly at the interruption in the first sign of true irritation he'd shown since he'd started his confession, "after my initial plan failed, I arranged for your gig to be damaged and tried to get Mr. de Lint to provoke you into breaking your own neck. Manufacturing the fight at your club was rather clumsy, but it worked as well as I had dared hope—except that, unfortunately, you survived the subsequent crash with relatively minor injuries. By then, though, you were bent upon your revenge, and while murder would not answer when you were Lord Wortham in England, it little mattered what happened to Señor Guerra in Italy."

Whitby turned his head as much as he could manage

while being half suspended by his collar. "If you would be so kind as to let me go, my story is finished," he said to de Lint.

De Lint loosened his grip—automatically, or so it seemed to Sebastian, out of surprise that the agent could make such a demand just after confessing so many crimes.

"Thank you," Whitby said, straightening. And then, without any warning, he leaned over the railing and did a sort of half somersault until he was hanging head-down over the edge. Before Sebastian could do more than gape, the agent let go.

And dropped.

Sebastian jerked at the crack of the man's head hitting the pavement, Sarah crying out softly behind him. The agent's body had crumpled as it hit the cobbles, and the impossible angle of his neck told him that there was no point in checking on the man. With that sound, all the anger, the deep-rooted fury that had festered since he had first discovered the attack on Adela, went out like a candle being snuffed. He stood numbly, feeling emptied out, afraid to see what was left now that the driving purpose of the past seven months of his life was gone.

De Lint made a disgusted sound, whether at his former friend or Whitby's unexpected suicide, Sebastian couldn't tell. "I should have you up before the magistrate for what you tried to do to me," he said.

Sebastian looked up at de Lint and saw him clearly, quite possibly for the first time in his life. He was not evil, exactly. Shallow, yes—self-centered, capable of many crimes in the name of self-indulgence and out of a feeling that the world was indebted to him. He was a man without compassion or love and with a streak of petty cruelty. But not quite a monster. He was not one to deserve any apologies, even if he was not deserving of Sebastian's planned revenge, had it succeeded.

And so Sebastian turned his back dismissively to the man, helping Sarah, who was still crouched, frozen, behind him, to her feet. She was shuddering, though whether from fear or from cold, he couldn't tell, and he pulled her protectively against him.

"I should have you up before the magistrate for what you tried to do to her," he said coldly to de Lint. "Consider your thrashing a stroke of luck."

"Ha!" De Lint snorted. "And who is she that anyone would believe her more than your precious little Adela?"

The words should have inflamed Sebastian, but his fury had died with Whitby. Now he ignored his old friend and turned to the woman who had saved him and stopped him in the middle of the revenge that, however wrongly, he had worked so hard for. *I love you,* she had said. Sebastian hadn't known he'd heard the words then, but now he remembered them. And he realized that she was everything he wanted.

Shivering, Sarah pulled away and looked up at Sebastian, still shaken by the whirl of revelations that had preceded the strange old man's abrupt suicide. Whatever the truth was, she had tried to destroy his revenge even when she had believed that Mr. de Lint had been as terrible as Sebastian had thought him to be. She had no hope of being forgiven, nor did she deserve it. Sebastian's face was so cold, so marble-smooth and shadowed, that she made herself cling to the thought that he still cared enough about her to rescue her from drowning. Surely he would not have saved her life only to destroy it. Her belly churned with fear and the canal water she had swallowed, making her want to vomit again.

"Do you love me?" he asked, his voice low and rough with indecipherable emotion.

Sarah started. What did he mean by asking that? "Yes," she said, forcing her gaze to remain steady though her voice shook out of her control. "You . . . you don't need to worry, though. I do not expect it to make a difference."

"That gunshot—" He broke off.

"It was meant for you," she confirmed, guessing what he meant to ask.

"You have saved my life twice, then."

"I-I must have done," she acknowledged, still unable to see where he was taking the conversation. "Just as you saved mine."

"You would have been in no danger if you had not kept Gian from shooting me." He nodded to his former employee, who still sat motionless against the wall. "It would have been a poor thanks to let you die saving me, don't you think?"

Sarah made some sort of noise, which he must have interpreted as the affirmative, for he continued, "And yet though I am worth so much to you that you would risk your life for mine, you stopped me from my revenge even when we both thought de Lint guilty of every crime he has been charged with."

"Yes," Sarah said, her stomach clenching. She longed to cling to Sebastian, to beg forgiveness. But she could not, for she was not sorry, nor could she be, no matter what happened between them as a result. "It was wrong to bring in Lady Anna." She lifted her chin, her voice breaking. "And I love you too much to let you do something that wrong."

His eyes bored into hers, but she could read nothing in them. "Even if I might hate you for it."

"Even if," she agreed, her voice scarcely a whisper.

Sebastian stepped closer to her, and her heart sped up so that she had to force herself not to back away from him. He caught her with one arm around her waist, one hand cradling the back of her neck. "And that, Sarah, is why I love you so."

For an instant, she didn't understand what he said. When she did, she stepped back involuntarily, but his hands tightened around her, pulling her against him. Her hands, pinned between them, bunched automatically around the fabric of his dripping tunic, warm with the heat of his body. "What are you saying?" she asked, hardly daring to believe her ears.

He groaned, burying his face against her neck, and she

clung to the sensations of his warm skin on hers, scarcely believing it was real. "Sarah, there are very, very few men in the world who have the honor of even meeting a person with a soul as beautiful as yours. You've spoken of wanting to shed beauty in this world, but you don't need to play the piano or speak a dozen languages to do it. It's part of who you are. I have the great honor of loving you, and if you will consent, I hope to have the even greater honor of having you as my wife."

Sarah jerked back, tearing herself away and looking at him wildly as her pulse raced and her head felt impossibly light. "I am not the kind of woman that an earl marries," she said tightly. "I understand that you are very . . . emotional right now, but you won't mean it tomorrow."

"Bloody hell, Sarah," he rasped, his face constricting. "You cannot imagine how much I mean it—today, tomorrow, and forever. Don't give me anemic arguments about society and expectations. Society allows almost anything an earl cares to do. It's one of the advantages of my position."

Sarah blurted, "But you can't do it. I have told you—I might even be barren."

Sebastian closed the space between them again, grabbing her shoulders and shaking her gently with both hands. "I do not care. Let the title pass to Daniel's children. I've scarcely done an admirable job of being a father thus far. I certainly don't need a dozen brats when I have you. Can't you understand that?" He took a deep breath. "Give me the answer that is in your heart. Would you like to be my wife?"

"We scarcely know each other, Sebastian. But I can't imagine that I could ever not love you." She bit her lip. "I have to say yes," she said, finally allowing herself to believe. "Oh, yes."

With a triumphant smile, Sebastian turned back up to face the portego loggia where Mr. de Lint still stood, crowded by a hundred guests. "This woman, ladies and gentlemen, is my future wife and countess. An insult to her is an insult to my title. I suppose that will be sufficient for you, de Lint?"

Eyes glittering, the man gave a small bow. "It looks like it must be," he said. And for the first time since Sarah had met him, he did not frighten her any longer.

Still smiling, Sebastian turned back to face her, his black, tempestuous brows eased with tenderness, his piercing eyes softened. "We shall be wed before we leave Venice—and before you have a chance to realize how much better you deserve."

And as she opened her mouth in reflexive protest, he chuckled and kissed her into silence.

Epilogue

Sarah stood at her private drawing room window, watching her guests and her new stepdaughter play croquet on the broad lawn behind Hartwald. This was her first time to be a hostess since she had become Sebastian's countess, and the event had been carefully planned as a low-key affair that included only Sebastian's cousin Mr. Collins, Maggie's family, Maggie's sister-in-law's family, and the family of one of Sebastian's tamest friends, who, Sarah discovered, was related to Maggie's sister-in-law by marriage.

Despite everything, Sarah had been completely unprepared for the stir that Sebastian's return from the dead caused—and with a wife of completely mysterious origins, no less. Aside from Lady Merrill's family, which was firmly silent on the entire affair, Maggie, Lord Edgington, and Lord Edgington's sister were the only ones besides Sebastian and Sarah herself in a position to enlighten the curiosity of society and the press, but they each knew well enough how to keep secrets.

So Sebastian had rapidly retired to the countryside with his wife and daughter, leaving all questions unanswered, and Sarah had made her first necessary forays into society by inviting a few very carefully chosen individuals to a quiet and decorous house party.

Sarah's meeting with Maggie had been painful, but Maggie had, with typical generosity, forgiven all of Sarah's lies of omission, and now Sarah felt closer to her than she had since they'd left the rookery behind them. She smiled down at her friend as the baroness bent awkwardly over her pregnancy to listen to some great secret that her young son wished to vouchsafe her. When her guests had first arrived a month before, Sarah had looked at the six children they shared between them with a mixture of envy and longing, but that emotion had quickly turned into a budding excitement of her own as the weeks passed and her growing suspicion became a certainty. The emotion was not unmixed, though, for she could not think of Sebastian's reaction without feeling the first stirrings of trepidation.

As if summoned by her thoughts, she heard someone walk into the room and turned to find Sebastian approaching. He stopped at her golden piano and sat, smiling at her as he began one of her favorite pieces. Though it still had the place of pride in her drawing room, Sarah now spent more time listening to Sebastian play than struggling through pages of music herself. She had spent many hours refurbishing the modest manor house, but she had finally discovered her true passion in the gardens, where she embraced the new, informal styles and the challenge of creating beautiful palettes that eased seamlessly from one season into the next.

"They seem very content," she observed, nodding at the people gathered on the lawn.

"You are a good hostess," Sebastian said.

"I did not know if I would be a good mother, though," Sarah said more tentatively. "Adela seems to love and respect me, though, and she seems to be very happy despite . . . despite everything, I mean."

"I was not a very good father to her," Sebastian said, frowning as the notes grew harsher.

"But now?" Sarah asked quietly.

"I think that I am beginning to redeem myself in some way," he admitted.

Sarah laced her hands nervously in front of her. "Do you ever wish that you might have another child? One with me?"

Sebastian stopped playing, his brows drawing together as he looked at her. "You have shown me that I don't have to repeat the mistakes of my father—or make worse ones. But I have you, and I am fulfilled, and I want nothing more."

"But what if you could have more?" Sarah asked. "What if—what if I were expecting a child?"

Sebastian stared at her for a long moment, his expression baffled. Then amazement replaced confusion, and he stood abruptly, shoving the piano bench across the soft carpet with the motion. Sarah involuntarily took a step back, bumping against the window's embrasure behind her.

"Are you?" he demanded. "But you said you were barren—"

"For three years, I lived as a whore and never became with child. What was I to think?" Sarah asked plaintively. "My courses have always been unpredictable and infrequent, and so I gave no thought to it when I was with you until we were on the boat returning from Venice. And then I had a miscarriage."

"It could not have been more than six weeks after we met," Sebastian objected. "How could you tell?"

"I've known enough women who have miscarriages to know the difference between regular bleeding and the remains of a child, even that soon," Sarah said, her voice barely above a whisper as she fought to keep it steady. "I can't even tell you how I felt. I had thought that being barren was just another mark of how much was wrong with me, and just knowing I conceived gave me such hope. . . . I was heartbroken that I had lost the child, and I was frightened that I would never have another. I was elated at the chance that I might—and terrified that you would think that I had lied to you. That you wouldn't want it after what happened to Adela, as you so often told me these past few months. That's why I didn't tell you. If I was not meant to bear a live child, you would never need to know." She took a deep breath. "But I did conceive again, and now enough weeks have passed that I am convinced this one will stay. In five or six months, we will have a child."

With that confession, Sarah closed her eyes, leaning against the embrasure for strength. There. She had said it— and now everything was up to him. She steeled herself for the worst.

Sebastian let out a long, slow breath of air. "I love you, Sarah. You know that." She felt rather than heard him approach, and she opened her eyes to find him gazing steadily down at her. She swallowed hard, waiting for the *but*.

It didn't come.

"And I am sure that I will love your baby—our baby— just as much," he continued, cradling her face in his hands. "Whatever selfish fears I might still harbor, I am glad for both of us. I am glad that you will have my child, and I only hope that I will be a father that he or she will be proud of."

"Really?" Sarah gasped, relief washing through her with such intensity that it made her knees weak.

"Good God, Sarah," Sebastian growled, a smile tugging at the corner of his beautiful lips, "must I convince you of everything I say?"

And then he kissed her and took her breath away.

Look for Lydia Joyce's latest gothic romance
filled with shadows and passion. . . .

Whispers in the Night

Coming in July 2006

Alcyone Carter was frightened.

She sat stiffly on the swaybacked mule, her hands clutching the pommel so tightly that her fingers had long ago gone from cramping to agony to final, blessed numbness. She had no use for the reins, and so they hung slack, slapping gently against her mount's neck with every steady step as it allowed itself to be drawn onward by the lead rope that stretched taut into the fog. Only that rope and the occasional muffled clop of a hoof assured Alcy that her invisible guide was still there ahead of them, and only blind, desperate hope allowed her to believe that he could have any idea where they were going.

Around her, the world closed in, as small and featureless as the inside of an egg. Her feet were swallowed in the swirling mist, and even her hands, scarcely two feet from her face, were shrouded. The few feeble rays of sun that penetrated the thick blanket were bounced around until they became a thin, even light, flattening shadows and erasing all sense of depth.

The sound of whispered prayers in French and the rattle of rosary beads grated from behind her like the dry scratchings of an insect's legs. Celeste, her lady's maid, had been terrified of the mules even without the danger of the precipitous drop on one side of the narrow trail, which had been the last thing they had seen before the fog enveloped them. Now she was nearly hysterical.

Alcy found herself split between annoyance and envy, weary of her maid's moaning litany and yet wishing that she, too, could bury her mounting anxiety in histrionics. She felt utterly powerless, and to make matters worse, she knew she looked a fright. She had worn her riding habit for six days straight, and even Celeste's nightly efforts could not keep the delicate gray silk and brilliant gold braid from showing the stains of mud and damp, the wrinkles of too much wear between ironings. The dress had been created for civilized two-hour jaunts in a well-tended park, not an endless journey through the wilderness. Her hair fared little better in the wind and damp, and she felt its rebellion from its pins and ribbons as a personal insult.

"How much farther?" Alcy called out in German to their guide. Her voice pierced the dead fog stridently, unnaturally loud. She tried again, attempting for insouciance. "When will we arrive? You said today was the last day."

"Now." The reply drifted through the whiteness.

Abruptly, Alcy sensed an openness around them, as if they had risen beyond the rocky slope that had sheltered them on one side as they climbed. Had they reached the mountain's crest?

As if in answer, a breeze pushed through the sullen air, tattering the fog into long streamers that fluttered like a thousand veils. The guide became visible in the shredding mist, and Alcy watched him pull his mount to a stop. Her own mule sauntered a few more steps before halting nose-to-tail behind him.

"Why are we stopping?" she asked, shoving her unruly hair from her eyes and hating the nervous shrillness of her tone.

"Be patient," the man said impassively. He had answered every question impassively for the last six days.

Alcy had no choice, and so she sat and waited, straining through the mist for some hint of what lay before them. The

breeze quickened to a wind, and through the rapidly clearing air, she traced the trail with her gaze as it sloped down
until it was swallowed where the rocky upthrust gave way to
the dark tangle of forest. From their vantage, she could look
out over the saw-toothed tops of the trees and see the opposite side of the valley . . .

. . . and the castle that loomed above it. It stood at the
edge of a cliff, only a little higher than the ridge crest where
they rested, iron gray and sheer-walled, its toothy crenella-
tions smiling indifferently down on the forest below. It
looked as ancient as the mountains, and as cold.

"Castle Vlarachia," the guide said. And then he nudged
his mule back into a walk as Celeste's prayers crescendoed
in panic.

Castle Vlarachia. It seemed impossible to Alcy that she
was facing it at last, which was strange because her father's
scheme had struck her as eminently sensible and achievable
when he had suggested it nearly a year ago. The plan had
still seemed practical and—Alcy was honest with herself—
rather romantic when she had exchanged a series of shy letters with the man she came to know as János. Her long trip
from England to Vienna and down the Danube had possessed the glitter of dazzling, girlish dreams, unshaken by
the ugly mundanities of transcontinental travel, but it had
seemed more real to her than anything she had experienced
in her life until that point.

But the fog had risen from the river when the barge
reached Orsova, wrapping Alcy in its insulating sense of unreality, and since the moment she had stepped onto the quay
there, she had not quite been able to make herself believe
that anything she experienced was truly happening. The
strange entourage that met her had only reinforced that sensation.

Someone will meet you at the docks, János' last letter had
promised her. And someone had. What János failed to warn
her was that her escort would not be a liveried coachman
with footmen to take her on a brief carriage ride to a manor

overlooking the town, but a strange, ruffianish pair who would lead her far into the depths of the wilderness on the back of a mule, with her baggage strapped onto two camels—two actual camels!—behind her. The camel driver spoke no language with which she was familiar, and the guide seemed to know a mere smattering of German, which he employed only grudgingly and usually to assure her that they were close to their destination—very close.

And now she faced it.

Alcy sank into a daze of confounded thoughts and emotions as they plunged once again into forest, feeling for the first time uncertain about the wisdom of her agreement to the scheme. Seeking to ground herself in what was real and chase away her phantom fears, she raised a hand to her necklace, her fingers curling around the miniature that hung from it. She had spent so much time gazing at that pendant over the past four months that she could now call to mind a perfect replica of its portrait. In England, she had thought the gentle, blurring glow around János' golden features to be rather dashing, but now its imprecision seemed to hint at grotesque possibilities.

She pushed the image from her mind and mentally paged through the affectionate yet distant letters he had sent her instead, trying to find the shape of the underlying personality in their careful forms. She was so preoccupied that her mule came to a stop before she realized they had somehow circled the cliff and arrived at the castle.

The trail had widened to a road only to be swallowed by an arching maw in the barbican. Directly in front of them, the gates stood shut tight as if to ward off an invading army, the oak blackened with age—and perhaps a little boiling pitch, too, that had splashed against the wood as it rained down upon the enemy. The vast curtain wall stretched away on either side of the gateway's towers, gray and bleak under the shroud of clouds that smothered the sky.

Were they just going to stand there until someone inside noticed them? Alcy wondered as her guide stared in mute patience at the battered oak. Just as she was beginning to think she ought to call a *hallo,* the gates started to creak open.

It was only then that Alcy remembered how frightful she must look, how travel worn and pale with her windblown hair and mud-stained skirts. *I cannot go in now!* She felt the first, fluttery stirrings of panic. She must look perfect to ensure a good first impression—however else she might be lacking as a lady, she knew she could at least look the part if given a chance, and all her future happiness might depend upon this initial meeting.

"Wait," she hissed to the guide.

He showed no signs of having heard her.

"I must refresh myself," she pressed on, a trifle more desperately. "I must change clothes, arrange my hair—"

By then it was too late. The gate had swung wide, revealing the servants who opened it—and beyond, a crowd of people who stared at her with wide eyes.

The guide entered, and her mule followed obediently behind. A broad, sere ward stretched out between the curtain wall and a massive square keep that stood proud of the warren of low gray additions sprawling from it in all directions. The space was filled with men, women, and children, and some automatic, distant part of Alcy's mind began to franticly add them up, losing its place only after it had passed two hundred.

Alcy sat ramrod-straight on her mule, her heart pounding wildly inside her chest, trying to project the cool, calm air of a born lady when she had never felt more like a tradesman's dressed-up daughter. For some reason, she had not thought of the local peasants and servants beyond the vague idea that there must be some—and if she had, she never would have imagined she would have to confront them all like this, at the moment of her arrival, and that they would be surveying her so weighingly. If she'd considered them at all, she would have envisioned them clothed in wholesome English calico dresses and decent wool coats and trousers. But the men wore short open waistcoats of an unfamiliar design, and the women's costumes struck her Leeds-bred eyes as tremendously exotic. Arches of white linen framed the women's faces, and wide aprons of the same material covered their dresses, both brightly embroidered in angular patterns that seemed almost barbaric. Alcy could easily believe these people to be the descendants of a tribe of horse nomads that had swept through the region centuries ago.

Before Alcy even consciously registered the pull, her gaze was dragged away from the gathered peasants to the one man who stood apart from the crowd. The sense of separateness that surrounded him was far more profound than could be credited to sublunary matters as the physical distance or differences in dress. It was rooted in who he was, what he was—and Alcy knew him to be the castle's lord.

He wore a coat cut in the height of French fashion, though from four or five years past, with matching trousers and a wine red waistcoat. The tailoring was exquisite, and it displayed a powerful frame, broad shoulders narrowing to lean hips, the muscles of his wide-planted legs apparent even through the cloth of his trousers. His body sent an instinctive reaction through her before she had even made out any details of his face, a reaction she had felt before when suddenly meeting eyes with a surprisingly handsome man, but this time it was compounded by the knowledge that there would soon be far more between them than idle glances. For Baron Benedek János was to be her husband.

Forcing her eyes upward as her guide pulled them to a stop, she discovered that he was inexplicably bareheaded, his chin shaven and hair worn long over his collar like a romantic poet from a generation past.

For an instant, he seemed like the young Apollo of his miniature, with his face turned into a wind that ruffled his pale hair. But then he turned to look at her, and she realized that his locks were not golden at all but silver, shot through with streaks of the darkest sable and surrounding an unlined visage that could be any age between twenty and fifty. His strong features were far from the dainty handsomeness of a fashion plate, but they were perfectly measured against one another and had an arresting quality that was almost other-worldly.

Alcy suddenly knew why the women of the old ballads always allowed themselves to be carried away by their faerie lovers. The man's gaze narrowed as it swept across her, and she felt her skin prickle with heat in its wake, the sensation waking an alarming sense of brazenness within her.

Celeste, who had gone silent, suddenly began to pray again in earnest, and out of the corner of her eye, Alcy saw her cross herself as if the man were a demon come to steal her soul. *Steal it? I'd like to see the woman who could deny him if he asked.*

The baron—she could not call this man by the Christian name she had been using freely in her letters for the last four months—strode toward them then, and Alcy sat frozen, watching him in dry-mouthed fascination as her body sang in awareness of every step he took. He moved with a kind of reined-in energy that she had never encountered before, riveting in its promise of excitement. His eyes were a cold, pale blue under the dark slashes of his brows, she saw as he drew near. She could not begin to sort through the thoughts that flickered within their depths, so quickly did they come and go, but it was clear he made no attempt to hide them. He was a man not accustomed to concealing his feelings, whatever they were—one who had never had the need. Alcy envied him suddenly and sharply.

Baron Benedek seized her stirrup, and she realized that he meant for her to dismount. Alcy swung down from the saddle, stiff after the long ride, her stomach fluttering with nervousness and attraction.

The baron caught her elbow as soon as her feet touched the hard-packed earth, and she felt a small, twisting pleasure deep in her center even though the thickness of his glove and her sleeve still separated them. His action might have been to steady her, but he used the motion to place her arm around his and pin it neatly to his side. She had the insane impression that he thought she might flee and was preemptively preventing any chance at escape. She mentally reviewed the miles of tangled trails they had traversed over the past six days. Flee to where? How? And what would make him fear that she might want to? The thoughts had a fine edge of hysteria.

Looking at her gravely, the baron spoke in some language that Alcy could not understand. She blinked and stared at him dumbly, letting the silence stretch out until she felt obliged to give some sort of reply or risk the appearance of rudeness. She cleared her throat, feeling heat creep up her cheeks as she remembered the many demurely tender letters she had sent him since their engagement had been formalized. Now, in his presence, those missives seemed impossibly naive, from another life, and she could not think of where to begin.

"Herr Benedek, I presume?" she asked tentatively in her schoolgirl German.

The baron's eyes narrowed, and Alcy feared she read a hint of contempt in their chilly depths. "In this part of the world, a noble is addressed by his full title," he replied in the same language. "A baron is never a 'lord.'"

Shamed at her mistake, Alcy swallowed hard against her roiling stomach. She had learned that Hungarians used their family names before their Christian; why had she not thought to research their titles as well? "Baron Benedek, then?"

"As you say." The words were without inflection. He looked her up and down again, possessively, assessingly, and she stiffened under his scrutiny even as she felt her cheeks heat even more, though now their warmth had nothing to do with embarrassment. "Welcome to Castle Vlarachia, Miss Carter. I am sure you are curious about your new home. I will arrange for a tour of the premises later, but right now we are wanted in the chapel. The priest has been waiting for some time." He began walking toward the nearest wing of the structure that sprawled from the hub of the keep.

"The priest?" she blurted, stumbling after him to keep from being dragged. He couldn't mean for them to be married now. She had only just met the man. She must recover from her journey and spend time getting to know him better, and even then there were so many preparations to be made—people to invite, wedding entertainments to arrange, and her first parties to plan for the neighboring nobility and gentry, not to mention the travel arrangements for their trip to the glitter and whirl of the imperial court in Vienna. Surely she misunderstood. . . .

"Indeed," he said as if he could imagine no difficulty with the prospect. "Why should we delay our happy union a moment longer than we must? After all, mine is a bachelor household, and it would be most improper for you to stay the night if we were not yet wed."

Just then, they passed through wide double doors in the end of the wing, entering a vast Romanesque hall. She was given no time to take it in, though, for the baron did not even slacken his pace in response to her hesitation, and she had to run a couple of steps to come even with him again.

"But I must wear my wedding dress," Alcy protested, the first coherent phrase she managed to pull from the welter of confused objections that tumbled through her mind.

"You may wear it for our marriage portrait," the baron assured her in the voice of an adult pacifying a child.

"But I am still an Anglican." Alcy seized upon another impediment, pushing down her irritation with his dismissive treatment of her first protest and her embarrassment at how vain it must have sounded. "I must convert before we can legally be wed."

"Do not worry," the baron said in a tone of bleak efficiency as they entered a narrow, shadowy corridor. "The priest will deal with that first. It will only be a matter of a few minutes." He gave her a sideways look, and once again the directness of those blue eyes stirred a trickling warmth deep inside her. "Surely four months is an engagement long enough for anyone's propriety. In England, it would be far in excess of the norm, would it not?"

"Yes." Honesty made Alcy agree, but she could not keep back the words that followed, implacably logical and thoroughly argumentative. "And yet this is hardly a usual English marriage, for we don't even know one another."

"Do months of correspondence mean so little to you, my little bird?" he asked. The endearment was straight from his letters, a play on the meaning of her name, but now the phrase had a sardonic twist.

"No. No, of course not," Alcy said, straightening her shoulders even as she grew more confused as to exactly what this man meant and what he intended. She felt as if she were engaged in some sort of battle with him, though for what, she couldn't say. She also felt, helplessly, as if he were cheating, changing meanings and twisting customs to suit himself, and yet she knew no acceptable way to call him on it.

"Good," the baron said with satisfaction, and Alcy knew she was beaten.

They turned down another near-lightless corridor, and Baron Benedek switched languages as he spoke again. This time, Alcy recognized the patterns of the Hungarian boatmen's speech.

"I do not speak Hungarian," she protested in German.

Baron Benedek made a noise halfway between a grunt of confirmation and a snort and changed languages again— and this time, she could decipher the words.

"Can you understand this, then?" he had asked as he guided her down another passageway.

"Only a little," she replied in classical Greek, markedly different from the modern vernacular he used.

He nodded. "And Russian?" he asked in that language.

"I read it better than I speak it." Was he testing her? Alcy wondered. To what purpose? And what answer did he want to hear? Belatedly, she considered that the baron might not care for a wife who knew more than the obligatory French, the German they had exchanged letters in, and perhaps a smattering of Latin, but it was too late now to pretend ignorance.

"French?" he asked, switching as if he'd read her mind.

"But of course."

He changed to another language, and then another and another, and Alcy merely shook her head helplessly as she did not recognize a word of any of them. The baron stopped without warning, and Alcy looked away from him, startled, to discover that the corridor reached a dead end at a dark, polished door in front of them.

"The chapel," Baron Benedek explained, in German again. He looked at her for a long moment, but the shadows of the unlit passageway were too deep for Alcy to read his expression. Still, his close attention was enough to send an edgy warmth buzzing through her, the sensation both heady and dangerous.

"I understand that it is customary for an Englishman to kiss his intended after she accepts his marriage proposal," he said. "There has been somewhat of a delay in our particular case, but I believe that it is a custom worth respecting."

For half a second, Alcy just stared at him, uncomprehending. Then he loosed his hold on her arm, slipped one arm around her back and the other behind her head, and pulled her towards him. Only then did she realize that he meant to kiss her.

She tried to jerk back automatically, but he held her too tightly. *Why resist?* she asked herself abruptly. There was surely nothing improper in it, as they were minutes from being wed, and yet as he drew her near, such a hot welter of sensation overcame her that she could not quite believe that it wasn't wicked, after all.

Their bodies met, the baron drawing her firmly against his hard stomach and chest, and his head began to descend. Light-headedly, she watched his face grow nearer, nearer, as her breath quickened and her heart raced. And then—his mouth found hers.

Polite, some distant part of her mind labeled that gentle contact, but it did not stay so for long. A rush of fire surged through her at that first brushing pressure, and she felt both heavy and weightless at once, her knees bending as she leaned against him, letting her head tilt back in invitation.

Which he took.

His gentle kiss hardened suddenly, and her lips parted eagerly at his tongue's urging. His touch inside her mouth was slick and firm, shockingly intimate, and the fire inside her roared up, flushing her skin with heat and making her head spin. When he finally pulled away, she wasn't ready, and she stumbled back, gasping for breath and blinking at him in the dimness that somehow seemed suddenly too bright.

Alcy thought, belatedly, that she might have shocked and repelled her future husband, but when she met his gaze, his expression contained more pleasure than even surprise. He raised a hand to her face, brushing the backs of his knuckles softly down her cheek.

"It seems that we have both gotten more than we expected," he said softly, cryptically, his voice roughened in a way that made Alcy shiver. "Come, bird. We have let the priest wait long enough."

Without waiting for her response, he took her arm on his again and opened the gleaming door.